John Clarence Cutter

Comprehensive anatomy, physiology, and hygiene

adapted for schools, academies, colleges and families : containing brief directions

for illustrative dissections of mammals, for elementary work with the microscope,

for physiological demonstrations of

I0740203

John Clarence Cutter

Comprehensive anatomy, physiology, and hygiene
adapted for schools, academies, colleges and families : containing brief directions
for illustrative dissections of mammals, for elementary work with the microscope,
for physiological demonstrations of

ISBN/EAN: 9783742812841

Manufactured in Europe, USA, Canada, Australia, Japa

Cover: Foto ©Andreas Hilbeck / pixelio.de

Manufactured and distributed by brebook publishing software
(www.brebook.com)

John Clarence Cutter

Comprehensive anatomy, physiology, and hygiene

PREFACE.

In accordance with the terms of my contract with the Imperial Japanese Government, it has been my pleasure to give instruction in Human Anatomy, Physiology, and Hygiene to five successive classes of English-speaking Japanese students. Experience with students whose knowledge of English had been wholly acquired in the day-schools of the cities of the Empire led me to depend in Anatomy less and less upon the text-book and more and more upon dissections before the class, and upon demonstrations from an active coolie and from microscopic preparations. By this method it was found that the students acquired a more definite, useful, and retentive knowledge of the form, color, position, and relations of the parts and organs than from the text-book used in connection with English and American charts. Also by demonstrations on the coolie and the students many physiological facts were made manifest. As the students experienced great difficulty in understanding the bearing of the *very general* statements in the sections of the text-books devoted to Hygiene, recourse was had to talks, giving concise and specific statements on the topics of air, water, ventilation, clothing, foods, etc. Furthermore, the question of *Alcoholics, Tobacco, Opium*, etc., had for them an intense interest, because of certain political and social problems of the day in the Far East. Their questions indicated a desire for unbiassed, definite, well-authenticated information concerning the effects of the use and abuse of stimulants and narcotics. As the college authorities were unable to procure a text-book containing such information, talks and lectures were introduced.

One of the great objects in the study of natural science, and especially of that of the structure and functions of the human body, is the cultivation of the observant faculties. A definite, though

1*

5

perhaps not extensive and deep, understanding of man is a most useful and most instructive form of knowledge. Such knowledge can be best acquired by observations on the living body, and, in the absence of subjects, by dissection of the bodies of mammals (dog, cat, rat, rabbit, etc.). Knowledge acquired through personal endeavor with the knife, the magnifying glass, the ear, and the hand is more definite, more tangible, and more useful in life than that acquired wholly through glances at charts and illustrations and the memorizing of sentences. By the practical method, the chief facts mentioned in the dissections and the text will be well impressed on the mind, and a conception of the mechanisms and phenomena of life may be obtained.

It has been my endeavor to make a *practical* treatise. The anatomical, histological, and physiological portions have been expressed in as direct and simple language as the nature of the subject seemed to admit. The directions for dissection, for microscopic work, and for demonstrations upon the human body have been so designed as to place their execution within the power of the average teachers in the American public schools. As far as possible the hygienic sections have been made concise, definite, and practical. The anatomy and physiology of a part have been given in contiguous paragraphs, rather than by a chapter upon the anatomy of a system followed by a chapter upon its physiology. The arrangement of the topics in each chapter, when the subject would admit, has been that which appeared most logical. The consideration of the motory and vocal systems was assigned to the later chapters, because of the intimate dependence of these systems upon the activities of the centres of the central nervous system. Numerous references from section to section have been introduced for the convenience of the teacher and for the assistance of the pupil. Chapter XV. has been designed to give, in a concise form, the best of the easily-executed methods of procedure in emergent cases, occurring in the school, in the home, in the workshop, on the road, and on the farm. The glossary has been made unusually full and complete, and is provided with references to the sections, the text of which serves to express more fully the meaning of certain terms. Quantities have been expressed in terms of the metric system, the equivalents of the same being placed within brackets. Questions have been provided for the sections printed in coarse type.

In the compilation of this elementary treatise, the latest and most reliable information has been sought. The writings of many of the leading instructors and practitioners of Europe and America have been consulted, and the knowledge contained therein has been freely employed. In so small a work it would be manifestly out of place to give proper credit for each fact so derived.

J. C. C.

Sapporo, Japan, June, 1884.

TO THE TEACHERS.

For *young scholars*, for *first-course* **students** in physiology, and for classes having thirty hours or less to devote to this branch of education, it is suggested that the entire time be confined to the study of the coarse-type paragraphs, and that the teacher, in the presence of the class, perform all dissections, all microscopic work, and all demonstrations as set forth in the text. *For advanced students*, and for students who may have studied this branch before, it is suggested that each paragraph in each chapter be studied in the order given; that the class be divided into sections of four to six students; that one of each section be assigned to act as dissector or demonstrator for the day; that, as far as possible, the microscopic work be done by the students, and that all be performed under the supervision of the teacher. If two consecutive school terms can be devoted to the subject, then it will be well to follow the course outlined for first-course students in the first term, and that outlined for advanced students in the second term.

Endeavor to make the instruction as actual as possible. Repeatedly call the attention of the pupils to the action of their own organs,—the heart, the conscious centre, the eye, the ear, the hand, etc. Familiarize them with the surface-markings and bony prominences of the body, so that they can localize arteries and the principal organs of the deep parts of the system. Direct especial attention to the weaker parts of the frame,—the temples, the supraclavicular spaces, the pit of the stomach, the exposed blood-tubes, the joint-flexures, etc.

The *topical method* of recitation may be conducted from the heads of paragraphs. To impress better upon the minds of the pupils the ideas expressed in the illustrations and diagrams, it is suggested that they be required to trace outlines of the principal cuts and then to write upon the tracing the names of the principal parts.

In teaching anatomy, outline anatomical charts and diagrams are as desirable for class-room use as maps in history and geography.

Where it is within the means of the school, I would suggest the advisability of purchasing a set of outline anatomical charts; also a set of Bock-steger models of the special sense organs, of a wired French skeleton, and of a manikin made in papier-maché by Auzoux, of Paris. These latter, when imported for school use, are not dutiable at the custom-house. J. B. Lippincott & Co., Philadelphia, will furnish descriptive price-lists for the latter on application.

Dissecting Instruments.—For the purpose of illustrative inanimation dissection, the student needs two or more scalpels, though crude work may be done with a sharp pocket-knife and a pair of Coxeter's dissecting forceps. The school will need, for occasional use, dissecting scissors, a meat saw, a cold-chisel, and a wood mallet. If a careful arterial dissection is to be made, then an injecting syringe and tubes and a few pounds of fine plaster of Paris should be procured. These instruments may be procured by mail of J. B. Lippincott & Co., Philadelphia.

Microscopes.—For the histological work outlined in this school-book the microscope should have a firm, low, metal base, a jointed bar, permitting the use of the instrument at any angle, a roomy stage, a diaphragm, suitable illuminating features, and a coarse and fine adjustment. The eye-piece and objective should always be of fine quality. One eye-piece (A or B), one $\frac{1}{5}$ or $\frac{1}{8}$ objective, and one $\frac{1}{4}$ objective is all that is required. An instrument combining all these features may be had in a suitable box at prices ranging from fifty dollars upwards. A neutral tint camera or a camera lucida, to enable the student to sketch from the object, should always be purchased and constantly used.

Materials.—One dozen glass slides, ground edges, two dozen glass cover-circles, one bottle of Woodward's Lilac Fluid, a few watch-crystals, and a couple of small shallow dishes. If much work is to be done, it would be well for the school to possess a microtome and a good section-knife. The student can make from glass tubing pipettes and dipping tubes and mount teasing needles in handles. Provided with a fine old razor, a pair of fine scissors, and the above, he is equipped for elementary work. Microscopes and materials may be procured from J. B. Lippincott & Co., Philadelphia.

General Directions.—(1) Remove all dust on the lenses of the eye-piece or objective with a camel's-hair pencil or a bit of soft silk. (2) Avoid unnecessary rubbing of the lenses. (3) For artificial illumination an argand burner may be used. Sunlight reflected from a white cloud is the best. Avoid direct sunlight. (4) With high powers employ the smaller holes of the diaphragm. (5) In focussing, run down the tube until the field-glass of the objective is within the focus, but not touching the cover-glass. With the eye at the eye-piece, *run up* the tube until the focus is reached. (6) Keep both eyes open when studying a specimen. (7) Observe the strictest neatness and the utmost cleanliness in work. Clean the pipettes, slides, and cover-glasses immediately after use. For this purpose employ water, alcohol, oil of turpentine, and occasionally mineral acids or strong alkalies. Keep the clean covers in 95 per cent. alcohol.

The tissues which make up the organs and intermediate structures of mammals do not differ materially from similar tissues in man. Hence the warm-blooded animals slain by butchers will furnish ample fresh materials for the study of microscopic anatomy. Use only minute portions of material. Soft, recent tissues may be snipped off with fine scissors or scraped from surfaces with a dull knife. With needles mounted in handles they may be teased out in shallow dishes containing a little water. Sometimes it is well to do the teasing under a ¾- or 1-inch lens mounted in a loop of wire, the handle of the wire being inserted in a vertical wooden rod, and the lens then forced into focus by pressure of the forehead. After washing, the teased specimens are floated on a slide, are wetted with a five per cent. salt solution, covered with a slip, and examined. Corpuscles, mucus, epithelia, pus, urea, etc., may be examined in their own media.

Each histologist has his peculiar method of procedure. The larger works, especially Frey's, contain minute directions for preparing the various tissues. The following is a ready method of procedure: In four large-mouthed bottles containing alcohol the specimens may be hardened preparatory to section-cutting. In No. 1, alcohol of 45 per cent.; in No. 2, alcohol of 60 per cent.; in No. 3, alcohol of 80 per cent.; and in No. 4, alcohol of 95 per cent. The cubes of tissues, each being properly labelled, are put into No. 1, and every fourth day changed to the next in turn. At the end of sixteen days the cubes in No. 4 will be ready for cutting. Embed them in mixed melted paraffin, one part, and pig's lard, one part, in the microtome-well. When hardened and cold, cut the mixture from the front and sides of the cube, and make numerous very thin sections; or, in cold weather, freeze the cubes, and then, with a sharp, cold razor, in a cold room, make sections. Keep the sections in alcohol. Remove a few sections to a little lilac solution in a watch-glass. After a few minutes, transfer to a solution of muriatic acid, one part, to 95 per cent. alcohol, four parts. After a few seconds, wash in alcohol and transfer to pure alcohol. From here they are placed in oil of turpentine, from whence they are floated on the slide, covered, and examined.

Books for Reference.—Leidy, Human Anatomy; Gray, Human Anatomy; Wilder, Animal Technology, a Guide to Dissection of the Cat; Foster, Text-Book of Physiology, 4th Eng. ed.; Beale, How to Work with the Microscope; Carpenter, On the Microscope; Phin, How to Use the Microscope; Parkes, Practical Hygiene; Wilson, Hand-Book of Hygiene; Huxley, Practical Biology; Foster, Practical Physiology; Howe, On Emergencies; Carter, Defects of Vision; Wilson, Healthy Skin; Eassie, Unhealthiness in Houses; Anstie, Stimulants and Narcotics; Anstie, Wines in Health and Disease; Kane, Drugs that Enslave; Acton, Reproductive Organs; Pavy, On Food; E. Smith, On Foods; Maudsley, Physiology of Mind; Ray, Mental Hygiene; Thomas, Medical Dictionary; Cutter, Anatomical Charts, 9 Plates; Marshall, Physiological Diagrams, 11 Maps.

CONTENTS.

CHAPTER I.

GENERAL REMARKS.

Definitions—Parts—Organs—Tissues—Chemical Composition . . . 15

CHAPTER II.

LIVING PROPERTIES OF THE ANATOMICAL ELEMENTS.

Amœba Cells—Protoplasm—Cell-Growth—Cell-Division—Growth—Granules—Life . . . 18

CHAPTER III.

THE FRAMEWORK AND ITS COVERINGS.

Dissection—Microscopy—Bones—Skeleton—Table of Bones—Flesh—Integument—Tissues—Membrane—Skin—Epidermis—Corium—Nail—Hair—Sebaceous Glands—Sweat Glands—Perspiration—Simpson's Bath—Functions of Skin—Hygiene—Clothing—Cold Feet—Light—Bathing—Soap 22

CHAPTER IV.

THE CONTRACTILE AND IRRITABLE TISSUES.

Elasticity—Striped Muscle—Unstriped Muscle—Cardiac Muscle—Ciliated Cells—Physiology of Muscle—White Nerve-Fibre—Remak's Nerve-Fibre—Nerve-Cells—Physiology of Nerve-Mechanism—Reflex Action—Automatism—Inhibition—Muscle and Nerve 48

CHAPTER V.

THE VASCULAR SYSTEM AND THE CIRCULATION.

Dissection—Microscopy—Thorax—Heart—Dissection—Auricles—Ventricles—Valves—Heart-Ganglia—Membranes—Arteries—Capillaries—Veins—Table of Arteries—Venæ Cavæ—Portal Vein—Pulmonic Ves-

PAGE

sels—Vasa Vasorum—Blood-Coagulation—Function of Blood—Course
of Circulation—Heart-Action—Work of Heart—Inhibition—Acceleration — Heart-Sounds—Blood-Flow—Vaso-Motor Influence—Catching
Cold—Capillary Blood-Flow—Interchange in Capillary Areas—Proofs
of Circulation—HYGIENE 55

CHAPTER VI.

THE RESPIRATORY APPARATUS AND RESPIRATION.

Dissection — Thorax — Vertebræ — Ribs—Sternum — Muscles — Thoracic
Contents—Pleura—Nasal Passages—Pharynx—Palate—Larynx—Tra-
chea—Bronchi—Air-Cells—Mucous Membrane—Mucus—Lungs—Tho-
racic Capacity—Thoracic Enlargement—Inspiration—Expiration—Dif-
fusion of Gases—Respiration—Blood-Changes—Hæmoglobin—Action
of Corpuscles—Action of Oxygen—Breathing—Statistics—HYGIENE—
Nasal Breathing—Normal Air—Air-Impurities—Effects of Vitiated Air
—Sewer-Gas—Contagia—Air-Contamination—The Home—Air-Space—
Ventilation—Open Fire—Sleeping-Room—Consumption—Fashionable
Compression 85

CHAPTER VII.

FOODS.

Plant Food—Animal Food—Definition of Food—Standard Food—Proteids—Fats—Starchy Class—Water and Salts—Accessory Foods—Diet
for Health—Water—Milk—Cooking—Meats—Table of Values—Cereals
—Legumens—Vegetables—Order of Richness—Fruits—Digestibility—
Table of Digestibility—Stimulants—Tea—Coffee—Cocoa—Alcohol . 11'

CHAPTER VIII.

THE DIGESTIVE ORGANS AND DIGESTION.

Dissection—Microscopy—Abdomen — Pelvis—Alimentary Canal — Gland
—Mouth—Demonstration—Teeth—Salivary Glands—Saliva— Mastication and Insalivation—Pharynx—Œsophagus—Deglutition—Stomach
—Gastric Juice—Action of Stomach—Small Intestine—Peristaltic Action—Vomiting—Large Intestine—Liver—Function of Liver—Pancreas—Function of Pancreas—Changes effected in Food Stuffs in the
Alimentary Canal — Osmose—Absorption — Lacteals—Chyle — Movements of Chyle—Summary—HYGIENE—Indigestion—Quantity of Food
—State of Food—Bad Teeth—Care of Teeth—Frequency of Eating—
Improper Food—Aids to Dyspepsia—Prevention of Dyspepsia—Constipation 135

CHAPTER IX.

THE LYMPHATICS, SPLEEN, THYMUS, ETC.—THE URINARY SYSTEM.

PAGE

Lymphatics—Vessels—Glands—Lymph—Function—Spleen—Function—
Suprarenal Bodies—Thyroid—Thymus—Kidneys—Urine—Function
of Kidneys—Bladder—Retention of Urine 165

CHAPTER X.

NUTRITION.

Assimilation—Glycogen—Fat—Urea—The Animal Machine—Manifestation of Force—Production of Force—Income—Outcome—The Energy
of a Living Diet—Heat—Energy—Heat-Production—Body-Heat—
Heat-Regulation—Excretion—Waste Products—Summary—HYGIENE
—Thirst—Appetite—Dietetics—Food-Excess—Food-Deficiency—Want
of Food—Human Endurance—Amount of Food—Diets . . 173

CHAPTER XI.

THE NERVOUS SYSTEM.

Dissection—Microscopy—Head—Face—Spinal Canal—Nervous System—
Fibres—Centres—Function—Impulses—Cerebro-Spinal System—Brain
—Cerebrum—Functions of Superior Parts of Brain—Rapidity of Cere-
bral Action—Functions of Superior Ganglia—Cerebellum—Spinal Cord
—Medulla—Pons—Membranes—Functions of Inferior Parts of Brain
—Cerebellum—Functions of Spinal Cord—Convulsions—Paralysis—
Sensory Nerve—Motor Nerve—Cranial Nerves—Table of Cranial Nerves
—Function of Cranial Nerves—Spinal Nerves—Sympathetic System—
Summary—Automatic Action—Co-ordination—Habit—HYGIENE—He-
redity—Normal Blood—Stimulants and Sedatives—Alcohol—Chloral
—Hashish—Opium—Tobacco—Regularity of Action—Mental Exercise
—Education—Harmonious Development—Occupation—Normal Sleep
—Work and Worry—Rest 190

CHAPTER XII.

THE SPECIAL SENSES.

Tongue—Taste—Nasal Passages—Smell—External Ear—Middle Ear—
Internal Ear—Sound—Functions of External and Middle Ears—Experi-
ments—Hearing—Auditory Sensations—Dissection of Eye—Microscopy
—Orbits—Protective Organs—Functions—Lachrymal Canal and Gland

PAGE

—Conjunctiva—Functions—Eyeball—Membranes—Media and Lens—
Functions — Experiments—Light—Refraction—Accommodation — Ex-
periment—Mechanism of Accommodation—Experiments—Near Limit
and Far Limit—Imperfections—Visual Sensations and Perceptions—
Color-Blindness—After-Images—Binocular Vision—Touch—Pressure
—Temperature—Localization of Sensations—Experiments—Muscular
Sense—Sense of Equilibrium—HYGIENE—Of Tongue—Of Nostrils—Of
External Ear—Management of the Eye: in Infancy; in Childhood; in
Student Life; in Adult Life—Illumination—Statistics—Myopia—Pre-
vention of Eye-Disease—Finger-Tips 240

CHAPTER XIII.

THE LARYNX AND VOICE.

Larynx—Cartilages—Cords—Production of Sound—Voice—Muscular Co-
ordination—Speech—HYGIENE 284

CHAPTER XIV.

THE MOTOR APPARATUS AND LOCOMOTION.

Dissection—Bone—Cartilage—Bone-Formation—Microscopic Characters
—Joint—Synovial Sac—Synovia—Ligaments—Interarticular Cartilage—Table of Muscles—Tendons of Muscles—Action of Muscles—Co-
ordinate Movements—Sensory Influence—Progression—Effects of Exercise—Deficiency of Exercise—Systematic Exercise—HYGIENE—Physical Culture—Swedish, English, and German Systems—Influence of
Physical Culture—Suppression of By-Motions—Conditions for Exercise
—Rest—Kinds of Exercise—Amount of Exercise—Posture—Training. 293

CHAPTER XV.

CARE OF THE SICK AND EMERGENT CASES.

Care of the Sick—The Watcher—Poisons—Table of Poisons and Common
Antidotes—Emergent Cases—Bleeding—Flesh-Wounds—Bleeding at
the Nose—Broken Bones—Burns and Scalds—Asphyxia: from Drowning; from Illuminating Gas—Silvester's Method—Prevention of Drowning—Bodies in External Ear—Particles on the Surface of Eyeball—
Frost-Bite — Hernia — Retention—Simpson's Bath—Wounds: Punctured, Mad Dog, Serpent, and Insect—Ivy-Poison—Sunstroke . . 326

GLOSSARY 345

INDEX 369

ANATOMY, PHYSIOLOGY, AND HYGIENE.

CHAPTER I.

GENERAL REMARKS.

1. ANATOMY is the science of organization. Human anatomy treats of the number, shape, situation, structure, and connection of the parts making up man. HISTOLOGY considers the minute structure of the tissues as made known by microscopic and microchemic studies. PHYSIOLOGY treats of the healthy operations which take place in living beings. HYGIENE embraces a consideration of the conditions most favorable for the healthy action of the parts and of the whole. CHEMISTRY treats of the nature and properties of every object accessible to man.

2. The body of man, as a whole, is readily seen to be composed of the *head, neck, trunk*, and *extremities*. These, under closer examination, offer the *scalp, forehead, eyes, ears, nose*, and *mouth*, of the head; the *thorax*, the *abdomen*, and the *pelvis*, of the trunk; the *arm, forearm, wrist*, and *hands*, of the upper extremity; the *thigh, leg, ankle*, and *foot*, of the lower. It is seen that different materials are employed in the construction of the varying parts, as *skin, hair, nails*, and *teeth;* that some parts are soft (fat), others firm (muscles), and still others hard and resisting (bone).

---

1. Define Anatomy. Histology. Physiology. Hygiene. Chemistry.

2. Give the general divisions of the body. Subdivisions of the head. Of the trunk. Of the extremities. Materials employed.

3. If the dead body be examined, it will be found to consist of a number of differing parts, called *organs* (such as the heart, brain); that the organs are made up of a limited number of materials, called *tissues* (like connective, nerve, muscular tissues); that the most complex organs are constructed of less than a dozen tissues, combined in varying numbers and proportions; and that the tissues are built up of *cells* and *granules*.

Demonstration.—Point out on the body of a boy the parts mentioned in paragraph 2. Request several of the students to demonstrate the same later. Bring into the class the heart of a chicken, calf, or pig. State its functions to the class. Show that it is made up of a number of materials, as of muscle, of areolar connective tissue, of nerve-masses, of blood-tubes, of white fibrous tissue, etc. Snip a small bit of areolar tissue. Under water, in a shallow saucer, tease it out with needles inserted in handles. Place on a slide in a drop of water under a cover-glass. Call attention to the membrane, or expansion, as a whole; then to the component fibres. If there are a few fat cells present, call attention to their form and limiting membrane. Then press on the cover and examine the oil-globules.

Place a drop of yeast on the slide. Spread out thin and cover. Call attention to the cells and groups of vegetable cells, their sizes, the contained protoplasm often showing a few shining dots. Run in a drop of magenta solution. The protoplasm will be stained.

4. *Chemical Composition.*—The normal body includes only fourteen chemical elements in its composition: oxygen, O; hydrogen, H; nitrogen, N; carbon, C; sulphur, S; phosphorus, P; fluorine, Fl; chlorine, Cl; Sodium, Na; potassium, K; calcium, Ca; magnesium, Mg; silicon, Si; and iron, Fe. Carbon, by weight, forms the principal element. It is the base of all organic substances. It is the chemical bond of all the various atoms which enter into the composition of the granules, cells, and tissues. The gases oxygen and nitrogen often are found in the tissues in a free state.

---

3. What makes up the body? Examples. Make-up of organs? Make-up of tissues? How many?

4. Name the chemical elements. What of carbon? Of oxygen? Of nitrogen?

5. In the living organism these fourteen elements are united into a series of complex chemical compounds. Owing to the presence of nitrogen in proportionably larger amounts than in plants, there is in the animal organism a great degree of chemical complexity and instability. The latter is shown in the quicker decay of animal tissues over vegetable tissues when once removed from the living organism, and the former by the marked predominance of ternary compounds (C, H, O) over proteid compounds (C, H, O, N, S, P) in the plant.

5. What of these elements? The difference between animal and vegetable compounds? Define proteid. (See GLOSSARY.)

CHAPTER II.

LIVING PROPERTIES OF THE ANATOMICAL UNITS.

Demonstration.—Amœba. Secure some stagnant water, or ooze from a pool, or make an infusion of animal matter and allow it to evaporate under direct sunlight. Search in the same for jelly-like organisms. Place one on a slide in a drop of water. Call attention to the outline, and to the structure, the nucleus, the contractile vesicle, the contained materials, the movements, and the formation of pseudo-podium.

6. The AMŒBA is a microscopic mass of living matter which inhabits fresh water. It is composed of jelly-like *protoplasm* containing granules. Its outer portion consists of a slightly consolidated transparent layer, and its inner portion of a more fluid, more mobile substance. The outer layer is highly extensile and contractile. The pseudo-podia (having false feet) are mainly made up of this layer. The inner portion contains the "nucleus," "contractile vesicle," and, at times, "food vacuoles." Food may be taken at any part of the surface and expelled from any part, after which the aperture closes up. There are no digestive, secreting, or excreting organs. There are no traces of a nervous system or of sense organs. The general surface recognizes contact with other objects. The mass moves itself by projecting out blunt finger-like processes, called *pseudo-podia.* These are projected at will from any part of the surface, and may be withdrawn at will. The nucleus appears at times as a clear granular body, or as a clear vesicle containing a nucleolus. New *individuals* are produced in several ways: 1. The organism may undergo self-division, each part becoming independent (Fig. 1, C). 2. A pseudo-podium may become detached and develop into an amœba. 3. A new mass may be produced in the interior, which may or may not be set free, but which develops into a perfect amœba (Fig. 1, B).

7. This little mass performs all the offices necessary to its grade of life,—growth and reproduction. This little mass is *contractile,—*

18

that is, it exhibits motion in its interior, as well as from place to place; it is *irritable* and *automatic*, for when disturbed it can move at will from its position; it is *receptive*, for it takes in food; it is *assimilative*, for out of the materials taken in it transforms and accepts a portion, and increases in size; it is *respiratory*, for gases interchange between it and its watery home; it is undergoing internal changes, and *secretes*, *excretes*, and *rejects* certain products; it is *reproductive*. In brief, all the major phenomena of life are exhibited in the amœba. All the physiologic phenomena of all the

Fig. 1.

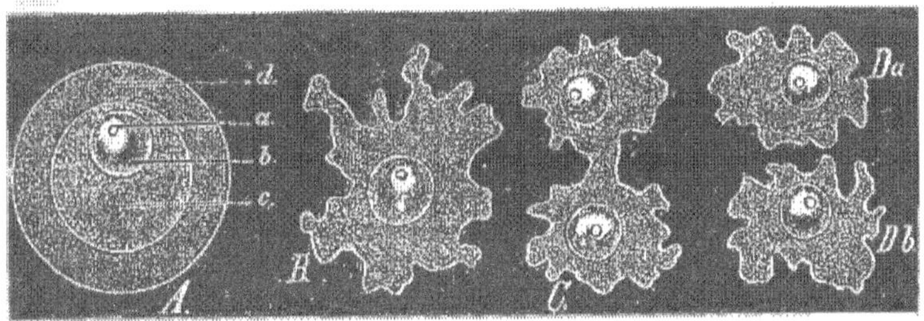

Fig. 1.—Amœba Sphærococcus (Letourneau). A, Amœba encysted; protoplasmic mass (c) containing nucleus (b) and nucleolus (a); enveloping membrane (d). B, Amœba free from enveloping membrane. C, Amœba commencing to divide. Da and Db, totally divided into two independent amœbæ.

higher animals are but the working out of certain acts by similar protoplasmic efforts. In the amœba grade of organization all is done by the protoplasmic units. In the higher grade of organisms there is division of labor, differentiation of duties. The many tissues and organs of the higher grades, like the simple mass of the lowest, work for a common purpose,—the building up, the protecting, the developing of the organism, and the continuance of the species.

8. CELLS.—The smallest known masses of living matter assume the spherical form. They present a colorless, soft, and, at times, granular appearance. Within the mass may be seen a clear, distinct, non-granular part or body, often enclosing, in turn, a still smaller body. Occasionally a thin layer of hardened material may be seen on its surface. The size of the masses is about 0.012 millimetre ($\frac{1}{2000}$ of an inch) in diameter. This is pre-eminently the

anatomical unit, and is known at present as *the cell.* The central mass is called the *cell-body;* the embedded, non-granular part, the *nucleus;* the body within the nucleus, the *nucleolus;* and the limiting layer, the *cell-wall.* By the activities inherent in the cell-body the food or pabulum received is converted into new cell-body material, which is later resolved into *formed* material, as cell-wall, fibres, tissues. All the formed or histological materials of the tissues pass through the cell-body stage of growth. The white corpuscle of the blood exhibits most of the characters, histological and physiological, of the anatomical unit (113).

9. Protoplasm.—The cell-body in the living state consists of a colorless, structureless material, which exhibits, under the microscope, slow movements. These movements originate in this transparent material; this material is called *Protoplasm* (or Bioplasm). The granular contents which are seen moving about in the mass are only minute suspended matters. The actual chemical composition of protoplasm is not known, because the processes of chemistry employed in the analysis destroy the *vital* or living feature, which is the marked characteristic of protoplasm. It probably contains fats, carbo-hydrates, protcids combined with certain inorganic salts, and much water. Protoplasm can absorb, excrete, secrete, grow, move, and multiply. The functions of the granules and nuclei have not yet been determined. Protoplasm is most easily studied in one of the simplest of the animal series,—the Amœba. Human white blood and mucous corpuscles also show a part of the above phenomena.

10. Cell-Growth.—Each living cell-body possesses the power of receiving into itself *foods,—i.e.,* materials different from itself,—in solution or in a state of fine division, and of working chemical and physical changes in the same until they become part and parcel of the cell-body. The matters received acquire properties and powers which the food alone did not have. The new matter is added to the mass not upon the outside, but in the inside,—that is, by *intussusception.* Cell-growth is an epitome of tissue-growth, of organ-growth, of body-growth.

11. Cell-Division.—If the materials received into the cell-body are in excess of its wants, and if it attains its limits of growth, then the formation of new living centres is induced. This tendency for change may come from within or from without. From *without,* it may start in an hour-glass-like contraction or elongation, with con-

traction of the cell-body continuing to the point of dividing the mass into two parts (Fig. 1, D); from *within*, by the appearance in the interior of the parent cell of one or more cell-bodies which may or may not be set free (Fig. 1, B). The new cells possess the properties and tendencies of the parent cells. In most cases the nucleus divides earlier than the cell-body.

12. GROWTH.—The increase in *volume* of the anatomical elements, together with their multiplication, accounts for the increase in size in tissues, organs, and the body,—that is, *growth*. The rapidity and energy of growth vary with the cell-body, its condition, its surroundings, and its food-supplies.

13. The GRANULES are the smallest known histologic elements. They may be suspended in fluids, may remain free with certain chemical elements, or perhaps enclosed in cells. They may be proteid or fatty in their nature. They vary as to color, size, and density. Their offices are not well understood: possibly they are food not yet ready to be made into the cell-body and the tissues.

14. In the *living body*, as in the *living cell*, there is a ceaseless internal motion and change of material. There is a constant removal of old or used materials, and a constant taking in of new materials, which are changed and modified in the organism, and then enter into its structure. The cessation of these changes in the cells or tissues constitutes *local death;* in the entire organism, *death*. The phenomena of life appear to imply the presence in the organism of a guiding, controlling, and dictating force. This force is modified in many ways by external and internal conditions; it is transmitted from generation to generation, and it appears distinct from, though working with, the common physical forces of nature. To this force have been applied the terms "germ force" and "vital force."

CHAPTER III.

THE FRAMEWORK AND ITS COVERINGS.

Direction for Dissecting.

TAKE the hind leg of a sheep, rabbit, dog, or rat. On the inside of the thigh make a clean cut from the groin to the second joint through the skin down to the muscle. This exposes, in section, the *hairs*, and their place of implantation, the *skin*. Now dissect off the skin to the right and left of the line, and remove it from the leg. We find the skin is attached to the parts beneath by a loose, extensible, elastic web, the *areolar* or *connective* tissue. In this loose web we find masses of *fat*, making up a more or less firm layer. Remove this. The white, glistening, membranous surface of the *fascia* is presented. This holds the red flesh-bands in their proper position. Make an incision through this, and dissect it off. The fleshy *muscles* and thin, white, firm *tendons* of connection come into view. With the handle of the knife, or the back of the blade, separate two of the large muscles, and we find that *areolar* tissue and a firmer *intermuscular* connective tissue or *septum* bind them together. In the gap, or an adjacent one, may be seen a whip-cord-like, hollow tube, the *artery*, one or two thinner, dark-colored, parallel tubes, the *veins*, and a clean, white, smooth cord, the *nerve*. Near the groin, and in the vicinity of the veins, may be seen a few roundish, softish, dark, pea-sized bodies, the *lymphatic glands*.

Remove the flesh from the bones. The bones will be found to be covered by a firm, white, close-fitting membrane, the *periosteum*. Beneath the periosteum may be seen a number of pits and holes. These admit microscopic blood-vessels to the interior. Break or saw the bone. At the line of fracture will be seen the frayed edge of the *periosteum*, the hard, pinkish white surface of the *bone*, and the spongy interior filled with a reddish, fatty matter, the *medulla* or *marrow*.

The *joint*. Remove the bits of fat, muscle, and areolar tissue. The bones will be seen to be held together by hard, firm, inelastic, flexible bands, the *ligaments*. These ligaments may be broad and flat, ribbon-like or round. Cut the ligaments and open the joint. A white, glairy fluid, the *synovia*, escapes. The ends of the bones are found tipped with a pearly white substance, a shaving of which can be removed by the knife. This is *cartilage*. Loose pieces of cartilage and internal ligaments may be seen within the joint, which is lined by the smooth *synovial membrane*.

Microscope Work.—Of the soft parts,—muscle, tendon, areolar tissue, etc.,—cut cubes about three-quarters of an inch on a side, and place in alcohol of one per cent. for hardening purposes. Take a small bit of areolar tissue or muscle, etc., place on a clean slide, add a drop or two of water, and carefully tease out with the needles. Do not hesitate to spend much time in the teasing. Breathe on the lower side of a cover-glass, apply the glass and adjust it in place, then place the slide on the stage and examine. Or take a drop of the fluids,—serum, blood, mucus, synovia, etc.,—as they occur, on a clean slide; put on a cover-glass; by slight pressure spread the drop, and examine by transmitted, by oblique, by direct light. Also observe the changes in form produced by slight changes of the focus, especially in examining the blood-corpuscles.

22

The Framework.

15. The framework of the human body consists of the *bones*, which, taken together, constitute the *skeleton*.

16. The BONES (501), when in the body, are moist, pinkish white in color, and covered with a tough, closely-adherent membrane, called the *periosteum* (*peri*, around, *osteon*, bone). The surface of bones is hard and compact. On the surface are many little holes, which lead to the interior. The interior usually has a spongy appearance. The spongy spaces chiefly contain a soft, reddish, fatty material, called *marrow*, or *medulla*.

17. The SKELETON gives general form to the body. It determines the height and the breadth; it supports and protects the soft parts of the interior; it gives effect and precision to the actions of the *muscles*, or ruddy flesh. Its separate pieces, two hundred in number (Gray), are held together by moist, strong, non-elastic, flexible bands, called *ligaments* (Fig. 2). The skeleton constitutes about sixteen per cent. of the body-weight.

18. The FLESH constitutes the soft, red portions of the body. It covers over in general the bones, and is attached to their surfaces at certain definite points. This skeleton-surrounding mass consists of about three hundred and seventy distinct fleshy masses, called *muscles* (75, 76). They are usually arranged in pairs. Their shape, size, form, and arrangement depend on the outline of the skeleton. They

15. Speak of the skeleton.

16. The appearance of a fresh bone. The surface. The interior. The periosteum. The marrow.

17. Use of the skeleton. Number of bones. Ligaments and their uses. Skeleton percentage of the body-weight.

18. Speak of the flesh. How many muscles? How arranged?

FIG. 2.

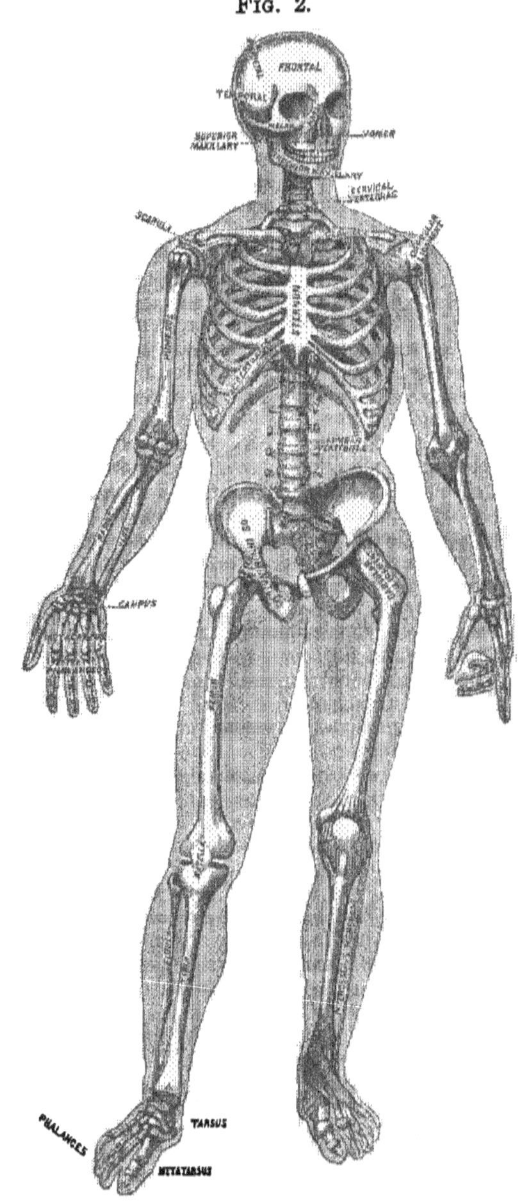

FRONTAL
TEMPORAL
SUPERIOR MAXILLARY
VOMER
CERVICAL VERTEBRÆ
SCAPULA
STERNUM
LUMBAR VERTEBRÆ
CARPUS
PHALANGES
TARSUS
METATARSUS

TABLE OF THE BONES.

HEAD (22)	*Skull* (8)	Frontal (forehead).
		2 Temporal (temples).
		2 Parietal (side).
		Occipital (posterior base).
		Sphenoid (base).
		Ethmoid (base of nose).
	Face (14)	2 Superior Maxillæ (upper jaw).
		2 Nasal (bridge of nose).
		2 Malar (cheek).
		2 Lachrymal (corner of orbit).
		2 Turbinated (within nostrils).
		2 Palate (posterior hard palate).
		Vomer (nasal partition).
		Inferior Maxilla (lower jaw).

CERVICAL REGION (8)
- 7 Cervical Vertebræ (neck).
- Hyoid Bone (base of tongue).

THORAX (37)
- 14 True, 6 False, 4 Floating Ribs.
- 12 Dorsal Vertebræ (back).
- Sternum.

UPPER EXTREMITIES (64)	*Shoulder*	Clavicle (collar).
		Scapula (shoulder-blade).
	Arm	Humerus (arm).
		Radius, Ulna (fore-arm).
	Hand	8 Carpal (wrist).
		5 Metacarpal (hand).
		14 Phalanges (fingers).

LUMBAR REGION (5)
- 5 Lumbar Vertebræ (loins).

PELVIS (4)
- 2 Innominata.
- Sacrum.
- Coccyx.

LOWER EXTREMITIES (60)	*Thigh*	Femur.
	Leg	Patella (knee-pan).
		Tibia (large bone).
		Fibula (outer bone).
	Foot	7 Tarsal (instep, heel).
		5 Metatarsal (arch).
		14 Phalanges (toes).

are arranged in layers, some *deep*, some *superficial*. On the back and abdomen they are broad; on the extremities, long and narrow; about openings, circular.

19. All muscles are held in their proper places by a

FIG. 3.

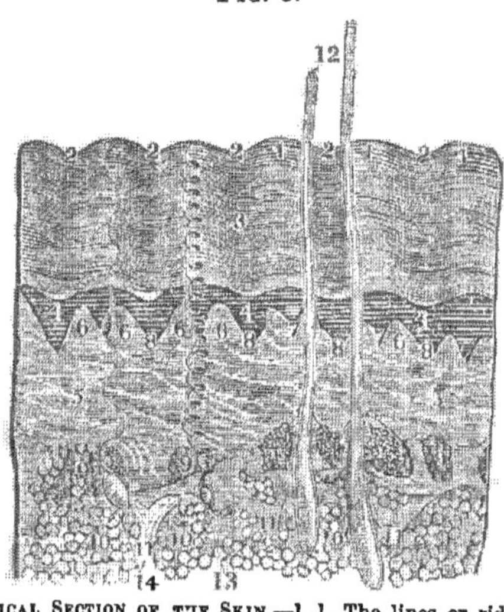

FIG. 3. A VERTICAL SECTION OF THE SKIN.—1, 1, The lines or ridges of the cuticle, cut perpendicularly. 2, 2, 2, 2, 2, The furrows or wrinkles of the same. 3, The epidermis. 4, 4, 4, Pigment layer. 5, 5, Dermis, or cutis vera. 6, 6, 6, 6, 6, Papillæ. 7, 7, Small furrows between the papillæ. 8, 8, 8, 8, Deeper furrows between each couple of the papillæ. 9, 9, 9, Cells filled with fat. 10, 10, 10, Adipose layer, with numerous fat vesicles. 11, 11, 11, Cellular fibres of the adipose tissue. 12, Two hairs. 13, A perspiratory gland, with its spiral duct. 14, Another perspiratory gland, with a duct less spiral. 15, 15, Oil glands with ducts opening into the sheath of the hair (12).

moist, whitish, web-like structure, called *inter-muscular connective tissue*. Muscles, being made up largely of *muscular fibre* (71), are endowed with the power of *contractility*, —that is, under certain stimulants (as heat, pinching, electricity, nerve-cell influence) the fibre becomes shorter, and on the removal of the stimulant regains its former state.

---

19. How are muscles held in place? Of what composed? Give an endowment of the muscles. Name some stimulants of the muscles. Muscular percentage of the body-weight.

The muscles of an adult (thirty-one years of age) constitute about forty-two per cent. of the body-weight.

20. The INTEGUMENT. Outside of the white, firm, resisting membrane called *fascia,* which holds many of the

FIG. 4.
FIG. 5.

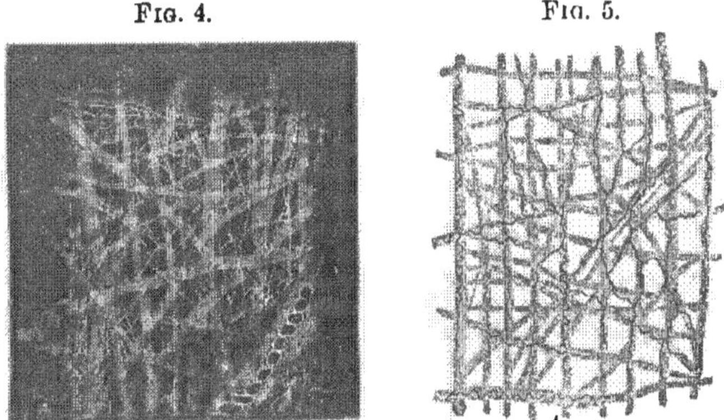

FIG. 4 (*Leidy*). PORTION OF CONNECTIVE TISSUE from the axilla, exhibiting its composition of bundles and filaments of fibrous tissue crossing in every direction. The rounded bodies represent a single row and a portion of small groups of fat cells. Magnified.

FIG. 5 (*Leidy*). 1, PORTION OF CONNECTIVE TISSUE from that which envelops the flexor tendons of the fingers as they pass beneath the annular ligament, treated with acetic acid. The pale, dotted portion is intended to represent the fibrous element fading away; the blacker, tortuous lines and nets represent the mixture of elastic tissue.

outer muscles of the body and limbs in position, is a layer or two of moist, fine, web-like *areolar* or *connective* tissue. In the meshes of the latter are seen little masses of semi-fluid *fat.* Outside of those layers, and intimately connected with them, is the *skin.*

21. The areolar tissue, the fat, and the skin, together, round off, fill up, and finish the contour of the whole surface of the body. The *fat* under the skin accumulates more rapidly than any other tissue, and is the earliest

20. What is fascia? Give its function. Speak of the areolar tissue. Where is the skin found?

21. What gives finish to the outlines of the body? Speak of fat. Its abundance.

removed under disease. It is a storehouse of food, and a good heat-retainer for the body. It is more abundant in children and in females than in males or in adults.

22. *Areolar connective tissue* consists of bands of white, also of *yellow, elastic* fibres, which interweave in every direction, leaving meshes or open spaces. It is loose, moist, flexible, and extensible. Its series of open spaces communicate with adjacent spaces, and so

FIG. 6.   FIG. 7.

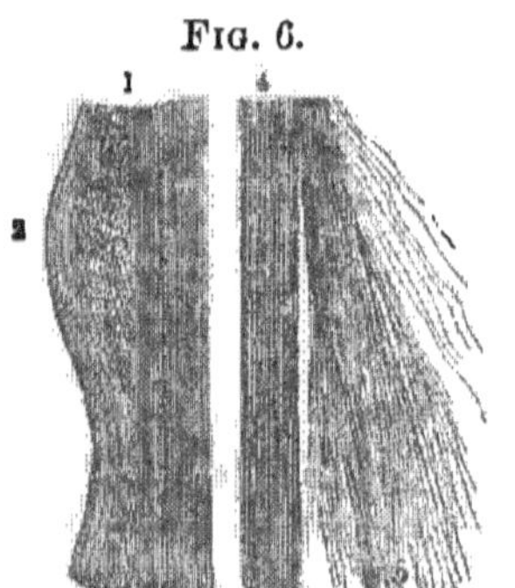
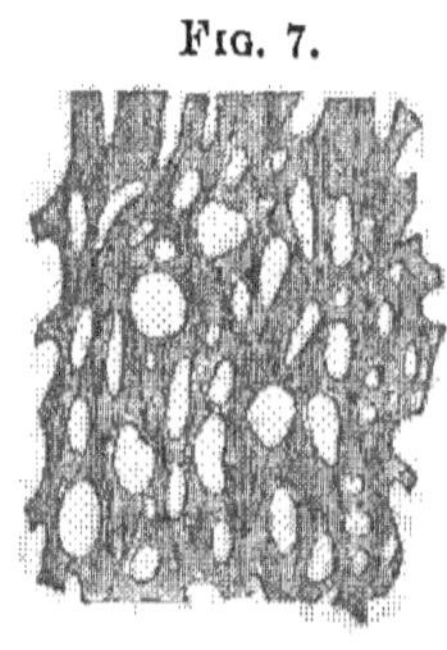

FIG. 6 (*Leidy*). FIBROUS TISSUE.—1, Portion of tendon, exhibiting its composition of prismatic bundles of fibrous tissue, the filaments all parallel to one another. 2, A few bundles drawn from the others, exhibiting their union by delicate crossing filaments of connective tissue. 3, One of the varieties of fibrous tissue. 4, A single bundle, more highly magnified, with a portion (5) of the filaments fretted out.

FIG. 7 (*Leidy*). ELASTIC TISSUE. Highly magnified.

on throughout the body. In these meshes are lodged the fatty tissues. In these spaces accumulate the fluids in general *dropsy* of the subcutaneous parts of the body. The function of this tissue is to connect organs and parts of organs, to support blood-vessels, lymphatics, and nerves, and to allow limited motion to adjacent muscles or organs.

23. The *white fibrous tissue* consists of fine white fibrils, usually arranged in parallel lines in the form of small bundles. It has a shining aspect, and is firm, resistant, and not elastic. It enters into the formation of membranes, tendons, and ligaments.

24. The *elastic* tissue has a yellow color. Its fibres are never quite parallel to one another, but often branch out and unite again. When cut, the ends of these fibres curl up. After this tissue has been stretched, it *retracts* like an india-rubber band. It is found in the

areolar tissue, in the inner coats of the arteries, in certain ligaments of the spine, and in the vocal cords.

25. *Adipose tissue*, or fat (309), is composed of numerous round or ovoid sacs, filled with an oily fluid. At the temperature of the living body the fat is fluid, but after the cooling of the body it becomes quite solid. In the state of emaciation the fat vesicles are emptied of fat, and the walls become shrivelled. This tissue is not formed within the skull, in the lungs, or in the eyelids, because its

Fig. 8.   Fig. 9.

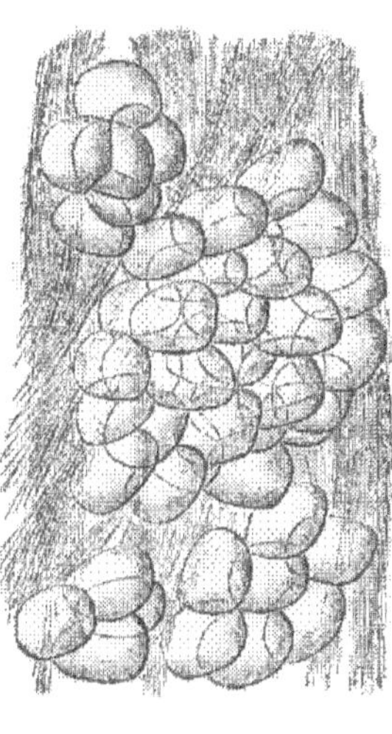

Fig. 8 (*Leidy*). Crossing Bands of fibrous connective tissue.

Fig. 9 (*Leidy*). Adipose Tissue, with Connective Tissue, from the superficial fascia of the abdomen. Highly magnified. The groups of fat vesicles are observed contained in the meshes of connective tissue.

accumulation alternating with its diminution would interfere with the functions of those organs. It is found under the skin (subcutaneous fat), about the kidneys, about the joints, about the heart, in the orbits, and in the omentum (21).

26. *Membrane* is the name given to the thin, supple, more or less elastic webs of the body. These webs are intended to separate, to envelop, or to form organs, or to bear certain cellular structures, called *epithelia* (156). The membranes are of three kinds,—*fibrous, serous,* and *mucous.*

3*

27. The *fibrous membrane* is firm, resisting, slightly elastic, white, sometimes pearly and glistening. It is made up largely of white fibrous tissue, though containing a slight admixture of yellow elastic fibre. It is sparingly supplied with blood-vessels and nerve-fibres. Its functions are to surround organs and to augment their solidity, like the capsule of the kidney, the sclerotica of the eye; to retain muscles in their proper positions, as the fasciæ of the arms and limbs; and to favor the motions of tendons and of the skin.

The *serous* membrane. (See 156.)

The *mucous* membrane. (See 164.)

The Skin.

28. The SKIN is the covering which invests the body. It is a flexible, extensible, elastic membrane. It is soft, smooth, and has an oily feel. Upon its surface, lines, pits, and depressions, and projecting hairs, may be seen. It varies in thickness, being thickest on the back, the palms, and the soles.

The skin consists of an external layer having no blood-vessels, the *epidermis*, and an internal deeper layer having many nerves, numerous blood-vessels and lymphatics, the *corium*, called also the *dermis*. The corium is the most important structure of the integument. In the deepest layers of the epidermis are soft cells in which the *pigment*, giving color to the skin, is deposited. A *blister* is an accumulation of fluid between the epidermis and the corium, causing the former to be raised from its bed.

29. The EPIDERMIS, or CUTICLE, is made up of layer upon layer of nucleated and non-nucleated cells. The cells of the external or upper layer are flattened, dry, firmly adherent, and transparent. This is known as the *horny layer*. The cells in the deeper layers

28. What is the skin? Speak of its layers. Where are pigment cells found? What is a blister?

resting on the corium are soft, granular, delicate, and nucleated, but have no cell-wall. This is called the *Rete Mucosum*, or soft epidermis. The epidermis is supplied with nervous filaments terminating in club-shaped extremities. In the deepest cells of this layer is deposited the *pigment*, which, varying in amount from the minimum in the Scandinavian to the maximum in the Guinea negro, gives color to the otherwise pink-white skin of health. The pigment in most skins, by exposure to the sun, becomes darker. The *freckle* consists of a circumscribed, increased amount of normal pigment.

30. The CORIUM, or TRUE SKIN, lies beneath the rete mucosum. It is a dense, moist, tough, and flexible web of fibrous and areolar tissue, and is of a pinkish-white color in all races. In this structure are found abundant blood-vessels and nerves, lymphatics, smooth muscles, hairs, oil glands, sweat glands, and fat cells. The upper portion of the corium is called the *papillary layer*, and consists of little conical projections, called *papillæ* (Fig. 10). These are most perfectly developed on the tips and inner surface of the fingers. They are of two kinds, the *vascular* and the *sensory*. The latter receive less blood than the former, but are largely made up of nervous elements.

FIG. 10 (*Leidy*). VERTICAL SECTION OF THE SKIN OF THE FOREFINGER ACROSS TWO OF THE RIDGES OF THE SURFACE; highly magnified. 1, Dermis, composed of an intertexture of bundles of fibrous tissue. 2, Epidermis. 3, Horny layer. 4, Soft layer. 5, Subcutaneous connective and adipose tissue. 6, Tactile papillæ. 7, Sweat glands. 8, Duct. 9, Spiral passage from the latter through the epidermis. 10, Termination of the passage on the summit of ridge.

31. During life the upper layers of the epidermis are

---

31. Changes of the epidermis. How affected in scalds and scarlatina? How is the callus made? How are corns produced?

being constantly worn off and as constantly replaced by the layers growing up from beneath. In scarlatina, and after scalds, the entire epidermis, as of the hand, may come off in large flakes or as a complete globe. If the skin is exposed to constant, moderate friction, then the epidermis may thicken, and a *callus* is formed. If the friction and the pressure take place over a limited portion of the toes, a hard, circumscribed growth of the epidermis is formed in the shape of a cone with the base upward. The pain is produced by the core of this growth, called a *corn*, pressing on the sensitive structures of the true skin.

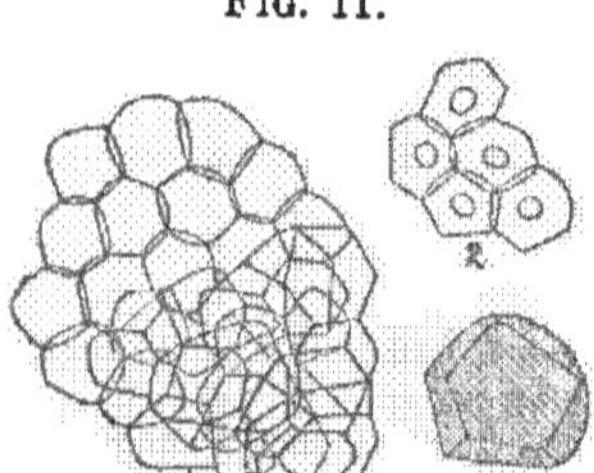

FIG. 11.

FIG. 11 (*Leidy*). SCURF FROM THE LEG.—A fragment of scurf, consisting of dried, flattened, non-nucleated cells. 2, A few cells with a nucleus. 3, A cell more highly magnified, to exhibit its polyhedral form.

32. If the epidermis is removed, as by a blister, then it will soon be restored to health. If the irritant or injury acts deeply enough to destroy the corium, then normal repair will not take place. The skin will be replaced by connective tissue, and a scar, or *cicatrix*, will remain. In large surface wounds, the surgeon often hastens repair and diminishes the tendency to the formation of a large scar by *transplanting* small bits of skin from healthy persons to the large denuded surface. Occasionally large bits of skin are transferred from one part of the body to another.

33. The NAIL is a modified part of the epidermis. It is horny, flexible, and translucent. It grows in length by

---

32. Give the effects of injury to the epidermis. To the corium. What causes a scar? What is transplanting skin? Its value?

33. Give the structure of the nail. Its formation.

additions at the root, in thickness by additions to the under surface. Its function is to protect the sensitive tips and to aid in seizing small objects.

34. The nail is continuous with the epidermis at the root and near the tip. The corium, on which the nail rests, is called the bed or matrix. The nail is made up of closely-connected plates containing nucleated fat cells. The *matrix* is very vascular, and the nail grows rapidly as long as the matrix is healthy.

35. *In-grown nails* usually result from boot-pressure from the outside, or the collecting of hard materials between the nail and the skin. Remove the cause. Clean the parts. Insert a little pledget of cotton or lint under the sharp edge of the nail, to keep it from the inflamed parts. In cutting the toe-nails, leave the nail square. The corners should not be rounded.

Fig. 12.

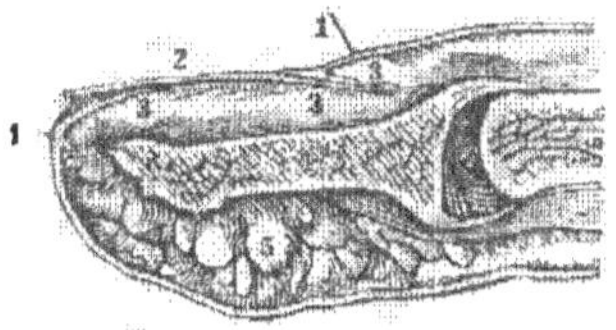

FIG. 12. A SECTION OF THE END OF THE FINGER AND NAIL.—4, Section of the last bone of the finger. 5, Fat, forming the cushion at the end of the finger. 2, The nail. 1, 1, The cuticle continued under and around the root of the nail, at 3, 3, 3.

36. The HAIRS have their seat in pits in the skin, called *hair follicles.* The hair *root* grows upon a pointed protuberance in the base of the follicle, called the *papilla.* The hair *shaft* is that portion of the hair projecting above the skin. In the Europeans, it is oval in cross-section; in the Japanese and Chinese, it is circular. Its length varies greatly. Hairs occur on most parts of the body, as is very evident in the Ainos, or hairy men of Japan.

---

35. Cause of in-grown nails. Management. The cutting of nails.

36. What are hair follicles? What is the papilla? The shaft? Give the shape, length, and distribution of hairs.

c

37. The hairs are usually seated obliquely in the skin, but their free ends are often elevated by shortening of the

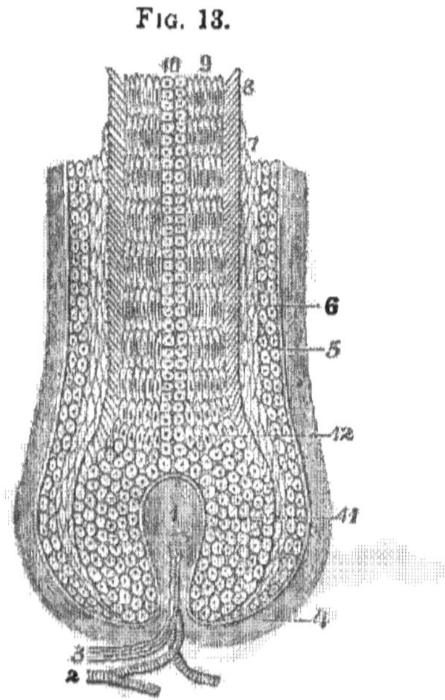

Fig. 13.

Fig. 13 (*Leidy*). DIAGRAM OF STRUCTURE OF THE ROOT OF A HAIR WITHIN ITS FOLLICLE.—1, Hair papilla. 2, Capillary vessel. 3, Nerve-fibres. 4, Fibrous wall of the hair follicle. 5, Basement membrane. 6, Soft epidermic lining of the follicle. 7, Its elastic cuticular layer. 8, Cuticle of the hair. 9, Cortical substance. 10, Medullary substance. 11, Bulb of the hair, composed of soft polyhedral cells. 12, Transition of the latter into the cortical substance, medullary substance, and cuticle of the hair.

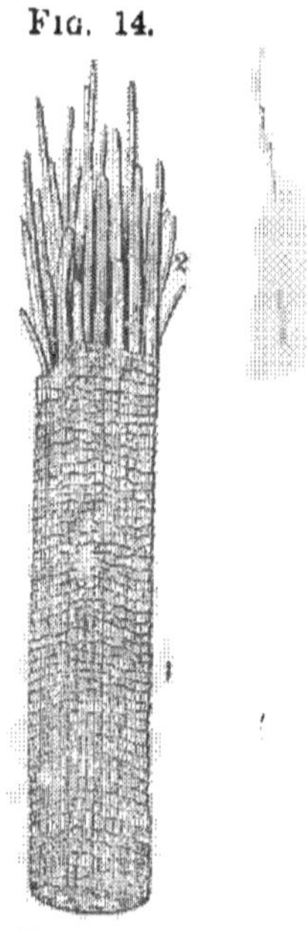

Fig. 14.

Fig. 14 (*Leidy*). PORTION OF A HAIR FROM THE OUTER PART OF THE THIGH, magnified. 1, Shaft of the hair, covered with transverse markings indicating the projecting edges of the cuticular scales. 2, Cortical substance at the end of the hair, broken up into coarse fibres, as the result of friction of the clothing.

little muscles in the skin. It is estimated that the normal scalp contains about one hundred and twenty thousand

37. How are hairs seated? Their number in the scalp? Color? Growth? Their function?

hairs. The numbers on the body vary with the locality, the person, and the race. The color depends on the presence of granular pigments. Hairs are nourished from the papillæ. They grow only in length. When cut off, if the papillæ be healthy, they soon grow out to their determinate length. Their function is protection.

38. The *hair follicle* is a minute depression of the epidermis and corium. At its base rises a conical, smooth body, a growth from the mucous layer, which is seen to extend into the base of the hair. This is the *papilla of the hair*, and into it enter blood-vessels and nerves. Upon this grows the hair *bulb* or *root*. The *shaft* consists of long, spindle-shaped, flattened filaments, striped longitudinally, which contain pigment granules. The filaments are bound together by a delicate investing membrane, called cuticle. The cuticle has a crossed, laminated appearance, not unlike the scales on a fish. The free ends of the scales point to the tapering free ends of the hair. On most hairs, a line of colored cells, called the *medullary substance*, runs lengthwise through the centre of the hair. Kaposi maintains that the accredited accounts of persons whose hair has changed color suddenly, under the influence of fear or other strong emotion, must all be rejected, since such changes are physiologically impossible.

39. The small flat muscles of the hair are inserted obliquely into the hair follicles below the ducts of the oil glands. The contraction of the muscles causes the oblique-lying hairs to become erect. Hairs are strong, extensible, and elastic. They absorb and give off water readily. Hairs consist of a nitrogenous substance containing sulphur, fats, and salts.

40. *Superfluous hairs* are best removed by the use of a mild galvanic current to destroy the papillæ. Strong caustics should not be used, as too often the hair is not removed, though the skin may be permanently injured. Hair- and whisker-dyes should be avoided. Most of these contain ingredients injurious to the hair as well as to the general health. *Cosmetics* too often contain ingredients like lead, bismuth, mercury, etc., and their continual use is injurious to the texture, softness, and health of the skin. Cases are on record where the use of cosmetics has led to wrist-drop and to general paralysis.

41. The SEBACEOUS or OIL GLANDS are always seated in the corium (Fig. 3). Their duct, as a rule, empties into the hair follicle. Each hair of the scalp is generally provided with two glands. The function of the fatty product is to oil the hairs, to keep the skin supple, and for protection.

42. The oil gland is pear-shaped and lobulated. The lobules are made up of minute membranous sacs, lined with *epithelium* (156). The epithelium elaborates an oily fluid, which is always mixed with cells from the gland-walls.

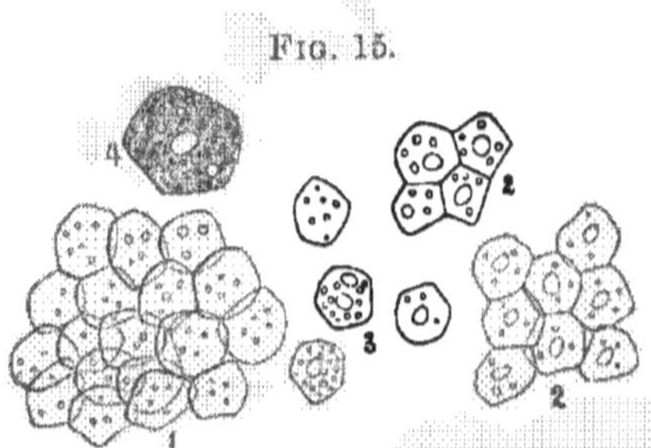

FIG. 15.

FIG. 15 (*Leidy*). FRAGMENT OF DANDRUFF FROM THE HEAD.—1, Portion of dandruff, consisting of non-nucleated cells. 2, Several fragments, consisting of nucleated cells. 3, Isolated cells, some with and some without nuclei. 4, A cell more highly magnified, exhibiting granular contents and a nucleus.

43. *Dandruff* is a scurf which forms on the head and comes off in small scales or particles. It consists of the dried products of the sebaceous glands and cells from their walls and ducts (Fig. 15). Its most frequent cause is impaired general health.

44. The SWEAT GLANDS are made up of tubes twisted in the form of a knot, leading to the surface by a long, sometimes spiral, duct (Fig. 10). These ducts terminate in openings on the surface of the skin, called *pores*. These glands are estimated to number upwards of 2,225,000. They give forth a clear, slightly saltish fluid. Their function is to eliminate water from the system, to expel certain

41. Where are the oil glands seated? Relation to the hair? Their function?

44. Describe a sweat gland. Number of these glands? Their function?

waste materials which collect in the blood, and, under the resulting evaporation upon the surface, to cool the body.

45. The *sweat glands* are situated deep in the corium, or in the subcutaneous connective tissue. The knotted tubes are lined with columnar epithelial cells, which are the secreting agents. The tissues beneath the secreting membranes are very vascular. These glands are found, with few exceptions, in all parts of the body. It is still an open question whether the sweat, as a whole, is furnished by the glands alone, or whether a considerable part may not transude through the epidermis. The secreting activity of these glands is aided by vascular dilatation, and diminished by vascular contraction (137). By the intimate relation of blood-supply and gland-activity, the temperature of the body is largely regulated (322). It is very probable that there are special nerves governing the activity of these glands. The amount of fluid passing away from the skin in twenty-four hours is considerable, varying from seven hundred to two thousand grains (one and one-half to four and two-fifths pounds).

46. The SWEAT or PERSPIRATION which is evaporated as fast as it is thrown out on the skin is called *insensible perspiration*, and that which accumulates on the skin, *sensible perspiration*. Most of the sweat passes off unknown to ourselves. The amount of sweat is greatly influenced by the temperature of the air, the clothing worn, the amount and kind of fluid taken, and the exercise indulged in. Other things remaining the same, an elevation of temperature favors, while a lowering of temperature retards, its secretion.

47. To excite the perspiratory action of the skin, as in the dry, hot skin of colds, the SIMPSON METHOD is to be commended. Fill six or eight bottles with hot water (not

---

46. What is sensible perspiration? Insensible perspiration? What is said of the amount of perspiration? What of the influence of temperature?

47. Describe the Simpson sweating-bath.

much above 150°), and cork tightly.   Wring six or eight woollen stockings out of hot water. Have them moist, not dripping wet. Draw one of the stockings over each bottle. Pack the encased bottles about the body and legs of the patient. Cover the patient well. After twenty to thirty minutes have elapsed, a thoroughly free perspiration will be effected. Remove the bottles, wrap the patient in a warm blanket, and allow the action to continue half an hour. Remove the damp blanket, and place the patient in a warm, dry bed.

FUNCTIONS OF THE SKIN.

48. The skin is the *protecting covering* to the whole body. It is the main part of the body concerned in the *sense of touch* (467). In the maintenance of the average temperature necessary for the continuance of healthy life (37° C. or 98.6° F.), the skin is the important *heat-regulating* organ. In twenty-four hours nearly seventy-eight per cent. of the heat lost by the body goes by the way of the skin. The thickness of the epidermis very much retards the *respiratory function* of this covering of the animal body, yet there is a small interchange of oxygen and carbonic acid gas. As a *secretory organ*, it gives forth the perspiration and the sebum. As an *excretory organ*, it may eliminate urea and other nitrogenous compounds (316), and thus lighten the work of the kidneys. As an *absorbing surface*, it can take in water to a very limited extent. If, however, the epidermis be removed, fluids and even solids find their way into the lymphatic and blood currents quite rapidly.

---

48. Give a function of the skin. What is the temperature of the healthy body ? How much body-heat is lost by the skin ? The respiratory action ? Secretory and excretory actions ?

HYGIENE OF THE SKIN.

49. CLOTHING.—The object of clothing, from a physiological point of view, is to protect the body against cold and heat. In hot countries the wearing of any kind of clothing is inconvenient, yet the people know from experience that the head must be shielded from the rays of the sun, and the abdomen protected against the hourly varying temperature, especially during the sleeping-hours; but in cold countries the use of clothing is essential for comfort and the preservation of life.

50. Clothing does not warm the body; it simply retards the radiation and conduction of the body-heat. Hence in cold climates the clothing should be designed to prevent the passing out of the heat from the body. In hot climates the clothing should be devised to protect against direct heat and to favor the escape of heat from the skin. In temperate climates the garments should be varied in form, material, and thickness in accordance with the changing seasons and temperatures. To the Esquimaux, furs are essential; to the laborer of the temperate regions, woollen; to the people of the "Middle Kingdom," cotton; and to the tattooed Siamese coolie the cotton breech-cloth is more than enough.

51. As to the use of clothes, Dr. Parkes sums up thus:

"*Protection against Cold.*—For equal thickness, wool is much superior to either cotton or linen, and should be worn

---

49. Object of clothing in hot countries? In cold countries?

50. The influence of clothing? The kind for cold countries? For hot countries? For temperate climes?

51. State the different qualities of clothing for protection against cold. Against direct heat. Against cold winds. Against excessive perspiration.

for all under-clothing. In case of extreme cold, besides wool, leather or water-proof clothing is useful. Cotton and linen are nearly equal.

"*Protection against Heat.*—Texture has nothing to do with protection from the direct solar rays; this depends entirely on color. White is the best color, then gray, yellow, pink, blue, black. In hot countries, therefore, white or light-gray clothing should be chosen.

"In the shade the effect of color is not marked. The thickness and the conducting power of the material are the conditions (especially the former) which influence heat.

"*Protection against Cold Winds.*—For equal thickness, leather and india-rubber take the first rank, wool the second, cotton and linen about equal.

"*Absorption of Perspiration.*—Wool has more than double the power of cotton and linen."

52. *The clothing should be loose-fitting.*—In warm weather thin, loose, and porous garments favor the radiation of heat and the evaporation or removal of the abundant perspiration. Dry air, dry fur, dry, well-meshed wool, and silk are excellent non-conductors of heat. Not only are such materials well adapted for cold climates, but where several thicknesses are worn the non-conducting layers of air favor the retention of body-heat. The astute Chinese gauge the weather by counting the number of cotton jackets they find it necessary to wear, as two-jacket weather, three-jacket weather, etc. By putting on our extra garments in a warm room some minutes before going out in the cold, we may secure a warm layer of air between our bodies and the over-garment.

---

52. The clothing, how worn? Kind of? Name good non-conductors of heat. Chinese gauge of the weather. Speak of over-garments.

53. *Water-proof* clothing is an exceedingly hot dress, because it prevents the passage of currents of air and condenses and retains the perspiration. Water-proof garments, boots, and overshoes should be worn only to keep out external wet, and then only during the time of exposure. A person using india-rubber clothing experiences less injury from the effects of the retained perspiration if he wears woollen under-clothing rather than cotton or linen. The Council of Health of the French army have persistently refused to allow the introduction of water-proof garments into the army.

54. *Cold and damp feet* cause much discomfort and not a little disease. If the boots "fit snug," perhaps "tight," then the blood-circulation is hindered and the conduction of heat facilitated. Wet leather is a good conductor of heat. If the boots fit tight and the leather be wet, then the heat of the feet will be removed faster than it is brought to or produced in them, causing cold feet, and inducing discomfort and, perhaps, disease. But when good skins are slowly tanned with "honest" bark, then "there is nothing like leather." Such leather does not readily absorb moisture, and is a bad conductor of heat. If the boots "fit easy," then a layer of air is around and about the foot, promoting warmth and comfort.

55. *Night clothing should be thicker than that worn during the day.*—1. The night is colder than the day. 2. The radiation of heat from the body is much greater during the sleeping than the waking hours. A wool or hair mat-

---

53. The effects of water-proof clothing. When injurious.

54. Influence of snug-fitting boots. Of wet leather. Of dry leather. Of an easy-fitting boot.

55. Why is more clothing required at night? Describe a healthy bed. Objections to feathers. The Italian idea.

tress, light, fleecy wool blankets, clean cotton sheets in ordinary weather, or woollen sheets in severe winter weather, make a healthy, sleep-inducing bed. Feathers above and feathers below make a very warm bed, but their influence is relaxing and enervating: besides, such beds do not admit of ready cleaning and airing. All bedding should be exposed to a current of air and to direct sunlight several hours each day. The Italian method of not making the bed until late in the day is to be commended, as it allows more time for the escape of the night's emanations.

56. *The clothing should be clean.*—As portions of the excretions and secretions from the skin, dust and moisture from the air, and small particles from the house and work-shop adhere to or are absorbed by the clothing, therefore the clothing should be frequently changed, often shaken, and well washed at near intervals. When taken from the body, all garments should be shaken, hung in a current of air, and at frequent intervals exposed to the direct sunlight. Under-garments should be changed every twelve hours,—that is, the night set should be aired and sunned during the day, and the day set aired during the night.

57. *Damp clothing is injurious.*—All articles from the laundry should be well aired before being worn. When the clothing is wet by accident or exposure, it should be changed immediately, unless the person is exercising so vigorously as to prevent the slightest chilly sensation. When the exercise ceases, the body should be rubbed with a dry crash towel till a thorough reaction takes place. Beds and bedding that have not been used for some weeks become damp, and should be aired before use.

---

56. What of the care of the clothing? Of the under-clothing?

57. Influence of damp clothing? Management of the body with wet clothing? Of the bed and bedding?

58. *Clothing in childhood, in age, and in disease.*—Persons in active employment need less clothing than those engaged in sedentary pursuits; the vigorous adult less than the child or the aged. The system of "hardening children," by furnishing them with an insufficient supply of warm clothing, is inhuman, and, "as our clothing is merely an equivalent for a certain amount of food" (Liebig), it is certainly unprofitable. For the latter reason the gift of flannels and blankets to the aged and infirm at the opening of winter is most appropriate. Persons suffering from headache, neuralgia, dyspepsia, consumption, and other chronic maladies need more clothing than healthy persons under the same circumstances of life and occupation.

59. *The clothing should be suited to the climate, the occupation, and the time of day.*—In the northern and central sections of the United States, merino (the weight and the amount of cotton admixture varying with the seasons) is undoubtedly the safest material for under-garments at all times. The change from thick to thinner garments should be made in the morning. The evening hour demands an increase of clothing, because of the coolness and dampness of the atmosphere and the less buoyant condition of the system. In certain sections of the country Boërhaave's maxim, "We should put off our winter clothing in mid-summer's day and put it on again the day after," should be put in practice. During the winter months the transition from the warm, every-day garments to the light "full dress," from active, exciting exercise in the hot, crowded

---

58. The amount of clothing? The axiom of Liebig? Clothing for the sick?

59. Adaptability of clothing for the sections of the United States? When should clothing be changed? Boërhaave's maxim? Dangers of transition in clothing and temperature?

dancing-hall to the sudden pause, from the close, stifling room to the exposed corridor or balcony, and especially at any hour after midnight, is, to say the least, very hazardous.

60. LIGHT exercises a very salutary influence upon the skin. It is no less essential to the vigor of animal than of vegetable life. Dwelling-houses should be built with reference to the free admission of sunlight and air into all occupied rooms. The absence of light favors the accumulation of dirt and the growth of moulds. "Dirt, debauchery, and death" are successive links in the same chain. Ladies often suffer seriously from too much exclusion of sunlight. Except in very warm weather, all should practise exercising in the full sunshine The health is often improved by sitting or reclining with the sun's rays falling on the back.

61. BATHING is indispensable to sound health, as well as to cleanliness. The skin soon becomes covered with a mixture of perspiration, oil, and dust, which, if allowed to remain, interferes with the action of the skin as an excretory organ. This increases the action of lungs, kidneys, liver, etc., which take upon themselves the excretory work which the skin fails to perform. By overwork they may become diseased. Again, obstruction of the pores prevents respiration through the skin, and deprives the blood of one source of its oxygen and one outlet of its carbonic acid (190).

62. *Bathing gives tone and vigor to the internal organs.*— When cool water (cool to the individual) is applied to the

---

60. Action of light? The arrangement of rooms? Influence of dark, damp rooms? Of direct sunlight?

61. The need for cleansing the skin?

62. The influence of cool water in bathing? What is reaction? Effect of reaction? What of the smooth muscles?

body, the skin instantly shrinks. This contraction diminishes the capacity of the cutaneous blood-vessels, and a portion of the blood is thrown upon the internal organs. The nervous centres are stimulated, and new impulses are sent to the whole system. This causes a more energetic action of the heart, and a consequent rush of blood back to the skin. This is the state termed *reaction*, and is the first object and purpose of every form of bathing. By this reaction the internal organs are relieved, respiration is lightened, the heart is made to beat more calmly and freely, the tone of the muscular system is increased, the appetite is sharpened, the mind is made more clear and strong, and the whole system seems to possess new power. Cold sponging and cold bathing are the gymnastics of the smooth muscles to a person of robust health. Regularity in bathing is necessary to produce permanently good effects.

63. *The simplest modes of bathing are by means of the sponge or the shallow bath.* The body may be quickly sponged over, wiped dry, and subjected to friction. The water may be warm or cold. If cold, the bath should be taken in the early part of the day and followed by exercise. The warm bath should usually be taken just before retiring. If taken at other hours, it should be followed by rest from half an hour to one hour under proper covering, followed by exercise.

64. *The shallow bath, in which the body is partly immersed in water,* is very pleasant and safe, provided the bather exercises in it by vigorous rubbing and does not remain too long. For a cold bath, it is not often safe to exceed five

---

63. Speak of the sponge bath. Of the cold bath. Of the warm bath. Precautions.

64. Duration of bath. Temperature of bath. Of friction.

minutes, and with delicate persons the time should rarely exceed two or three minutes. A bath is considered cold when below 75°; temperate, from 75° to 85°; tepid, from 85° to 95°. This and every other form of bath should be followed by thorough friction with a coarse towel or flesh-brush.

65. *The hour for ablution is of importance.* It should neither immediately precede nor immediately follow a meal. The same is true of severe mental and muscular exercise. The bath is less beneficial in the afternoon than in the forenoon. The best time for sea-baths is two or three hours after breakfast. The system is then at "flood-tide," while from that time till the retiring-hour the tide is ebbing: hence the worst time for a cold bath is at bedtime. Then friction with the flesh-brush can be substituted. For those who cannot choose their time, the hour of rising will answer very well,—that is, for many persons, especially if they become accustomed to the use of water by beginning at another and a better hour. If the mind and body are brightened by the early bath, and an exhilaration follows, the bath is beneficial; if, on the contrary, languor follows, and the skin looks blue or too pale, it is injurious. That the bath is to be followed by exercise must not be forgotten.

66. *In diseases of the skin, and in many chronic ailments of the internal organs, bathing is a remedial measure of great power.* In disease which has baffled the skill of physicians, depending wholly upon internal remedies, the effect of a systematic course of baths is often surprising. Like other curative means, the baths should be directed by those who

---

65. The bathing-hour. The flood-tide of the system. Symptoms following a beneficial bath. Following an injurious bath.

66. Bathing in disease of the skin, and in other diseases. Give the simple rules.

thoroughly understand the use of water as a remedial agency.

A few simple rules must be observed in bathing. The face and head should be wet in cold water before the bath. Cool baths should not be taken when the person is chilly, perspiring, or greatly fatigued. All general baths should be taken briskly, and the skin well rubbed and quickly dried, inducing a healthy glow over the whole body. Exercise should follow most baths.

67. *Soap* is admirably adapted to the removal of dirt from the skin; but if it is too freely used on the general surface of the body it dissolves the oily secretion of the sebaceous glands, leaving the skin dry and harsh. The external epithelial cells may be removed too rapidly when soap is used in excess, leaving the skin without its proper protection. The best kinds of soap should always be employed.

---

67. What of the use of soap?

CHAPTER IV.

THE CONTRACTILE AND IRRITABLE TISSUES.

68. THE *nerve* and *muscular* tissues are irritable,—that is, when they are stimulated, a certain amount of energy, latent in their protoplasm, is set free as heat, motion, impulse, etc. *Muscle* alone is contractile,—that is, under the influence of a stimulus it is capable in itself of causing changes in its own form. The contractile tissues embrace the *striped* muscle, the *unstriped* muscle, the *cardiac muscle* fibre, and the *ciliated cells*.

69. When a piece of an india-rubber band is pulled out by the exercise of force, the particles of the rubber tend to resume their former position. When a piece of muscle is so stretched, the same tendency is noticed, but in a less degree. If now one end of the band or the muscle be set free, then the stretched elements resume at once their former quiescent position. This shows the property of *elasticity*.

70. When a bit of fresh muscle, slightly weighted, is stimulated, as by heat, or acid, or electricity, then the muscle shows changes in form, in length, and a wave-like line of progression, and the weight is moved. As often as the muscle is stimulated up to the point of exhaustion, these changes will be noticed. These movements result from the setting free of energy latent in the muscular tissue, and not from an external force. This property of the fibre is called *contractility*. If a rubber band be similarly stimulated, no contractions follow.

71. The STRIPED MUSCULAR fibre (Figs. 16, 17) consists of fine long filaments, which break up into smaller fibrillæ. Fine, alternate dim and bright cross-bands are seen passing through the whole thickness of the fibre. The cross-marks are called *striæ*. The fibrillæ are seen to be made up of fine disk-like bodies, called *sarcotic elements*. The fibres are surrounded by a delicate, transparent sheath of tissue, called *sarcolemma*. This kind of fibre contracts with rapidity, because the shortening and lengthening are seen to

48

be under the control of the will. It is called *voluntary muscular fibre*. The great muscles of the body are made up of this kind of fibre (512).

FIG. 16.   FIG. 17.

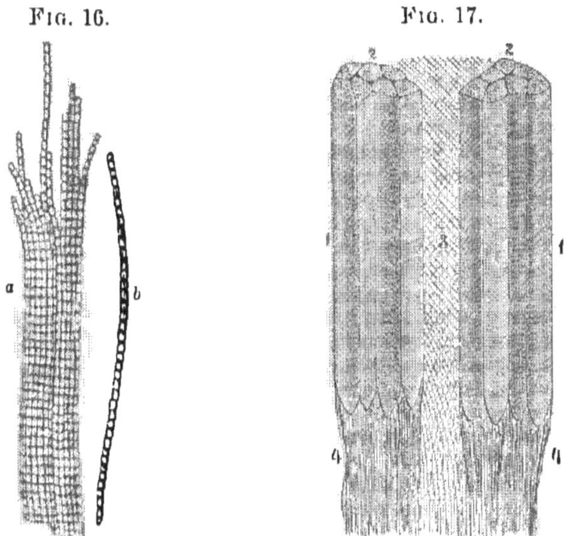

FIG. 16 (*Leidy*). FIBRILS FROM A MUSCULAR FIBRE OF THE AXOLOTL, A BATRACHIAN REPTILE; highly magnified. *a*, Bundle of fibrils. *b*, An isolated fibril.

FIG. 17 (*Leidy*). TWO PORTIONS OF A MUSCULAR FASCICULUS, from the trapezius muscle; highly magnified. 1, Two portions of a muscular fasciculus, composed of prismatic striated fibres terminating below, in rounded extremities, among the fibrous tissue of the commencing tendon. 2, Cut extremities of the fibres, showing their prismatic form. 3, Delicate sheath, composed of obliquely-crossing filaments of areolar tissue. 4, The fibres of the commencing tendon. Partly a diagram.

72. The UNSTRIPED MUSCULAR fibre appears as long, pointed-at-both-end cells, containing granules and nuclei. The fibres are flat, and are arranged in the form of bundles. No cross-markings are to be seen. This kind of fibre contracts slowly. The contraction and relaxation are independent of the will: hence it is called *involuntary* muscular fibre. Such muscular bands are found in the intestines, the ducts of glands, and the larger blood-tubes.

73. The CARDIAC MUSCULAR fibres show the cross-striæ which are seen in the voluntary muscle, but they are arranged in long bands. These fibres frequently anastomose, and often have branches. There is no sarcolemma. Nuclei are to be seen at quite regular

spaces. This form of contractile tissue is found in the muscle of the heart.

74. CILIATED CELLS.—Upon certain surfaces of the body are found cells which are furnished with very actively vibrating hair-like processes, or *cilia*. The cilia bend their ends in a given direction, but recover slowly. They work together, and, as a result, the fluids resting upon their surfaces move in definite currents. These motions continue after the cells are removed from the body. The ciliary motion is probably due to changes going on in the protoplasm of the cell-body. The cilia found in the air-passages assist in the respiratory changes, causing movements in the smaller air-passages of the lungs (164, 183).

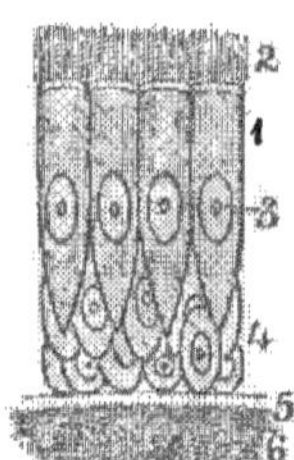

FIG. 18.

FIG. 18. DIAGRAM.—1, Columnar ciliated epithelial cells. 2, Cilia. 3, Nuclei. 4, Young cells. 5, Basement membrane. 6, Fibrous layer.

75. PHYSIOLOGY OF MUSCLE.—If muscular fibres be *stimulated*, as by heat, acid, pinching, or nervous impulse, contractions are to be seen. If the stimuli be removed, the fibres resume their earlier form and position. After the contact of the stimulus there is a brief rest, after which the fibre shortens slowly, then more rapidly, later more slowly, followed by relaxation and the taking of the earlier position. If the stimulus is repeated rapidly, the fibre may remain in a constant state of contraction, or *tetanus*. In the living muscles, contractions are usually excited by nervous impulses. The muscle also exhibits electric currents. The movements are due to the contractile energy inherent in the muscular elements, not to an external agent.

76. Muscular contraction produces an elevation of the temperature, and if the contractions occur in rapid succession sounds may be heard. During the action, acid is set free. Repeated contractions exhaust the muscle-energy, and the point is readily reached at which the fibre refuses to contract under the given stimulus; but if a stronger or a new kind of stimulus be used, the muscle again responds. Rest alone restores the contractile power. Rest and proper muscle-food, however, restore the power sooner. The shortening of the muscle may be as much as three-fifths of its length. The exact function of the striæ has not been determined.

77. The eminently *contractile* muscular fibres and cilia-cells, and the eminently *irritable* tissues, nerve-cells, and nerve-fibres of the

body, are the most important tissues.   The nerve and muscular tissues of the body are the master-tissues.   The relations between them are so intimate that it is desirable to consider their action and their relations in the same section.

78. THE WHITE or TUBULAR NERVE-FIBRES consist of an outer, thin, transparent, limiting layer of connective tissue (22), enclosing a layer of transparent fluid fat. This latter is the *white substance of Schwann.* Within this is a darker, firmer, denser, albuminoid core, called the *central band axis.* This latter, like the copper core of the submarine cable, is the important part of the fibre.

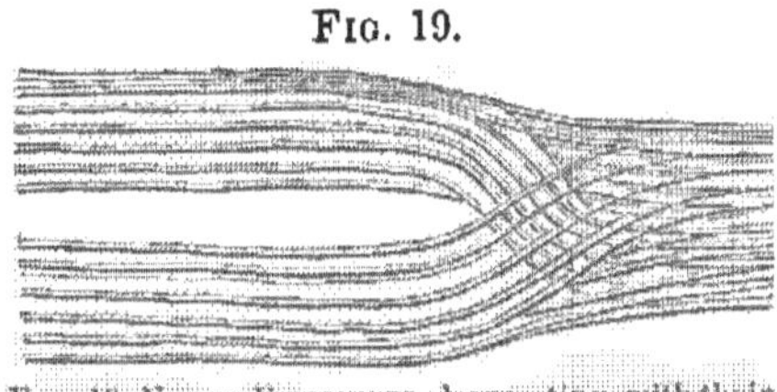

FIG. 19.

FIG. 19. NERVE-FILAMENTS, decussating, with their sheath.

This kind of fibre composes the white parts of the brain and spinal cord (345), and the chief substance of the nerves.

79. The GRAY or REMAK'S NERVE-fibres are pale, soft, granular, and somewhat flat in appearance.   They have no distinct investing structures.   They contain many dark nuclei.   These fibres are abundant in the nerves of the sympathetic system (386).

80. The NERVE or GANGLION CELLS consist of finely-granular cell-bodies, sometimes colorless, sometimes pigmented, which contain large, round, vesicular nuclei, and are limited by a thin membrane.   In the isolated ganglia other investing membranes are to be made out.   Many of these cells exhibit one or more tail-like prolongations (unipolar, bipolar, multipolar cells), while others have none.   Nerve-cells are found in the brain, spinal cord, and other ganglia.

81. PHYSIOLOGY of the NERVE-CELLS and FIBRES.—A simple ideal nerve system may be conceived to be composed of—1, a sensitive *nerve-cell* or receiving-cell on the surface of the body; 2, an *afferent* or sensory nerve-fibre (inward transmitting line); 3, a central *nerve-cell* in the interior; 4, an *efferent* or motor nerve (outward transmitting line), ending in, 5, a muscular fibre cell.   The fibres of nerves act like the conductors in the electric cable; the receiving-cells, like the telephonic transmitter; but the central cells perform a duty not yet delegated to clever mechanisms and physical forces,

—that of receiving impulses and then of originating and sending out differing impulses.

82. REFLEX ACTION.—If the receiving surface of a system similar in principle but more complex in structure than the ideal system (81) should be excited, as by the prick of the skin, an impulse passes over the afferent fibres inward. This impulse, reaching the central cells, induces changes in the protoplasm of the same,—that is, the impulse is recognized, acted upon, and perhaps registered, in the cell-structure. The changes in the protoplasm induce the sending of a *different* impulse over the *efferent* fibres, which impulse, acting

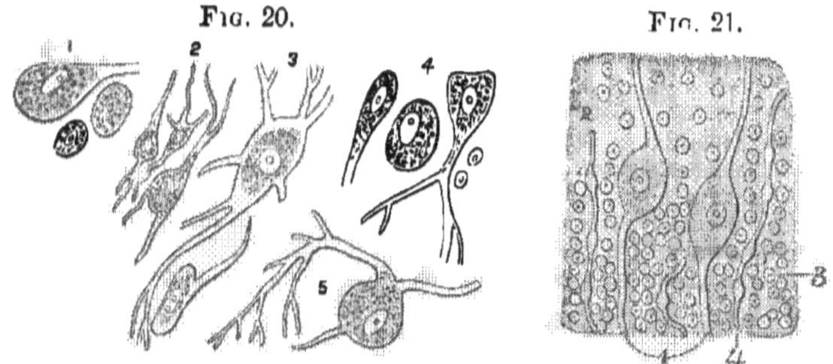

FIG. 20 (*Kölliker and Hannover*). 1, Nucleated cells from a sympathetic ganglion. 2, Branched or stellate cells from the gray substance of the spinal cord. 3, Branched cells from the medulla oblongata. 4, Simple and branched cells from the convolutions of the brain. 5, A large cell from the gray substance of the brain. Magnified one hundred diameters.

FIG. 21 (*Leidy*). PORTION OF GRAY SUBSTANCE, FROM THE EXTERIOR OF THE CEREBELLUM.—1, Two nerve-cells with bipolar prolongations. 2, Granular matter. 3, Nuclear bodies. 4, Nerve-fibres.

on the proper receiving apparatus, as the cells of a series of muscles, gives rise to motions. This, in outline, is an explanation of the complicated phenomena of reflex action. The brain and spinal cord are the chief seats of reflex action. The majority of these phenomena are very complicated, as in the muscular movements made by a sleeping person to remove a fly from a part of the face, or the series of coughs, varying in intensity and rapidity, employed to remove dust from the air-passages.

83. Experiments show that the impulses from the receiving surface towards the interior, and from the central cells outward, are transmitted equally well; that only a small amount of energy is

expended in the transit; that the rate of motion is much slower than electricity; and that varying conditions of the nerve-fibres and of the system in general retard or accelerate the rate. No chemical or physical changes in the fibres resulting from the passage of impulses have been detected. Natural electric currents pass over the fibres. The changes in the central cells are probably accompanied by the expenditure of much energy, being manifest to us by waste of tissue and weariness. Also, it is probably true that the peculiar make-up of the nerve-cells, their repeated duties, and their condition of ease or disease, exercise an influence on the quality, quantity, and degree of force of the new impulse generated therein.

84. **AUTOMATISM.**—A series of nerve-cells grouped together constitute a *nerve-centre* or *ganglion*. Distinct centres have been localized in parts of the spinal cord, the brain, the muscles of the heart, and the intestinal muscles. The protoplasm of nerve-centres appears to possess the power of originating vital impulses. This power of developing an impelling vital force is called *automatism* (390). The impulses so arising, when transmitted outward, may be made known to us as muscular movements, in volition, in speech. The peculiar, worm-like, progressive action of the muscular fibres of the intestines (265), and the motions of the heart (94), are the best examples of *automatic* action.

85. **INHIBITION.**—When nerve-cells or groups of cells are already in action, as of the heart-ganglia, causing the contractions of the muscles of the heart, a new impulse may arise, and so act upon the cells or their activities as to modify the impulses. This new impulse may increase, or it may decrease, the former action; in the heart, it may diminish the number of beats, may change the force of each contraction, or it may have the opposite effect. The retarding of the influence of a group of cells is called *inhibition*. This is well shown in the control of certain centres in the brain over the action of the heart (128).

86. *Muscle* and *Nerve*.—Late investigations show that, in the striped muscle, the nerve-fibres penetrate the sarcolemma and end beneath it in a fine, granular, plate-like, nucleated substance, in close contact with the contractile elements. The method of ending in the unstriated muscle is not yet settled, though the nerves end in many fine meshes in certain cases, and by fine terminal fibres in the contractile fibre cells in others.

5*

87. To account for the contraction of a living muscle, a theory
has been advanced, that—1, an impulse arises in a nerve-cell; 2, a
nervous impulse is transmitted along the nerve to the muscle; 3,
the nervous impulse is changed into a muscle impulse; 4, the sending of this new form of impulse along the muscular fibre gives rise
to the *contraction*. The change in the form of the muscular fibres
is accompanied by chemical changes, the exact nature of which is
not yet known. This much is known, that carbonic acid and lactic
acid become more abundant. The source of muscular energy is the
chemical decomposition of chemical substances in the muscle. The
immediate muscle food-material, stored up partly, at least, in the
muscle, is mainly non-nitrogenous and carbo-hydrates. During
muscular contraction there is an increased consumption of oxygen
(181, 182), and an increased elimination of carbonic and lactic
acids: the fact that the latter compounds are relatively larger than
the oxygen received at that time, will account for the needed rest
(529). The nitrogen-elimination is but slightly increased during
exertion. During the contraction, heat and muscular energy are
made manifest.

CHAPTER V.

THE VASCULAR SYSTEM AND THE CIRCULATION.

88. THREE great cavities are formed in the framework of the body: the skull (Fig. 38), the chest or thorax

FIG. 22.

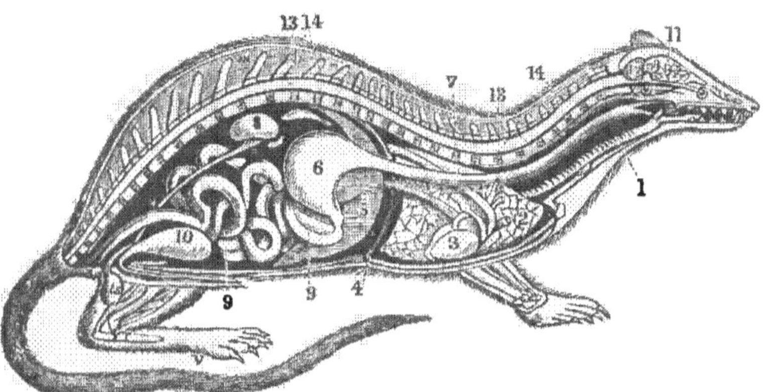

FIG. 22. SECTION OF A SMALL MAMMAL.—1, Trachea. 2, Lungs. 3, Heart. 4, Diaphragm. 5, Liver. 6, Stomach. 7, Œsophagus. 8, Kidney. 9, 9, Intestines. 10, Bladder. 11, Cerebrum. 12, Cerebellum. 13, 13, Medulla spinalis. 14, 14, Vertebræ.

(Fig. 22), and the abdomen (Fig. 22). There is a longitudinal cavity in the spinal column (Fig. 75) continuous with that of the skull.

DISSECTION.—Place a rabbit, dog, or rat on its back. Make an incision in the middle line of the body from the lower jaw-bone to the pubes. Dissect up the skin as far back as possible on each side, and pin or tie it back with threads. The *ribbed* part exposed is the *thorax*, and the soft part the *abdomen*. Observe the external muscles of the front thorax, the *pectoralis* and the *serratus*, the former being the thicker and attached to the

88. Name the three great cavities of the body. What of the spinal column?

that central bone, the *sternum*, and to the arm-bone, the *humerus*, and the latter having numerous saw-like digitations for insertion. The ribs are seen to be connected with the sternum by means of a white, gristle-like material, the *costal cartilages*. Cut through, on each side of the sternum, the white cartilages, making the cut as near the blue hard rib as possible. At the inferior end of the sternum raise the bone and cut away the muscle, the *diaphragm*, which holds it in place. The freed end is now to be raised, freed from its under parts with a few nicks of the knife, turned over towards the chin, and the ligamentous attachments of the sternum to the right and left upper ribs severed.

Dissect the skin and subcutaneous tissues from the neck parts. On the front neck, to the right and left, we see a thin tube holding dark blood, the jugular vein. In the middle line cut through the thin muscle, *platysma*, and draw it to the right and left. Remove the layers of tissue beneath until you expose the white, ring-like tube, the *trachea*, and the cartilaginous enlargement above, the *larynx*. Just above the larynx can be felt a V-shaped bone (the *hyoid bone*), and below the larynx, a fleshy mass on each side of the trachea, the *thyroid body*. By drawing the muscles and connective tissue from the trachea, there will be brought into view, running nearly parallel to it, a firm, whip-cord-like tube, the *carotid artery*; near it, thinner tubes, containing dark fluid, the *veins*, and a white, string-like fibre, the *pneumogastric nerve*. If the larynx is followed upward, it is found to end in a musculo-membranous cavity, the *pharynx*. Beneath and to one side of the trachea is to be seen a collapsed tube with thick fibrous walls, the *œsophagus*, which is seen to open into the pharynx above.

Now cut the larynx free from the pharynx, then raise and separate the parts from the œsophagus and the muscles of the neck below, and pull towards the thorax. The trachea will easily be removed from contact with the œsophagus. Put two strings around each jugular vein, about an inch apart; tie them so as to compress the tubes, and sever the veins between the *ligatures*. Sever the carotids; but, as they are empty, ligatures are not needed. Now observe the contents of the *thorax*,—two lateral compartments, formed by the thin, smooth-surfaced *pleura*, lining the chest-walls, each compartment containing a shrunken, pinkish-white, spongy organ, the *lungs*, of which the right is the larger. Tie a tube in the trachea, and fill the lungs with air, by blowing into the tube. Notice the deep lines dividing the lungs into *lobes*, and the irregular lines marking *lobules*, situated just under the pleura. Between the lungs is a sac, the *pericardium*, containing fluid and a firm, pear-like, fleshy organ. Projecting and arching into the thorax from the abdomen is seen a muscular and fascia-like partition, the *diaphragm*. The pericardium is attached to this, and should be cut free; but the lungs are not attached to the diaphragm.

Open the pericardium with the scissors. It is seen to contain a small amount of *fluid*, and to be lined by a smooth, close, serous membrane. Floating in this pericardial fluid is a firm, pear-shaped, muscular organ, the *heart*. Its apex, or free point, is turned towards the ribs, and its broad, tube-attached base towards the back.

Now continue the separation and elevation of the trachea, arteries, and veins, in a mass, down into the thorax. After the large tube, the *aorta*, is cut below its arch, the lungs and the heart can easily be raised out. The *trachea* is seen to divide into two tubes, the *bronchi*, which in turn divide and subdivide as they enter the *lungs*. From the heart are seen tubes, *arteries* and *veins*, running into the lungs in company with the bronchia. Rising from the base of the heart is seen a large, round, gaping tube, the *aorta*, which arches, gives off several branches, among them the *carotids*, and passes downward along the backbone of the animal, where it is called the *thoracic aorta*. This latter gives off many branches to the right and left, and passes out of the thorax through a hole in the diaphragm. If the lungs and trachea are now separated from the heart and vessels, and thrown into water, the lungs will be seen to float and the heart or the tubes to sink. If a bit of the lungs be held under water and then squeezed, small bubbles of air will rise

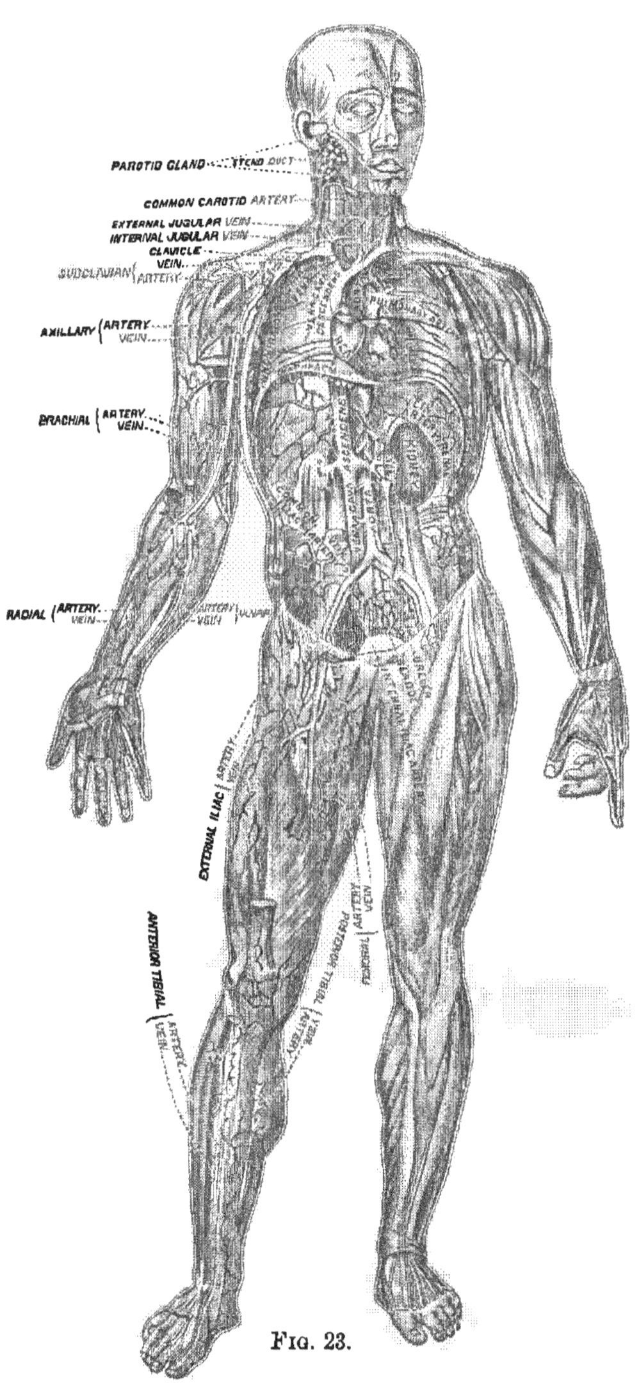

FIG. 23.

THE VASCULAR APPARATUS AND THE CIRCULATION.

to the surface. If a bit of the lungs be pinched, a peculiar sensation, called *crepitation*, will be noticed. It is thus shown that the collapsed lung still holds a certain amount of air in its smaller tubes and cavities.

There will now remain in the thorax the parietal pleura, the pericardium, the œsophagus, the thoracic aorta, and the *thoracic duct*, which latter may be found, after careful dissection, in the left side of the chest, near the backbone. The œsophagus, the thoracic duct, and a large tube with thin walls, the *ascending vena cava*, are seen to enter the abdomen through perforations in the arching diaphragm.

Microscopic Work.—Cut cubes of the organs as before, and place in alcohol No. 1 for hardening. Examine a bit of the muscle of the heart after careful teasing. Compare with intercostal muscle. Make thin sections of the aortic walls, of the valve-tissues, etc. Examine heart and vein. Prick your finger. As soon as possible, transfer a drop to a clean slide. Breathe on the lower side of the cover-glass, and cover at once. Spread the drop so thin that little color is visible. At first use a 1-inch objective; then a ¼-inch. Study the *red corpuscles*. (1.) They tend to take the shape of rouleaux. (2.) Focus down; they appear clear on the outside and dim in the centre, then clear in the centre and dim outside,—*i.e.*, they are biconcave. (3.) In profile they are dumb-bell shape. (4.) Near the edge of the glass they appear crenate, owing to evaporation. Their size is about $\frac{1}{3200}$ of an inch. Find a *white corpuscle*. It is somewhat adhesive, has an irregular form, is colorless and granular, has a transparent nucleus. To a fresh drop add dilute acetic acid; the *red* corpuscles swell up, but show no nucleus; the *white* show granules and an irregular nucleus. Add a drop of five per cent. sodium chloride solution, the red become shrivelled and crenate. Note between the rouleaux minute interlaced filaments of *fibrin*.

89. The THORAX (148) is a framework of bones and cartilage filled in with soft tissues. It is conical in shape, the base being towards the abdomen. Its capacity during life is continually undergoing changes. It contains and protects the central *organs* of *circulation* and *respiration*.

DISSECTION OF THE HEART.—Procure the heart of a sheep, ox, or dog. The front of the heart may be recognized by a groove filled with fat. Hold the heart with the front towards you. The *right ventricle* in your left hand is more yielding, because its walls are thinner, than the *left ventricle* in your right hand. Observe the gaping *pulmonary artery* rising near the middle line, and back of it the large, elastic, tubular *aorta*. Tie a tube in the pulmonary artery and fill it with water. The fluid does not enter the heart, it being stopped by the *semilunar valves*. Test the aorta in the same manner. If the valves are uninjured, the water will not pass into the heart.

Lay open the *ascending* and *descending venæ cavæ*. Allow the cuts to meet in front of the right auricle. Note the size of the venæ cavæ, the thinness of the walls, and the absence of valves between them and the auricle. Observe the size, form, and thickness of the walls of the *auricle* and its dog-ear appendage. Cut away most of the *right auricle*. Holding the ventricles in the left hand, pour some water suddenly through the opening into the ventricle. The *tricuspid valves* will float up and close the opening. Allow the water to pass out through the semilunar valves. Introduce the scissors between two of the folds of the tricuspid valve, and cut a slit through the ventricular wall to the apex, then

89. What is the thorax? Shape? Capacity? Contents?

turn the scissors and cut alongside of the septum towards the pulmonary artery. Observe on the ventricular side of the tricuspid valves the many thin fibres attached to the folds of the valves, the *chordæ tendineæ*, and their attachment at the other end to the *columnæ carneæ*, or muscular pillars.

Hold the heart-ventricle. Pour water into the *pulmonary artery*. Raise the ventricular flap, and observe from below the form and mode of closing of the *semilunar valves*. Then continue the last incision, and lay open the semilunar valve and the pulmonary artery. Notice the little nodules in the free edge of each flap, the *corpora Arantii*, and the little pouches in the arterial walls opposite each flap, the *sinuses* of *Valsalva*.

Lay open the *left auricle* in the same manner as the right. Study the mitral valve, and use water as before. Note the thickness of the walls of the *pulmonary veins* and of the *auricles*. Lay open the *left ventricle* in the same manner as the right. Note the very thick walls and the great firmness of the tissues near the apex. Compare the walls of the auricles and ventricles as to thickness and firmness. Observe the *mitral valve* from the ventricle. Notice its greater thickness and rigidity as compared with the tricuspid, also the increased size and strength of the chordæ tendineæ and the columnæ carneæ. Lay open the aorta. Examine its coats, their layers, thickness, and elasticity. Study the semilunar valve, the corpora Arantii, and the sinuses of Valsalva, and note their entrance to the coronary. Observe the entrance to the *coronary arteries* (the nutrient arteries of the heart-muscle) in the anterior sinuses.

THE HEART.

90. The *heart* is the great central pump of the vascular system. In the adult man it is about the size of the closed fist. Its base is connected with the large blood-vessels, and is directed upward and backward. Its apex is free, and points downward and forward to the left of the sternum. It is a hollow muscular organ. It is divided by a longitudinal septum into two chambers, the *right* and the *left* heart. After birth these two chambers do not communicate. Each chamber is divided into two cavities, the *auricle* and the *ventricle*. The auricle and ventricle of the same side communicate.

91. The AURICLES are placed at the base of the heart. Their walls are thin. They receive blood from the veins and propel it into the ventricles. The VENTRICLES are

--- ---

90. What is the heart? Size? Shape? Apex? Chambers? Cavities?

91. What of the auricles? Of the ventricles? That of the right? That of the left?

situated below the auricles. Their walls are quite thick, that of the left being about three times thicker than that of the right. From each ventricle extends a tube called an *artery*, that of the right leading to the tubes of the lungs, and that of the left to all parts of the body by many branches.

Fig. 24.   Fig. 25.

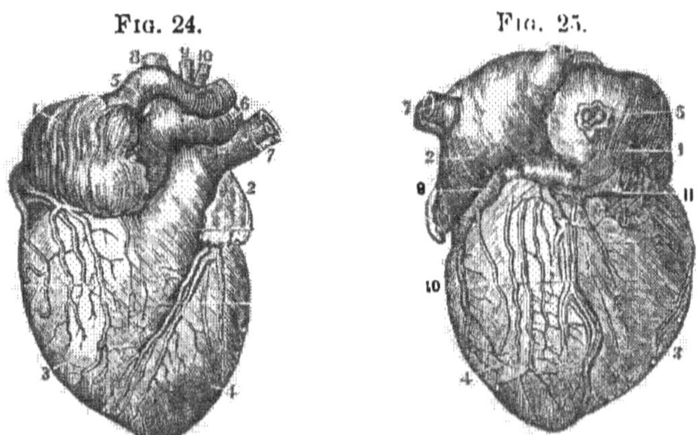

Fig. 24. A FRONT VIEW OF THE HEART.—1, The right auricle of the heart. 2, The left auricle. 3, The right ventricle. 4, The left ventricle. 5, 6, 7, 8, 9, 10, Vessels through which the blood passes to and from the heart.

Fig. 25. A BACK VIEW OF THE HEART.—1, The right auricle. 2, The left auricle. 3, The right ventricle. 4, The left ventricle. 5, 6, 7, The vessels that carry the blood to and from the heart. 9, 10, 11, The vessels of the heart.

92. *To direct the currents of blood* in the proper course, valves are placed in the heart. Between the *right* auricle and ventricle is a valve, composed of three pointed, membranous curtains, the *tricuspid valve*. The valve opens *towards* the ventricle. Between the ventricle and the artery leading to the lungs is a valve, composed of three semicircular, membranous folds, named *semilunar* valve. This valve prevents the blood from returning to the right heart.

92. Object of the valves. Describe the tricuspid. The semilunar.

93. Between the *left* auricle and ventricle is a valve, formed of two segments or curtains, named *mitral* valve. These curtains and their adjuncts are stronger and thicker than those of the right side. The opening from the ventricle to the *aorta* is provided with a *semilunar* valve which is thicker and stronger than that of the right side. This valve prevents the return of the expelled blood from the aorta to the ventricle.

94. HEART MOTIVE POWER.—The heart propels the blood from the interior of its ventricles into the tubes leading to all parts of the lungs and the system, by means of successive regular contractions of its ventricular walls. The immediate source of the motive power is the contractility of its muscular tissue. The muscular contractions are caused by impulses which arise in the heart itself. The impulses arise in and are due to changes in the *nerve-ganglia* scattered in the heart-substance (84).

95. The chambers of the heart are lined with a very fine,

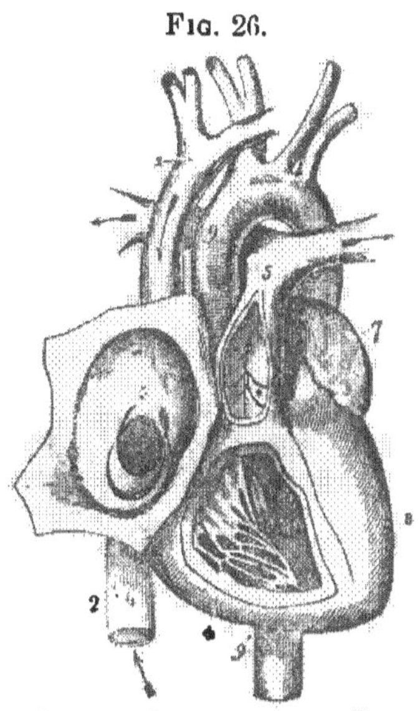

FIG. 26. DIAGRAM OF THE HEART AND GREAT BLOOD-VESSELS.—1, Superior vena cava. 2, Inferior vena cava. 3, The right auricle laid open. 4, The right ventricle laid open, showing segment of tricuspid valve, chordæ tendineæ, and papillary muscle. 5, Pulmonary artery. *, Two semilunar valves. 7, Part of left auricle. 8, Left ventricle. 9, Aorta, with the branches from the arch. 9′, The thoracic aorta, The arrows show the course of the blood in the veins.

smooth membrane, called *endocardium*. This membrane is continuous with the lining membrane of the large blood-tubes. The heart is suspended in the folds of a serous sac, called the *pericardium* (156). The *serum* between the heart-layer and the outer layer (mediastinal) permits of great ease of movements.

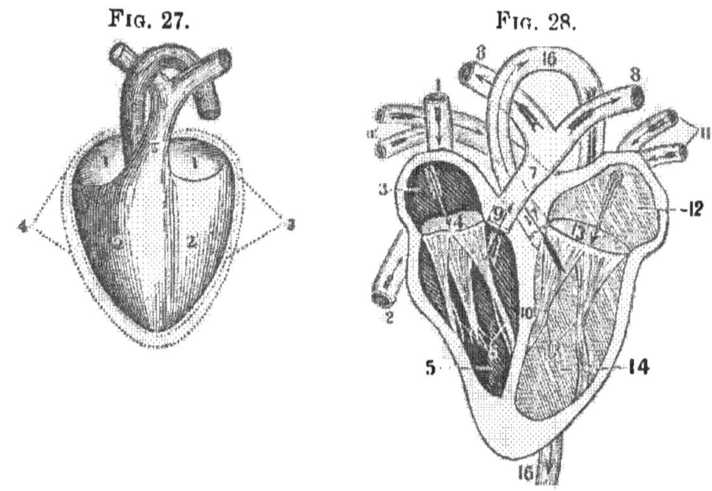

FIG. 27. DIAGRAM OF THE HEART, WITH ITS INVESTMENTS.—1, 1, Right and left auricles. 2, 2, Right and left ventricles. 3, 4, Pericardium. 5, Pulmonary artery. 6, Aorta.

FIG. 28. DIAGRAM OF THE HEART AND VALVES.—1, Descending vena cava (vein). 2, Ascending vena cava (vein). 3, Right auricle. 4, Opening between the right auricle and the right ventricle. 5, Right ventricle. 6, Tricuspid valves. 7, Pulmonary artery. 8, 8, Branches of the pulmonary artery that pass to the right and left lung. 9, Semilunar valves of the pulmonary artery. 10, Septum between the two ventricles of the heart. 11, 11, Pulmonary veins. 12, Left auricle. 13, Opening between the left auricle and ventricle. 14, Left ventricle. 15, Mitral valves. 16, 16, Aorta. 17, Semilunar valves of the aorta.

96. HEART-STRUCTURE.—The walls of the right auricle average two twenty-fourths of an inch in thickness; the left, three twenty-fourths; the right ventricle, three twenty-fourths, and the left, nine twenty-fourths. The left increases in thickness as life advances. The heart muscle-fibre (73) is striated, often branched, and often joined to adjacent fibres. The fasciculi of these fibres interlace,

and the sarcolemma is, as a rule, absent. There is scarcely any
areolar tissue between the fibres, and hence the peculiar firmness of
the contracted heart. The arrangement of the bands of muscular
fibres is very complicated.

97. To the margins and ventricular surfaces of the tricuspid and
mitral valves are attached numerous fine, inelastic cords, the *chordæ
tendineæ*, the other ends of which are attached to the *papillary muscles* projecting from the heart-wall in the interior, or directly to the
ventricular walls. Their combined functions are to prevent the curtains of the valves from being crowded into the auricular cavities
during severe contractions. In the middle of the free edge of each
fold of the semilunar valve are little nodules of fibro-cartilage.
The free margins also contain tendinous fibres, and behind the
folds in the walls of the arteries are little pouches, the *sinuses of Valsalva*. When the valve is open, the nodules prevent the folds from
being flattened against the tube; but when the systole is over, a
little of the reflux blood, with that already in the pouch, starts the
folds towards closing, and the great reflux closes them with a sharp
click.

98. The CAPACITY of the cavities of a hollow muscular organ
is difficult to determine. The estimates given for the left ventricle vary from one hundred and twenty to one hundred and
ninety-five grammes (four to six and one-half ounces). The
capacity of the auricle is equal to or a little smaller than that of
its ventricle. It is inferred that each contraction sends the same
amount out of the right side as is sent out of the left. The heart-
muscle receives its food from the aortic system, but the tissues adjacent to the endocardium may receive a small amount from the
contents of the heart. The substance of the heart contains numerous nerve-ganglia, and upon its surface are sympathetic nerves and
ganglia (386). It also receives fibres from the pneumogastric nerve
(383).

99. The *arteries* are firm, membranous, cylindrical tubes,
arising from the ventricles of the heart by two trunks : that
from the left ventricle, named the *aorta*, is the systemic

---

99. What are arteries ? Describe the aorta and its branches.

trunk, and that from the right ventricle, named the pulmonic *artery,* is the lung trunk.

The *systemic* trunk, or aorta, divides and subdivides into finer and finer arteries, like the branches from the trunk of a tree, excepting that these branches communicate with one another in a finer net-work, till the ultimate ramifications, too minute to be seen by the naked eye, extend to every nook and corner of the body. These final branches are called *capillaries.*

100. The CAPILLARIES serve to connect the terminations of the arteries with the beginning of the *veins,* so that it is impossible to tell just where the artery ends and the vein begins.

101. The VEINS thus commencing with the capillaries unite into larger and larger veins, converging towards the heart, like the roots of a tree towards its trunk, till the final union in two trunks (the ascending and descending *venæ cavæ*), that connect with the right auricle of the heart.

102. The SUPERIOR VENA CAVA derives its branches from the heart, neck, upper extremities, and walls of the thorax. It terminates at the upper back part of the right auricle of the heart. The INFERIOR VENA CAVA collects the blood from the lower extremities, pelvis, and abdomen, and terminates in the right auricle.

103. The PORTAL VEIN is a short trunk, about three inches in length, derived from the convergence of the veins of the stomach, spleen, pancreas, and intestines; this passes into the liver, where it divides and subdivides,

---

100. What is the use of the capillaries?

101. What of the veins?

102. Speak of the superior vena cava. Of the inferior vena cava.

103. The origin of the portal vein. Its distribution. Course of its blood.

being distributed throughout the organ. This blood, with that of the hepatic artery, is returned to the general circulation by the hepatic veins (270).

104. The PULMONIC or lesser circulation, from the right ventricle through the lungs to the left auricle, has a similar set of vessels: the trunk leaving the right ventricle is named the *pulmonic artery*, and corresponds to the aorta; those trunks conveying the blood to the left auricle, and corresponding to the venæ cavæ, are named the *pulmonary veins.*

105. ARTERIES are strong, yellowish-white, branching tubes. They have thick, elastic walls, and consist of three coats. The outer coat is of firm areolar and elastic tissue (22); the middle, of unstriped muscular fibre (72), arranged circularly around the tube and elastic fibres; and the inner is a very thin, smooth membrane. When cut across, an artery remains open. If a string is tied tightly around an artery, it crushes the inner and middle but not the outer coat, which is very tough. Hence, by the use of ligatures, severe bleeding from a vessel can be controlled until nature has time to close up the tube with a living plug. Arteries, especially in the extremities, frequently *anastomose.* Hence, if an artery becomes plugged by disease or operation, the blood can be carried around the obstruction to the part beyond. Arteries are usually placed deeply between the muscles, and are shielded by membranes and bones.

106. The smaller arteries have relatively more muscular tissue, and the larger relatively more elastic tissue, in their walls. The outer coat, and perhaps the middle coat, is supplied with nutrient

---

104. Speak of the pulmonic circulation. Of its arteries. Of its veins.

105. Describe an artery. Its coats. Its action when cut across. What is a ligature? What is anastomosis? Position of arteries?

TABLE OF THE PRINCIPAL ARTERIES, WITH THEIR BLOOD-DISTRIBUTION.

Aorta . . . .
- Coronary (Heart muscle).
- Innominata (Right head, arm, and chest).

Arch of Aorta . . .
- Carotid . . . .
  - External . . . .
    - Occipital (Scalp).
    - Lingual (Tongue).
    - Facial (Lower part of face).
    - Temporal (Scalp and face).
    - Internal Maxillary (Deep parts of face).
  - Internal . . . .
    - Ophthalmic (Eye and its orbit).
    - Cerebral (Brain).
- Subclavian . . . . . .
  - Vertebral . . . .
    - Spinal.
    - Cerebellar (Lower brain).
  - Inferior Thyroid (Larynx).
  - Axillary (Shoulder), Brachial (Arm) .
    - Radial (Forearm), Deep Arch (Hands, Fingers).
    - Ulnar, Superficial Arch.

Thoracic Aorta . . .
- Bronchial (Lungs and Air-tubes).
- Œsophageal (Gullet).
- Intercostal (Muscles of the Chest).

Abdominal Aorta . .
- Phrenic (Diaphragm).
- Cœliac Axis . . .
  - Hepatic (Liver, Stomach).
  - Splenic (Stomach, Pancreas, Spleen).
  - Gastric (Stomach).
- Superior Mesenteric (Small Intestines, Ascending Colon).
- Renal (Kidneys).
- Inferior Mesenteric (Colon, Rectum).
- Lumbar (Lumbar Muscles).

Aorta, Iliacs . . .
- External Iliac, Femoral (Thigh) . . . . . .
  - Profunda.
  - Pudic.
  - Popliteal (Knee).
    - Muscular.
    - Anterior Tibial (Leg and Foot).
    - Posterior Tibial (Foot).
    - Peroneal (Leg).
- Internal Iliac . . . . .
  - Vesical (Bladder).
  - Gluteal (Buttocks).
  - Pudic (Pelvis).
  - Sciatic (Thigh).

Fig. 29.

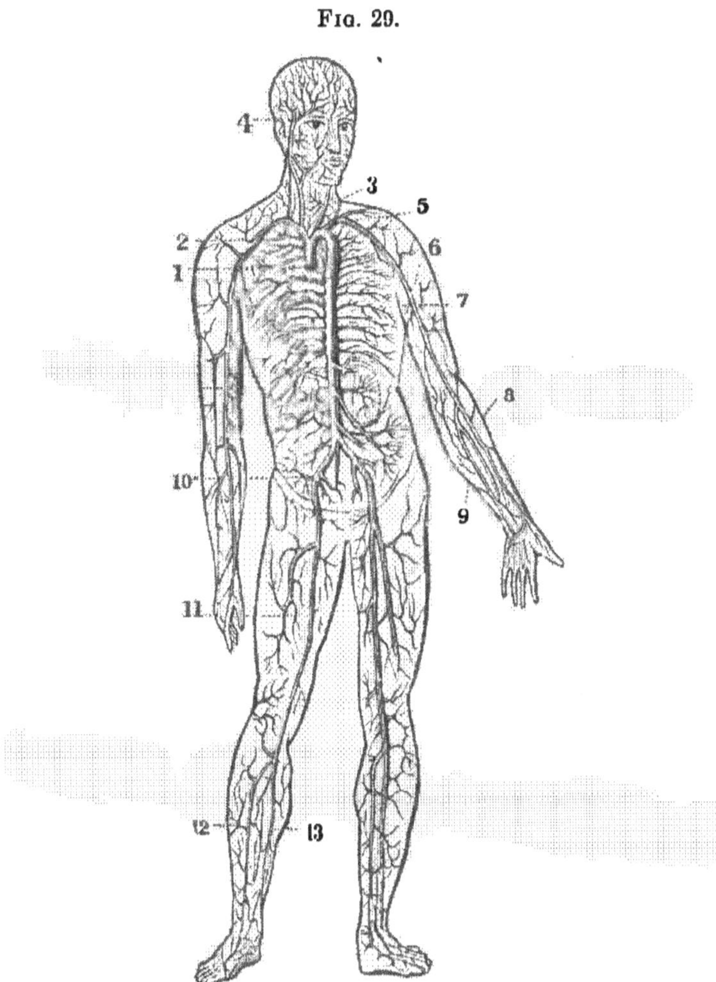

FIG. 29. THE AORTA AND ITS BRANCHES,—1, The commencement of the aorta. 2, The arch of the aorta. 3, The carotid artery. 4, The temporal artery. 5, The subclavian artery. 6, The axillary artery. 7, The brachial artery. 8, The radial artery. 9, The ulnar artery. 10, The iliac artery. 11, The femoral artery. 12, The tibial artery. 13, The peroneal artery.

blood-vessels, *vasa vasorum*. The arteries have nerve-fibres from the sympathetic system. Hence the diameter of the lumen of the arteries can be changed under the action of the nervous system upon the fibres of the muscular coat. By the sending out of certain nerve-impulses, the muscular contractions diminish the lumen of the artery; by the relaxation of the muscular tonicity, the action of the elastic tissue causes the lumen to be increased. Thus the flow of the blood in the smaller arteries and in the capillaries is regulated.

107. The VEINS have thinner walls and are more yielding than arteries. When cut across, they collapse. Within certain veins, at intervals, are found little folds or flaps, called *valves*. They are most numerous in the lower limbs, and assist materially in the flow of the blood. The small veins occur quite irregularly under the skin, but deeper in the tissues they accompany the arteries and bear the same names.

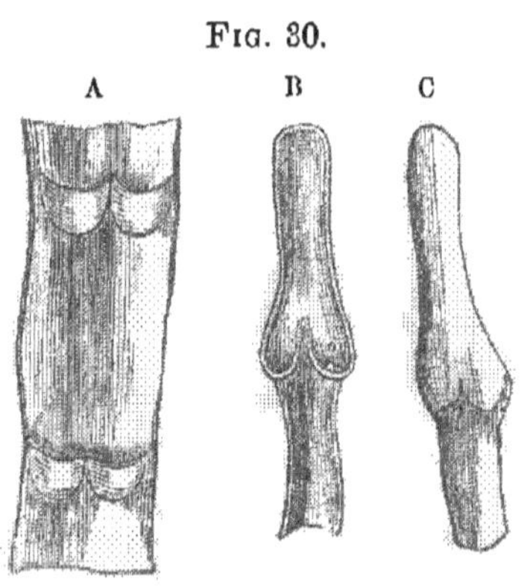

FIG. 30.

FIG. 30 (*Leidy*). DIAGRAMS EXHIBITING THE ARRANGEMENT OF THE VALVES OF VEINS.—A, Vein laid open, showing the valves in pairs. B, Longitudinal section of a vein, indicating the mode in which the valves, by apposition of their free edges, close its calibre. The dilated condition of the walls behind the valves is also seen. C, Vein distended, showing how the sinuses behind the valves become dilated.

108. Valves are not found in the cranial, spinal, renal, portal, hepatic, or pulmonary veins. Their folds may be single, double, or triple. Their free edge is always towards the heart. Veins have *vasa vasorum* and a few nerves.

---

106. What is said of the smaller arteries? How is the flow of the blood regulated?

107. Differences between veins and arteries? Valves? Position of the veins?

Experiment.—Tie a string around the forearm below the elbow, but not so tightly as to stop the radial pulse. The veins at the back of the hand soon become distended. Little venous prominences, about an inch apart, may be seen. These indicate very nearly the position of the valves. On one vein press on the finger side of the valve, then stroke the blood to beyond the next valve, and the intermediate portion of the vein will lose its distention,—that is, the valve prevents the reflux of the blood. Remove the finger-pressure, and the tube again appears, owing to the fact that the heart is constantly pumping blood into the veins. If the compression is continued for some time, the hand becomes painful, cooler, and bluish in appearance. Hence all obstruction to the venous flow of the blood is injurious.

109. The fine *net-work* of minute CAPILLARY tubes in which the arteries end and the veins begin has very thin, nucleated, membranous walls. These walls permit the nutritive material of the blood to pass freely into the neighboring tissues and spaces (143). The heart, arteries, capillaries, and veins form a closed system of chambers and tubes, in which the blood is contained.

110. The walls of the capillaries are formed by the fusing together of very thin and flat nucleated cells. The capillary net-work is of various forms,—in the muscles, elongated; in the skin, loop-like; in the intestines, close-meshed, etc. The tubes are the smallest, and the meshes finest, in the lungs. The smallest, however, permit the passage of the red corpuscles. The joint cartilages, the cornea of the eye, the enamel of the teeth, the epidermis, the nails, and the hair have no capillaries.

BLOOD.

111. PHYSICAL APPEARANCES.—The blood in the living human body is a fluid varying in color from a brownish red to a bright red. It has a peculiar odor. It constitutes by weight about one-thirteenth of the body: thus, a man weighing 75 kilograms (165 pounds) would have about 5.8 kilograms (12.7 pounds) of blood.

109. What of the capillary walls? What passes through their walls? Where may blood be found in the normal body?

111. Appearances of blood? The amount?

112. MICROSCOPIC APPEARANCES.—A drop of blood under the microscope shows a pale-yellowish fluid, *plasma*, in which float a large number of disks, *corpuscles*, of which the red are more numerous than the white. The *red* corpuscles have rounded edges, are circular, are concave on the upper and lower surfaces, and when seen on edge appear dumb-bell-shaped. If 3400 were placed side by side in a line, they would fill a linear inch; if about 14,000 were placed one upon another, they would occupy a vertical inch. It is estimated that 83,000,000 exist in a cubic inch of normal blood.

113. The *red* corpuscles have a homogeneous appearance, and show no nucleus. If they roll together they often assume an appearance like a roll of coins. The *white* corpuscles are not uniform in size, as are the red; they are granular and contain a nucleus, they tend to adhere, and they are more abundant after meals. They frequently change their forms, and at times exhibit a remarkable appearance, with changes of position, called *amœboid movements* (9, 6). Transparent net-works of fine fibres, called *fibrin*, are sometimes seen between the red corpuscles.

114. CHEMICAL COMPOSITION.—The living fluid consists of from one-third to one-half of its weight of corpuscles, and the rest of plasma. The gases oxygen, nitrogen, and carbonic acid are mechanically mixed with the blood. The *plasma* is made up of a small percentage of fibrin, C, H, O, N, S (4), and a yellowish fluid called serum.

115. The *serum* is composed of water (H, O), ninety parts; serum-albumen (C, H, O, N, S),—a transparent fluid, very similar in appearance to the white of an egg,—seven to eight parts; fats (C, H, O), extractives like urea (C, H, O, N), sugar, lactic acid, etc. (C, H, O), and salines, sodic and potassic chlorides (Na, K, Cl), calcic, magnesic, sodic, potassic phosphates, carbonates, and sulphates (Ca, Mg,

---

112. Microscopic appearances? Describe the red disks. Their size and number.

113. What of the red corpuscles? Of the white corpuscles? Of the amœboid movements? Of the fibrin?

Na, K, O, H, P, C, S), one to two parts.   The most abundant salines are the salts of sodium, especially common salt (sodic chloride).

116. The *red corpuscles* consist of about fifty-seven per cent. water, and the rest mostly of organic solids, of which *hæmoglobin* (C, H, O, N, S, Fe) constitutes the larger part.   This compound is the great iron-containing material of the body, and acts as the oxygen-bearer of the blood (180).

117. The corpuscles contain the same salines as the serum, but the potassic salts and the phosphates are relatively in larger proportions.

118. The exact chemical arrangement of the fourteen chemical elements (4), especially the atomic grouping of the carbon compounds, is not known.   The means of research now in use do not enable us to grope into the combinations of the *living* fluids and *living* solids of the body.   Most of the chemical changes taking place in the living blood and tissues can, as yet, only be conjectured.

119. The origin and fate of the corpuscles are debated questions. The *red* may arise from certain colorless nucleated bodies in the blood, similar to, if not identical with, the white corpuscles of the blood, from the small nucleated corpuscles of the spleen-pulp (298), or from the transitional cell-like forms seen in the red medulla of the large bones.   The spleen is supposed to be the grave of many red corpuscles, and the breaking up of the corpuscles to form the biliary coloring-matter, the end of others.   The *white* corpuscles may arise from division of the colorless cell-bodies, but more probably from the lymphatic glands and other adenoid tissue (296). Their function appears to be to give birth to the red corpuscles.

120. COAGULATION OF BLOOD.—If a little fresh blood is collected and allowed to remain in a clean vessel, it is seen to pass through a fluid, a viscid, and a jelly-like stage in turn; then a few drops of a yellow fluid appear on this jelly-surface, about the sides and below; finally, a central, dark, contracting mass floats in the yellowish fluid.   This mass is called the *clot*.   The process of clot-formation is called *coagulation*.

---

120. Describe the changes occurring in blood-coagulation.   Of what is clot composed?   Write out a scheme of the changes.

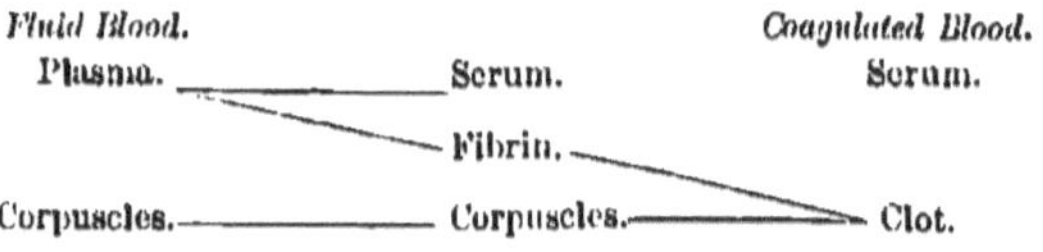

121. If a little fresh blood is whipped with fine sticks or wires, a fine felt-work of elastic, pale, granular fibres adheres to them. These fibres are *fibrin*. The *clot* consists of the corpuscles imprisoned in the slowly-forming fibrin.

122. *Coagulation is favored* by exposure to the air, motion, and the presence of obstacles and rough objects. Blood does not coagulate in the healthy living blood-tubes. It may coagulate in diseased, enlarged, or contracted blood-tubes, or in the heart. When a blood-tube is ruptured or cut across, as after an injury, the stream of blood is hindered, and in most cases arrested, by the forming of a clot. This is one of Nature's methods of stopping *hemorrhage*. Later, minute vessels appear in the plug, and it soon becomes *organized*, and a part of the living blood-tubes; thus there is no recurrence of the bleeding.

123. FUNCTION OF THE BLOOD.—Blood is the great medium of interchange between the tissues. They are bathed and permeated by it. It takes to them the necessary foods, and removes from them their waste and effete matters, which it conveys to the proper excreting organs, as the kidneys, lungs, etc. Its fluidity enables it to pass through fine tubes into all organs. Its plasma passes through the healthy coats of the tubes into the cellular spaces. The vitality of the tissues depends upon the presence of this very complex fluid. Its chemical composition, and its physical appearance, color, density, etc., are constantly changing. The *white* corpuscles appear to have no special function; the *red* have a special respiratory duty (181); and

---

123. What is the blood? What does it accomplish? What changes does it undergo? What are the functions of the red corpuscles? Of the white? Of the plasma?

the *plasma* acts a nutritive part, as well as that of a corpuscle and a gas-bearer.

CIRCULATION OF THE BLOOD.

DIRECTIONS.—With tapes fasten a live frog on a piece of stiff card-board. Near the toes of one outstretched hind limb cut a hole in the card three-quarters of an inch in diameter. Attach threads to two adjacent toes. So arrange the threads that the stretched web comes over the centre of the hole. Place a drop of water on the web, and over the same a thin cover-glass. Use on the microscope a 1-inch or ¾-inch objective. If you desire greater magnifying power, lengthen the tube with blackened Bristol-board. Observe the moving bodies; the *red* and the *white* corpuscles; the comparatively small number of the latter; the walls of the channels; the rapid central current; the slow wall-current; and the pigmented granules in the web.

FIG. 31.   FIG. 32.

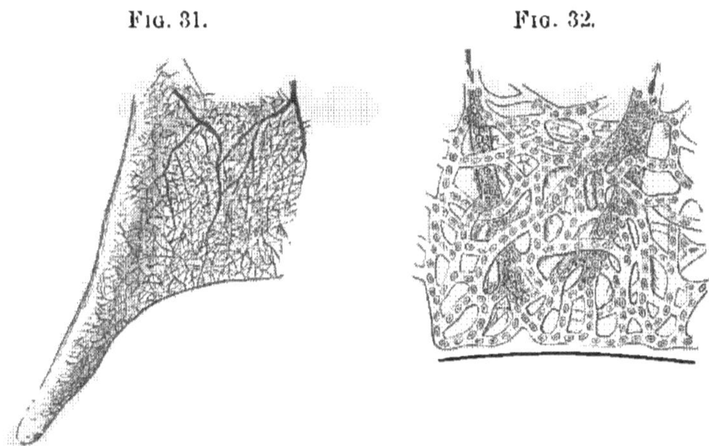

FIG. 31 (*After Wagner*). A PIECE OF THE WEB OF A FROG'S FOOT, slightly enlarged, showing the fine capillary net-work connecting the terminations of the arteries with the commencement of the veins.

FIG. 32 (*Allen Thomson*). A MINUTE PIECE OF THE MARGIN OF THE FROG'S WEB, showing the ultimate capillaries, connecting the end of a small artery with the beginning of a minute vein. The oval blood-corpuscles are seen in these vessels, and the arrows entering and passing out of the artery and vein indicate the course of the blood-current. Magnified about thirty diameters.

124. COURSE OF THE CIRCULATION.—The blood in the living body is always in motion. It moves in certain defi-

---

124. What of the blood in the living body? Describe the systemic circulation. The pulmonic circulation.

nite tubes and in certain directions. Propelled from the left *ventricle*, passing through the *aorta* and its arterial branches, the blood reaches the *capillaries* in every part of the body; now entering the little *veins* which empty into the larger veins, it finds its way to the right *auricle*. This is called the SYSTEMIC CIRCULATION. Dropping into the *right ventricle*, it is propelled through the *pulmonic artery* and its branches to the lungs. Flowing through the capillaries, it collects in the *pulmonic veins*, and, passing through the left auricle, it reaches the left ventricle. This is called the PULMONIC CIRCULATION.

125. *The chief cause of the circulation* of the blood is the contraction of the muscular walls of the heart upon its fluid contents. The motion is also influenced by the elastic and muscular walls of the arteries (105), the intermittent pressure of the body-muscles on their adjacent veins, and the movements of the chest in breathing. The effects of the muscular pressure are entirely due to the presence and direction of the valves in the interior of the veins. The influence of the respiratory movements on the circulation is very complicated, and cannot well be described in an elementary book.

ACTION OF THE HEART.

DIRECTIONS.—With tapes bind a living frog on the card-board or "frog-plate." Make an incision in the abdominal median line from the lower jaw to the pubis, and from the middle of this line two transverse cuts. Lift up the sternum, cut off its lower quarter, and then slit the sternum up to the neck. Pin back the right and left parts. The heart will be seen moving within its sac, the *pericardium*. Slit open the pericardium. Observe the contraction of the right and left auricles at the same time; just later, the contraction of the right and left ventricles at the same time. During the contraction, or systole, the ventricle becomes pale, hard, rigid, conical, and the apex rises. Then occurs a pause, the *diastole*, during which the heart-chambers resume their uncontracted state. Again

---

125. The chief cause of the motion? Aids to the motion? Influence of muscular action?

Fig. 33.

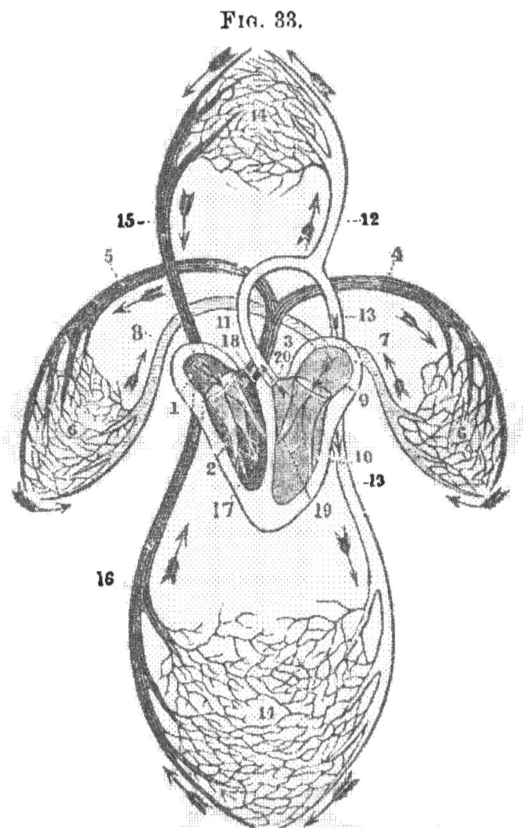

Fig. 33.   An ideal view of the circulation in the lungs and system.—From the right ventricle of the heart (2), the dark, impure blood is forced into the pulmonary artery (3), and its branches (4, 5) carry the blood to the left and right lungs.   In the capillary vessels (6, 6) of the lungs, the blood becomes of a red color, and is returned to the left auricle of the heart (9) by the veins (7, 8).   From the left auricle the pure blood passes into the left ventricle (10).   By a forcible contraction of the left ventricle of the heart the blood is thrown into the aorta (11).   Its branches (12, 13, 13) carry the pure blood to every part of the body.   The divisions and subdivisions of the aorta terminate in capillary vessels, represented by 14, 14.   In these hair-like vessels the blood becomes dark-colored, and is returned to the right auricle of the heart (1) by the vena cava descendens (15) and vena cava ascendens (16).   The tricuspid valves (17) prevent the reflow of the blood from the right ventricle to the right auricle.   The semilunar valves (18) prevent the passage of blood from the pulmonary artery to the right ventricle.   The mitral valves (19) prevent the reflow of blood from the left ventricle to the left auricle.   The semilunar valves (20) prevent the reflow of blood from the aorta to the left ventricle.

the auricles and the ventricles contract, and the large vessels become turgid with blood. Note that after the auricle contracts the ventricle is redder and more distended than after the latter contracts.

126. ACTION OF THE HEART.—The normal human heart contracts at regular intervals, ranging from sixty-five to seventy-five beats per minute in the adult. The right and left auricles contract together. The auricles contracting empty their contents into the ventricles. Almost immediately the *tricuspid* and *mitral* valves close and the ventricles contract, forcing the blood beyond the *semilunar* valves, which then suddenly close. A *pause* now occurs, during which the auricles fill with blood and the ventricles resume their uncontracted state. Then occur another series of contractions, a pause, a filling, and a dilatation. This rhythmic action commences in fœtal life and continues until the hour of death. The work of the auricles is light, that of the ventricles severe, and hence the latter, especially the left, have thicker walls.

127. WORK OF THE HEART.—At each beat it is supposed that the ventricles are entirely emptied. It is estimated that at each systole the left ventricle empties into the aorta one hundred and eighty grams (six ounces) of blood. A quantity equivalent to the whole blood passes through the heart in thirty-two contractions or beats. Supposing the heart to beat seventy-two times per minute, the day's work of the heart amounts to about seventy-five thousand kilogram-metres (about equal to the raising of one ton weight to the height of thirty-nine inches eighty-two times). The diastole is the period of rest for the heart-

---

126. Describe the heart's action. What valves act at the same time? What occurs during the pause? What of the work?

127. The work of each beat? Frequency of the blood-passage through the heart? The heart's work? The heart's rest?

muscle. For each beat it is nearly one-third of a second, or about nine hours per day.

128. HEART-INHIBITION is the stopping or checking of the heart's pulsation. Colonel Townsend, by an act of the will, could hold his breath for such a length of time as to lessen his heart's action. Czermak, by pressing his pneumogastric (vagus) nerve (383) against a small bony tumor in his neck, could stop the beating of his own heart at will. An interrupted electric current passed over the vagi causes the beats to diminish, and even to cease. Mechanical and chemical stimulation of the divided nerve, or certain diseased conditions or injuries of the brain, may induce inhibition. The fainting from emotion or from severe pain is the result of a reflex inhibition acting through the brain on the vagi nerves.

129. ACCELERATION of the pulsation of the heart may be induced by direct electric stimulation of the cervical spinal cord. The nervous impulses started by a sensation, an emotion, or a thought may accelerate or retard the heart's action. The introduction of alcohol and of certain drugs into the system, acting upon the muscle, ganglia, or inhibitory apparatus increases the frequency of the beats; some other drugs, on the contrary, retard the frequency of the pulsations.

130. The *modifications* of the heart, through the influence of the vagi nerves and the general nervous system, enable this organ to accommodate itself to the varying demands and the changing conditions of the entire system. By means of the nervous system, the action of the heart and blood-vessels is co-ordinated. As the blood of the body is not sufficient to keep all the organs in full activity at the same time, and as only a part of the organs must be in full activity at a given time, the nervous mechanism of the heart and vessels, by modifying the force of the heart-beat and the calibre of the vessels, regulates the supply in accordance with the demands. When the digestive organs are in full activity, the brain works sluggishly, the muscles do not contract vigorously, and certain minor functions are in abeyance, for the nervous control limits the supply to the brain and muscles, but increases the supply to the intestinal organs.

131. HEART-SOUNDS. *Observation.*—Place the hand on the bare chest of a boy over the fifth and sixth ribs, about two inches to the left of the sternum. A slight concussion, the *impulse* of the heart, is felt. This coincides with the *systole* of the ventricles. Put

two fingers on the wrist-pulse of the boy (the artery-beat may be felt on the thumb side of the wrist over the lower end of the radial bone, palmar side), and place the ear on the impulse-area: a deep, dull, long sound is heard at the time of the impulse and just before the pulse at the wrist. This is the *first* sound, and coincides with the ventricular systole and the closure of the mitral and tricuspid valves. Then place the ear to the left of the sternum over the space between the second and third ribs; a sharp, high-toned, ringing, short sound is heard directly after the duller first sound. This is the *second* sound, and coincides with the closing of the semilunar valves. These sounds are somewhat obscured by the sound of the rush of blood, the muscular sounds, and the impulses. With colored chalk or ink, mark on the skin the course of the main arteries of the neck, arms, and legs. Call special attention to the places over which the "field tourniquet" may be applied to control bleeding. (See Chapter XV.)

132. BLOOD-FLOW IN THE ARTERIES.—When an artery is severed, the flow of bright red blood is not equable, but it comes in jets from the side towards the heart. These jets correspond with the heart-beats; yet the flow does not cease between the jets. The larger the artery and the nearer to the heart, the greater the force of the jet and the more marked the intermittency. The velocity of the arterial stream is greatest in the large arteries, and diminishes from the heart to the capillaries. Its average rate is estimated at twenty-five centimetres (about ten inches) per second in the common carotid.

133. The rhythmic beat of the heart, combined with the resistance of friction in the tubes and points of branching and the smallness of the lumen of the capillaries, keeps the arteries in a state of permanent distention. Then each beat propels into the overfull artery a new increment of fluid, thus increasing the pressure and giving rise to an expansion of the elastic tube. When the beat is over, and the semilunar aortic valve's closure prevents the return of the fluid, then the elastic coat contracts, giving rise to a slight pulsation, followed by a continued pressure on the fluid. Hence the flow in the artery is intermittent from the heart's action, but the stream is kept continuous by the elastic after-pressure on the contents of the overfull arteries.

---

132. The blood-flow from an artery? What of the intermittency and force? Of the rate of motion?

134. Vaso-motor Action.—The middle coats of all arteries contain circularly-arranged plain muscular fibres (72). Nerve-fibres from the sympathetic system (386) are distributed largely to the arteries. Experiments show that by the mechanical stimulation of certain of these nerve-centres the arterial muscular coat may be made to contract, causing the calibre of the arteries influenced to become smaller. Then, if the stimuli be removed, the muscular contraction diminishes, the elasticity of the vessel-wall increases the lumen, and more blood passes through the vessel. In snowballing, the contact of snow with the hand so affects the nerve-centres controlling the distribution of the blood to the hand as to diminish the arterial lumen. Later, this new action is overcome, the centres lose power over the muscular fibres, and the vessels become unduly dilated, giving rise to the increased glow and warmth of the skin.

135. Experiments indicate that a centre of *vaso-motor* activity, presiding over and regulating the local centres, exists in the medulla (373), and regulates the calibre of the vessels of the system at large by keeping the muscular fibres of the vessels in a state of *tonic* contraction; that the blood acting on this centre causes the generation of certain impulses which incite the muscular fibres to greater or less contraction, thus modifying the calibre of the vessels, and, as a result, the amount of blood sent to a part is gauged to the wants of that part. Experience shows that the vaso-motor centre and the local centres may be depressed or exalted by varying influences coming from the various sentient surfaces or the brain. When the right hand is dipped in cold water, the temperature of the left hand falls, owing to a reflex constriction of the vessels of the skin of that hand; when one eye is injured, the other not infrequently becomes diseased, being a result of reflex vaso-motor action; when a certain thought or emotion arises in the brain, it depresses or exalts that portion of the vaso-motor centre controlling the vessel-areas of the neck, and thus *blushing* or *pallor* is induced. The thought of food often causes an increased amount of blood to be sent to the glands about the mouth, inducing a copious secretion of saliva, —*i.e.*, "the mouth waters."

136. The amount of the constriction of the minute arteries may in a great measure be dependent on the blood-pressure itself, though this is not fully demonstrated. There are reasons for believing that the vaso-motor centre is directly affected by the quality of the blood

passing through it. If the quantity of oxygen in the blood is reduced, the contraction of the muscular fibres of the vessels is increased, and arterial constriction, with a rise of blood-pressure, results. If the oxygen is increased, the action of the centre is lessened, the vessel is dilated, and the pressure falls.

137. *The vaso-motor system is of great regulative value.* By local dilatation in one area the flow of blood is encouraged, and the consequent reduction of pressure lessens the amount of blood sent to other areas. By local constriction in one vascular area the blood-pressure is raised, the calibre of the vessels is diminished, and the mass of the blood is thus forced to other areas. These vaso-motor centres respond to external or to internal stimuli, acting through the blood or the nervous tracts, and thus the supply of blood to this or to that organ or tissue is regulated. In cold weather the vessels of the skin are constricted, the flow of blood is diminished, and thus undue loss of heat is prevented. In warm weather the cutaneous vessels dilate, the blood-flow to the skin is increased, the perspiration is augmented, and the loss of heat from the skin is thus encouraged. In health, the harmonious inhibiting and exalting of these centres keep the mass of the blood in those parts where it is most needed.

138. COLDS are very frequently caused by a portion of the skin being exposed to a current of cold air, or by the wearing of damp clothing. The nerves of the skin, acting on the vaso-motor centre (135), incite the latter to send forth such impulses to the muscular coats as lead to a diminution of the calibre of the cutaneous vessels. This causes a rise in the blood-pressure, and the crowding of an abnormal amount of blood into the internal organ areas, inducing internal "determination of blood," followed by "congestion." The internal overplus of blood is made known to us by a feeling of uneasiness, followed by a more or less copious discharge of mucus and fluids,—in the cold season by bronchitis and nasal discharge, in the warm season by diar-

---

138. The cause of colds? The influence of the vaso-motor centre? Results of the overplus in certain areas? The proper treatment?

rhœa.   Hence in such maladies we seek to induce the skin vascular areas to receive more blood, by employing friction, external heat, extra merino under-clothing, and a flannel band (eight or ten inches wide) for the abdomen.

139. BLOOD-FLOW IN THE CAPILLARIES.—The flow is constant, equable, and regular.   The motion is most rapid in the centre of each stream.   The velocity has been estimated at one-thirtieth of an inch per second in the systemic capillaries, and one-fifth of an inch per second in the pulmonic capillaries.   This slow rate affords time for the interchange between the blood and the air in the lungs.

140. *The retardation of the flow* is due to the increased capacity of the capillary area over the arterial common trunks.   The arterial blood-pressure is always greater than the venous, and the blood flows through the capillaries to the part offering the least resistance; that is, towards the veins.   The heart-beat pulsation is not transmitted to the capillary current.   The elastic rebound of the arterial walls crowds the overplus of each ventricular systole in a steady stream into the venous system, and, by a nice adjustment of the nerve-influence of the vaso-motor centres, as much blood is discharged into the veins as is received at each systole.   If the heart ceases to beat, the elastic walls of the arteries force enough blood through the capillaries to equalize the pressure of the arterial and venous systems, and then all motion ceases.   Hence, after death the large arteries are found nearly empty.

141. BLOOD-FLOW IN VEINS.—When a vein is severed, the dark blood flows from the end near the capillaries in a continued stream, with little force and slight velocity.   The velocity increases from the capillaries towards the heart. The velocity of the flow is said to average from one-third to one-half of that of the corresponding arteries.

139. The flow of blood in the capillaries?   Its velocity?   What changes occur?

141. The flow of blood from a cut vein?   The velocity of the venous flow?

f

142. *The primary force* in the movement of the blood in the veins is the heart's action, modified by the elasticity and recoil of the arteries. The movements are aided by pressure of the muscles acting on the veins having valves, and the thoracic respiratory movements. *Expiratory* movements, as coughing, sneezing, holding the breath, retard the venous flow. The *inspiratory* movements facilitate the entrance of the blood to the auricles, but not to the ventricles, because of the semilunar valves. The rate of motion in the veins is more subject to disturbing influences, as rapid or slow breathing, pressure of garments, bands, boots, gloves, etc., than any other part of the circulation.

143. INTERCHANGES IN THE CAPILLARY NET-WORK. —All the tissues of the body live on the blood of the body. It is in the capillary areas that the blood is the seat of constant additions and constant subtractions. It is while slowly moving here that the blood does its *nutrition* and *de nutrition* work. By some as yet unknown process, each tissue selects and withdraws from it the materials which it requires, and gives up to it effete materials to be conveyed away. We only know that the blood coming from the capillary areas is different from that entering, and that definite changes have occurred, as is shown by repair, by growth, or by continued ability to perform functions.

144. The PULSE is the name given to the impulse transmitted to a finger placed tightly upon an artery running over a bone, as the radial at the wrist, or the temporal in front of the ear. It is due to the intermittent additional distention which the artery experiences after each systole of the ventricles. In health it is present only in the arteries.

145. PROOFS OF THE CIRCULATION are the anatomical

---

143. What occurs in the capillary area?   What do the tissues do? How is the blood changed?   What result in the tissues?

144. What is the pulse?   Its cause?

145. Proofs of the circulation in the living body?   What did Harvey prove?   What did Malpighi see?

connection and the continuity of the heart, arteries, capillaries, and veins (109); the different direction in which the blood escapes from a cut artery (132) and a cut vein (141); the effect of ligature upon the veins (108); the direction of the valves of the heart (92) and veins (107); and the observation of the blood moving in the web of the frog's foot (Fig. 32), and retina (451) of the human eye. In 1628, William Harvey, of England, demonstrated the real course of the blood; in 1661, Malpighi demonstrated the capillary circulation in the web of the frog's foot; and the problem which had baffled their predecessors was then first settled.

HYGIENE.

146. *The clothing should be loose*, especially about the neck and limbs, in order that the flow of blood in the great venous vessels be not impeded in the least. In changeable weather woollen under-garments should always be worn, thus preventing the undue accumulation of blood in one part of the body at the expense of other portions. By the use of the flannel abdominal band during warm weather, diarrhœa can usually be avoided; by the judicious distribution of the clothing on the limbs and trunk, many coughs, colds, and subsequent maladies can be prevented.

147. Persons suffering from diseases of the vascular system should take a proper amount of exercise daily; should eat plain, nutritious food; should avoid tea, tobacco, and also mental disturbance and all hasty, sudden exertions. *Alcoholics* ought not to be used, as they derange the

---

146. What relation has the clothing to the veins? Why should woollen be preferred? What of the abdominal flannel band?

147. What of the management of disease of the heart or blood-vessels? Speak of the effects of alcohol on the circulation.

vaso-motor system. The action of the heart is disturbed, the pulsations are increased, and hence results increased work for this vital organ. Alcoholics also relax the capillaries, especially those of the skin and the nervous system, causing an early sense of warmth and exhilaration. This abnormal accumulation of blood in the skin and the nerve-centre areas deprives other areas of their proper share. The temporary exhilaration, mental and physical, is commonly followed by a corresponding depression, more especially under exposure to cold (245). Frequent repetitions of the unnatural over-distention of the nervous capillary areas tend to produce permanent perverted nutrition and diseased action in the nerve-centres, as is strikingly shown in alcoholism (408). The facts of vaso-motor physiology testify against the use of alcoholics. Cold or tepid sponging is often beneficial. It is most important that the sleeping-room be cool, commodious, and well ventilated.

(For the treatment of wounds, hemorrhages, etc., see Chapter XV.)

CHAPTER VI.

THE RESPIRATORY APPARATUS AND RESPIRATION.

Direction for Dissection.

WHEN the thorax of a dog or rat is opened (88), air enters the pleural cavities; the lungs, which had hitherto filled the large right and left chambers of the thorax, shrink somewhat. Before removing the thoracic viscera, bend two straws of broom-corn into a sickle shape, pass one into each nostril, and then urge them gently forward to their whole length. Open the mouth, gently move the soft curtain attached to the back part of the roof of the mouth to one side, and the two straws will be seen projecting into a cavity or open sac, the *pharynx*. The passages in which the straws lie are separated from each other by a long and cartilaginous septum, and from the mouth by bone and a soft fleshy curtain. The latter is called the *uvula*, or *soft palate*, and the former the *hard palate*. If the musculo-membranous pharynx be laid open, *five* openings will be easily seen: two leading to the nostrils, one to the mouth, one to the larynx, and one to the gullet. The fleshy uvula is seen to be capable of closing either the passage to the nostrils or that to the mouth, while the stiff, nearly vertical *epiglottis* can close down over the entrance to the larynx if pressed upon. At rest the mouth is completely filled and the entrance to the œsophagus is closed.

Remove the larynx, trachea, lungs, and heart, as directed in Chapter V., 88. At the upper or anterior part we encounter the *larynx*, an irregular cartilaginous box, opening above into a membranous sac, the *pharynx*, and below into a cartilaginous tube, the *trachea*. Observe on the upper front of the larynx a stiff, elastic, projecting, tongue-like mass, the *epiglottis*. Press this down, and it is seen to close over a slit-like opening in the larynx, the *glottis*. Lay open the larynx by an incision on the œsophageal side. The broad right and left cartilages, the *thyroid*, and the cut edges of the lower ring-like cartilage, the *cricoid*, are brought into view. In the interior, from above downward, note: the *mucus* on the surface, the two contiguous surfaces forming the upper *slit*, two right and left pits, the *ventricles* of the *larynx*, and two thin, contiguous surfaces, forming the *true vocal cords*, and the cut *cricoid*, with the two *arytenoid* cartilages resting thereon.

The *trachea* is found to be nearly a complete open tube. The front three-fifths of this tube is of horseshoe-shaped cartilages, while the posterior portion and the uniting parts of the semi-rings are made of fibro-muscular elastic membranes. The trachea divides into two partly cartilaginous tubes, the *bronchi*, which in turn, as a rule, divide and subdivide by twos. The cartilages in these latter soon disappear, they only being represented by membrane. The lumen of these tubes grows smaller and smaller, and is lost to sight in the soft, elastic, pinkish mass called the *lung*. Entering the lung-mass, side by side with the bronchi, are seen the open, firm *arterial* tubes, and the numerous dark, thin, flattened *veins*. These bronchi, arteries, and veins, together with the accompanying nerves, lymphatics, and connective tissue, constitute the *root of the lung*. The smooth outer surface of the lung-mass is the *pulmonary pleura*. By a dainty scratch a portion of a thin membrane, the *pleura*, may be raised into view. The smooth lining of the empty thorax is the *parietal* pleura, and the moisture the *pleural fluid.* Squeeze a portion of fresh lung-mass, and there arises a sensation called *crepitation ;* throw a bit into water, and it is seen to float ; hold a bit under water, squeeze it, and bubbles will be seen to arise,—the *residual air* of the lung.

Microscopic Work.—Cut out cubes of the soft tissues, and place in alcohol of one per cent. Examine the lung-tissue after careful teasing. Make thin sections of the cartilages, and examine at leisure.

THE THORAX.

148. The THORAX is made up of an open cage-work of bones and cartilages, with the intervals filled with muscles, membranes, tubes, and other soft parts. The bones consist of twelve bones of the *vertebral column* behind, twenty-four ribs (twelve pairs), extending to the right and left from the column, and the flat, thin, and broad *sternum* in front.

149. The VERTEBRAL COLUMN (343) is composed of a series of bones, called *vertebræ*, and disks of firm elastic material placed between the vertebræ, called the *intervertebral cartilages.* The vertebræ are bound together by flexible, elastic, and inelastic ligaments (509), and hence limited motion is possible, as in bending or twisting the spine. In the thorax the spine curves backward.

150. The RIBS are long, flat, round-edged, curved bones. Behind they are attached to pits in the vertebræ, from whence they curve downward and forward. The upper ribs are most curved. The seven upper pairs are attached directly to the sternum ; the three next pairs indirectly, by means of long cartilages ; while the two lowest pairs are free in front.

---

148. Speak of the thorax. The bones of the thorax.

149. What of the vertebral column ? Of the cartilages ? Of the ligaments ? Of the motions ?

150. Describe a rib. How attached ? Kinds of ribs ?

FIG. 34.

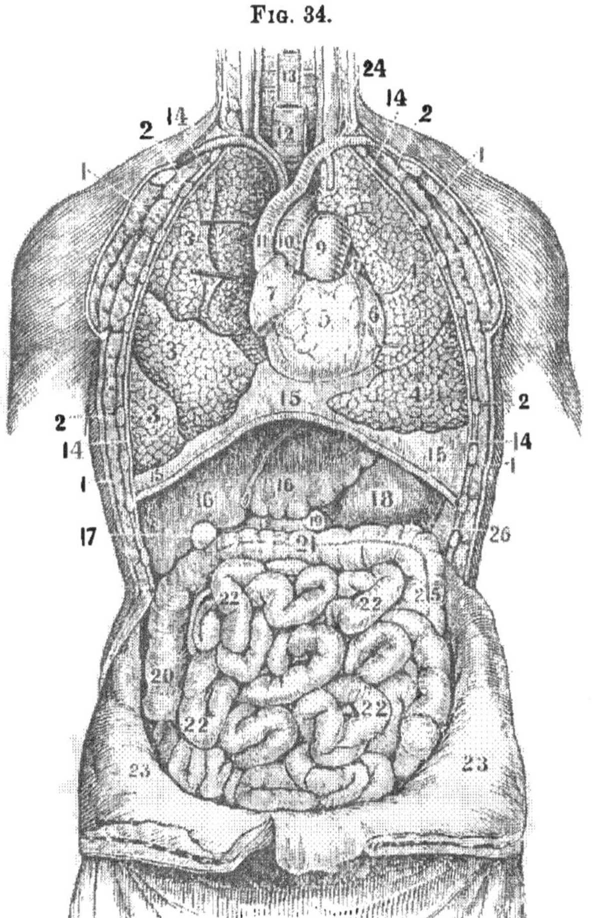

FIG. 34. A FRONT VIEW OF THE ORGANS OF THE CHEST AND ABDOMEN.—1, 1, 1, 1. The muscles of the chest. 2 2, 2, 2, The ribs. 3, 3, 3, The upper, middle, and lower lobes of the right lung. 4, 4, The lobes of the left lung. 5, The right ventricle of the heart. 6, The left ventricle. 7, The right auricle of the heart. 8, The left auricle. 9, The pulmonary artery. 10, The aorta. 11, The vena cava descendens. 12, The trachea. 13, The œsophagus. 14, 14, 14, 14, The pleura. 15, 15, 15, The diaphragm. 16, 16, The right and left lobes of the liver. 17, The gall-cyst. 18, The stomach. 26, The spleen. 19, 19, The duodenum. 20, The ascending colon. 21, The transverse colon, 25, The descending colon. 22, 22, 22, 22, The small intestine. 23, 23, The abdominal walls turned down. 24, The thoracic duct, opening into the left subclavian vein.

151. The Sternum is flat and broad.   It has eight pits on each side, seven for the ribs and one for the *clavicle*, or collar-bone.

Fig. 35.

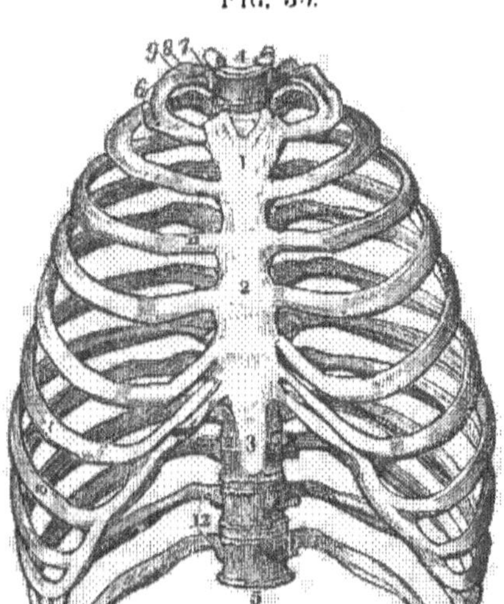

Fig. 35. The Front View of the Thorax.—1, 2, 3, The sternum. 4, 5, The spinal column. 6, 7, 8, 9, The first rib. 10, The seventh rib. 11, Cartilage of the third rib. 12, The floating rib.

152. The cage-work of bones is filled in with twenty-two pairs of MUSCLES.   The eleven outer pairs (external intercostals) run obliquely between the ribs, and in contracting raise the ends of the ribs and roll the lower edges inward, thus diminishing the capacity of the chest.

153. The FORM of the thorax is conical. It is narrowest above, where the tubes and soft parts going to the neck

----

151. Describe the sternum.

152. How many thoracic muscles?   Speak of the external set. Of the internal set.

153. Form of the thorax?   What of the diaphragm?   What tubes perforate it?

nearly close it. It is widest below, where it is separated from the abdomen by the *diaphragm*. The latter is a broad, thin, almost circular muscle, having in its central portion some fibrous tissue. It arches up in the thorax, because of the constant pressure of the abdominal viscera and muscles.

154. The chief contents of the thorax are the *heart* and *lungs*. These are the great central organs of circulation

Fig. 36.

Fig. 37.

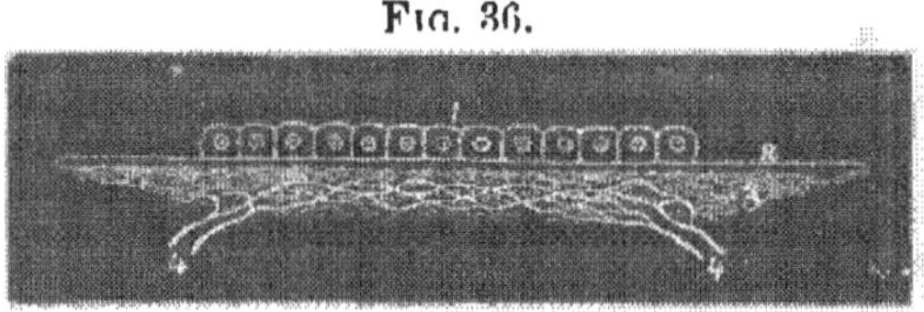

FIG. 36 (*Leidy*). DIAGRAM EXHIBITING THE RELATIVE POSITION OF THE COMMON ANATOMICAL ELEMENTS OF SECRETING MEMBRANES.—1, Epithelium, composed of nucleated cells. 2, Subjacent layer. 3, Areolar layer, in which the arteries and veins (4) ramify in a capillary net-work.

FIG. 37 (*Leidy*). DIAGRAM EXHIBITING THE RELATION OF A SEROUS MEMBRANE (*the pleura*) TO THE ORGAN IT INVESTS AND THE CAVITY IT LINES.—1, Lung. 2, Root of the lung, which is the only attached portion of the organ, all others being free. 3, Side of the thorax. 4, Diaphragm. 5, Parietal pleura. 6, Pulmonary or reflected pleura. 7, Cavity of the pleura. Magnified.

and respiration. The lungs occupy the right and left sides, and the heart the left central portion. The former are found in the *pleural* cavities, and the latter in the *pericardial* cavity.

155. The PLEURA is a thin, moist membrane, in the form of a *closed sac*, enclosing a fluid called *serum*. A portion of the outside of one sac is closely attached to the outer surface of one of the lungs and its root, and the other portion to the inside of its proper thoracic wall, while the

154. Contents of thorax? What cavities?
155. What is the pleura? Use of serum?

serous enclosed fluid lubricates the pleural surfaces, permitting the lung-portion to move smoothly over the thoracic portion. The lung is therefore outside of the sac of its pleura. The pleuræ are two in number, and form two chambers.

FIG. 38.

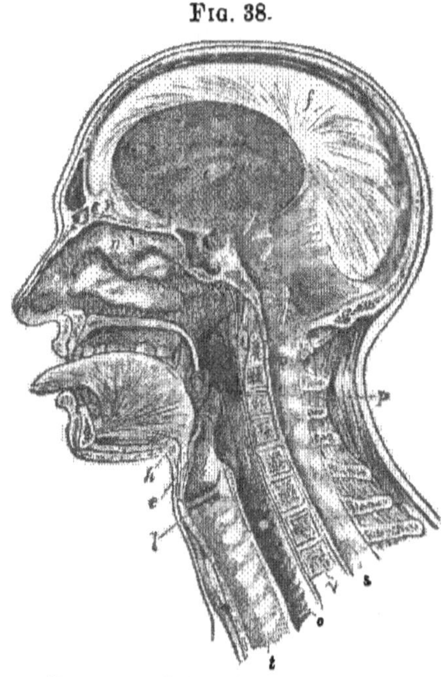

FIG. 38. VERTICAL SECTION. c, Cavity of skull. f, Falx. s, Spinal canal, leading from cavity of skull. n, Right nasal cavity. Below the hard and soft palate, the cavity of the mouth, the teeth, tongue, and lips. p, Pharynx. o, Œsophagus. h, Section of hyoid bone. l, Larynx. e, Epiglottis. t, Trachea. v, Section of cervical vertebræ. (*Marshall.*)

156. A SEROUS MEMBRANE consists of epithelial cells, a delicate subjacent web of tissue, on which the epithelia rest, and some areolar tissue (22) beneath, containing the blood-vessels and nerves. The *epithelial cell* consists of a delicate limiting structure, enclosing protoplasm, which contains nuclei and granules. Serous membranes are usually in a single layer, and are most frequently of the pavement variety (Fig. 42). The *subjacent tissue,* or basement mem-

brane, in cross-section appears little more than a faint line. The protoplasm of the epithelia elaborates a thin, slightly albuminous fluid, called *serum*. This kind of membrane is formed into a closed sac, having the epithelia on the inside. The principal membranes of this class are the pleura, the pericardium (95), and the peritoneum (246).

THE AIR-PASSAGES.

157. The NASAL PASSAGES are two in number. They are separated from each other by the bony and cartilaginous septa of the nose, and from the mouth by the *hard* palate and the *soft* palate, or *uvula*. They open behind into the *pharynx*. They are lined by mucous membrane, which is very vascular. In the upper portion of these passages are located the nerves of *smell* (429). (Fig. 38.)

158. The PHARYNX (259) is a musculo-membranous open sac. It is wider above than below, and is suspended from the base of the skull like a bag under a grain-funnel. It has seven openings,—above the soft palate, the two leading forward to the nostrils, the two to the middle ears (Eustachian tubes); below the soft palate, one to the mouth, one to the œsophagus, and one to the larynx.

159. The SOFT PALATE descends like an apron from the back edge of the hard palate, and is largely composed of muscles. The mucous membrane covering it above is like that of the nasal passages; below, like that of the mouth. The uvula can close either the opening to the nasal passages or the opening from the pharynx to the mouth (Fig. 38).

160. The LARYNX (487) is a hollow chamber, which is

suspended from the *hyoid bone* at the base of the tongue. It opens into the pharynx above and the trachea below. The framework is made up of cartilages held together by small ligaments, and forms the projection called "Adam's apple." At the upper opening is a curved, upright, elastic plate, called the *epiglottis*, which, during swallowing, closes down over the entrance to the larynx and prevents the admission of foreign materials.

161. The TRACHEA is situated in the middle line of the neck, commencing at the larynx and terminating in two smaller tubes called bronchi. It is from three-fourths

FIG. 39.   FIG. 40.

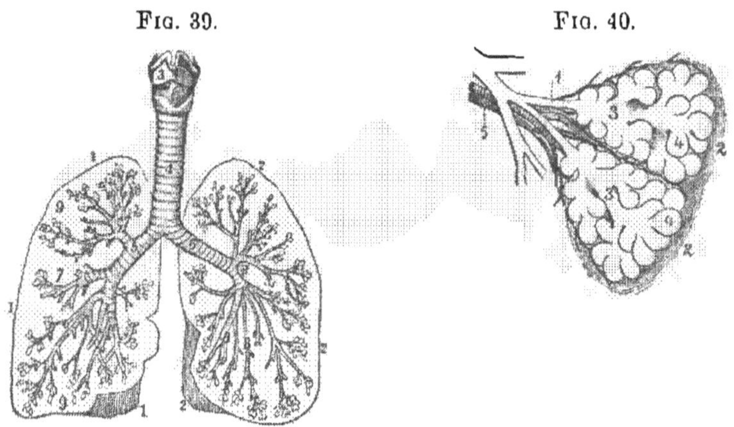

FIG. 39. THE BRONCHIA.—1, Outline of right lung. 2, Outline of left lung. 3, 4, Larynx and trachea. 5, 6, 7, 8, Bronchial tubes. 9, 9, Air-cells.

FIG. 40. (*Leidy*). DIAGRAM OF TWO PRIMARY LOBULES OF THE LUNGS, magnified. 1, Bronchial tube. 2, A pair of primary lobules connected by fibro-elastic tissue. 3, Intercellular air-passages. 4, Air-cells. 5, Branches of the pulmonary artery and vein.

of an inch to one inch in diameter, and is always open. It is made up of from sixteen to twenty independent, transverse, incomplete rings of cartilage, which are held together

---

161. Describe the trachea. Its position.

by muscular and elastic fibres. Behind, the tube is completed by a musculo-fibrous membrane.

162. The BRONCHI are two in number. Their structure is similar to that of the trachea, the cartilage hoops being incomplete. On entering the lungs the bronchi divide and subdivide, usually by twos, into smaller tubes, called *bronchia*, and then the whole appears like a tree with many branches. In all the larger and medium-sized bronchia, bits of cartilage are interspersed in the elastic fibrous membrane of the walls, in order to keep the tubes open.

163. AIR-CELLS.—The finest bronchia divide within the lobules of the lung from four to nine times. These finally terminate in the air-sacs. These air-sacs have nu-

FIG. 41.   FIG. 42.

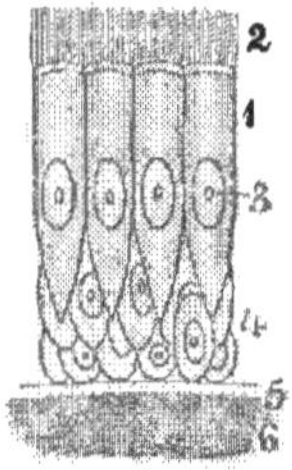

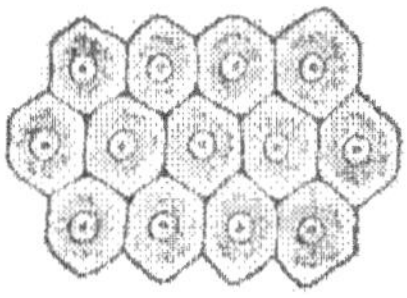

FIG. 41. DIAGRAM OF A VERTICAL SECTION OF THE BRONCHIAL MUCOUS MEMBRANE.—1, Columnar ciliated epithelial cells. 2, Cilia. 3, Nuclei. 4, Young cells. 5, Basement membrane. 6, Fibrous layer.

FIG. 42 (*Leidy*). PAVEMENT EPITHELIUM, from a serous membrane, highly magnified, and seen to consist of flat, six-sided nucleated cells.

merous cup-shaped depressions, called *air-cells*. The walls of the cells, in which blood-vessels, lymphatics, and nerves ramify, are transparent and very thin, and are lined with a delicate mucous membrane.

---

162. What are the bronchi? The bronchia? Function of the pieces of cartilage?

163. Speak of the air-cells. Form. Walls.

164. The air-passages from the nose to the air-cells are lined by MUCOUS MEMBRANE. Throughout most of the tubes it has an epithelium (156), showing free-moving, hair-like projections, called *cilia* (74). In a portion of the pharynx and in the air-cells the epithelia of this membrane elaborate a watery material, more or less viscid, called MUCUS. In places within the air-passages are *glands*, which secrete a thicker and more abundant mucus.

165. The *mucous membrane* consists of one or more layers of epithelium, resting upon a transparent and delicate subjacent or basement layer of tissue. This merges beneath in a layer of areolar and elastic tissue, in which ramify blood-vessels and nerves (Fig. 36). Mucous membranes open directly or indirectly on the surface of the body. The chief and most extensive one is called the *gastropulmonary*, because it forms the lining membrane of the digestive apparatus and the air-passages.

166. *Mucous glands.*—In some parts of the trachea, bronchi, and bronchia the mucous membrane is recessed into little tubes or sacs, which are called *glands* (250). The secreting surface is thus very much increased in a small space. The mucous crypts of the air-passages secrete an abundantly thick bronchial fluid, called bronchial mucus. The protoplasm of the epithelia is the secreting agent (156).

167. The LUNGS are two in number, and occupy completely and accurately the pleural chambers of the thorax. Each lung is free in all directions, except at the *root*, which chiefly consists of the bronchi, arteries, and veins connecting the lung with the trachea and the heart. The lungs are porous, spongy organs, the tissues of which are very elastic.

168. Each lung is of a conical shape, the apexes of which are blunt and project into the neck from an inch to an inch and a half

---

164. What lines the air-passages? Kinds of epithelia? Their secretion? Gland-secretion?

167. Speak of the lungs. Position. Root. Structure.

above the first rib. The base is broad and concave, and rests on the *diaphragm* (153). Each lung is divided by a deep fissure into upper and lower lobes. The upper lobe of the right side is imperfectly divided into two lobes, making three in the right and two in the left lung. The lobes are made of many closely-packed lobules. Each lobule is composed of a terminal branch of an air-tube, possessing a cluster of air-cells. In the fine interstitial areolar tissue of the lobule ramify the pulmonary vessels, the nutrient vessels, the lymphatics, and the nerves (Fig. 40).

169. The CAPACITY of the chest, and, therefore, of the lungs, varies. In a man of average height, after a forced inspiration, the chest contains about 5380 cubic centimetres (328 cubic inches) of air. After a violent expiration, followed by a violent inspiration, a healthy man of average stature (five feet eight inches) can take in about 3700 cubic centimetres (225 cubic inches). This is known as his *vital capacity*. This amount increases by about one hundred and thirty cubic centimetres (eight cubic inches) for each inch of stature above the average. In ordinary breathing, five hundred cubic centimetres (thirty cubic inches) of air are taken in and expelled with each complete respiration.

Directions for Demonstrations.—Let a healthy boy remove the apparel covering his neck and chest, except a close-fitting undershirt. Have him stand easily erect and execute four or six full respirations in a deliberate manner, the class, meanwhile, watching the movements attentively.

Place a tape snugly around the chest, about three inches below the armpits. Notice the difference in circumference during a full inspiration and a complete expiration,— 1st, in normal breathing; 2d, in labored breathing. Notice that the right half-circle of the chest is usually larger. If a spirometer can be procured, test the air-capacity of the lungs. Place the forefinger flat on the wall of the chest. Tap this finger smartly with the first two fingers of the other hand. Test different parts of the chest in front and in the rear in the same manner. A clear sound denotes the presence of air in the organs beneath: a dull sound, the presence of solids or liquids. The healthy lung-areas give forth a clear sound. By this method, the limits of the lungs, the heart, the liver, and the intestines may be approximately mapped out.

Place the ear on the skin over the region of the trachea in front; a blowing sound is heard both in inspiration and in expiration. Then place the ear on the shirt over the lung-

169. Capacity of the chest after inspiration? Vital capacity? Ordinary variation?

areas, pressing the latter smoothly and closely on the chest-walls. Listen in one place during several respirations. Shift the ear to different parts of the chest, and listen. A soft, low, murmuring sound is heard, being most marked over the front and upper parts of the chest and during inspiration. The murmur is mainly caused by the air passing in and out of the air-sacs and air-cells.

Take a clean glass (fruit) jar with cover; fasten a piece of candle, with wire or a small nail, near the end of a stick twenty inches long. Lower the lighted candle into the jar: it will burn freely. Reverse the jar; shake after the taper is withdrawn. Now have some person take a full inspiration, retaining the air, for a time, in the lungs; then steadily expel it from the lungs into the jar, directing the current to one side; cover; soon breathe again in the same manner into the glass vessel, and lower a lighted candle. The flame will be extinguished, because the carbonic acid, the watery vapor, and other gases from the lungs have so vitiated the air in the jar as to prevent combustion. Such air will not sustain life. (Before entering deep wells or caverns, a lighted taper should be lowered.) Place a little fresh lime-water in a jar; breathe several times into it; cover, and shake the lime-water. Instead of a clear liquid, there will be formed the white carbonate of lime. Put a live rat in a jar. Regulate the supply of air by the cover, giving a liberal supply, a limited supply, and then total exclusion of air, and notice the results.

Breathe on the cool surface of a clean mirror, and *watery vapor* will be condensed from the saturated exhaled air. Take a clean, cool mirror into the recitation-room. In a few minutes examine the moist surface. If onions or leeks have been recently eaten, ether or chloroform inhaled, or alcoholics recently drunk, or if persons have decayed teeth, the expired air will give forth odors easily detected. When air vitiated by respiration passes through strong sulphuric acid, the latter becomes darkened; through a solution of permanganate of potassa, the solution is deodorized; through distilled water, the water becomes offensive in odor and taste. These tests show the changes produced in air by respiration.

PHYSIOLOGY OF RESPIRATION.

170. ENLARGEMENT OF THE THORAX.—In normal breathing there are two principal means of enlarging the internal capacity of the thorax: the descent of the diaphragm and the elevation of the ribs. When at rest, the muscular diaphragm is arched into the thorax; but when contracted, it becomes flatter (Figs. 43, 44). This movement of the diaphragm presses upon the abdominal contents, causing the abdominal walls to project, but enlarging the capacity of the chest from above downward. The elevation of the ribs enlarges the front-to-back and side-to-side diameters of the chest. *Abdominal* or diaphragmatic

170. Means of enlarging thoracic capacity? Action of diaphragm? Elevation of ribs? Abdominal inspiration? Thoracic inspiration?

respiration is most marked in males; the *thoracic*, in females.

FIG. 43.   FIG. 44.

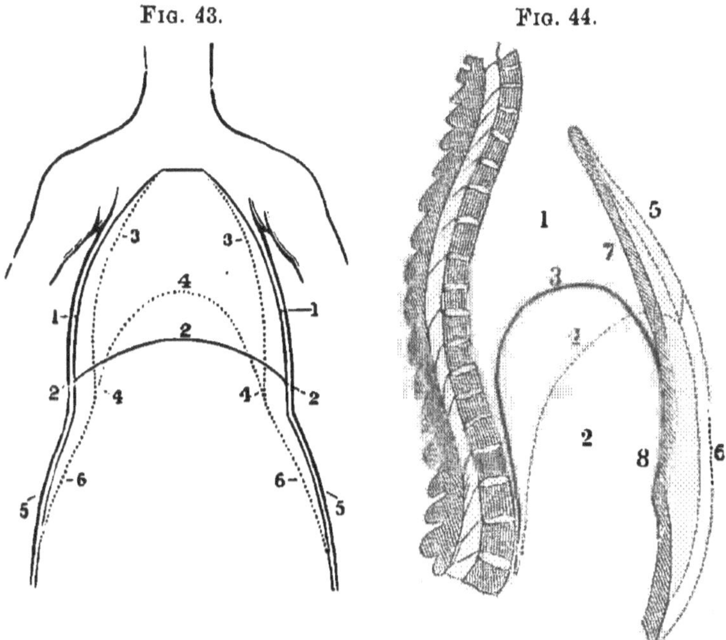

FIG. 43. A FRONT VIEW OF THE CHEST AND ABDOMEN IN RESPIRATION.—1, 1, The position of the walls of the chest in inspiration. 2, 2, 2, The position of the diaphragm in inspiration. 3, 3, The position of the walls of the chest in expiration. 4, 4, 4, The position of the diaphragm in expiration. 5, 5, The position of the walls of the abdomen in inspiration. 6, 6, The position of the abdominal walls in expiration.

FIG. 44. A SIDE-VIEW OF THE CHEST AND ABDOMEN IN RESPIRATION.—1, The cavity of the chest. 2, The cavity of the abdomen. 3, The line of direction for the diaphragm when relaxed in expiration. 4, The line of direction for the diaphragm when contracted in inspiration. 5, 6, The position of the front walls of the chest and abdomen in inspiration. 7, 8, The position of the front walls of the abdomen and chest in expiration.

171. In respiration, the movements of the ribs are complex. Principally by the contraction of the seven upper intercostals (152), the sternal ends of the ribs are elevated and carried forward (Fig. 45). As all the ribs at rest have a downward, slanting position, when their sternal ends are elevated the elastic sternum and the cartilages are thrust forward and upward, and thus the antero-posterior diameter of the chest is increased (Fig. 44). The

E   g   9

first pair of ribs are fixed. Each succeeding rib is moved, and with an increasing amount of movement over the one above it, so that there is a transverse enlargement, due to the increase of the sweep of the costal arches from the first to the seventh.

172. In *labored inspiration* additional muscles are brought into action. The *scaleni* of the neck raise the first and second ribs, and the *posterior superior serrati* render the four lower pairs of ribs more fixed, and thus the diaphragm, from its insertion, can more easily force down the contents of the abdomen. In violent breathing most of the muscles of the chest and some of the neck are brought into service.

173. INSPIRATION. —The enlarging of the cubic capacity of the chest reduces the pressure of the air in the lungs, for the elastic lung expands as the thorax enlarges, and hence the air outside rushes in through the nostrils or mouth until an equilibrium of pressure is established between the outside air and that in the lung. This constitutes *inspiration*. If a puncture or opening be made through the walls of the chest, then will the air, on the enlargement of the chest, enter the pleural cavity rather

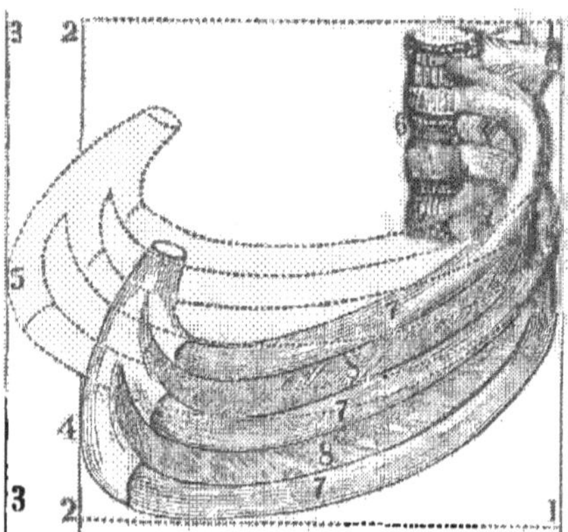

FIG. 45.

FIG. 45. 6, Four of the vertebræ, to which are attached three ribs (7, 7, 7), with their intercostal muscles (8, 8). These ribs, in their natural position, have their anterior cartilaginous extremity at 4, while the posterior extremity is attached to the vertebræ (6), which are neither elevated nor depressed in respiration. 1, 1, and 2, 2, parallel lines, within which the ribs lie in their natural position. If the anterior extremity of the ribs is elevated from 4 to 5, they will not lie within the line 2, 2, but will reach the line 3, 3. If two bands extend from 1, 1, to 2, 2, they will effectually prevent the elevation of the ribs from 4 to 5, as the line 2, 2, cannot be moved to 3, 3.

than the lung, and, as a result, the lung will be compressed and unable to do its proper duty. Under such a condition, the respiratory movements will mostly move the air in the pleura.

174. EXPIRATION.—In normal, easy breathing, expiration is principally an effect of elastic reaction. By the inspiratory act the elastic portions of the tissues have been extended. This stretched condition lasts as long as the muscular contraction continues, but, on the cessation of the latter, the elastic fibres contracting on the air in the lung-tubes drive out a portion of the same,—that is, about five hundred cubic centimetres (thirty cubic inches). The elasticity of the sternum, the weight of the ribs, and the pressure of the abdominal walls acting through the contents of the abdomen and the diaphragm, all combining cause the capacity of the thorax to be diminished.

175. A little expenditure of muscular energy may be necessary to bring the thorax to its former condition. The internal intercostals, the triangularis sternum, and the abdominal muscles probably effect this. In *labored* respiration the abdominal muscles come into action. In *violent* expiration all the muscles which can depress the ribs or press upon the abdominal contents are forced into service.

176. DIFFUSION OF GASES.—If two gases or vapors, of the same or of different density, which do not act chemically upon each other at common temperatures (like oxygen and nitrogen, or watery vapor), are placed in the same vessel, they will be found, after a certain time, to be uniformly mixed. This is known as diffusion of gases. This action of gases is of the greatest importance in the economy

174. Describe expiration. Amount of air expelled? Aids to expiration?

176. What is gas-diffusion? Influence in nature?

of nature. It principally keeps the atmosphere in a uniform state, prevents the accumulation of poisonous gases and exhalations in houses and towns, and renders the interchange of gases in the living tissues possible.

177. RESPIRATION.—The inspiratory and the expiratory act taken together constitute a *respiration*. The fresh air introduced by inspiration into the upper air-passages contains more *oxygen* and less *carbonic acid gas* than the air then in the small passages. By diffusion the new air gives up some of its oxygen to and takes some carbonic acid gas from the old air in the tubes, and is then expelled. Hence, respiration introduces oxygen, a food, into the lung-tubes, and removes carbonic acid gas, a waste product, from them. By the ebb and flow of the upper air, and the action of diffusion between the upper and the lower air, the contained air in the lungs is being constantly renewed.

178. When the air enters the bronchial passages it makes exchanges with that already there, and, as a result, the expired air is warmer, contains much more moisture, is about one-fiftieth less in volume, and contains about five per cent. less oxygen and four per cent. more carbonic acid gas than the inspired air. The expired air also contains small amounts of impurities, most of which have a bad odor and undergo rapid decay.

179. CHANGES IN THE BLOOD.—When the dark purple blood coming from the right ventricle (124) passes through the lung capillaries, it undergoes a change. When it reaches the left auricle, it appears of a bright scarlet hue. But now,

177. What is a respiration? What is introduced? What occurs? What is expelled? What results?

178. Difference between inspired and expired air?

179. What change in the lung capillaries? In the systemic capillaries? What is the difference between arterial and venous blood?

passing from the left ventricle, and flowing through the capillaries of the system at large, it returns to the left auricle, having a dark purple color as at first. The principal difference between the scarlet, or arterial, and the purple, or venous blood, is in the relative proportions of the oxygen and carbonic acid gases contained in each. One hundred volumes of blood exhibit about the following proportions:

	Oxygen.	Carbonic Acid.	Nitrogen.
Arterial blood	20 vols.	39 vols.	1 to 2 vols.
Venous blood	8 to 12 "	46 "	1 to 2 "

180. HÆMOGLOBIN.—In natural arterial blood but little oxygen can be obtained from the serum. The oxygen in the blood is found to bear a definite relation to the red corpuscles. *Hæmoglobin* is the distinguishing feature of red corpuscle, and constitutes ninety per cent. of the dried corpuscle (116). When it has lost a part of its loosely combined oxygen it becomes of a purple hue. If the purple hæmoglobin is exposed to oxygen gas, it soon becomes of a scarlet hue. By using oxygen-reducing agents and free oxygen properly, this play of colors can be repeated again and again. This adding to and taking away from the hæmoglobin does not disturb its molecular character.

181. ACTION OF THE CORPUSCLES.—The red corpuscles of the blood are *oxygen-bearers* (123). Its hæmoglobin, as it passes through the lung capillaries, combines with the oxygen, forming *oxy-hæmoglobin*. This oxygen passes from the air-sac, through the walls of the sac and of the capil-

---

180. Oxygen in serum? What of hæmoglobin? What of its color-changes? To what due?

181. What occurs in the lung capillaries? How does it occur? The change in the tissue capillaries? What of the oxygen?

lary, and through the serum of the blood, to the red corpuscles. When the oxygen-bearing corpuscles in the arterial stream reach the capillaries of the tissues, a portion of the oxygen is left, and a portion of the oxy-hæmoglobin is reduced to hæmoglobin. Thus the blood becomes *venous* in character. It is believed that the oxygen is stored away, in part, in the tissues for future use, and not all used in direct combustion.

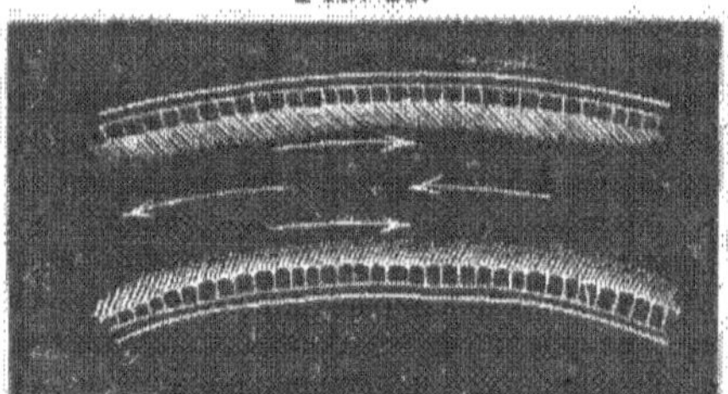

FIG. 46.

FIG. 46.   DIAGRAM OF A SMALL BRONCHIAL TUBE, showing outward and inward current produced by ciliary cell action.

182. ACTION OF OXYGEN. — The activities of the oxygen in the tissues have not yet been traced. All evidence goes to show that the union of the oxygen with the elements of the tissues takes place, not in the adjoining blood, but in the tissues. Sooner or later it appears in combination with carbon and other elements, but especially as carbonic acid gas. This latter gas appears to be continually formed in the tissues, and as constantly to be passed into the capillary blood-current and swept on to the lungs, where it is partly expelled into the air-sacs.

183. The tension of the carbonic acid gas in the air-cells being less than that in the capillaries, the latter passes through the capillary and air-sac walls into the air-sacs. From here, by diffusion and the movements of the cilia (164, 74), it reaches the bronchia and mingles with the air that is passing out in the movements of

---

182. Where does the oxygen combine ? What is produced ? What of the product ?

183. What results from over-tension ? The movers in the bronchia ? The result ?

expiration. Thus one of the great products of tissue-disintegration is passed out of the system; thus the smoke of the myriads of vital furnaces is eliminated.

184. BREATHING is an involuntary act. It takes place, on an average, eighteen times per minute during the waking hours. Although the diaphragm and other inspiratory muscles can be caused to contract more frequently by an act of the will, yet these regular contractions occur independently of it. Though we lose consciousness, the respiratory movements continue at regular intervals. For healthy breathing, certain muscles must contract, each at its proper moment, each in its proper order. How are these movements co-ordinated? By the activity of the nerve-cells of the *respiratory centre of the medulla* (373).

185. All the brain above the medulla (369) may be removed, yet breathing will continue. If the spinal cord be cut through just below the medulla, all the chest movements cease, yet the facial and laryngeal muscles of respiration continue as before. If the medulla be removed, all thoracic, facial, and laryngeal respiratory movements cease. Again, if only a certain small portion of this tract be destroyed, all these co-ordinated muscular movements cease. After destruction of this centre, death results at once. This portion of the cord was formerly known as the " vital knot," but at present is termed the "*respiratory centre.*"

186. When one *vagus* (383) is cut, the breathing becomes slower. If both be cut, the breathing becomes very much slower, deeper, and fuller. Hence it is evident that impulses arising in the lungs, working through the vagi, act on the respiratory centre. If the stump of the cut vagi be stimulated, normal respiratory movements will occur, but they cease on the removal of the stimulus. If the superior laryngeal branch of the vagi be stimulated, the vagi being uncut, the respiratory movements will be retarded, even stopped. The same stimuli, passing over different fibres of the same nerves,

---

184. What of breathing? Influence of the will? Function of the respiratory centre?

may cause an acceleration or a retardation of the central action, or modify each other's action. Stimuli arising in the cerebrum may thus affect the respiratory movements, causing yawning, sighing, laughing, etc.; or the application of cold to the skin will prominently affect the breathing.

187. Experiments show that the conditions of the blood affect the respiratory centre strongly. The less arterial the blood, the greater is the activity of the centre. Thus, under great exertion, or during the inhalation of air containing carbonic acid gas, the respiratory centre sends out its impulses at an accelerated rate and with increased power, and the breathing then becomes labored and even violent. Under such conditions the impulses may be generated so rapidly and sent out so frequently as to exhaust the centre, causing cessation of respiration. If, however, the blood becomes too highly oxygenated, the centre may remain quiescent (*apnœa*) until oxygen is reduced to the proper amount to excite the impulses due to the action of venous blood. The opinion now is that this activity of the centre is due to the direct action of the blood upon it.

188. If an animal breathe an air of carbonic acid gas and nitrogen, the going out of the carbonic acid gas is not impeded, and the blood shows no abnormal amount of carbonic acid, yet the animal dies with the phenomena of *dyspnœa*,—exaggerated movements, labored expiration, violent expiratory movements, general convulsions, exhaustion, long intervals of inspiration, and death. This is attributed to the want of oxygen. But if the air breathed, though highly charged with carbonic acid, has abundance of oxygen, the animal does not suffer from dyspnœa. It, however, becomes drowsy, sleepy, and finally unconscious; that is, the carbonic acid acts on the cerebrum as a *narcotic*, and not on the respiratory centre. In brief, the reason the venous blood causes the respiratory centres to send out impulses is not the presence of carbonic acid gas in the blood, but the deficiency of oxygen.

189. PULMONARY STATISTICS.—If we assume that an average person, at rest, respires fifteen times per minute, and that at each respiration he takes in half a litre (30 cubic inches) of air, then in a day he will use 10,800 litres (374 cubic feet) of air. As the air in respiration loses 5.4 per cent. of oxygen, the total quantity taken up by the lungs in twenty-four hours is equal to 583.2 litres (20.4 cubic feet), or 833.9 grams in weight (12,867 grains). The amount

of carbonic acid excreted from the lungs is 4.3 per cent. of the volume of the air breathed, and for twenty-four hours is 464.4 litres (16.25 cubic feet), or 910 grams (14,043 grains). The amount of water carried off in twenty-four hours averages about 255 grams (9 ounces). The total daily loss of heat from the body by the lungs is estimated at 10.7 calories,[1]—7.2 in evaporating the water of the breath, and 3.5 in warming the inspired air.

190. Oxygen can be taken into the blood not only through the lungs, but from the skin and the alimentary canal. The carbonic acid passes away from the skin through the various secretions, as well as from the lungs.

HYGIENE.

191. In order that each tissue and organ shall be able to perform its functions properly, the blood must convey to them a sufficient supply of oxygen; that the blood may receive its due amount of oxygen, the lungs and air-passages must be in good condition, and not impeded in their action; and that the gases entering the system shall not do injury, the air offered the lungs must be *pure*. Not only should pure air be supplied to the lungs, but all the impurities communicated to the air from lungs, skin, and excretions should be at once dissipated by the fresh-air dilution and air-motion.

192. *Breathe through the nostrils.* The hairs at the entrances, acting as a sieve, the structure of the nostrils, of the nasal passages, of the uvula, of the open pharynx, and the nature of the epithelium (ciliated) of the mucous membrane lining the air-portions of these passages, indicate their

---

191. What of the oxygen-supply? Of the air-passages? Of the air? Of air-impurities?

192. Why breathe through the nostrils? Objections to breathing through the mouth?

[1] A calorie is as much heat as will raise the temperature of one kilogram (2.2 pounds) of water 1° C. (1.8° F.).

respiratory function.   In addition, the comparatively long, irregular, and tortuous passages of the nose (Fig. 38) enable the entering air to be warmed in passing over the extended, highly-vascular surfaces, and to be moistened by the copious, thin mucus of the same.   Hence the entering air on reaching the lung air-passages is moist and of an agreeable temperature.   Breathing through the mouth is noisy, gives rise to bad odors, is unhealthy, and, in cold weather, introduces the cold air too quickly to the upper air-tubes, chilling their surfaces, deranging the blood-supply to the same, and thus giving rise to catarrhs, and perhaps to bronchitis and pneumonitis.

193. *Of all the causes of death which usually are in action, impurity of air is most important.*   The chief causes of the larger death-rate in the cities over the country are impurity of air from overcrowding, want of cleanliness, and imperfect removal of excretions, gaseous, liquid, and solid.   The evidences of injury to health from impure air are not always manifested suddenly and in a marked manner. The usual effect is a steady deterioration in health; an increase in the number of sick days per year; an increase in the severity of many diseases unconnected with the breathing function, and a higher death-rate, especially among the children.

194. NORMAL AIR is a mixture of about twenty-one volumes of oxygen and seventy-nine of nitrogen, together with small amounts of carbonic acid gas, watery vapor, and organic matters in either a living or a dead state.   The amount of carbonic acid is from two to five parts in ten thousand, and

---

193. Effect of air-impurity?   Cause of large death-rate in cities? Effect of continued bad air?

194. What is normal air?   How much carbonic acid?   How much moisture?

the watery vapor from forty per cent. of saturation up to complete saturation, the best for health being estimated at sixty-five to seventy per cent. of saturation. The air of an expired breath is usually nearly filled with watery vapor. By some authorities all organic matter is considered an impurity.

195. AIR-IMPURITIES.—A large number of substances, solids, vapors, and gases, continually pass into the air and mix with it, such as that breathed by man and other animals, the carbon compounds from fires, lamps, and animals, dust, and vegetable decay. Many of these substances may be smelt or tasted at first, but soon the senses become so blunted that they are not noticed, as when a person, coming from the outer air, enters a close room containing several persons, and detects the bad odors at once, but in a short time does not notice the odors, as his senses have lost their delicacy. The non-odorous gases, like the highly-injurious carbonic oxide, pass unrecognized into the air-passages, enter the blood, and work for evil or for good. The solid particles entering in the air may stop in the mouth, nose, larynx, trachea, giving rise to irritation, coughing, or catarrhs, or pass on to the bronchia and finest tubes, like the particles of coal in the " miner's lung," or the bits of stone in the " mason's lung," or the leather dust in the " buffer's lung." If these materials remain, they cause coughing and expectoration, and may induce disturbance of nutrition in the parts, giving rise to profuse fetid expectorations, formation of cavities, bleeding, and *phthisis.*

196. *The air of inhabited rooms is rendered impure* by the carbonic acid coming from the lungs and skin; the carbonic acid and carbonic oxide coming from lamps and im-

---

195. Name the chief air-pollutions. How detected? Why not detected? What of solid particles? What are dangerous trades? What diseases follow?

perfect stoves or grates; the watery vapor from the human system; portions of epithelium from skin, mouth, lungs, etc.; organic gaseous emanations from body excretions and from decomposing animal and vegetable materials; particles of arsenic from green hangings, and, perhaps, portions of the dried sputa or secretion from the lungs of phthisical persons, or the contagium of certain skin maladies. A large amount of carbonic acid in an audience-room causes the lamps to burn dimly and the people to become drowsy and dull. The carbonic oxide is a rapid poison, as it replaces the oxygen in the lungs and is not readily removed from them. The watery vapor tends to saturate the air with moisture, and thus hinders the elimination of certain products (48) from the skin. The organic particles contaminate the air,—at one time conveying disease, at another giving rise to objectionable odors, and *at all times constituting the most dangerous factor of air that has been breathed.*

197. *The effects of breathing air rendered impure* by respiration are quite marked. The common effects are a sense of heaviness, headache, inertness, and, in some cases, nausea. When the employment is sedentary, and the air moderately impure and breathed for hours at a time and day after day, then the unfortunates become pale, partially lose their appetite, and after a time a decline is seen in muscular strength and mental buoyancy. Of the special diseases following such conditions of life the lung maladies are most common (consumption). When the air is rendered

---

196. The impure air of occupied rooms? What from the person? From the heaters? From the walls? What of carbonic oxide? Of moisture? Of organic matters?

197. Early effect of vitiated air in a room? Later effect? Special diseases? The poisonous agents?

very impure, as in the "Black Hole of Calcutta," or the Cooper "Round Tower," the effect is rapidly fatal. The poisonous agencies are the fetid organic matters and the want of oxygen.

198. In the "Black Hole of Calcutta," in 1756, one hundred and forty-six Englishmen were crammed into a room eighteen feet square, having two small windows. During the night one hundred and twenty-three perished. After the battle of Austerlitz, three hundred Austrian prisoners were confined in a cavern, and in a short time two hundred and sixty died. In 1848, the captain of an Irish steamer, during a storm, confined one hundred and fifty passengers in a small cabin. In the morning seventy were found dead, and the others in a wretched state. In 1857, Commander Cooper, of the British army, confined two hundred and eighty Sepoy prisoners in a round tower. The next morning two hundred and thirty-seven were *dragged out* and butchered, under military orders, the others having died during the night from heat, organic emanations, and want of air.

199. SEWER-GAS.—The effects of breathing air rendered impure by gases and effluvia from cesspools and sewers are languor and loss of appetite, followed by vomiting, diarrhœa, colic, and prostration. When sewer-air continually penetrates a house, and especially imperfectly-ventilated sleeping-rooms, there arise in children loss of appetite, pallor, languor, and even diarrhœa; in adults, headache, malaria, and feverishness, followed, perhaps, by typhoid fever in its worst form.

200. The *contagious particles* which are at the foundation of certain dreadful diseases, though often too minute to be detected by the most powerful microscopes or by

---

199. Effect of much sewer-gas? Of moderate continued amounts on children? On adults?

200. State the effect of contagious particles upon the system? What specific medicine? Management in epidemics?

the most subtile chemical analysis, are carried about in the air or in the clothing, reach an appropriate human soil, and make known their presence by their violent effects. The germs of typhoid, typhus, and yellow fevers and cholera have not yet been isolated. No specific has yet been found to render their action harmless. In *epidemics*, the most powerful agents to be used are *free ventilation*, *pure water*, externally and internally, and *simple, nutritious food.*

201. CONTAMINATION OF AIR.—Air to be used by men or animals should not be exposed to sources of contamination. All rubbish, all decaying animal and vegetable matters, and all excretions, solid or liquid, should be removed at once from the vicinity of the houses or stables, for the air, in passing over them, cannot avoid becoming tainted. To prevent the ascent of bad air from the ground under the house and near the house-walls, the cellar should be thoroughly under-drained, and, if possible, the bottom and sides should be cemented. The waste-pipes—water and sewerage—should not connect directly with the sewer main. There should be a large air-tube (reaching above the roof, at least), as well as a self-acting, efficient trap, outside of the walls of the house, to prevent sewer-gas being forced into the house. To prevent disease and discomfort, the cellar should be provided with many ventilating windows, and it ought to be cleaned at frequent and regular intervals. "Mould and decaying vegetables in a cellar weave shrouds for the upper chambers." The cold air for the air-chamber of the furnace should not be taken from the cellar, but from an air-tight flue coming from the outer

---

201. How is outer air made impure? Action of cellar-air? Care of the cellar? Of furnace-air?

air, the entrance of which should be three or more feet above the surface of the ground.

' 202. THE HOME.—Gravel hillocks are the healthiest of all sites, as most natural gravels and sands are healthy. Deep vegetable or garden mould, and "made land," especially that filled with city and town waste, should be avoided, for noxious compounds may be generated in the moist, decomposing mass, and, forcing their way into the cellar, rise and vitiate the air of the rooms. The subsoil should always be drained, and, if possible, the cellar paved. Positions near the top of a slope, on the sunny side, are advantageous, on account of the natural drainage and the freer circulation of currents of air. The subsoil of all sites should be "pipe-drained." The upper drain should be so arranged as to remove rapidly all roof, surface, and sewage waters. Herbage is healthy, and ought to be encouraged near the buildings, as it absorbs and fertilizes waste organic materials and purifies the soil. Trees ought not to be recklessly removed, particularly in a new country; yet they should not be left so thick as materially to impede the entrance of sunlight and the movements of the air. The almost complete extinction of malaria in England, and its decrease in sections of America, have been brought about by proper drainage and cultivation of the soil, also by the wise preservation and planting of trees. The walls of the house ought to be so constructed as to insure dryness. Building-material ought to be porous, to permit free circulation of air. Brick is more porous than lime or sand-stone, but less permeable than pine wood and mortar. If you have an enemy, says an Italian proverb, let him

---

202. Mention healthy sites. What of preparation of site? Of trees? Objects to be secured in building a home?

occupy your new house the first year of its erection. The objects sought for in a healthy house are purity and perfect cleanliness of air (201), freedom from too abundant moisture, ample, direct sunlight (60), abundance of pure water (227), and quick removal of solid, liquid, and gaseous waste products. When these have been obtained, comfort, convenience, and adornment may be considered.

203. AIR-SPACE.—The British army regulations allow each *healthy* man 17 kilolitres (600 cubic feet) of barrack-room, and the sick, in hospitals, 34 kilolitres (1200 cubic feet). The space allowed for each person in civil life, as all are not in health, should be not less than 18.7 kilolitres (800 cubic feet), yet 34 kilolitres (1200 cubic feet) would be better. The sick should be allowed 34 to 56.6 kilolitres (1200 to 2000 cubic feet) space. In addition, arrangements are necessary to renew this air frequently, and to renew it so as not to give rise to uncomfortable currents. The larger the space allowed each person, the less noticeable will be the incoming and outgoing currents. The amount of air allowed to enter a room should be such that a person entering from the outside shall detect no odors and not suffer from the closeness of the room.

204. VENTILATION is the removal, by a current of pure air, of the exhalations of the lungs and skin of men and animals and the products resulting from the lights of a room. Practically, however, impurities from other sources must be removed by the air-currents. In summer, the forces of nature, diffusion (176) and the action of winds, can be relied upon. The former alone is not efficient. Air moving

---

203. Malaria. Army air-space. Civil air-space. Why larger air-spaces? Air-currents? Amount of air?

204. What is ventilation? What are nature's agents? Effect of heat? Speak of inlets and outlets for the air. Position of flues.

at two miles an hour (almost imperceptible), and allowed to pass freely through a space 6.55 metres (20 feet) wide, will change the air five hundred and twenty-eight times in an hour. In the winter, warming and ventilation must, in most houses, work together. If the air of a space or room be warmed by persons or by artificial heat, the air expands and is forced upward by the in-rush of a similar mass of colder and heavier air. This continues until an equilibrium of density and temperature is established. Hence, in cold climates, small houses can be efficiently ventilated by taking advantage of the currents induced by artificial heating. The outlets should be placed near the ceiling, if specially warmed outlet-flues are not constructed, and they should be slightly larger than the inlets. The inlet tubes and passages should be short, and so placed as to be readily cleaned. The inlets and outlets should be numerous, but not of large size (inlets not larger than 48 square inches, outlets, 144 square inches). If the incoming air is not warmed, the inlet-tube should open from 1.21 to 2.42 metres (4 to 8 feet) above the floor.

205. The *open fire* is a healthy method of warming a room. The heat from it is pure heat, not the drying, parching, impure air-warmth of the stove, furnace, or steam-pipe. The open fire is, however, more efficient as a ventilator than as a warmer. An ordinary fireplace and chimney will sufficiently ventilate a room suitable for four to six persons, as the outflow is from 170 to 566 kilolitres (6000 to 20,000 cubic feet) per hour. If the room is small and the fire brisk, the currents of cold air along the floor cause the sitter much discomfort, which can, however, be

----

205. Advantages of the open fire? Disadvantages? Influence of open fire on health?

mitigated by the use of screens. Still, with its minor discomforts, its tendency to produce draughts, and its expense, the open fire is the best method of warming a sitting- or sleeping-room. Persons who use an open fire, as a rule, are less subject to coughs, colds, headaches, neuralgia, and petty bodily ills than those who keep their rooms close and warm with stove- or furnace-heat. Rooms warmed by stove or furnace can be made more cheerful, more agreeable, and more healthy by having a " hearth-fire's ruddy glow."

206. Rooms warmed by iron stoves, wood or coal, may be fairly ventilated by putting a board about ten centimetres (four inches) wide, and extending from one side of the window-frame to the other, under the elevated sash of each window; or by having a wire screen so arranged as to follow down the upper sash when it is lowered; or by using double windows, keeping the lower outer and the inner upper sash partly open. These methods admit of changes of air, yet avoid the making of strong draughts. In a sitting- or sleeping-room the stove should have no back-damper, in order that the passage of the products of combustion to the chimney shall not be impeded in the least. As the air of rooms warmed by stoves is too dry, water-vessels should be placed near the fire, not on the cold, ornamented top, so that the water may be abundantly evaporated. The upper sash of all windows should be so constructed as to be easily lowered. In kitchens it is advisable to have a large outlet just over the stove, so that the steam and vapors can readily pass away. In cold climates, and in most houses, if outlets for the warm air be provided, as by lowering the upper sash, cold air will enter

---

206. Methods of ventilating common rooms? What of the back damper? Of the water-urn? Of kitchen outlet? Of ordinary inlets?

through defects in carpentry and under the doors and windows; but, as such air may flow through an outhouse or an impure cellar, it is better to provide clean inlet-tubes, opening into each room at some distance above the floor.

207. The *sleeping-room*, in which one-third of life is passed, ought to be so placed as to receive the direct sunlight for several hours each day. Each person ought to be allowed 18.7 kilolitres (800 cubic feet) of air-space. If the sleeping-room is not provided with a fireplace in which there is a fire or light several hours in every twenty-four hours, then the upper sash should be kept lowered all the time, severe weather alone excepted. These precautions are most important, for during the day our senses are active, and can so warn us that we may avoid breathing impure air, but during sleep, smell and taste do not give us early and efficient warning of the presence of impure air, as sewer-gas or illuminating-gas, and hence much injury may result ere we are warned or awakened. It is best for every person to occupy a separate bed. There are many facts which go to show that a healthy person, constantly sharing a bed with a consumptive, sooner or later contracts the same disease, and that when two persons in ordinary health share the same bed the influence is not for the best health of either.

208. CONSUMPTION.—Persons suffering from disease, and especially thoracic disease, need pure air in abundance. Pure air is not necessarily cold air, but is air free from all mechanical or physiological impurities. The consumptive wants not drugs, not stimulants, not medicated pillows, not

---

207. Location of sleeping-room? Size? Ventilation? Why very important? Single or double beds? Why?

208. Of air for the sick? Needs of the consumptive? What common factor in the production of consumption? Remedy?

medicated air, but pure air of an agreeable temperature, a sun-bath daily in a warm room (the exposure of the surface of the body to sunlight), milk, meat, whole wheat bread, and fruits (60). The best climates for a consumptive are those which permit the greatest number of hours to be spent in the open air. The common factor in the causation of destructive lung-disease in all climates has been found

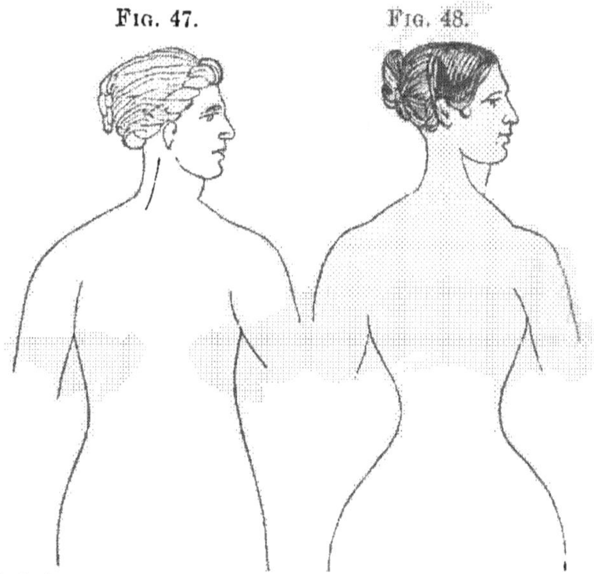

FIG. 47. FIG. 48.

FIG. 47. A CORRECT OUTLINE OF THE VENUS DE' MEDICI, tho *beau-idéal* of female symmetry.

FIG. 48. AN OUTLINE OF A WELL-CORSETED MODERN BEAUTY.

One has an artificial, insect waist; the other, a natural waist. One has sloping shoulders; the shoulders of the other are comparatively elevated, square, and angular. The proportion of the corseted female below the waist is also a departure from the symmetry of nature.

to be the breathing of air rendered impure by respiration. When the air-space has been enlarged, when the methods for the removal of the bad air have been improved (all other conditions the same), there has been a marked decrease in the death-rate from phthisis in all parts of the world.

209. *Compression of the Thorax and Abdomen.*—By wearing snug-fitting or close-fitting garments, by straps, belts, and corsets, the natural movements of the walls of the

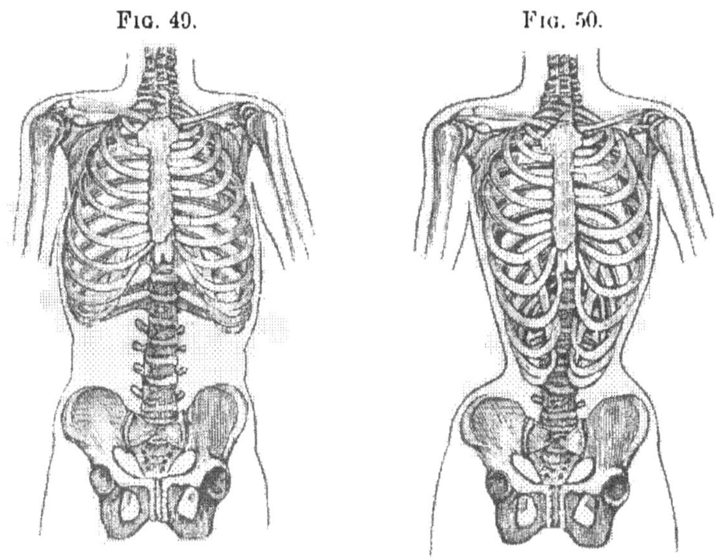

FIG. 49.   FIG. 50.

FIG. 49. A CHEST well proportioned.
FIG. 50. A CHEST fashionably deformed.

chest and abdomen can be impeded. All impediments to the enlargement of the cavity of the thorax (169) diminish the air-capacity of the lungs, hinder the aëration of, and excretion from, the blood, and thus act injuriously upon the entire system. The healthiest mothers in the world are the women who do not wilfully impede the movements of the walls of the thorax and abdomen by external compression; and the healthiest men are those who do not bind down their thoracic walls with close-fitting vests and coats. The use of the corset is injurious to health, whether

209. What of compression? Of healthy mothers? Of healthy men? Of the corset? Of Chinese *vs.* American custom?

employed by male or by female. Fashion ordains that the Chinese lady shall deform her feet so as to be unable to walk, and that the European or American woman shall compress her chest and abdomen to such an extent as to impede the vital functions of digestion, circulation, and respiration, as well as locomotion. Which civilization, in a series of generations, will produce the more vigorous race?

Individuals may have small chests from birth, this being, to the particular individual, natural. That like produces like is a general law. If the mother has a small, tapering waist, either hereditary or acquired, the form may be impressed on her offspring, thus illustrating the truthfulness of Scripture, which declares that the sins of the parent shall be visited upon the children unto the third and fourth generations.

The question is often asked, Can the size of the chest and the volume of the lungs be increased when they have been once compressed? Yes. The means to be used are a full inflation of the lungs at each act of respiration, and a judicious exercise of them by walking in the open air, reading aloud, singing, sitting erect, and practising appropriate gymnastic exercises. Unless these exercises are systematic and persistent, however, they will not afford the beneficial results desired.

CHAPTER VII.

FOODS.

210. In general, *plants* feed on the carbonic acid gas (194) of the atmosphere and a series of chemical compounds made up of a few elements (C, H, O, N, K, Na, Ca, Mg, Fe, S, P, Fl, Cl, Si) found in the soil. Under the influence of the sunlight the living plant changes these soluble (in water) soil-foods and air-foods into plant-tissues, cells, and granules. In certain parts of the structures, notably the seeds, stems, and roots, plants accumulate a store of material fitted to become the food of man or animals, such as starch, sugar, fats, and proteids.

211. The higher animals do not possess the power of changing the compounds of the air and soil into animal tissues. They feed upon the products of plant-growth, directly or indirectly, by eating flesh of other animals, and build up the complex animal muscle, fats, starches, and proteids, which are suitable for the food of man.

212. A Food is a substance which, during its destruction in the system, gives forth heat or energy (312). Foods furnish the materials which build up, repair, and sustain the living body.

---

210. Food of plants? Influence of sunlight? What is stored up?

211. What cannot animals do? Food of animals? What is made?

212. What is a food? What, in the living body, is derived from food?

213. *Foods* are of two kinds: 1. Those substances which are capable of uniting in the body with oxygen, of giving up oxygen, or of splitting up into simpler chemical compounds, and in the process manifesting heat, mechanical energy, formative power, etc., and thus serving the purposes of healthy life (starches, fats, proteids). 2. Those substances which aid or permit these manifestations of energy by preparing the conditions for chemical changes (water, salt, and other mineral compounds). Neither class is of itself alone capable of manifesting energy. The full powers of foods are only manifested when certain substances belonging to the same class exist together. Thus, a proteid alone, like lean meat, will not sustain healthy life, but it must be combined with fats, starches, and salts, in certain proportions.

214. MILK contains all the necessary food-elements, and in the best form : 1, the *nitrogenous* or *proteid* substances (C, H, O, N, S, P, Ca), like casein, albumen, etc.; 2, the *fats* and *oils* (C, H, O), as in cream; 3, the *sugars* (C, H, O), like lactin; 4, water (H, O), and the chemic salts of magnesium (Mg), calcium (Ca), potassium (K), sodium (Na), iron (Fe), in combination with fluorine (Fl), chlorine (Cl), and the oxygen acids of sulphur (S, O, H), phosphorus (P, O, H), and silicon (Si, O, H).

215. The PROTEID or NITROGENOUS food-stuffs (C, H, O, N, S, P, Ca) are principally derived from the flesh of animals, birds, and fishes; from eggs and milk-cheese; from peas, beans, and vetches; and from wheat, barley, oat, and maize (corn) flours. They are formed exclusively in plants. They undergo but little alteration when consumed as food and stored up by animals.

216. The *proteid aliments* are blood fibrin, muscle fibrin, vegetable

---

214. What does milk contain ? Name its principles.
215. Sources of proteid foods? By what formed? Changes in animals ?

fibrin, albumen in various forms, vegetable and animal casein, and globulin. They contain about sixteen per cent. of *nitrogen*, and usually calcium phosphate. They can replace one another in nutrition, but do not have the same nutritive value.

217. *Animal fibrin* has a filamentous structure, and is quite elastic. It occurs abundantly in lean meats. *Vegetable fibrin* occurs as a grayish-white, tough, elastic mass. It is found in most plants, and is especially abundant in the cereal grains. It is also known as *gluten.* *Animal casein* occurs most plentifully in milk. It is readily coagulated by a solution of rennet from the calf, and thus separated from milk, as is seen in the process of cheese-making. *Vegetable casein*, or *legumin*, is found chiefly in the seeds of the Leguminosæ, as in peas and beans. It is precipitated from its juice by rennet solutions. *Albumen* is a white or yellowish-white, transparent substance. It occurs abundantly in the fluids of animal bodies and in the white of eggs. It is found in nearly all vegetable juices, especially in the potato and the wheat. *Globulin* is a whitish, transparent substance. It occurs in the blood-corpuscles and in the connective tissues (22).

218. The FATS and OILS (or hydro-carbons, C, H, O) are found in the diet-lists of most peoples,—the fats in the cold and temperate, the vegetable oils in the warm regions. The fats are principally derived from the blubber of sea-animals, from the bodies of animals and birds of the chase and of domestication, and from milk. The oils are mostly derived from fish, the palm, the olive, the rape, the cocoa-nut, and cotton. Maize is rich in oils; the other grains, however, contain only small quantities.

219. The *animal* and *vegetable* fats and oils are all quite similar in chemical composition. They are mostly composed of the base called *glycerin*, united into varying compounds with *oleic, palmitic, butyric, margaric,* and other acids. Their difference in nutritive value depends in a great measure upon the physical form, size,

---

218. What are found in the diet-lists of most nations? Sources of fats? Of oils? How derived?

and grouping of the component oil-drops. Some fats, like cream and cod-liver oil, are more easily digested, more easily assimilated into the blood, than others, like fish or cotton-seed or olive oil, and hence have a higher value as foods.

220. The STARCHY class (or carbo-hydrates, C, H, O) is a most important part of a normal diet. Its substances are mostly derived from the vegetable world and from the bulk of the food of the people of the temperate and tropic regions. This class embraces the starches of the grains, roots, and tubers; the sugars of the cane, fruits, and milk; the vegetable acid salts (citrates, tartrates, malates, etc.), the cellulose of plants, and certain vegetable extractives. Chemically, they contain carbon, hydrogen, and oxygen, like certain of the oils; but they are physiologically distinct from the latter (335).

221. The SUGARS possess a sweet taste, are soluble in water, and, undergoing fermentation, form alcohol (241). They are derived principally from the cane, the beet, the maple, the fruits, and, to a limited extent, from milk. The STARCHES are principally derived from the grains and potatoes of the temperate regions, and the marantas (arrow-root), cassavas (tapioca), and palms (sago) of the tropics. The starches of the grains are found in the meshes of the cellular tissue, which acts as a protective. The starch-grains appear to the naked eye as a white, glistening, softish powder. They are insoluble in cold water or alcohol. Under the action of direct heat, or of boiling, the grains burst, and their contents are more easily acted upon by acid and alkaline solutions at the temperature of the body: hence the importance of heat-cooking. Human saliva, malt, and dilute acids, under conditions of warmth and moisture, convert the starch into *grape-sugar*, or glucose. *Cellulose* is the main constituent of the vegetables, herbs, and greens used by man. Chemically it is allied to the starches, but physiologically it is

- - - — — —

220. What of the starchy or carbo-hydrate class? What does it include? What resemblance to fats?

quite different, in that it affords little or no nutriment. It is useful, because its bulk distends the alimentary canal, and thus the digestive juices can have a greater action on the starches.

222. The WATER and SALTS class (H, O, K, Na, Ca, Mg, P, S, Cl, Fl, C, Si, Fe) has the simplest atomic grouping. It is as essential for healthy nutrition as the proteid class. If a normal diet is furnished, all of these constituents will be present in sufficient quantities, with the exception, perhaps, of common salt (NaCl).

223. Of the *salts*, those of potassic and calcic phosphate and sodic and potassic chloride are most important. Calcium is absent from no tissue. A deficiency of lime salts (calcic) in the foods leads to the growth of impaired muscle and nerve and of soft and deformed bones (rickets).

224. Besides the four classes above considered, there are substances used by men which may be called ACCESSORY FOODS. The various condiments, salt, vinegar, spices, relishes, etc., tea, coffee, cocoa, and alcohol, are the chief materials of this class. Of their exact action in nutrition but little is definitely known. It is a general fact that most peoples use some one or more of them habitually, in connection with the other classes of foods.

225. DIET FOR HEALTH.—In a cold climate and with great exercise, or under severe exposure, a man can keep healthy on a diet consisting largely of proteids, with fats, salts, and water. It has not been shown that health can be maintained on a diet of proteids, carbo-hydrates, salts, and

---

222. The need of the water and salts class? How provided? The exceptions?

224. Name the chief accessory foods. Their use in nutrition? Name a general fact.

225. What of a diet without starch? Without fat? Without vegetable acids? What is scurvy? What of a perfect diet?

water without fat. Health is not sustained on a diet of proteids, salts, and water, nor on one wanting in one or more of the lactates, citrates, tartrates, malates, etc., which are found in fruits, potatoes, fresh vegetables, and certain preserved foods. The want of these is manifested in *scurvy*, the former scourge of merchant-ships and frontier garrisons. The experience of men in all parts of the world, and the results of careful experiments, show that a certain amount of each of the four classes must be present in a perfect diet.

226. WATER enters largely into the constitution of all animal tissues. It constitutes sixty-eight per cent. of the entire human body. It is the great constituent of meats, fresh bread, vegetables, and fruits (233). As a beverage, it is one of the most important parts of human food. Good water has the following chief characteristics: cleanliness, freedom from odor and taste, good aëration, coolness, and a certain degree of softness, so that the cooking of vegetables can be properly performed.

227. Good water cannot be derived from an impure source. It can be rendered impure by the entrance of impurities into its storage-wells, tanks, or pipes. The impurities most deleterious to health are human and animal excrements, products of the decay of animal and vegetable materials, and lead. The animal and vegetable impurities find easy access to the streams and lakes from which town-waters are taken, and to the shallow wells of the country. Many sudden and severe outbreaks of cholera, typhoid fever, diarrhœa, and dysentery have been traced to the use of water tainted by human sewage and cesspool-water. The most efficient artificial filtration leaves behind much matter, invisible to the naked eye, and is therefore no effective safeguard against these most dangerous impurities. The boiling for half an hour of water rendered impure

226. What of the presence of water in the body? In foods? Characters of good water?

by excrement, organic decaying matters, and disease-germs, is probably a means of destroying its power of communicating disease. The latrine and sewage arrangements of China, Japan, and India are very defective, yet the use of boiled water, with a little tea, in the former two countries, accounts for the fact that cholera is less prevalent in them than in India. The continued use of water having traces of lead often induces neuralgic pains, nervous troubles, colic, and even "wrist-drop."

COMPARATIVE VALUE OF WATERS.

Wholesome. { 1. Mountain springs. 2. Deep wells. } Very palatable.
3. Upland surface. } Moderately palatable.
Suspicious. { 4. Stored rain. 5. Surface-water of cultivated land.
Dangerous. { 6. River-water liable to sewage access. 7. Shallow well-water.

Prof. Frankland.

228. MILK contains all the food-elements needed by the body. It is the best food for the young, the convalescent, and the aged, because its proportions of fats and proteid materials are relatively large, its digestion is easy and rapid, and its nutritive power is great in that the residuum left in the intestinal canal is small. Milk is best taken in the fresh state. Persons who cannot take new milk are often able to use milk which has been heated to a temperature of 100° F. Its tendency to curdle in the stomach may be corrected by the use of lime-water. Its constipating effects may be corrected by taking it with Seltzer water. It should be derived from healthy cows which are kept under favorable conditions of air, water, and food.

229. One pint (.568 litre) of the milk of the cow contains in round numbers nearly 55.6 grammes (2 ounces avoir.) of water-free food. An adult man requires for the average manifestation of his working powers 650 grams (23 ounces) of water-free food in twenty-

228. Milk as a food? Methods of using? Precautions? Quality?

four hours. To procure this from cow's milk would require the consumption of about 6.2 litres (11 pints). This would give a man far too much water, and the fats would be in excess of a normal diet (338).

230. COOKING.—The use of fire in the preparation of food is peculiar to man. Its use, whether direct, as in roasting, baking, and broiling, or indirect, through the agency of water in boiling or of fat in frying, changes the physical and chemical condition of the cooked substances: the proteid bodies are more or less coagulated or partly swollen or gelatinized; the fat-cells are ruptured, and the fats rendered more fluid; the starch-grains become more or less pulpy; the cellulose and the lignin of vegetable tissues are more or less broken up, and their contents set free; and peculiar empyreumatic flavors and odors are developed. The foods are thus rendered softer and more finely divided, and hence can be more readily masticated and digested. By the use of sugar, salt, spices, vinegar, etc., the relish of the food is increased.

231. METHODS OF COOKING.—Animal flesh (oysters excepted) and starchy and cellulose substances (certain ripe fruits excepted) should be cooked before eating. The simplest methods of cooking make the most healthful food. *Boiling*, in the case of vegetables, effects the solution of the sugars, the rupture and partial solution of the starch-grains, the coagulation of the proteids, and a softening of the cellulose. In boiling meats, first plunge the meat into boiling-hot water, and retain it there until a protective layer of coagulated albumen forms on the surface. This requires

---

230. What food-preparation is peculiar to man ? Methods of cooking ? Effects ? Use of condiments ?

231. What should be cooked ? Boiling of vegetables ? Of meats ? Of wasting of meats ? Of vegetables ? Objections to frying ?

a few minutes only; then cook slowly in water having a temperature of 160° F. This method retains in the meat most of the soluble nutritive portions. *Roasting* and *broiling* are the best methods of cooking meats. The heat at first should be intense, in order to form a protective layer to retain the juices, and then more moderate, but long continued. By this method but little is wasted, and more nutrient materials are retained than by other methods of cooking. The roasting of fruits and potatoes renders them more palatable, digestible, and nutritious. The baking of flour renders it sweeter, breaks the starch-grains, and makes it more digestible. *Frying* is the most objectionable method of cooking, for the heated fats permeate the foods and render them difficult of access to the digestive fluids.

232. MEATS.—The advantages of these food-substances are the large amounts of proteids, united with much fat, and the presence of the salts of potassic chloride, phosphate, and carbonate, and iron. They are easily and rapidly cooked, are more easily digested than vegetables, and are very largely assimilated (236). Meats are, however, wanting in the starches, and are therefore well supplemented with rice or bread. *Salt meats*, as far as nutrition is concerned, are but little better than meat from which a good soup has been extracted. Canned meats are excellent when fresh meat is not to be had. The eating of raw or partly-cooked flesh or fish exposes the system to dangers. Fresh pig's flesh may contain the trichinæ or the cysticercus of the tape-worm (*Tænia solium*); fresh ox flesh, the cysticercus of the tape-worm (*T. medio-canellata*); and fish, the eggs of intestinal worms. The eggs and the immature worms found in the flesh are not destroyed by a temperature under 212° F.: hence prolonged roasting is the best method of cooking flesh. *Eggs* are easily cooked, and are very nutritious. Hard-boiled and fried eggs are more difficult of digestion than soft-boiled and whipped eggs. *Fish* is well adapted to supplement cereal foods, and is used most extensively in rice-countries. It is rich in phosphates and proteids, and the latter occur in a form easily appropriated by the human system. Many kinds of fish are deficient in fats.

TABLE OF COMPARATIVE FOOD-VALUE.[1]

Medium beef	100	Fresh cod	68
Fresh milk	23.8	Eel	95
Skimmed milk	18.5	Shad	99
Butter	124	White-fish	103
Cheese	155	Salmon	101
Hens' eggs	72	Salt mackerel	111

Prof. Atwater.

233. *Wheat* is very nutritious in small bulk, and is rich in soluble albumen and casein. Its starchy substances are large in amount and are easily digested. Its salts are principally phosphates. The fine flour made from wheat is wanting in fats, salts, and part of the albumen. Decorticated wheat flour contains all these ingredients, and is a more healthful food than finely-bolted flour. Bread, pudding, etc., made from decorticated wheat flour are sweeter, more nutritious, and more wholesome than those made from fine white flour. *Barley* contains a larger amount of digestible proteids than wheat. It is very rich in phosphates and iron, and is a nutritious food-stuff. The athletes of ancient Greece were trained on a barley diet. The *oat* has not only a large amount of proteids, but also is rich in fat. Though it cannot be made into bread, yet it is more readily cooked than wheat or barley. It makes an excellent food for sustained mental or physical labor. Oatmeal, made into the form of a thin gruel, forms a most sustaining and cooling drink for men exposed to great heat (as the stokers on the Oriental steamers, and soldiers in hot countries). Cracked wheat, oatmeal, and milk should occupy a prominent place in a student's diet. *Maize* contains a large quantity of yellowish fat. It is an excellent food-stuff for hard labor and for cold climates. It requires longer and more careful cooking than wheat or oats. *Rice*, as an article of diet, has the advantage of being the most easily digested and the most perfectly assimilated of the starch-grains. It is poor in fats and salts. The Japanese rice is the richest in gluten of any produced in the East. Rice is four times as nutritious as potato (König), and is also more uniform in quality. It constitutes the great food of nearly one-third of the human race. The *potato* has a very low nutritive rank, although its starch is very digestible. It contains the citrates of soda, potassa, and lime. It is the great antiscorbutic vegetable, and constitutes a food of which man rarely

[1] Equal weights, no bone.

tires (225). *Beans* and *peas* are distinguished from other vegetables by containing a large amount of proteid substances, principally in the form of *legumin*, a vegetable casein. They contain much sulphur and phosphorus. They make an excellent food for men with robust digestion engaged in severe labor. In the rice-countries, beans and peas are largely used. Their disadvantage is the long cooking which they demand, and their comparatively great indigestibility.

ORDER OF RICHNESS IN THE UNCOOKED STATE.

Proteid substances.	Fats.	Starch carbo-hydrates.	Mineral salts.
Beans.	Maize.	Rice.	Beans.
Peas.	Oats.	Rye.	Oats.
Wheat.	Barley.	Maize.	Peas.
Oats.	Peas.	Wheat.	Wheat.
Rye.	Rye.	Barley.	Barley.
Maize.	Beans.	Oats.	Maize.
Barley.	Wheat.	Peas.	Rye.
Rice.	Rice.	Beans.	Rice.

Arranged from analysis of Profs. *Wolff* and Knop.

234. *Fruits* are most valuable for their vegetable acid salts and watery constituents. Their solid nutriment is small. A moderate amount of ripe fruits in their season is beneficial. Unripe fruits contain starch which has not yet been converted into sugar. Cooking often removes the hygienic objections to the use of unripe fruit. Rather than use sugar in excess to neutralize the acidity, add about one-eighth of a teaspoonful of carbonate of soda, or potassa, to a pound of fruit.

235. DIGESTIBILITY.—Fitness for digestion depends partly on the hardness, cohesion, or chemical nature of the food, and partly on the changes it may have undergone in passing through the system of a food-animal or under the processes of preparation and cooking. A pound of bread contains more solid nutritive matter than a pound of beefsteak; but, with an ordinary man, it does not do as much

---

235. Upon what depends the digestibility of food? Of bread? Of beefsteak? Of salmon? Of cheese?

i

nutritive work, because the cooked meat is more digestible and is more completely assimilated than the bread. The same is true of equal weights of salmon and cheese, of venison and lean pork.

Cooked rice, cooked tripe, whipped eggs, cooked sago, tapioca, barley, boiled milk, raw eggs, roasted lamb, parsnips, and potatoes are the most readily digested of foods, and in the order given. Cooked in the most favorable manner, beef, mutton, oysters, veal, fowl, and white wheat-bread, with butter, are rather less digestible. Fresh pork, salt pork, and salt beef require still more time and energy for digestion.

236. As a rule, animal food is digested sooner than starchy food, and in proportion to its fineness of division and its tenderness of fibre. The admixture of the different classes of foods, as of fat and lean meats with starchy and accessory foods, aids digestion. We should seek for variety in foods of the same class, as of beef, mutton, eggs, fish, etc.; beans, peas, cereal grains; rice and potatoes. As sameness clogs, changes in the combinations of the food are essential. Cooking requires skill, which in reality assumes the importance of no inferior art.

TABLE OF DIGESTIBILITY.

(Giving the Percentage which is incorporated into the Human Body and the Percentage which is rejected.)

	Incorporated.	Residuum.			Incorporated.	Residuum.
Meat	96.7	3.3		Maize	93.3	6.7
Rice	96.1	3.9		Potatoes	90.7	9.3
Eggs	94.8	5.2		Milk	88.9	11.1
White bread	94.4	5.6		Black bread	88.5	11.5

Prof. Voit.

237. STIMULANTS.—A stimulant has the power of exciting the organic action of the human body. It calls forth the stored-up forces of the system, and enables them to be used at once. It goads the system on to an increased exertion, mental or physical, and thus enables a person to draw on the reserves of his vital bank. When the deficit in the reserves is promptly made up by rest and appropriate nourishing foods, the vital bank appears to suffer no

---

236. Advantages of animal food? Of variety in foods? The art of cooking well?

physiological impairment; but if the deficit steadily increases, then mental and physical bankruptcy will result after a longer or shorter period. The principal stimulants in use are tea, coffee, cocoa, and alcohol (407, 408, etc.).

238. TEA is used by peoples whose food consists largely of carbohydrates, like the Chinese and Japanese. Its active principle, *thein*, gives to food something which it did not before contain. Tea seems to enable persons to do work on a smaller diet than would otherwise be required. It has the power of putting away sleep, and it enables a person to draw on the stored-up resources of the body for an increased exertion. It is thus largely used by the under-fed and overworked seamstresses of the large cities. The action of the thein, combined with the warmth of the infusion, braces up the nervous system, but no marked depression follows. It is a stimulant, but not an intoxicant. The hot infusion is potent against cold and heat (inducing perspiration), and is useful under great fatigue in hot countries. Tea, as made in America, should not be used by children. The excessive use of strong-made tea leads to nervousness, neuralgia, and indigestion.

239. COFFEE makes a pleasant, stimulant beverage. It removes the sense of commencing fatigue during exercise. It is very serviceable against cold. In the British Antarctic Expedition it was found superior to spirits. According to the Algerian and Indian army reports, it has been found well adapted to keep up the men in a campaign under a tropic sun, in that it affords an invigorating nervous stimulation and increases the action of the skin. Coffee does not give rise to the nervous symptoms which follow the excessive use of tea. It should, however, be excluded from the diet of children and of youth of both sexes, on account of its peculiar stimulant action. It is said that in Brazil, where coffee is largely drunk by all classes, alcoholism (408) is almost unknown.

240. COCOA contains a large amount of fat and proteid substances. It has been compared to milk, but it is inferior as a food. It may profitably be substituted for tea and coffee by persons of a spare habit. It is a valuable drink for adults under circumstances requiring great exertion.

241. ALCOHOL (ethyl-alcohol, C_2H_6O) is made from sugar by fermentation, or from starches which have been

changed into sugar. The grains, fruits, grapes, and potato are the principal source of the starches so used. Pure alcohol is a colorless, limpid fluid. It is lighter than water, and has a pungent, agreeable taste and odor. Spirits, wines, and beers owe their stimulating and intoxicating properties to the alcohol they contain. The amount of alcohol in them varies from 1.28 per cent. in small beer to 54.32 per cent. in Scotch whiskey.

242. There is a wide-spread consumption of alcohol in the world. All civilizations have their means of acting on the nervous centres,—of transporting their people into a more exalted condition of mental activity and physical buoyancy, the excessive and evil manifestations of which are called *intoxication*. From the drinks made by the women of the Polynesian islands by chewing pepper and spitting the profuse saliva into a bowl (the contents of which are drunk by the warriors), the pulque of Mexico, the talluh of Abyssinia, the koumis, saké, and arrack of Asia, to the vodki, spirits, wines, and beers of Europe and America, —everywhere man has devised stimulants and intoxicants. The more civilized a nation becomes, the greater appears to be the variety of its alcoholic beverages. This craving for stimulants is not only world-wide, but there are reasons for believing that it is on the increase. Where the use of alcohol has been restricted, it has been found that the consumption of other stimulants, like opium, ether, tea, and coffee, has vastly increased.

243. ACTION OF ALCOHOL.—Alcohol is a carbo-hydrate. Taken into the system in small quantities, it is destroyed in

---

241. The sources of alcohol? Characteristics? Percentage in beverages?

242. Of the use of alcoholics? The action desired? Kinds of drinks?   Of the craving? Of the use of other stimulants?

the body, and generates force and heat. It restricts tissue-waste, and in some cases favors the accumulation of flabby adipose tissue. Alcohol decreases the elimination of carbonic acid and the excretion of urea. It thus tends to retain these waste products in the blood (324). It quickens the functions of the organs of circulation (147), and modifies the nerve-centre control (paralysis). In small doses, it aids feeble digestion; in large doses, long continued (especially undiluted spirits), it ruins the digestive function. Alcohol induces a marked disease-process in the liver and kidneys. The continued use of alcoholics probably induces an abnormal condition in all the soft tissues of the body, as shown by the hues, textures, and functions (408), though after death the changes escape detection, except the striking fibrin-changes evident in the "gin-drinkers' liver," in the "alcoholic-contracted kidneys" (305), and in the thickened leathery walls of the stomach. The alcohol not consumed in the system is eliminated by the kidneys, skin, and lungs.

244. Alcoholics, occasionally and judiciously used, enable a person to employ his reserves of force by setting free body-energy not called out by ordinary nerve-cell action. There are conditions—not quite diseased conditions—which are improved by the temporary use of a little alcohol. After exposure and great exertion, the shelter having been reached, a small amount of alcohol or spirits in hot water is often beneficial. Selected spirits, at times, are useful additions to the food of invalids, but should be taken with

243. Give the action of alcohol. What effect on the waste products of the system? On digestion? On all the soft tissues? How shown? How eliminated?

244. Uses of alcoholics? Does taking alcohol prevent contracting disease?

the food, and not alone. The abstemious derive the best effect when a dose of alcohol is administered. As a rule, alcoholics should never be used except for a specific purpose and under the continued advice of a physician of integrity. Alcohol is not a preventive of disease, but the reverse.

245. *Alcohol is injurious* to the young or immature of either sex. Its evil effects are more marked in females than in males. In hot climates it is a fertile source of disease, and has no compensating advantage. Before or during severe exertion, or before or during exposure to low temperatures, alcohol ought not to be taken. The Russians will not permit a man who has recently indulged in the use of spirituous liquors to undertake a cold march. In health, alcohol is not a necessity, and the majority would be more vigorous did they not use it in any form. As now used by mankind, it is more powerful for evil than for good. It is a "genius of degeneration," moral, mental, and physical (408). Its baneful influence is not confined to the generation that uses it, but the deterioration induced on the nervous system has a peculiar tendency to *hereditary transmission*. Insanity, idiocy, instability of mind, weakness of will, and a *craving for alcoholics* occur more frequently in the offspring of the habitually intemperate than in those of water-drinkers (401).

---

245. To whom, in particular, is alcohol injurious? In hot climates? In cold climates? What is said of the Russians? Influence on this generation? On succeeding generations? Results?

CHAPTER VIII.

THE DIGESTIVE ORGANS AND DIGESTION.

Directions for Dissection of Abdomen.

SECURE the animal (preferably a dog or cat; a rat may be used) on its back by means of blocks. Make an incision through the skin from the sternum to the pubes. From near the *umbilicus* (navel) make two incisions at right angles to the first, extending nearly to the *lumbar vertebral processes.* Fasten back the skin after it has been dissected from the underlying muscles. Observe the pale *abdominal muscles;* the glistening *fascia* of the muscles, forming in the middle line the *linea alba;* the fibres of the *external oblique* muscle. Cut the fascia near the median line of the body, elevate the fascia, and expose the *rectus* muscle. Dissect off the external oblique muscle, and expose the *internal oblique* muscle, having fibres running in a different direction from the external.

With scissors, divide in the median line the walls. A large cavity, lined by a smooth moist membrane, the *peritoneum*, is exposed. This membrane lines the abdominal cavity, and is reflected over the intestines and organs contained therein, and serves to keep the latter in their proper places. Without cutting or tearing, but by simply turning over or pulling aside, trace the *alimentary canal* from near the left inferior side of the diaphragm, viz., the narrow *œsophagus*, the dilated *stomach*, the convoluted small *intestine*, the large, dark, sacculated *cæcum*, with its worm-like *appendix*, the large *intestine*, containing balls of excrement, and the *rectum*. Trace out the *mesentery*, made of two folds of the peritoneum, enclosing blood-vessels, lymphatics, and nerves, which connect the alimentary canal to the vertebral region. If the dog is in good condition, a loose, mesenteric, fatty apron, the *great omentum*, will be seen hanging from the lower border of the stomach. Notice the dark-purple-colored long body lying near the broad end of the stomach, the *spleen*. Observe the form, the lobes, the tubes entering, and the attachments of the large, dark-red solid organ, the *liver*. Now turn over the stomach, slightly stretch the small intestine, and notice within the mesentery the long, hammer-like, pale-red, lobated *pancreas*. Trace the *duct* from the pancreas to its entrance into the small intestine, about a foot from the stomach.

Turn the stomach and intestines to the right side (towards the liver side of the animal). Notice the abdominal *aorta* at its exit from the diaphragm. Follow its branches to the principal organs. On the surface of the œsophagus may be seen a few fibres of the *pneumogastric nerve*. Turn the stomach and intestines to the left side. Trace the flaccid tubes (containing dark maroon blood) from the mesentery, spleen, and stomach until they unite in a single trunk, the *portal vein*, which is seen to enter the liver. Observe the *vena cava ascendens* as it enters the diaphragm, receiving blood from the liver. Turn the dark-red liver up towards the diaphragm, and its greenish *gall-bladder*, with its *cystic duct*, and the *hepatic duct* (from the liver), forming one *common duct*, will be brought into view.

Place a double ligature around the rectum, and divide between the cords. Put a single ligature on the hepatic veins, close to their entrance to the vena cava, and divide **close**

Fig. 51.

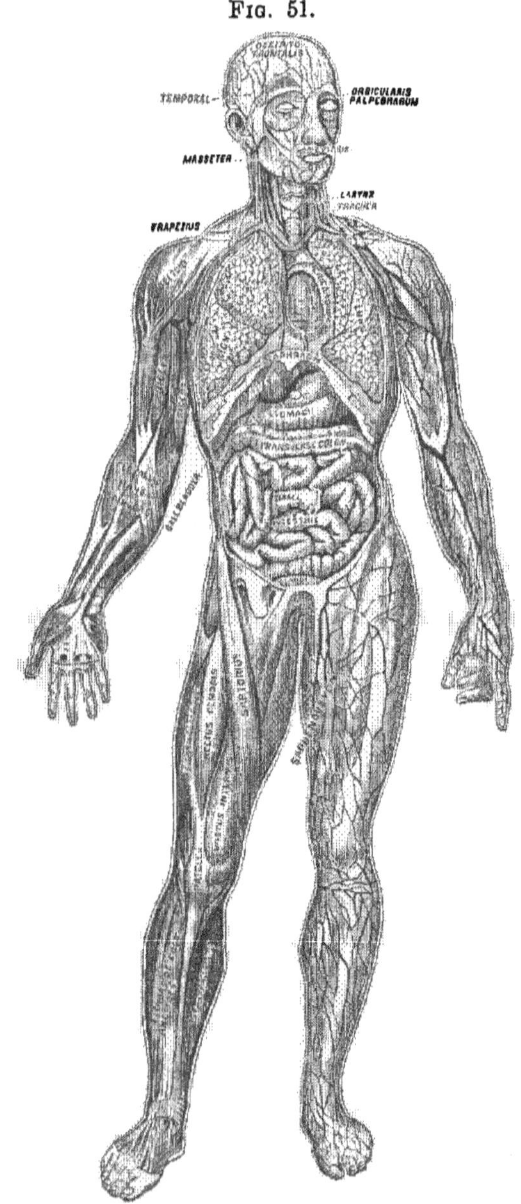

THE DIGESTIVE ORGANS.

to the liver. Put a ligature on the œsophagus, and divide on the thoracic side of the same. Remove the alimentary canal and its appendages by cutting the mesentery free from the posterior walls of the abdomen, then carefully trim the mesentery from the alimentary canal. Examine the tube externally from the stomach to the rectum.

Sever the stomach from the intestines, lay open, throw away the contents, and wash. Place it in a shallow basin of water, the interior upward, and observe the structure of the lining *mucous membrane*. Treat portions of the intestines later in the same way. Attach the alimentary canal to a water-tap, and wash out the interior. Pass bristles through the pancreatic and biliary ducts. Lay open the *duodenum* (the upper portion of the small intestines), find the bristles, and study the mucous membrane. Lay open the next five or six feet of intestine, wash, spread out in a shallow basin of water. Notice, with a lens, the projecting, velvety *villi*. Cut out a portion of the large intestine, treat in the same way, but no villi are to be found.

Cut open the *liver*. Trace a *hepatic vein* from the vena cava into the substance of a lobe. Try to distinguish the *portal vein* from the hepatic vein by the small artery and duct running alongside the former. Cut open the *spleen*. Note its fibrous investment, its pulpy contents, and the absence of a duct. Separate the long, pale-red *pancreas*, and note its friable, lobulated character. Observe to the right and left of the backbone a compact, roundish, solid organ, invested by areolar, tissue-holding fat, the *kidney*. Note that the left kidney is nearer the pelvis than the right. Trace from the backbone the *renal* artery and vein leading to and from the kidneys. Notice the *ureter*, a pale, firm-feeling duct, running from a depression in the kidney towards the middle line into the *pelvis*, and ending in the *bladder*. Note the soft body capping the kidney, the *suprarenal body*. Tear the kidney out of its sheath, dissect the ureter, artery, and vein about an inch, then cut away the kidney. Lay open the kidney by a longitudinal incision parallel to the flat side. Note the dilated ureter, the *pelvis* of the kidney, the projecting *papillæ*, the incised *pyramids*, the *medullary substance*, and the *cortical* layer (see Fig. 69).

Divide the pubes, and stretch open the pelvis. Lay open the *bladder*. Within and near the pelvis are the organs of generation.

Microscopic Work.—Cut out cubes of the various organs and place in No. 1 alcohol. Later make sections.

THE ALIMENTARY CANAL AND ITS APPENDAGES.

246. THE ABDOMEN.—The essential organs of digestion occupy nearly the whole of the *abdomen* (Figs. 51, 34, 23). The abdomen is walled in by broad muscles, fasciæ, and skin, except behind, where the projecting processes and the bodies of the five *lumbar vertebræ* assist (Fig. 49), above by the vaulted diaphragm, and below by the bones of the *pelvis*, the cavity formed by the latter being supplementary to the abdomen. The capacity of the abdomen varies,

---

246. Where are the chief organs of digestion found? Boundaries of the abdomen? The pelvis? The peritoneum?

owing to the nature of its walls.   It is lined by a closed serous sac (156), the *peritoneum*, whose visceral layer is reflected over the contained viscera, forming the thin external *serous coat*.

247. The BONY PELVIS is composed of four bones,— the two *innominata*, which bound it on each side and in front, and the *sacrum* and *coccyx*, which complete it be-

FIG. 52.

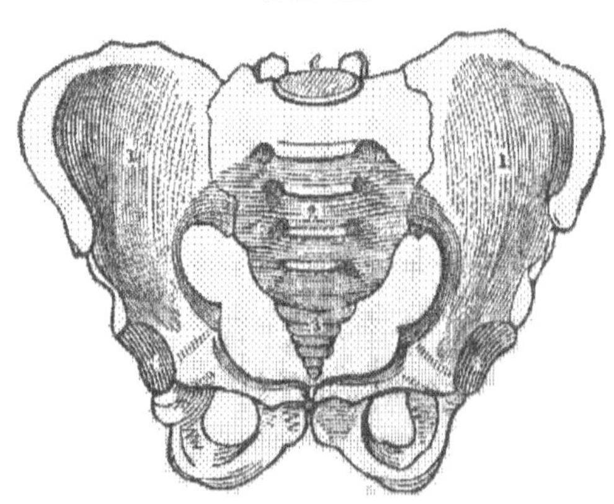

FIG. 52. FRONT VIEW OF THE PELVIS.—1, 1, The Innominata. 2, The sacrum. 3, The coccyx. 4, 4, Socket. *e*, The junction of the sacrum and lower lumbar vertebra.

hind. It is a strong and massive ring of bones placed between the lower end of the *spine*, which it supports, and the lower extremities, on which it rests. Its position, inclined to the spine in standing, enables it to sustain the superincumbent viscera. Its large and projecting surfaces are used for muscular attachments, and they afford leverage for those muscles which pass upward from the lower limbs, serving to balance the pelvis upon the thighs (Fig. 128). The sides and base of the cavity are completed by

247. The bones ? Form ? Position ? Attachments ? Object ? Contents ?

muscles and fasciæ. It holds the rectum and bladder and some of the organs of generation.

248. The DIGESTIVE APPARATUS consists of a mechanism for dividing and crushing the food (in the mouth), of a long musculo-membranous passage, variable in size, lined with mucous membrane, and extending from the base of the skull to the end of the rectum, called the *alimentary canal*, and of certain accessory organs called *glands*.

249. The ALIMENTARY CANAL, lying in the neck, in front of the spine, passes through the thoracic cavity (148), perforates the diaphragm, and runs a tortuous course through the abdomen and a straight course in the pelvis. It is about thirty feet long, and has variable diameters. It embraces the *mouth, pharynx, œsophagus, stomach, small intestine*, and *large intestine*. Its lining mucous membrane (165) is modified in each region according to the functions of the part, and is continuous at both extremities with the skin. Its muscular fibres are mostly of the unstriped variety (72), and are arranged lengthwise and circularly in the tubular portions. Its layers—serous, muscular, areolar, and mucous—are abundantly supplied with blood-vessels. The tube has nerve-ganglia (345), and receives fibres from the central and sympathetic systems (386). In the abdomen the tube has much freedom of motion, owing to its mesenteric attachments (264).

250. A GLAND (166) is a term applied to those softish, more or less granular and lobated organs composed of blood-vessels, nerves, areolar tissue, and secreting tissues. The latter tissues are epithelial (159) in nature, being in most positions modified mucous membrane. The function of these tissues is to take blood into

---

their structures, to build up for themselves, and out of or through their protoplasm to produce materials, usually fluid, different in properties from the blood, or to secrete and modify from it substances already there in solution (275). Such organs are provided with *ducts* or tubes, to convey away the gland-products, as the pancreatic duct, Steno's duct of the parotid. Certain of the glands have sacs or pouches, in which the secretion collects, like the gall-bladder of the liver.

251. The MOUTH (Fig. 38) is bounded by the lips in front and the soft palate and arches behind; above, by the hard palate; below, by soft structures; and on the sides, by the cheeks. It is lined by mucous membrane. It contains the *tongue* and *teeth*. When shut, the cavity is completely filled. It is the main entrance to the alimentary canal, and, with its appendages, is of great service in speech. The TONGUE is made up of many muscles and considerable fat. Its apex, sides, upper surface, and lower front part are free. Its muscles are attached to the *hyoid bone* and the *lower jaw* principally. Its upper surface is covered by peculiarly developed papillæ or eminences. It contains the nerves which are chiefly concerned with the sense of taste (427). Into the mouth open the ducts from three pairs of glands, and upon its lining surfaces is discharged much mucus.

Directions for Examination of the Mouth Parts.—Request a boy having a good set of teeth to stand before the class. Call attention to the *lips*: line of junction of skin and mucous membrane, contour, angle of junction, mobility. *Dental arch:* upper and lower jaw,—form of arch, insertion of teeth, the gums, order of teeth from the median line,—*incisors, canines, bicuspids,* and *molars;* variations in the cutting surfaces; of the grinding surfaces; points of decay. *Movements of the lower jaw:* forward, backward, to the right or left, and combinations of movements. While cutting a firm object, feel the masseter muscle and the angle of the jaw. Place the finger in front of the ear, over the jaw articulations, then move the jaw slightly, then stretch open; notice the degree of motion. *Hard palate:* notice its hard surfaces, with ridges, the soft posterior portion terminating

---

251. Limits of the mouth? Contents? Functions? The tongue? Muscles? Papillæ? Taste? Ducts?

in the soft palate, or *uvula*. *Tongue:* its free apex, its bridle, its veins prominent on the lower surface. On its upper surface note the numerous minute, conical *filiform papillæ*, the irregularly scattered, large, round eminences, having a deep red color, the *fungiform papillæ*, and near the posterior part, arranged in a V shape, eight or ten flattened *circumvallate papillæ*. Observe the variety of movements which the tongue can execute. *Throat:* Request the boy to stand in the sunlight, mouth wide open, head slightly thrown back, and then to articulate slowly, Ah—ah—h—h. Thus the *soft palate* will be elevated, the palatine arches widened, and the throat parts brought into view; the *soft palate* in the middle line, over the dorsum of the tongue, the right and left *anterior parts;* behind them the right and left almond-shaped *tonsils*, then the *posterior pillars* and the posterior wall of the *pharynx* in the central field. Observe that the mouth and pharynx are lined with mucous membrane, and that the surfaces are bathed with mucus. If the mouth is suddenly opened, a jet of fluid may come from near the second upper molar tooth,—saliva from the *duct of Steno* (parotid), or, if the tongue is raised, from the floor,—saliva from *Wharton's ducts*. Wipe the mouth and tongue. Hold a bit of cracker. Remove. Move the mouth parts a few minutes, and then insert a new bit of cracker and hold a few moments. What changes have taken place in each case?

252. The UPPER JAW consists of two bones, meeting in the middle line, called the *superior maxillæ* (Fig. 73, 7). Each half in the adult contains sockets for eight teeth. The *hard palate* is mostly formed of the lower portions of these bones joined in the median line. These bones are firmly attached to the adjacent bones of the face. The lower jaw, or *inferior maxilla*, is the only movable bone of the face. It consists of a horseshoe-shaped base, having two nearly vertical rami, ending in a process and an *articulation*. The upper surface of the base offers sixteen sockets for teeth. This bone forms a hinge-like joint with the temporal bone (Fig. 73, 9). By the action of certain muscles the bone may be

FIG. 53.

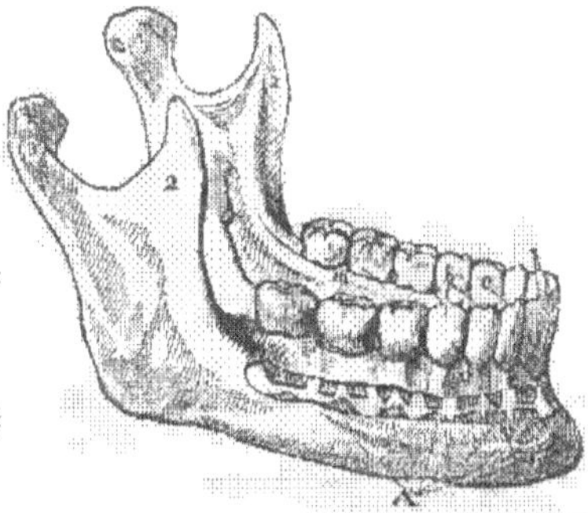

FIG. 53. 1, The body of the lower jaw. 2, Ramus, or branch of the jaw, to which the muscles that move it are attached. 3, 3, The processes which unite the lower jaw with the head. *i*, The lower and lateral incisor teeth of one side. *b*, The bicuspid teeth. *c*, The cuspids, or eye teeth. *m*, The three molar teeth. A, shows the relation of the permanent to the temporary teeth.

moved up and down, forward and back, laterally, and in combinations of these movements.

253. A TOOTH consists of an exposed part, called the

crown; a part concealed in the gum and jaw, called the *root* or *fang,* and at the junction of the fang and crown a constricted portion, called the *neck.* The teeth differ in size, in form of crown, and in number of fangs. They are, in the adult, thirty-two in number, and are divided into *incisors, canines* or *cuspids, bicuspids, molars,* and *wisdom.*

Fig 54.

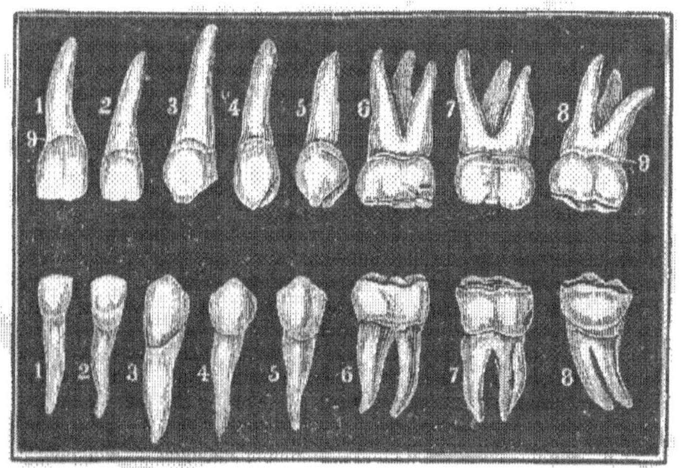

Fig. 54. THE ADULT TEETH.—1, 2, The cutting teeth (incisors). 3, Canine (cuspid). 4, 5, Small grinders (bicuspids). 6, 7, 8, Grinders (molars). 9, 9, Neck of the tooth.

254. The *incisors* have one fang and a wide, thin, chisel-shaped crown, and are well adapted for cutting purposes. The *canines* have a sharp-pointed crown and one long, single fang. The *bicuspids,* or *pre-molars,* have two pointed cusps on the crowns. The single fang in the lower jaw is deeply grooved, but in the upper is partly cleft. The *molars,* or *grinders,* have large, cuboidal crowns, with four or five cusps. The two front molars of each side in the lower jaw have two fangs; in the upper, three; while in the wisdom tooth they are usually united in a mass. The teeth are firmly secured in the socket by the firm, fibrous, pinkish structure called the *gum.*

253. Parts of a tooth? Differences? Number? Kinds?

255. The *milk* teeth are twenty in number, ten in each jaw:
$\dfrac{m.\ 2 \quad c.\ 1 \quad i.\ 4 \quad c.\ 1 \quad m.\ 2}{m.\ 2 \quad c.\ 1 \quad i.\ 4 \quad c.\ 1 \quad m.\ 2} = 20.$ They begin to appear about the seventh month, and are completed about the twenty-fourth month. These teeth are shed, and are succeeded at intervals by the *permanent* teeth, thirty-two in number, sixteen in each jaw:
$\dfrac{m.\ 3 \quad b.\ 2 \quad c.\ 1 \quad i.\ 4 \quad c.\ 1 \quad b.\ 2 \quad m.\ 3}{m.\ 3 \quad b.\ 2 \quad c.\ 1 \quad i.\ 4 \quad c.\ 1 \quad b.\ 2 \quad m.\ 3} = 32.$ The permanent teeth appear earlier in the lower than in the upper jaw. The incisors, the earliest, appear between the fifth and seventh years, the wisdom teeth between the seventeenth and twenty-fifth years, and the others at variable dates between these limits.

256. The hard portion of the tooth is composed of dentine, cement, and enamel. The *dentine* forms the greater part of the tooth. It contains more mineral matter and is harder than bone. It consists of microscopic tubes, called *dental tubuli*, which have hard walls and are bound together by a hard intermediate substance. The *cement* is a layer of true bone (505), which covers the fang. Its outer surface is attached to a fibrous, sensitive membrane analogous to the peritoneum (16), which serves to fasten the tooth in the socket. The *enamel*, the hardest of all animal textures, is the white substance which protects the crowns of the teeth. It contains 96.5 per cent. of mineral matter. It is made up of minute, hexagonal, prismatic rods, arranged closely together on the dentine. On the crown the enamel rods are vertical, but on the sides they are at first oblique and then horizontal. Near the dentinal surfaces are minute interstices, which are supposed to be for nutritive permeation. In the interior of the tooth is a cavity, which contains a soft substance called the *pulp*. The pulp consists of areolar tissue, supplied with vessels and nerves entering through

FIG. 54*a*.

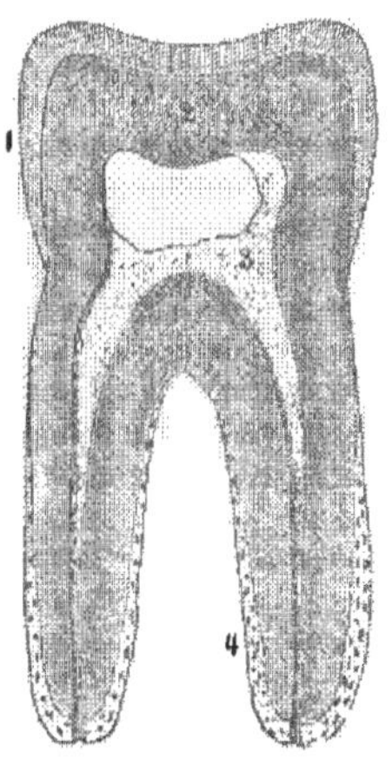

FIG. 54*a* (*Leidy*). VERTICAL SECTION OF A MOLAR TOOTH, moderately magnified. 1, Enamel, the lines of which indicate the arrangement of its columns. 2, Dentine, the lines indicating the course of its tubules. 3, Thin lamina of the dentine forming the wall of the pulp-cavity, the dots indicating the orifices of the dental tubuli. 4, Cement.

the fang, and is the remains of the papillæ on which the tooth was originally formed.

257. THE SALIVARY GLANDS embrace three pairs,—the *parotid*, seated on the sides of the face, between the ear and the lower jaw; the *submaxillary*, beneath the horizontal part of the lower jaw; and the *sublingual*, beneath the tongue. The glands consist of numerous lobes and lobules. The product of its secreting tissues, the *saliva*, is conducted

FIG. 55.   FIG. 56.

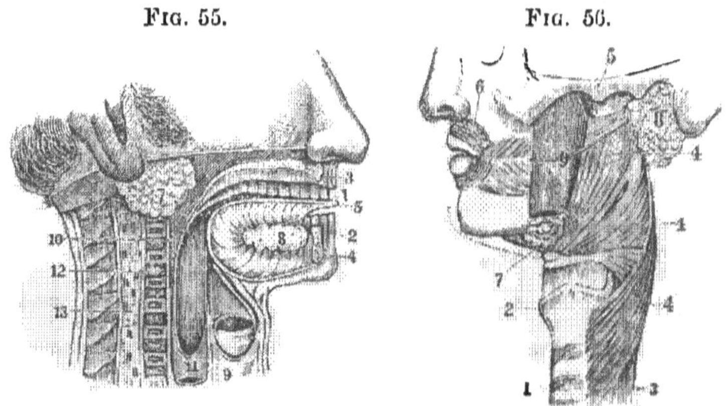

FIG. 55. THE MOUTH AND NECK LAID OPEN.—1, The teeth. 3, 4, Upper and lower jaws. 5, The tongue. 7, Parotid gland. 8, Sublingual gland. 9, Trachea (windpipe). 10, 11, Œsophagus (gullet). 12, Spinal column. 13, Spinal cord.

FIG. 56. A SIDE-VIEW OF THE FACE.—1, 2, Trachea. 3, Œsophagus. 7, Submaxillary. 8, Parotid gland. 9, Duct from the parotid gland. 4, 4, 4, 5, 6, Muscles.

to the mouth by ducts. In the mouth, the SALIVA is a glairy, frothy, limpid fluid. It contains but a small amount of solids. It serves to moisten the food, to assist in mastication and swallowing, and to commence the change of the starch into grape-sugar.

[*Experiment.*—Place a bit of dry bread in the mouth, hold it there a few minutes; then notice the change produced.]

257. Of the salivary glands? Number? Position? Composition? Secretion? Appearances of saliva? Uses?

258. MASTICATION AND INSALIVATION.—This process is performed by parts of the mouth, consisting of the teeth, the jaws, the muscles which move the lower jaw on the upper and those which act on the cheeks, lips, tongue, and pharynx, and the glands. It consists in the cutting, crushing, and grinding of the food-substances, the mixing of the same with air, saliva, and mucus of the mouth, and the forming of the materials into a soft, pulpy mass. The action is quite complicated, but each part, muscle, and secreting tissue is so arranged as to perform its proper action at the correct moment, the muscles moving the jaws, the tongue, lips, and cheek keeping the mass between the proper teeth, the glands, under the stimulation of the motions, giving forth abundant fluid, and the soft palate keeping the entrance to the palate closed, so that breathing through the nostrils may not be impeded during the process.

259. The PHARYNX (158) is the musculo-membranous canal into which the mouth opens behind. It is provided with three pairs of constrictor muscles (Fig. 56, 4, 4, 4). It opens below into the œsophagus and larynx, and is common to both food and air in its middle portion.

260. The ŒSOPHAGUS, or *gullet*, is a musculo-membranous tube leading from the pharynx to the stomach. It is the narrowest portion of the alimentary canal.

261. SWALLOWING, or DEGLUTITION, is divided into three stages. (1.) The mass of food is forced by the tongue through the fauces into the pharynx. This is under the

---

258. What parts are engaged in masticating food? The action? Duties of each part? Breathing?

259. Describe the pharynx. The muscles. The openings.

260. What of the œsophagus?

261. Swallowing: first stage? second? third? When does the will act?

control of the will.   (2.) In this stage the bolus must pass through the portion of the pharynx common to food and air,

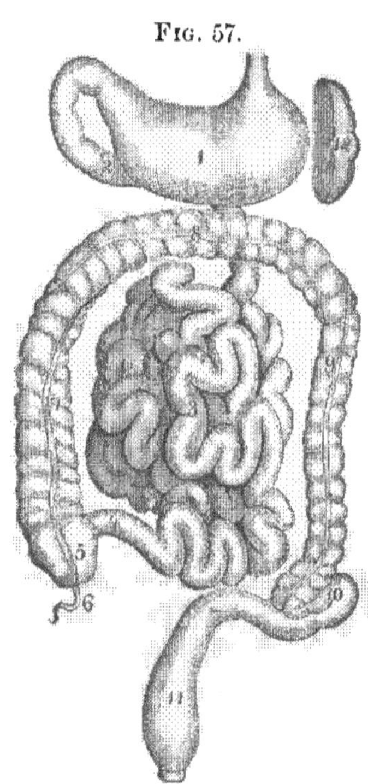

Fig. 57.

Fig. 57 (*Leidy*). THE STOMACH AND INTESTINES.—1, Stomach. 2, Duodenum. 3, Small intestine. 4, Termination of the ileum. 5, Cæcum. 6, Vermiform appendix. 7, Ascending colon. 8, Transverse colon. 9, Descending colon. 10, Sigmoid flexure of the colon. 11, Rectum. 12, Spleen.

and hence it must be quickly performed.   It is done by a series of contractions controlled by the reflex centres, not by the will.   (3.) The passage through the gullet is done by progressive muscular contractions, peristaltic, from above downward, and is independent of the will.

262. The STOMACH, the dilated part of the alimentary canal into which the œsophagus opens above, is a somewhat pear-shaped sac.   It is placed on the left side of the abdomen, and under the diaphragm.   The larger end is towards the left side, while the smaller or *pyloric* part, which ends in the small intestine, points to the under side of the liver.   Its capacity is variable, ranging from a teaspoonful up to about three pints.   Its walls are composed of four layers.   The outer or *serous* layer—thin, transparent, and smooth—is a part of the peritoneal lining of the abdomen.   The fibres of the *muscular* layer are arranged lengthwise, circularly,

262. The stomach: shape? Position? Capacity? Layers or coats? Glands? Secretion? Characters of the juice?

and obliquely. The *areolar* layer contains blood-vessels and lymphatics. The *mucous* or inner layer is provided with multitudes of glands, which secrete the GASTRIC JUICE. This fluid is colorless and watery, and has a sour taste and odor. It contains free hydrochloric acid, and a ferment-body called *pepsin*.

263. FUNCTION OF THE STOMACH.—Its secretion, gastric juice, has the power of changing the insoluble *proteids* (beef, eggs, legumin) into soluble and diffusible substances,

FIG. 58.   FIG. 59.

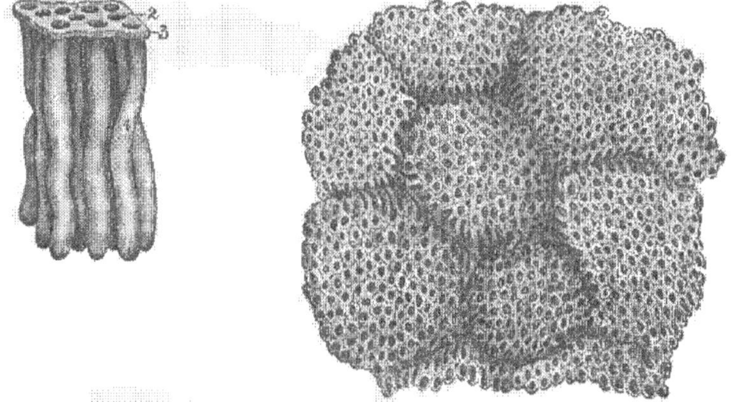

FIG. 58 (*Leidy*). SMALL PORTION OF THE MUCOUS MEMBRANE OF THE STOMACH, WITH THE EMBEDDED GASTRIC GLANDS.—1, The glands. 2, Orifices of the glands. 3, Epithelium of the mucous membrane. Moderately magnified.

FIG. 59 (*Leidy*). MAMMILLÆ OF THE MUCOUS MEMBRANE OF THE STOMACH, moderately magnified, exhibiting the orifices of the gastric glands.

called *peptones* (274). The muscular contractions churn the contents of the stomach and thoroughly mix the food with mucus and juice. These motions are independent of the will. When a portion of the food is reduced to a soft pulp, it is forced into the intestine.

---

263. Action of gastric juice? Of the muscles? Further action of the foods?

264. The SMALL INTESTINE extends from the *pylorus* of the stomach to a valve-like opening at the entrance of the large intestine, near the right groin. It is about twenty feet long, and lies in coils in the middle and lower part of

FIG. 60.   FIG. 61.

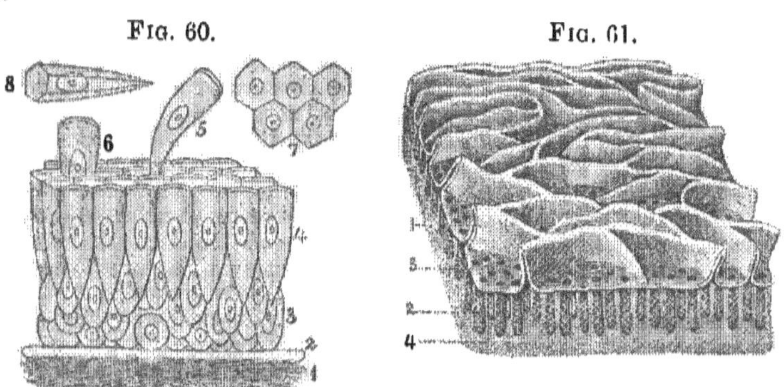

FIG. 60 (*Leidy*). DIAGRAM OF A VERTICAL SECTION OF THE MUCOUS MEMBRANE OF THE SMALL INTESTINE, highly magnified.—1, Fibrous layer, in which the blood-vessels are distributed. 2, Basement membrane. 3, Young nucleated cells. 4, Layer of columnar cells. 5, 6, Cells in the act of being shed or thrown off. 7, Free ends of the columnar cells, exhibiting their six-sided form. 8, A single columnar cell, exhibiting its form at all parts.

FIG. 61 (*Leidy*). MUCOUS MEMBRANE FROM THE JEJUNUM.—1, Villi resembling valvulæ conniventes in miniature. 2, Tubular glands: their orifices, 3, opening on the free surface of the mucous membrane. 4, Fibrous tissue. Magnified.

the abdomen. It is from one to one and three-fourths of an inch in diameter. It is supported and held in place by a broad double fold of the peritoneum (246), enclosing blood-vessels and nerves, called the *mesentery*. The first ten inches of this intestine is known as the *duodenum*, into which the ducts from the pancreas and liver empty. The *jejunum* includes the upper two-fifths of the remainder, and the *ileum* the lower three-fifths. The interior of the tube shows many transverse projections, extending half or two-thirds around the tube, the *valvulæ conniventes*, and

---

264. Small intestine: extent? Length? Position? Size? Mode of suspension? Divisions? Valvulæ conniventes? Villi? Glands?

an immense number of minute thread-like processes, the *villi* (see Fig. 63). When immersed in water, these villi stand up, and thus resemble the pile of velvet. There are many glands in the mucous membrane layer.

265. The movement forward of the contents of the intestine depends upon the longitudinal and circular muscular fibres of the tube. This *peristaltic* (84) *action* consists of slow, successive, wave-like contractions, chiefly of the circular fibres, extending from the upper part gradually to the lower part of the canal. The series of contractions force the intestinal contents along. These contractions may occur, as in a portion cut out of the body, independently of the central nervous system. Their essential stimuli arise in the nerve-ganglia seated in the intestinal walls, but the movements are modified by influences passing over the vagi (383) and sympathetic nerves (386).

266. In *vomiting*, the œsophageal opening of the stomach is dilated, and the increased pressure of the abdominal walls, together with holding back the breath, forces the contents of the stomach out. The pylorus is usually closed. When the gall-bladder is full, a large flow of bile takes place into the duodenum, especially during vomiting, and this gall may find its way to the stomach and be subsequently ejected. The nervous mechanism of vomiting is complicated, and as yet but little understood. There appears to be a *vomiting reflex centre* in the medulla, near the respiratory centre (185). This centre may be excited by thoughts, odors, brain-disease, tickling of the fauces, irritation of the stomach (mustard-water), drugs, irritation of the intestine (hernia), or renal or bile stones.

267. The LARGE INTESTINE is from five to six feet long, from one and a half to two and a half inches wide, and has a wrinkled and sacculated appearance. Its mucous membrane is smooth, and has, in depressions, a few glands. There are no villi.

268. Commencing near the right groin, it ascends on the right

267. Large intestine: length? Size? Appearance? Lining?
268. Course? Divisions? Value? Vermiform appendix? Function of the latter?

side to the liver, passes across behind the *umbilicus* to the left side, descends to the iliac hollow of the left innominata, makes a double curve, enters the pelvis, and passes down, resting on the sacrum and coccyx. The portion in the pelvis is known as the *rectum*, and the other portion as the *colon*. Between the small intestine and the colon is a valve of two segments, which prevents the contents of the colon from returning to the small intestine. Projecting from the lower end of the first part of the colon is a narrow, coiled, and tapering tube, called the *vermiform appendix*. In this cherry-stones and round objects sometimes stop, giving rise to pain and even inflammation. The appendix has no definite function in man.

FIG. 62.

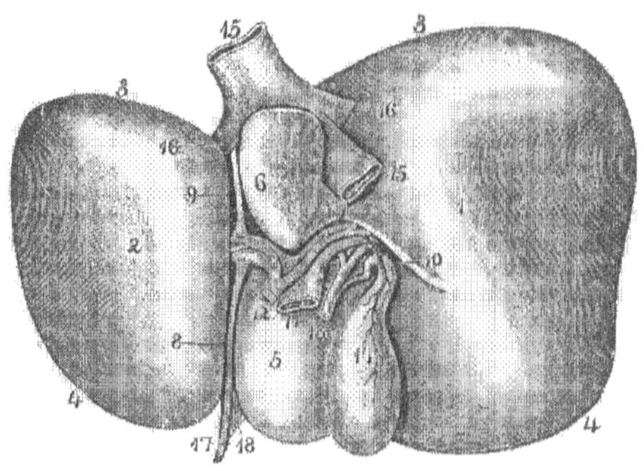

Fig. 62 (*Leidy*). INFERIOR SURFACE OF THE LIVER.—1, Right lobe. 2, Left lobe. 3, Posterior margin. 4, Anterior margin. 5, Quadrate lobe. 6, Caudate lobe. 7, Isthmus, or caudate process, connecting the latter with the right lobe. 8, 9, Longitudinal fissure. 10, Transverse fissure. 11, Portal vein. 12, Hepatic artery. 13, Common biliary duct, formed by the union of the hepatic and cystic ducts. 14, Gall-bladder. 15, Inferior cava. 16, Hepatic veins. 17, Round ligament. 18, Anterior part of the suspensory ligaments.

269. The LIVER is a solid organ, of dark reddish-brown color. It weighs nearly four pounds, and contains in its tubes nearly one-fourth of the blood of the body. It is placed under the diaphragm, on the right side of the abdo-

---

269. Liver: color? Weight? Contents? Position? Gall-bladder?

men (Fig. 34). The GALL-BLADDER is a pear-shaped sac, lodged in a groove on the lower side of the liver. It serves to hold bile until it is needed.

270. The *liver* is made up of a multitude of little lobules, each of which has an artery, a vein, a portal canal, and a duct, all bound together by areolar tissue, containing *hepatic* or *liver cells*. Hence the liver has three sets of blood-vessels,—the *hepatic artery*, bringing nutriment to the liver-tissues; the *portal vein* (103), bringing blood to be acted on by the liver; and the *hepatic veins*, to take away all the blood. The ducts from each little lobule run into and form a single duct, the *bile-duct*, which, about two inches from the liver, divides, one branch leading to the gall-bladder, and the other to the duodenum.

271. FUNCTION OF THE LIVER.—(1.) It forms *glycogen* (308) from the sugar and peptones of the portal blood, and stores it up in the liver. (2.) It gives out the glycogen, when it is wanted, in the form of sugar, which sugar is used in the nutrition of the body. (3.) It works over and changes the form and condition of the proteids of the blood. (4.) It forms from the blood the yellowish-green, viscid, bitter fluid, called *bile*, which aids in the absorption of fats (274). (5.) It forms *urea* (310) out of proteid compounds existing in the blood.

272. The PANCREAS is a long, narrow, pinkish gland. It is found behind the lower border of the stomach. In structure it resembles the salivary glands. Its duct discharges into the duodenum.

Its secretion is viscid, colorless, odorless, and of an alkaline reaction. The pancreatic juice rapidly converts *starch* into grape-sugar, *proteids* into peptones (274), *fats* into an

---

271. Of glycogen? Of its storage? Of the proteids? Of the bile? Of urea?

272. Pancreas: characters? Position? Resemblance? Duct? The secretion? Its action on starch? On proteids? On fats?

emulsion or a soap, and it is therefore remarkable for acting on all the principles of the food-stuffs (225).

CHANGES EFFECTED IN THE FOOD-STUFFS IN THE ALIMENTARY CANAL.

273. The mixed food-stuffs, cooked or uncooked, in passing along the alimentary canal, are subjected to the action of certain secretions, such as the salivary, gastric, and pancreatic juices. Under the influence of warmth, moisture, and motion, these secretions produce such changes in the ordinary foods that, from being largely insoluble, they become largely soluble,—the starches being converted into sugars; the proteids, into peptones; and the fats, into emulsions, or soaps,—and the major part directly or indirectly enters the blood-current, and the lesser part is discharged as *excrement.*

274. CHANGES.—*In the mouth,* the mixed food, as flesh, bread, vegetables, etc., is broken into small pieces, is moistened with saliva, mixed with air and saliva, and formed into a bolus for swallowing (258). Some of the *starch* is at once converted into soluble grape-sugar. *In the stomach,* the presence of the food, made more or less alkaline by the saliva and mucus, excites the glands of the stomach to great activity. The contents of the stomach become more and more acid; the change of starch into sugar is lessened or arrested; the fats remain unchanged; the proteid envelopes of starches and fats are loosened; the natural bundles of flesh and vegetables fall asunder, and the fats, starches, oils, and protoplasm become more exposed; the

---

273. What juices act on the food-stuffs? What changes are induced? What results?

274. Changes in the mouth? In the stomach? What is a peptone? Appearance of chyme? Changes in the small intestine? In the large intestine?

protoplasm is dissolved, and the *proteids* (215) are converted into peptones. A PEPTONE is a proteid. It is soluble in water, is highly diffusible,—*i.e.*, it passes through moist animal membranes with ease,—and is not coagulated by heat. The food is now imperfectly dissolved, and forms a turbid, grayish liquid, called *chyme*. This latter, together with large lumps, is from time to time ejected through the pylorus into the duodenum. *In the small intestine*, by the action of the bile (271), the pancreatic juice (272), and the intestinal secretions, together, the remaining *proteids* are converted into peptones, the *starches* into sugar, and perhaps into lactic acid, and the *fats* are made into an *emulsion*, or into a *soap*, and are thus in a state which enables them to be taken into the portal blood-vessels (103) or into the lacteals (277). *In the large intestine*, the contents again become acid, owing to fermentation. A certain amount of cellulose (221) may be here digested. The great work, however, is absorption of the liquids contained in the fluid mass passed through the *ileo-cœcal valve*, so that when the mass reaches the rectum it has become firm, closely packed, and somewhat dry.

275. OSMOSIS.—When two different liquids, as blood and chyme, are separated by thin membrane, as the mucous membrane and the thin capillary walls, it is noticed (1) that the liquids mix through such membranes, and (2) that the quantities passing in opposite directions are unequal. The mixing of the fluids through membrane is called osmosis. In the case of blood and chyme, the greater current is towards the blood, owing to the relative physical and chemical conditions of the fluids. Watery solutions usu-

---

275. What occurs through membranes? What is osmosis? Direction of the currents? What osmose easily?

ally osmose readily. Colloids, like gelatin, other proteids, starches, and fats, osmose slowly, or not at all.

276. ABSORPTION.—The *water*, the soluble *salines*, and *crystalline organic compounds* may be absorbed from any part of the canal through osmosis of the veins and capillaries. By the help of the circulation, an almost unlimited quantity of fluid may be absorbed. The *sugars* and *peptones*, in part, are taken into the blood-current through the vessels in the walls of the stomach. The largest and most

FIG. 63.

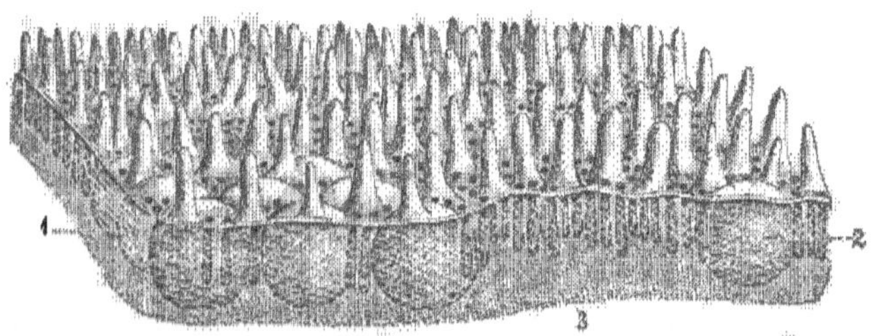

FIG. 63 (*Leidy*). PORTION OF THE MUCOUS MEMBRANE FROM THE ILEUM, moderately magnified, exhibiting the villi on its free surface, and between them the orifices of the tubular glands.—1, Portion of an agminated or clustered gland. 2, A solitary gland. 3, Areolar tissue.

important part of the digested material leaves the canal during its passage along the small intestine, partly into the portal vessels (103) and partly into the lacteals. A considerable quantity of *peptones* and *sugars* passes into the portal vessels. The great mass of the *fats* which enter the system from the intestines passes through the lacteals.

277. The LACTEALS commence within the villi of the small intestine (264) by closed extremities. They consist

277. Commencement of the lacteals? Their structure? Nature of villi? Appearance of chyle? Ending of lacteals? Describe the thoracic duct.

276. Place of absorption of watery solutions? Of sugars? Of peptones? Of the fats? Where is absorption most active? What two chief channels?

277. Commencement of the lacteals? Their structure? Nature of villi? Appearance of chyle? Ending of lacteals? Describe the thoracic duct.

either of a net-work of tubes, which, at the base of the villi, pass into larger tubes, or of a single, closed, dilated, minute tube, ending in a net-work of tubes. The villi contain some muscular fibres and an arterial and venous twig, which form a net-work outside the lacteal. During intestinal absorption, these lacteals are seen to be distended with a whitish or bluish fluid, called *chyle*. Leading from each villus are tubes, which run into larger tubes lying in the mesentery (264). These tubes terminate in firm, ovoid or roundish bodies, called *mesenteric glands*. From these glands thread-like tubes lead to a larger tube, the *thoracic duct*, lying in front of the vertebral column. This duct is from eighteen to twenty inches long, has numerous valves opening towards the neck, and empties into the left subclavian vein (Fig. 64, 3).

278. CHYLE.—In a fast-

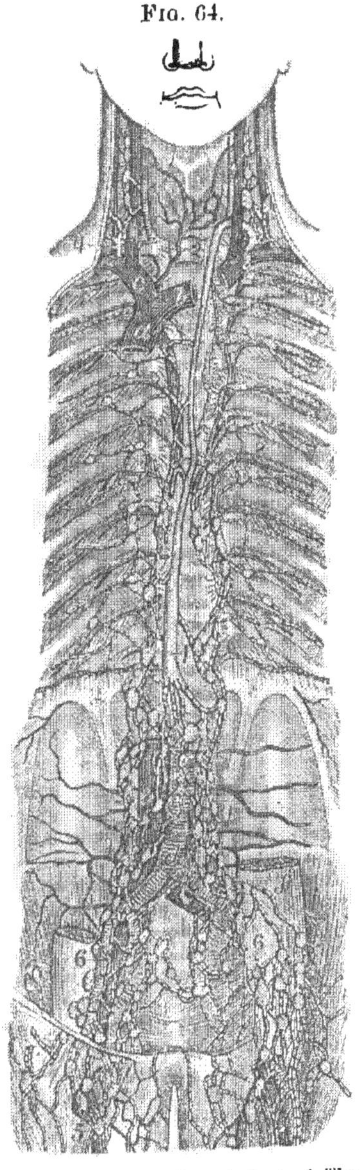

FIG. 64.

FIG. 64 (*Leidy*). VIEW OF THE GREAT LYMPHATIC TRUNKS.—1, 2, Thoracic duct. 4, The right lymphatic duct. 5, Lymphatics of the thigh. 6, Iliac lymphatics. 7, Lumbar lymphatics. 8, Intercostal lymphatics. *a*, Superior cava. *b*, Left innominate vein. *c*, Right innominate vein. *d*, Aorta. *e*, Inferior cava. 3, Left subclavian vein.

ing animal, the contents of the thoracic duct are clear and transparent. Shortly after a meal they appear milky and opaque. Chyle is a mixture of the lymph (295) coming from the rest of the body and of the white fluid seen in the lacteals. Chyle readily coagulates, like blood (120),

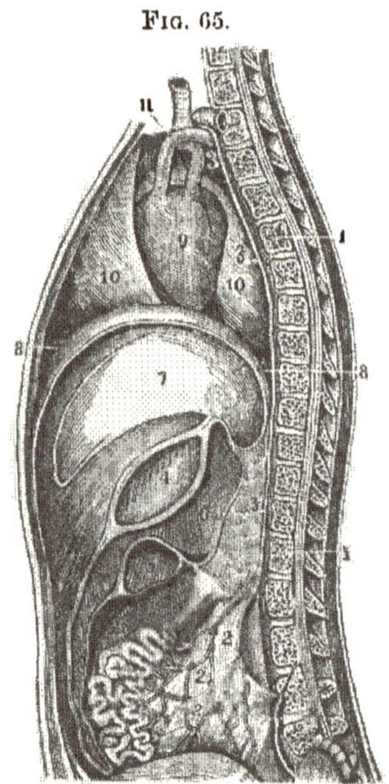

Fig. 65.

Fig. 65.—1, 1, Vertebral column. 2, 2, 2, Lacteals. 3, 3, 3, Thoracic duct. 4, Stomach. 5, Colon. 7, Liver. 8, 8, Diaphragm. 9, Heart. 10, 10, Lungs. 11, Large vein into which the thoracic duct opens.

but the clot is not firm. It assumes a pinkish color on standing. It consists of fibrin, of a large number of white corpuscles, of a small number of red corpuscles, and of many oil globules. It mixes with the blood in the left subclavian vein.

279. MOVEMENTS OF CHYLE. —Though the villi may act as a kind of muscular suction-pump, yet the exact method of the transit of the fat from the intestines, through the walls of the villi and of the intervening tissues, to the lacteals, is not known. Having reached the interior of the mesenteric tubes, the liquid contents are directed by the numerous valves, and their flow is aided by the general muscular movements, the suction of the subclavian vein (owing to the lessened blood-pressure ruling therein), by the influence of the inspiratory movement, and by the continual pressure of the intestinal contents. All these forces working to-

278. Appearance of chyle? Composition? Characters? Where does it mingle with the blood?

gether cause the contents of the lacteals and of the lymph-ducts (295) to be discharged into the general blood-current.

280. SUMMARY OF DIGESTION.

In the mouth:
  Mastication and insalivation.
  Starches partly changed to sugar.
In the stomach:
  Thorough mixing of ingredients.
  Breaking up of the proteid envelopes.
  Setting free of starch, fats, and protoplasm.
  Proteids changed to peptones.
In the small intestine:
  Starches changed to sugars.
  Proteids changed to peptones.
  Oils emulsified or saponified.

SUMMARY OF ABSORPTION.

From the mouth:
  Water, salts, sugar.
From the stomach:
  Water, salts, peptones.
From the small intestine:
  (*a*) Portal veins,—water, sugar, peptones.
  (*b*) Lacteals,—emulsions, soaps.
From the large intestine:
  Water, salts, sugar (?), peptones (?).

HYGIENE.

281. INDIGESTION, OR DYSPEPSIA.—Difficulty and imperfection in the digestive process arise under a variety of

---

280. Summary of digestion?   Of absorption?
281. What is dyspepsia?   Causes of indigestion?

circumstances. Indigestion may occur with certain articles of diet (cheese, oysters, strawberries, etc.), or with disturbances located in the stomach or intestines, or in both. Among the common causes of indigestion are excessive eating (334), too rapid eating, insufficient mastication or insalivation, irregularity of meals, too frequent occurrence of meals, or the reverse, improper quality of the food, the drinking of too much cold water during or immediately after taking food, the excessive use of tea (238), the abuse of alcohol (245), and the injudicious use of condiments.

282. The QUANTITY OF FOOD necessary to the system varies, being affected by age, occupation, temperament, habits, temperature, amount of clothing, health, and mental state. The supply must equal the waste of the system (338), and, in children, the demands for growth (337). The supply should be in the form of plain food, plainly served, and eaten in moderation. The quantity should be kept well within the digestive capacity of the individual. The object to be kept in view in the use of food is not the development and maintenance of a 'fat, plump body, but of a *sound* body. On the diminution or cessation of active employment, especially physical, practise self-denial, as regards the amount of food, until the system has become accustomed to the new conditions. On the advent of warm weather reduce the amounts of fat and proteids in the diet, and by so doing indigestion and "biliousness" may be prevented.

283. PHYSICAL STATE OF THE FOOD.—The more finely

---

282. The amount of food, how affected? The supply? In what form? Object in feeding? Management under less bodily work? In the spring?

283. The conditions for easy digestion? About eggs? Advantages of flesh? Spallanzani's experiments? What suggestion?

divided the food, the less the proteid portions are sheltered by insoluble envelopes, like the cellulose of vegetables and grains, and the more thoroughly it is mixed with air and the saliva, the more rapid and easy is the gastric digestion. Well-beaten white of eggs is more easily digested than boiled white, hard-boiled yelk than boiled white, and hard-boiled white than fried white (231).   Hard-boiled eggs are more difficult of digestion than roasted or boiled flesh, because the gastric juice can only attack the former on its outer, impervious surfaces; but the flesh, under the action of warmth, moisture, and motion, breaks up into its fibres and muscular disks (71), and thus more surface is exposed to the action of the juice.   Spallanzani's experiments with perforated tubes containing food, placed in the stomach of animals, gave the following results : food moistened with saliva was most quickly digested ; then food moistened with water ; and, lastly, food not moistened at all.   Hence the importance of careful, wise cooking, of fine division, and of complete insalivation of all kinds of food.

284. BAD TEETH are a fertile source of dyspepsia.   A person having very irregular, decayed, or defective teeth is unable to divide his food thoroughly or to incorporate the same well with saliva, and, as a result, extra digestive labor is thrown upon the stomach and pancreas.

285. The dentist and cook may be of much service to the person having defective teeth.   Teeth having cavities ought to be cleaned and plugged.   The best filling is gold foil.   Badly-decayed teeth should be removed, as their presence is hurtful to the adjacent teeth, taints the breath,

---

284. Influence of bad teeth?

285. What can the dentist do?   Of artificial teeth?   What can the cook do?   Of management of food in the mouth?

and acts injuriously on the food passing over them. It is better for the health, in the absence of natural teeth, to use artificial ones than to struggle along without them. A good cook, by the judicious selection and careful preparation of the food, can be of much assistance to persons having defective teeth. Light puddings, soups, minced meats, eggs, milk, etc., require little mastication. They should not, however, be "bolted," but ought to be well rolled about in the mouth, in order to mix considerable quantities of mucus and saliva with them before swallowing.

286. CARE OF THE TEETH.—The teeth should be kept clean by cleansing them with tepid water after each meal. Quill, wood, or ivory picks are preferable to those of metal. The teeth should be carefully brushed, outside and inside, morning and evening. The occasional use of a fine soap, followed by careful rinsing, is advisable. No coarse or acidulated tooth-powders should be employed. Avoid sudden extremes in temperatures of food and drink. The cracking of hard objects with the teeth is not judicious. *Tobacco* injures the enamel, discolors the teeth, debilitates the gums, and taints the breath, while it offers no compensating advantage to the digestive functions (412).

287. FREQUENCY OF EATING.—Man in a savage state feeds with great irregularity. When the food is abundant, he devotes himself to eating, drinking, and sleeping; but when it is scarce, he contents himself with one meal a day. In either case the quantity taken is enormous. A good calf, weighing two hundred pounds, makes only one meal for four or five Yakuti; a reindeer, a meal for three only

---

286. Teeth-cleansing? Toothpicks? Soap? Powders? Temperature? Hard substances? Tobacco?

287. Frequency of eating in the savage state? In Japan? In Rome? In Europe? Distribution of food?

(Cochrane). The Japanese "jinriki," confined to a diet of beans, millet, rice, and dried fish, eats five or six times daily; the boatmen, four to six; the field-laborers, three to five; and the official class, two to four. The Romans had two meals a day,—the dinner at 9 A.M. and the ceremonious supper at 4 P.M. Until recent times there were but two meals a day in civilized Europe. Experience shows that in America three meals, each meal being of simple quality, is the best division for efficient activity. The distribution of the day's food, according to Dr. E. Smith, should be about one part for the evening meal, one and one-half parts for breakfast, and two parts for dinner.

288. Under ordinary circumstances, it is best for healthy persons to *take no food between meals.* Children should have their food oftener than three times in the twenty-four hours. Invalids ought strictly to follow the diet-directions of their medical adviser. Light conversation, enlivening wit, and genial humor promote digestion. Unpleasant topics, labored discussions, business affairs, etc., should be banished from table-conversation.

289. IMPROPER FOOD.—To a certain person, the improper quality of a food may depend upon the nature of the food itself, upon the manner in which it has been prepared, or upon its having undergone changes, like decomposition or fermentation.

The food which is suitable for the soldier, sailor, or laborer may be, and is often, very unsuitable for the student or the professional man or woman. Articles which the

---

288. Of eating between meals? Intervals for children? For invalids? Influence of conversation?

289. Causes of improper quality of food? Of differences in individuals? Of a diet for students? Prevention of dyspepsia? Suitable foods?

former class can take with impunity, digest with ease, and derive energy from, would cause pain, loathing, and digestive troubles and be of no advantage to the latter. Other things remaining the same, the student, the professional man, the seamstress, and others engaged in sedentary pursuits need a higher grade and more readily assimilable kinds of food than do the classes engaged in active, out-of-door pursuits.

The *cooking* of the food for the sedentary classes demands more care, wisdom, and skill than are commonly given to it. To prevent dyspepsia, or to remedy dyspeptic conditions, the regulation of the diet-list is the chief thing demanding attention. In all cases of early indigestion, articles known to be difficult of digestion—pastry, cheese, certain fruits and vegetables, fresh white bread, and most fancy dishes— must be avoided. Pork, veal, and salted meats are to be used with caution. Fresh beef and mutton, not too fat, and carefully baked or boiled, are most suitable meats. Light soups, chicken, game, white fish, yolk of eggs, milk, rice, barley, and oat-meal are to be commended.

290. AIDS TO DYSPEPSIA.—Sedentary habits, as ex- hibited in the lives of most students, lawyers, seamstresses, etc.; undue exercise, mental or physical, just before or just after meals; habitual constipation; the abuse of opium and other narcotics; the constant use of "pills;" the injudicious use of tobacco, tea, and alcoholics; excessive study; emo- tional disturbances, and many forms of mental shock,—one and all tend to induce dyspepsia, by influencing the *secretory* and *motor functions* of the stomach and alimentary canal.

Persons should abstain from eating at least three hours before retiring for sleep. It is no unusual occurrence for persons who have eaten heartily immediately before retiring to have unpleasant dreams, or to be aroused from their unquiet slumber by colic pains,

---

In such instances the brain becomes partly dormant, not imparting to the digestive organs the requisite amount of nervous influence; this being deficient, the unchanged food remains in the stomach, causing irritation of this organ.

291. Prevention of Dyspepsia.—To counteract the tendency to dyspepsia, *interesting* physical exercise (riding, rowing, lawn-tennis, etc.) should be taken daily, and at regular hours, though not immediately before or after a meal. The ventilation of the working- and sleeping-rooms needs constant attention (204). Abstinence from injurious habits, such as excessive smoking of tobacco and intemperance in the drinking of tea (238) and alcoholics, must be observed. The action of the skin is to be encouraged by cool baths, the skin quickly dried, and by douche-bathing, with occasional warm or Turkish baths. The wearing of flannel next to the skin must not be neglected, as it not only prevents the chilling of the abdomen, but tends to relieve constipation.

The functional exercise of any organ abstracts fluids, sanguineous and nervous, from other parts of the body, thus weakening those parts for the time. Severe exercise of muscle concentrates the forces in the muscle; severe exercise of the brain concentrates the forces in the brain; and so with the vocal and other organs. After severe exercise, from thirty to forty minutes should be allowed before eating, for restoring equilibrium to the system. The student, farmer, or mechanic who hurries from his toil to his dinner to "save time" will, in the end, lose more time than he saves. After eating, the digestive organs need, for a time, the chief use of the vital forces, and if these are habitually expended elsewhere, as in study or labor, digestion will be arrested, the chyle cheated of its proper elements, and headache, dulness, and general derangement will follow. Moderate exercise of the muscles, a social chat and a hearty laugh, aid digestion, and tend "to shake the cobwebs from the brain." These directions are particularly applicable to the am-

<hr>

291. Influence of exercise in dyspepsia? Of ventilation? Of abstinence? Of bathing? Of clothing?

bitious student who feels that he must "save time" and "must have the lesson." Let him try the experiment, and he will soon find that in the after-dinner hour his lesson is better learned when he spends half the hour in recreation and the other half in close application. Many students are obliged to give up their course of study, from simple neglect of these rules.

292. CONSTIPATION is very prevalent among sedentary persons, as students, writers, females, clerks, and operatives in factories. The main causes are want of daily, active exercise, inattention to a proper diet, and neglect of nature's needs. In a majority of cases, constipation can be remedied by eating well-cooked white flour compounds, cracked wheat, oat-meal, hominy, etc., sub-acid fruits, and a moderate amount of boiled or roasted lean meats. The habit of going to the stool daily at the same hour, even though at first there is no response to the effort, should be persevered in. For children and the majority of persons, soon after breakfast is suggested; for those suffering from evident rectal diseases, as tumors, piles, and fistulas, just before retiring. A recumbent position mitigates rectal pain. Active exercise, which calls all portions of the body into service, ought to be practised daily. As a remedial agent, body-flexion (533) should be practised at least three times daily. These movements accelerate the portal circulation (103), unload the congested, tense rectal veins, strengthen the muscular fibres of the rectum, and stimulate the rectal glands. Daily evacuation of the intestines may be aided by friction over the abdomen, followed by faithfully kneading the abdominal walls, by a suppository of hard soap, or by an enema. The continued use of laxative and purgative drugs injures the system.

___

292. Cultivation of habit in constipation? Change of diet? External agents? Drugs?

CHAPTER IX.

THE LYMPHATICS.—THE SPLEEN, THYMUS, ETC.—THE URINARY SYSTEM.

THE LYMPHATIC SYSTEM.

293. THIS system includes the *lymphatic* **vessels**, the *glands*, and the *lacteals* (see 277). The LYMPHATIC VESSELS consist of delicate tubes of nearly uniform size, presenting a knotted appearance because of the presence of valves. They are found in nearly every texture and organ of the body. The *superficial* set are placed just under the skin, and in the submucous tissues of the gastro-pulmonary and urinary tracts. The *deep* sets accompany the deep-lying blood-vessels.

294. The LYMPHATIC GLANDS vary in size from a hempseed to an almond. They are round or oval in form, have a pinkish-gray color, and are made up of *adenoid tissue.* They are situated in the course of the lymphatic vessels and the lacteals. They may be easily found in the neck, in the armpit, in front of the elbow, in the groin, in the mesentery, and near the large blood-vessels. Occasionally, after an injury, bright-red streaks extend from the injured spot up the limb to certain small, firm, painful enlargements.

---

293. What does the lymphatic system include? Describe the vessels. Where located? Of the two sets?

294. The glands: size? Shape? Location? How recognized? Appearance after injury?

Fig. 66.

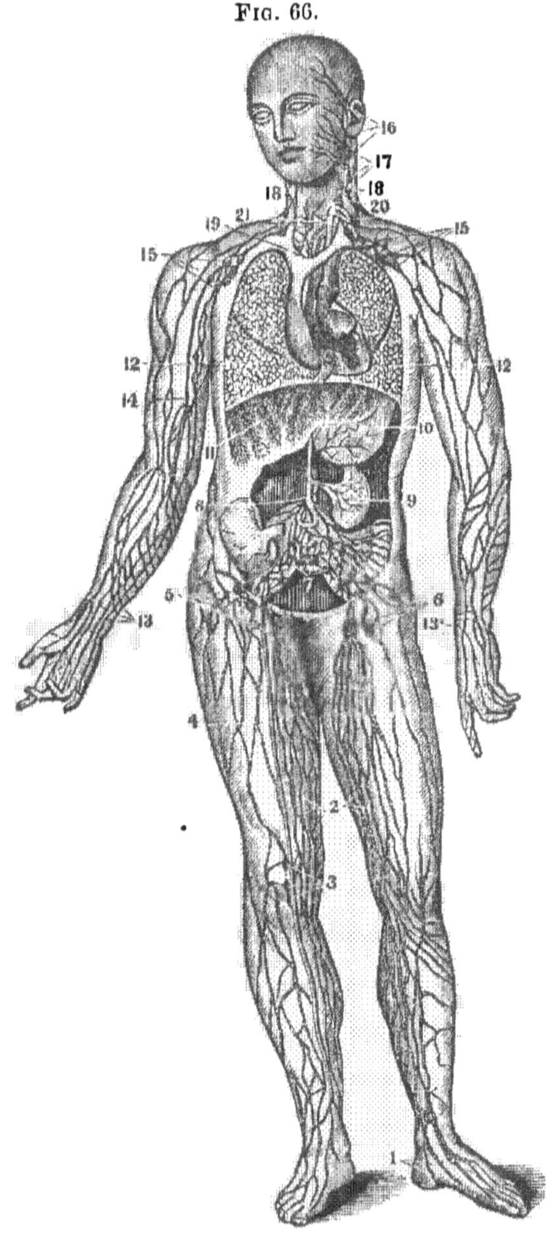

The red lines indicate the course of the superficial set of lymphatics of that part, and the enlargements the glands.

295. The LYMPH is a clear, colorless fluid found in this system of vessels. In general terms, it is blood without its corpuscles. This fluid passes from most tissues through the delicate walls of the tubes into the vessels, and is by

FIG. 67.   FIG. 68.   FIG. 69.

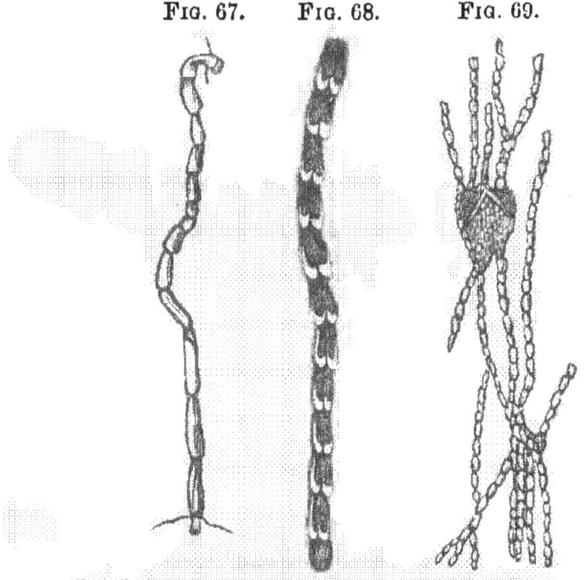

FIG. 67. A SINGLE LYMPHATIC VESSEL, much magnified.
FIG. 68. THE VALVES of a lymphatic trunk.
FIG. 69. A LYMPHATIC GLAND, with several vessels passing through it.

them conducted to the general blood-current. The lymphatics of the right thorax, the right side of the head and neck, and the right arm, empty their contents into the right

FIG. 66. A REPRESENTATION OF THE LYMPHATIC VESSELS AND GLANDS.—1, 2, 3, 4, 5, 6, The lymphatic vessels and glands of the lower limbs. 7, Lymphatic glands. 8, The commencement of the thoracic duct. 9, The lymphatics of the kidney. 10, Of the stomach. 11, Of the liver. 12, 12, Of the lungs. 13, 14, 15, The lymphatics and glands of the arm. 16, 17, 18, Of the face and neck. 19, 20, Large veins. 21, The thoracic duct.

295. What is lymph? Its movements? What system of tubes?

lymphatic duct (Fig. 64, 4), and those of the rest of the body into the thoracic duct (277).

296. FUNCTION.—The lymph continually passes into the blood-current a crowd of white bodies, which for the most part appear in the vessels after they have emerged from the glands. These adenoid glands may be one of the birthplaces of the white corpuscles (119). The lymph also carries back to the blood materials present in the interstices of the tissues, which may again be used in nutrition. Through slight abrasion of the skin or mucous surfaces, the virus of specific diseases (smallpox, vaccinia, farcy, and poison from a dead body) quickly enters the lymph-channels, is conveyed to the blood, and, through the latter, infects the whole system. Hence the importance of using adhesive plaster to cover scratches or broken surfaces of the skin when handling dead bodies.

297. The SPLEEN (MILT) (Figs. 57, 34) is a soft, dark-bluish body attached to the cardiac end of the stomach. Its size and weight vary more than those of any other solid organ of the body, owing to the variations in the quantity of blood which it contains. It has a strong, fibro-elastic coat, and is divided by numerous slender bands into spaces which contain a soft, bluish-red mass, called *splenic pulp*. The spleen has few lymphatics, and no duct.

298. FUNCTION.—It has been removed from man without producing any marked permanent change in the economy. After a meal it increases in size, remains enlarged for some hours, and then returns to its normal size. This peculiar action may be connected with the manufacture of white corpuscles (119) and the destruction of the red. Evidently, active changes associated with digestion

---

296. What appear beyond the glands? Speak of the birth of corpuscles. What is also carried in the lymph?

297. What of the spleen? Of its structure?

take place in the spleen, but exact information as to their nature is wanting.

299. Of the functions of the SUPRARENAL BODIES, found cap-'ping the kidneys, nothing is definitely known. The same may be said of the THYROID BODY, seen on the front and sides of the trachea, below the larynx, and of the .THYMUS GLAND, a temporary organ seated in the lower part of the neck of infants. This organ continues to grow until the second year, after which it gradually wastes away.

THE URINARY SYSTEM.

300. The KIDNEYS are two dense, dark-red, solid organs, situated in the back part of the abdomen, between the eleventh rib and the innominate bone. Their shape is not very unlike that of the kidney-bean. They are placed back of the peritoneum, and are surrounded by areolar tissue having much fat, which serves to keep them of a uniform temperature. The artery (*renal*) leading to each kidney is short, but large, and is accompanied by a large vein. Leading from the cavity of the kidney is a musculo-membranous tube, the *ureter*, which terminates at the base of the bladder. This tube conveys the excretion called *urine* from the kidney.

301. If a longitudinal section of the organ is made (Fig. 70), the solid substance is found to consist of an outer *cortical* portion and a deep-seated *medullary* portion. The conical masses of the medullary portion, from fifteen to twenty in number, form the *pyramids*. The apexes of the pyramids projecting into the *renal pelvis* (the funnel-shaped dilatation of the kidney) are called *papillæ*. The substance of the kidney is made up of minute, closely-packed tubes, the *tubuli uriniferi*, with blood-vessels, lymphatics, and nerves, held together by a soft material. It has been estimated that there are two million tubuli in each kidney. The tubuli are lined with pavement or spheroidal epithelium (Fig. 42).

---

300. Kidneys: Color? Shape? Position? Coverings? Vessels? Tubes?

302. URINE.—Healthy urine is a clear, yellowish fluid, of a peculiar odor. It has an acid reaction, and a specific gravity of 1.020.

FIG. 70.   FIG. 71.

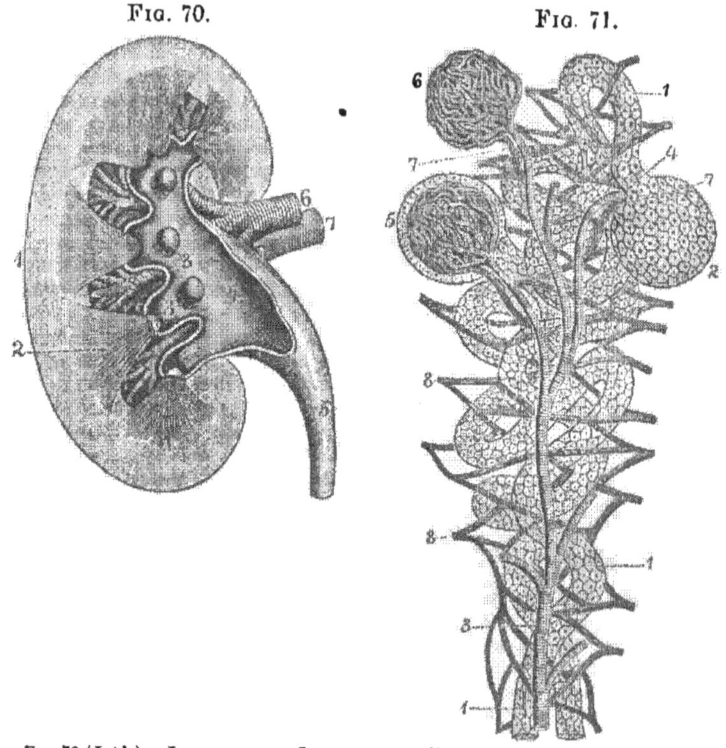

FIG. 70 (*Leidy*). LONGITUDINAL SECTION OF A KIDNEY.—1, Cortical substance. 2, Renal pyramid. 3, Renal papillæ. 4, Pelvis. 5, Ureter. 6, Renal artery. 7, Renal vein. 8, Branches of the latter vessel in the sinus of the kidney.

FIG. 71 (*Leidy*). DIAGRAM OF THE STRUCTURE OF THE KIDNEYS.—1, Two uriniferous tubules of the cortical substance lined with pavement epithelium. 2, Dilatation of a tubule at its extremity. 3, Branch of the renal artery ending in vessels which enter the dilatations as seen at 4, 5. 6, Knot of blood-vessels freed from its investment. 7, Veins emerging from the vascular knots. 8, Plexus formed by the latter veins among the uriniferous tubules, from which plexus originate the branches of the renal vein.

303. FUNCTIONS OF THE KIDNEYS.—The kidneys are excretive organs. Their function is to eliminate certain

---

303. Describe the kidneys. Their function? How affected? What relation between the kidneys and the skin? How is urea separated? What may also occur? What of the urine?

substances produced by the activity of other tissues. The waste inorganic and organic salts existing in the blood in solution are *filtered*, under varying blood-pressure (140), from the blood entering by the renal artery. There is an intimate correlation of the kidneys and the skin. When the blood flows freely in the skin, as in the summer, the perspiration is abundant, but the amount of urine voided in twenty-four hours is diminished; in cold weather the converse is noticed. Urea (310) is always present in the blood. The protoplasm of the epithelial cells lining the tubuli withdraws the urea from the blood and discharges it into the tubuli. This does not appear to be filtration, but a true *secretion* process. The epithelium of the kidney may also change various nitrogenous matters existing in the renal blood into urea, and then remove it from the blood. The urine is continually produced, and finds its way, drop by drop, from the pelvis of the kidney, through the ureter, into the bladder.

304. The BLADDER is a muscular sac, lying, when empty, in the pelvis behind the pubic bones (Fig. 51). The medium capacity is two hundred and fifty cubic centimetres (about half a pint). It is lined with mucous membrane. The two ureters enter it at the base, and the URETHRAL TUBE passes out through its neck. Its function is to hold the urine continually entering by the ureters, and to expel it at proper intervals.

305. The *retention* in the blood of the nitrogenous prod-ucts of tissue-waste, owing to deficient or suppressed action of the kidneys, gives rise to headache, dizziness, nausea, con-

---

304. Bladder: structure? Position? Capacity? Lining? Openings? Function?

305. Effect of retention of nitrogen compounds in the blood? Of urine in the bladder?

fusion of ideas, and, if continued, a disease called uræmia. One of the most common factors in the production of disease of the kidneys is the steady use of alcoholics, especially distilled liquors,—whiskey, rum, gin, etc. (243). The *forced retention of urine* in the bladder leads to severe pain and over-distention. The latter may result in an inability to empty the bladder, in inflammation of the lining membrane, or in overflow. Hence the importance of obeying at once nature's pressing demands for the evacuation of this organ.

The office of the lymphatics may also include another,—assimilation. Disintegration of the tissues is everywhere taking place. Every respiration, every heart-beat, every muscular movement, every thought, is produced at the expense of the life of some of the tissues; but, says Carpenter, "The *death* of the tissues by no means involves their immediate and complete destruction; and there seems no more reason why an animal should not derive support from its own dead past, than the dead body of another individual. Whilst, therefore, the matter that has undergone too complete a disintegration to be again employed as nutrient material is carried off by the excretory process, that portion which is capable of being again assimilated may be taken up by the lymphatic system."

CHAPTER X.

NUTRITION.

306. THE study of the preceding chapters has shown that certain materials known as *foods* (Chapter VII.) enter the blood, after undergoing more or less change, by venous absorption or lacteal absorption from the alimentary canal (280), by osmosis through the lung-tissues (177), and by absorption through the skin; that the blood, in circulating through the organs of the system, especially the lungs and liver, is changed in its chemical and physiological characters; that this blood in the capillary areas parts with certain portions and receives additions (143); that certain of these materials received in the capillary areas are of no further use to the system, and that these materials are *excreted* from the system by the way of the kidneys (303), the lungs (178), and the skin (48).

307. NUTRITION, or ASSIMILATION, embraces the process or the change which the food-elements in the blood-current undergo for the production of energy and heat, and also for conveying from the system portions of waste matter. The forms in which the foods enter the system, and the conditions most favorable for their entrance, have been treated in Chapter VIII. The changes which they undergo in

---

306. What of the entrance of foods into the blood? Of changes in the blood? Of the gains and losses of the tissues? Of the modes of excretion?

307. What does nutrition embrace? What is really known? What products have been partly studied?

the system, in the repair, building up, and reproduction of parts, and in the production of heat and other energy, are for the most part unknown (143).   Glycogen, fat, urea, and uric acid have been only partly considered.

308. GLYCOGEN (271) is a sugar-producing substance, appearing in a pure state as a white, amorphous powder.   It is found in the hepatic cells of a normal liver.   It is elaborated from the portal blood, containing proteid foods or starch foods, but not from fat foods.   It is stored up during active digestion, and thus acts as a reserve store of carbo-hydrates.   According to the demands of the system, the insoluble glycogen is changed in the liver into the soluble sugar which appears later in the hepatic veins.   The part which this sugar, gradually set free by the liver, plays in energy- and heat-production has not been elucidated.   A certain amount of sugar is normal to the blood.   An excess appears to be injurious. This excess is removed in two ways: (1) by the kidneys, giving rise to *diabetes*, or sugar in the urine; (2) by the liver-cells, changing the excess in the portal blood into insoluble glycogen.   Experiments indicate that the glycogenic function of the liver is subject to the central influence of a nerve-centre located in the medulla, near the *vaso-motor* centre.

309. FAT.—Of all the tissues of the body, the fat fluctuates most (21).   It is formed the most quickly, and the most quickly removed. Experiments and observation show that it is formed by the active agency of the protoplasm of the fat-cell, and that it is stored up as fat granules or drops.   Under suitable conditions, the fat of the food may be stored up in the body as fat.   In most cases it is formed in the system out of something which is not fat, as shown in the milk- and fat-production of cows.   The carbon elements of the fat may be derived from proteids, from carbo-hydrates (starches and sugar), from fats, or from a mixture of the same.   Experience shows that carbo-hydrates are most efficacious in producing an accumulation of fat.   A decrease of hæmoglobin (180) favors its accumulation.   When demanded by the system, it appears to be discharged in a manner more or less mechanical.

310. UREA (303).—The history of the early stages of urea has not yet been made plain.   The antecedents of urea appear to be *kreatin* ($C_4H_9N_3O_2$), a constant constituent of muscle-juices, and

leucin ($C_4H_{13}NO_2$) and *tyrosin* ($C_9H_{11}NO_3$), two of the principal products of the decomposition of nitrogenous matter, especially in pancreatic digestion. Their change into *urea* ($(NH_2)_2CO$) may take place in the liver (271), the kidney (303), or the spleen; but of the method of change we are yet ignorant. In the production of heat and other energy from the tissue-constituents, many intermediate products are formed. All the *non-nitrogenous* substances yield carbonic acid and water, and the *nitrogenous* ultimately yield carbonic acid and water, uric acid, and urea. Urea is a crystallizable body, and is the characteristic ingredient of urine. It exists in the blood, and has been detected in the saliva and chyle. It contains all the nitrogen and part of the carbon and hydrogen of the proteids from which it is derived.

311. *Uric acid* ($C_5H_4N_4O_3$) is normally present in the spleen, pancreas, and liver. It is found only in slight amounts in the urine of man. It is a product of proteid change, less oxidized than urea. It is not, however, an antecedent of urea. Like urea, it is eliminated by the kidneys.

PRODUCTION OF HEAT AND ENERGY.

312. In general terms, the human body is a machine for converting the latent energy stored in the foods into the active energy manifested in the heat and the work of the living body. Though the animal economy may combine simple compounds into complex compounds, as in the building up of complex tissues, yet in general it is engaged in reducing the complex compounds received as foods into the simpler compounds excreted as waste. In the process of breaking up of compounds, either by the union of oxygen with certain elements or the splitting of a complex compound into simpler ones, *force* and *heat* are evolved. Every ingredient of food contains a fixed amount

312. What is the purpose of the human body? Speak of its general action. What is evolved in the process? What does food contain?

of force or energy; every one of the simpler compounds into which it may split up in the body also contains its smaller but yet definite amount of force; and the difference between the force in the latter and that in the original substance expresses the amount of force or energy which that substance contributes to the body.

313. MANIFESTATION OF FORCE.—Plant-life, working under the influence of the sunlight, builds up the tree, which yields wood. If this wood be heated to a certain extent, as by rubbing two dry sticks together, the carbon of the wood unites with the oxygen of the air. The wood disappears, but heat, light, smoke, and carbonic acid gas and water-vapor are produced. In this change, called *oxidation*, two forces, called heat and light, are made manifest to our senses. If similar bits of wood had been exposed to the atmosphere and allowed to decay, the oxygen of the air would have united more slowly with the carbon elements, not producing always carbonic acid at first, but certain intermediate products, which ultimately would become carbonic acid and water. In this latter case the heat and light would not be readily recognized by us, yet the amount of energy set free in either case would be the same. In both cases the complex carbon compound—wood—was oxidized; in both cases carbonic acid and water were produced; and in both cases the same amount of energy or force was liberated. In the one case the energy was liberated in a brief space, and thus attracted the attention of the senses; in the other, the liberation was spread over such a length of time and so attenuated as not to attract the notice of the senses.

---

313. What does the plant build up? The results of quick oxidation? Of slow oxidation (decay)? Of the results in either case? Differences of the manifestations?

314. The PRODUCTION OF FORCE in the human body
has been compared to the operations of the boiler and
steam-engine. In the cold boiler, the water is quiescent
and exerts no force, except pressure on the bottom and
sides of the boiler. If the iron be heated, as by the burning of wood under it, the heat-energy of the wood is transmitted to the liquid water, causing the latter to assume the
form of steam. If now the steam be admitted into a cylin-
der, with a piston and valves, its expansive power is changed
into mechanical motion. As the steam may be used for
heating, for propelling machinery, for drawing water, etc.,
so in the human body the energy set free by the oxidation
of the materials of the food, or of certain materials in the
tissues, may appear partly as heat or partly as motion, in
the form of muscular work, electrical currents, tissue-con-
struction, tissue-changes, etc.

315. In the human body, the complex compounds of the tissues
may, under oxidation, split at once into simple compounds, like
water, urea, and carbonic acid, or they may give rise to intermediate compounds, like lactic acid, kreatin, and tyrosin. The amount
of force set free in either case will be the same, but the period of
its evolution will be longer. The *ultimate oxidation* of the *proteids*
produces urea (310) and carbonic acid and water; of the *fats*, carbonic acid and water; and of the *carbo-hydrates*, carbonic acid.
During this process energy is made manifest.

316. The INCOME of the body consists of C, H, O, N, S, P, and
the saline matters contained in the proteids, the fats, carbo-hydrates,
salts, and water of the food, and the uncombined oxygen and nitrogen entering by the lungs, the skin, and the alimentary canal. The
OUTCOME consists chiefly of carbonic acid and water, passing out
by the lungs, skin, and alimentary canal; the water and salts (the
small amount of urea and uric acid may be neglected), by the
skin; and the water, salts, and, practically, all the nitrogen com-

---

314. Comparison of the human body with the steam-engine? Speak
of steam-production and its uses. Of energy- and heat-production.

m

pounds, by the kidneys. Of these, the carbon, the nitrogen, and the uncombined oxygen are by far the most important factors.

317. A Living Diet and its Energy.—

	MOLESCHOTT.	PETTENKOFER.	RANKE.
	Grammes.	*Grammes.*	*Grammes.*
Protoids	30	148	100
Fats	84	103	100
Starches, etc. . .	404	378	240
Salts	30		25
Water	2800		2600

Moleschott's diet is derived from a comparison of a large number of public diets, and, as seen, the cheaper carbo-hydrates are used in place of the dearer fats. Pettenkofer's is calculated for soldiers, and hence has more of the stimulating proteids and less of the bulky starches. Ranke, a man weighing seventy-four kilogrammes (one hundred and sixty-three pounds), found himself in good health, neither gaining nor losing on his diet. For purposes of calculation, Ranke's is best. When the ingredients of the first three items (the other two, salts and water, are left out of the calculation, as they contribute in themselves little or no force, but simply make the conditions for the action of the force-producers) are perfectly oxidized, Professor Frankland's data of combustion (Foster, p. 367) would make their energy equivalent to the following "gramme-degrees C. units of heat" and "metre-kilogrammes units of force."[1]

Grammes.	Gramme-degrees.	Metre-kilogrammes.
100 Protoid	436,800	185,000
100 Fat	906,900	384,100
240 Starch, etc. . . .	938,880	397,680
Total income . . .	2,282,580	966,780

---

[1] A *unit of heat* is the amount of heat required to raise the temperature of a given weight of a given substance through a certain thermometric space. The heat required to raise one kilogramme of water through 1° C. constitutes the French or "gramme-degree C. unit of heat." The heat required to raise one pound of water through 1° F. constitutes the English thermal unit.

A *unit of work* is the amount of force required to raise one kilogramme through one metre, which is called "metre-kilogramme unit." A unit of work (English) is the amount of force required to raise one pound weight through one foot = "foot-pound unit."

One metre-kilogramme = 7.233 foot-pounds.
One foot-pound = .138254 metre-kilogramme.
One English thermal unit = (pound 1° F.) = 772 foot-pounds.
One French thermal unit = (kilogramme 1° C.) = 424 metre-kilogrammes.

318. *The energy set free in the body* appears in two forms,
—HEAT and MECHANICAL LABOR. The normal expenditure for internal mechanical labor of an average adult is
80,000 metre-kilogrammes. A good day's *work* is put
down at about 150,000 metre-kilogrammes. The external
work, 70,000 metre-kilogrammes, is equivalent in walking
to a twelve and one-half mile course for a man weighing
one hundred and fifty pounds, or the raising of seventy-
five pounds six feet high one hundred times an hour for
ten hours. The normal energy-income of the adult body
has been estimated in round numbers at 1,000,000 metre-
kilogrammes (317). The normal expenditure in the form
of *heat* has been determined by subtracting the mechanical
labor-expenditure from the total energy-income. It is
about 850,000 metre-kilogrammes. Hence from one-sixth
to one-fifth of the total energy-income of the body is expended as mechanical labor, and from four-fifths to five-
sixths leaves the body as heat. The best steam-engines
utilize in mechanical work only about one-tenth of the
energy of the fuel employed in them. In this respect the
body is an economical machine.

319. *The human body loses energy* in the performance of
muscular work, as in running, walking, climbing, etc., in
all kinds of manual and bodily labor, in respiration, and
in speech. This is equivalent, in a hard-working adult, to
about 70,000 metre-kilogrammes. The internal work of
the body—the labor of the internal muscular apparatus, the
labor in the molecular changes in the nervous, gland, and

---

318. How does the energy appear? What is the value of the internal work? Of the external work? Of the heat? What of the
economy of the human machine?

319. How is energy expended? Its value? What of the internal
work? How is heat lost?

other tissues—appears as heat before it leaves the body. The body loses heat by *conduction*, removed directly by solids, fluids, or gases in contact with the body-surfaces, by *radiation*, thrown off into the surrounding atmosphere, after the manner of rays, and by *heating* the egesta,—the outgoing air, gases, water, and excrement.

320. HEAT-PRODUCTION.—The larger part of the heat is due to the oxidation of carbon in the system. The chief sources of heat-production are seated in the muscles and the abdominal viscera, especially the liver, which contains nearly one-fourth of the blood. The blood of the hepatic veins in a dog was the warmest in the body (40.73° C.), while that of the right heart was 37.7° C. Wherever changes in protoplasm are taking place,—in the brain, the nerve-centres, the glands, the heart-muscle, the general muscular system,—heat is generating. The heat is *lost* in about the following proportions (Helmholtz), by the various channels :

In warming excrement and urine, 2.6 per cent. ;

In warming expired air, 5.2 per cent. ;

In evaporation of water of respiration, 14.7 per cent. ;

In conduction and radiation and evaporation by the skin, 77.5 per cent.

321. BODY-HEAT.—In ordinary health, the temperature of man, as registered by a thermometer placed in the axilla, varies between 36.25° and 37.5° C. (97.25° and 99.5° F.). There is a diurnal variation of temperature, the maximum occurring from 9 A.M. to 6 P.M. The variation produced

by the taking of food depends on the nature and the temperature of the food. Alcohol, as its earlier effect, appears to produce a fall of temperature. Exercise and ordinary variations of external temperature cause very slight changes. The temperature of the inhabitants of the tropics is practically the same as that of those living in Arctic regions. Prolonged study and other mental efforts cause a slight depression. Fasting lowers the temperature, and in starvation the fall in temperature becomes very rapid in the last few days of life. The thermometer enables the physician to determine whether or not *fever* is present, and, at times, the nature of the fever. The fever temperature ranges from 37.8° to 41.2° C. (100° to 106° F.). A temperature holding for hours above 41.6° C. (107° F.) is almost a certain forerunner of a fatal issue. In a case of cerebral rheumatism having a temperature of 43.4° C. (110° F.), the patient survived. Bernard places the lethal body-temperature of a mammal at 45° C. (114.8° F.). In extreme collapse, followed by recovery, the temperature rarely falls below 33° C. (92° F.).

322. **REGULATION OF BODY-HEAT.**—The great heat-regulator is the skin (45). The blood circulating through the skin is cooled by heat-loss, due partly to the radiation and conduction from the skin, but much more to the evaporation of the water of perspiration. The larger the amount of blood flowing through the skin-vessels, the greater will be the heat-loss, and, as the amount of blood in the heat-producing areas (the muscles and the abdominal viscera) is at the same time in like degree lessened (320), less heat will be produced; hence a fall of temperature will result. The

---

322. How does the skin largely regulate the body-temperature? What controls the calibre of the arteries? The conditions produced in cold weather? In warm weather? What may be a controlling factor?

calibre of the vascular tubes of the heat-production and heat-loss areas is under vaso-motor influence (137). In cold weather this influence keeps the skin white, anæmic, and cold, in order to retain the bulk of the blood in the heat-production areas; in warm weather, when the heat-production and heat-reception (from influences of the external temperature) elevate the internal temperature, this influence contracts the internal vascular apparatus, enlarges the cutaneous blood-vessels, and the mass of the blood flows to the skin; the latter becomes high-colored and glowing, and the activity of the perspiratory glands is encouraged, followed by great heat-loss. The influence of an increase or decrease of heat-production through tissue-changes in its action on heat-regulation has not yet been well determined. There may, however, be a tissue-change-controlling mechanism, quite comparable to the vaso-motor mechanism, but it has not as yet been well established.

323. In *cold climates* man uses padded cotton garments, many garments (having air-layers between each garment), fine-meshed woollens, and skins, to retain the body-heat and to retard heat-loss (50). In *hot regions* he diminishes heat-production by restricting his proteid diet, and encourages heat-loss by the use of larger amounts of liquid or fruit foods and the wearing of gauzy garments. In FEVER we endeavor to reduce heat-production by encouraging the action of the skin (sweating emetics); by diminishing tissue-change (alcohol, morphia, quinine, salicylic acid); by diminishing the heart's action (digitalis, aconite, veratria); and at the same time to encourage heat-loss by tepid bathing, alcohol- and water-sponging, application of ice, internally

---

323. What is a common-sense management in cold climes? In hot climes? The scientific management in fevers?

and externally, cold-sheet-pack, cold baths, etc., as well as the internal administration of perspiration-exciting drugs.

324. EXCRETION.—The purpose of excretion is to rid the body of the compounds which are formed in the actions of living tissues. These compounds are given to the blood during its movements through the capillary areas (143). They are, for the most part, of no further use to the living economy. Most of them are injurious to healthy life, and, if not rapidly removed, produce evil, if not fatal, results. These materials are removed from the blood by the epithelia of certain organs and tissues. Some of them are eliminated at once, like carbonic acid and water, from the lungs and the skin; others are kept in sacs for a time, to be later passed out, like the urea and excrement.

325. WASTE PRODUCTS.—Broadly speaking, the waste products of the animal economy are urea, carbonic acid, salts, water, and excrement.

326. The total daily excretion of *carbonic acid* in an average man was determined by Pettenkofer and Voit to be 800 grammes, or 406 litres, containing 218.1 grammes (3365.8 grains) of carbon and 581.9 grammes (8980 grains) of oxygen. The oxygen consumed during the determination was about 700 grammes (10,802 grains). Of these exertions, only 10 grammes (154.3 grains) were passed out by the skin. The quantity of oxygen consumed, and that of carbonic acid given out, vary widely, the former ranging from 680 to 1285 grammes, and the latter from 594 to 1072 grammes.

327. The total daily average excretion of *urea*, as determined by Parkes, was 33.18 grammes (512 grains). The daily excretion of urea on an exclusively animal diet was found to be 53.14 grammes (820 grains); on a mixed diet, 32.40 grammes (500 grains); on a vegetable diet, 22.48 grammes (347 grains); and on a completely non-nitrogenous diet, 15.35 grammes (237 grains). The urea is

---

324. What is the function of excretion? Influence of waste matters in the system? How are they removed?

325. Name the chief waste products.

formed largely from the food. The amount derived from the tissues is less than half the ordinary daily amount excreted. The nitrogenous waste of the body is almost entirely excreted by the kidneys, traces only ordinarily escaping by the lungs and the skin.

328. The total daily average excretion of *salts* in the urine, as determined by Parkes, is 37 grammes (570 grains). Of 100 parts of these salts, 53 parts are sulphates, 24 phosphates, 23 chlorides, and the rest salts of the organic acids. The chief base is soda, then potassa, ammonia, magnesia, lime, and traces of iron and silica. Most of these salts are derived directly from the materials of the food, only a small portion arising in the tissue-changes of the twenty-four hours. By the *skin*, a small amount of chloride of sodium, and traces of other inorganic salts, are eliminated. By the *rectum*, considerable amounts of salts are passed out.

329. The *water* eliminated from the body varies largely within the limits of health. The average daily amount appearing in the *urine* is 1500 grammes (53 ounces); exhaled from the *skin*, about 742 grammes (30 ounces); and lost in respiration, 370.7 grammes (15 ounces).

330. The *excrement* contains the indigestible and undigested constituents of the food, shreds of elastic tissue, cellulose from vegetable food and areolar tissue from animal food, fragments of muscle-fibre, fat-cells, and starch-grains. The amounts of these vary with the nature and the quantity of the food. From the digestive canal and glands the excrement receives mucus, fatty acids, a peculiar ferment, also *excretin* (a crystalline body containing sulphur), and salts, especially of magnesia.

331. SUMMARY.—The average man receives daily *foods* estimated at 1,000,000 metre-kilogrammes:

Proteids in flesh, cheese, beans, etc.

Fats in butter, lard, oils, etc.

Carbo-hydrates in starches, sugars, fruits, etc.

Salts in normal foods and condiments.

Free oxygen *via* lungs and skin.

Water in foods and drinks.

---

331. Give the summary of man's daily food. What is evolved? What is excreted? From whence excreted?

Evolution of heat and force:

Heat estimated at 850,000 metre-kilogrammes.

Force estimated at 150,000 metre-kilogrammes.

Average excretions:

Carbonic acid *via* lungs, skin, and alimentary canal.

Urea *via* kidneys and skin.

Water *via* kidneys, lungs, and skin.

Waste *via* rectum and skin.

Of the entire *excreta*, 32 per cent. pass off by the breath; 17 per cent. by the skin; 46.5 per cent. by the kidneys; 4.5 per cent. by the alimentary canal.

332. THIRST is a sensation referred to the tongue and palate. It is dependent on a general state of the system, as it is readily distinguished from dryness of the mouth. This general state of the system is caused by a deficiency of water in the blood. Thirst is soonest and most successfully quenched by water, and especially by ice-water in small quantities at frequent intervals. The sensations of APPETITE and HUNGER seem to be dependent upon a general condition of the system. The former is agreeable, the latter painful. They are both referred to the stomach, but the presence or absence of food in the stomach does not wholly account for the sensation, since it is relieved by nutrient materials injected into the blood or the rectum. Hunger is not so readily relieved as thirst, but its demands can be more comfortably deferred than those of thirst. In healthy organism, appetite and hunger are the sensations which impel man to seek food, and, in general, they are safe guides as to the amount of food needed by the healthy system.

332. Upon what does thirst depend? How best satisfied? Speak of the sensations of appetite and hunger. To what referred? How satisfied? Their influence?

333. Dietetics comprises the rules to be followed for preventing, relieving, or curing disease by means of food. Tendencies for health or for disease, tendencies for evil or for good, can be modified by diet. The bear at Giessen was gentle when fed on bread, but a few days' diet of flesh made him savage and dangerous. The boys in the reformatory institutions of France were found to be improved physically, mentally, and morally by the more liberal diet secured them by M. Metz. The energy of the American over the Asiatic workman is largely due to his more liberal diet. The diseases chargeable to food form the most numerous order arising from a single class of causes. Hygiene has been considered by some writers to be almost a branch of dietetics.

334. Excess of Food.—If food is taken in too large quantities, the excess is not digested, and cannot be absorbed. It remains in the warm, moist, intestinal canal, undergoes chemical changes, putrefies, and forms large quantities of gases. As a result, irritation, pain, slight fever, vomiting, or diarrhœa may result. If the habit of over-eating is continued in moderation for long periods, dyspepsia and constipation ensue. Excess of proteid foods taken consecutively leads to fulness and enlargement of the liver, to plethora of the system, to imperfect oxidation of food and tissue-elements, as shown in gout and certain kidney diseases. Excess of the starches tends to acidity and flatulence, and of the sugars and fats, joined with a deficiency of exercise, to a weakening of the muscular system. Excess

---

333. What is understood by dietetics? What is the influence of food on bears? On boys? On laborers? On health?

334. What is the effect of an undigested excess? Of continued over-eating? Of excess of proteids? Of starches? Of sugars and fats?

may consist in taking too great a quantity at one time, in taking too large an amount in twenty-four hours, or in the too frequent taking of food.

335. DEFICIENCY OF FOOD.—If the proteids be completely withdrawn from the diet of a healthy man, after a few days a great loss of muscular strength, often mental weakness and want of decision, some feverishness, and indigestion are noticed. This is succeeded by a falling off in the quality of the blood, and by general prostration. If the withdrawal of proteids be only partial, there is a lessening of physical and mental activity, followed by a weakened condition of the system and a tendency to malarial affections, typhoid fever, and pneumonitis. The deprivation of both fat and starch produces illness in a few days. Under a diet containing no starch, but having fat in moderate quantities, the condition is sustained for a long time. The absence of all fat in food is not well borne. It has not yet been proved that starches can take the place of fat in nutrition. A deficiency of mineral ingredients produces marked results, as in rickets and bone-softening.

336. WANT OF FOOD.—Shipwrecks and famines have afforded numerous examples of the complete deprivation of food, with its terrible history of pain over the region of the stomach, thirst, weakness of mind and body, sinking, intense debility, loss of voice, delirium, convulsions, and death. It is generally supposed that a healthy person, deprived of both solid and liquid food, would not live longer than ten days.

---

335. What is the effect of withdrawing proteids from the diet? Of partial proteid deficiency? Of starch deficiency? Of fat deficiency? Of mineral deficiency? Can starches replace fats?

336. What are the symptoms induced by total want of food? How long can life be thus sustained?

ENDURANCE.—On March 22, 1880, Master Soma, aged fourteen years, with two companions, aged fifteen and seventeen respectively, left Tsuishicari, Yezo, to walk to Sapporo, a distance of about twelve miles. Before setting out, they partook of a lunch of cold rice, pickled radish, and tea. Each took in his belt about two handfuls of rice, and Soma, in addition, enough ginger-relish for two meals for one person. That afternoon they lost the trail in a snow-storm, and were soon unable to proceed. Before going to sleep, they ate all the rice, most of the ginger, and some snow. They were lightly clad in cotton or bark tunics and leggings, wore open straw sandals, and had half a light blanket each. They had no materials to make a fire. That night the temperature, as registered at Sapporo, was 24° F. The next morning they could not walk, their extremities having been frozen. Soma states that the eldest died on the sixth day and the other on the seventh day. During the period of exposure there was much snow, sleet, and winter rain, considerable wind, and very little clear sky during the day. Guided by the crows, the soldiers found Soma on April 19, twenty-eight days from the time he left Tsuishicari.

He was brought to the Kaitakushi Hospital, at Sapporo, at 5 P.M. of that day, and came under my charge. He could not speak; movements of the chest were scarcely to be detected; no pulse at the wrist; impulse of the heart very feeble, and valve-sounds indistinct. The brain-torpor was profound. The body was excessively emaciated, the abdomen retracted, and the eyes deeply sunken in the orbits. There was no reflex action from the hands. The lower extremities were black and dead to the middle of the legs. On the 22d, he was able to articulate a few indistinct sounds. After the first ten days he made steady progress towards health, and later both stumps were amputated in the middle third of the legs. At the present writing (March, 1884), the young man is living at Kotoni, and enjoying good health.

337. AMOUNT OF FOOD.—The diet of the child to the ninth or tenth year of age should be mainly milk, well-cooked oat-meal, decorticated wheat, simple puddings, and, occasionally, small amounts of roasted or boiled meats (231). The proportion of food required by a growing child is much greater per pound weight than is demanded by an adult (three times as much of carbonaceous and six times as much of nitrogenous), for the child has to form tissues and to build up its structures.

338. After the tenth year, children may partake of the usual food of the family, tea, coffee, and sharp condiments excepted. At this time it will require half as much in quantity as an adult woman, and at fourteen years, quite

337. What is the best diet for a child?

338. What of the diet after the tenth year? For youth and for women? For a man? What proportions?

as much. In general, women require one-tenth less food than in-door workmen, and from one-fourth to one-third less than out-door workmen. A healthy, vigorous man consumes about nine hundred and seven grammes (two pounds) of dry solid matter daily, and of water (free and combined) 2494.8 grammes ($5\frac{1}{2}$ pounds or pints). The relation of the carbonaceous (starches, sugars, fats) to the proteid (flesh, eggs, vegetable cascin, etc.) is about 6 or $6\frac{1}{2}$ to 1 in a working diet. The best proportion for the common wants of the adult human system is about 9 of fat, 22 of proteids, and 69 of starches and sugars. Experience shows that different races, by various combinations, have sought such an average dietary.

The daily ration of the United States soldier, given below, is the most generous army ration in the world:

Bread or flour (20 ounces common meal)	22 ounces.
Fresh or salt beef (or pork or bacon, 12 ounces). . . .	20 "
Potatoes (three times per week)	16 "
Rice	1.6 "
Coffee (or tea, 0.24 ounce)	1.6 "
Sugar	2.4 "
Beans	.64 gill.
Vinegar	.32 "
Salt	.16 "
Molasses, pepper, etc.	

CHAPTER XI.

THE NERVOUS SYSTEM.

Remove the skin from the head and neck of the animal, as of a dog, cat, rat, or rabbit. Cut out and remove the lower jaw and its appendages. If possible, allow the parts to become thoroughly frozen. With a cold saw, in the median line saw vertically between the nostrils, through the bones of the face, of the skull, and vertebræ as far as the fifth or sixth cervical vertebra. At this part saw in at right angles and remove one-half. Remove all splinters, loose tissue, etc. Such a section will expose the corresponding parts, as in Fig. 38. The parts thus brought into view are the *scalp*, or the movable, hairy portions over the vertex; the *periosteum* of the cranial bones; the *cranial bones*, exhibiting in places two layers of compact bone, with an intermediate cancellated layer; lining the interior of the cranial vault, a hard, firm, resisting membrane, the *dura mater*, which dips down from the vertex near the median line, forming a divisional fold between the right and the left brain, the *falx*, and, projecting from the sides, forms a partition between the great and the little brain, the *tentorium*. Beneath the free edge of the falx is seen the cut surface of a band of white nerve-matter connecting the right with the left brain, the *corpus callosum*. Beneath the corpus callosum will be seen a right and a left depression, the *lateral ventricles*.

With the handle of the scalpel loosen the cranial contents of one side from its case. Turn it out gradually, severing, as they present, the nerves leading to the nose, eye, etc., near the base, the tentorium, the posterior cranial and the spinal nerves. The larger mass, the *cerebrum*, is somewhat triangular, and presents on its gray surface a number of *convolutions*, with depressions, called *sulci*, and beneath a number of white, projecting fibres, the *cranial nerves*. Behind the larger brain, separated from it by a deep depression, is a smaller mass, the *cerebellum*, whose cut surface presents a tree-like appearance, in gray material. Its outer surface is gray, like that of the cerebrum, but is arranged in more or less parallel ridges. Connecting the cerebrum and cerebellum and the medulla is a mass of nerve-substance, the *pons*, or "bridge." Leading back from this is the *spinal cord*, the enlargement of which, near the cerebellum and lying within the skull, is called the *medulla oblongata*. Leading from the inferior aspect of the cerebrum, pons, and medulla are seen numerous fibres, the *cranial nerves*, and from the cord a pair of nerves for each intervertebral space, the *spinal nerves*.

The outer surface of the brain is smooth and moist. Dipping down into all the sulci will be seen a web-like membrane, abundantly provided with blood-vessels, the *pia mater*. The smooth, firm membrane lying in the cranium is the *dura mater*.

In the frozen brain make a vertical incision with a sharp, thin-bladed knife parallel to the median surface, about half an inch from the falx border. This section shows that the convolutions and ridges are made up of gray nerve-matter, in the form of a much-puckered layer; that the bulk of the cerebrum and cerebellum is composed of white

190

Fig. 72.

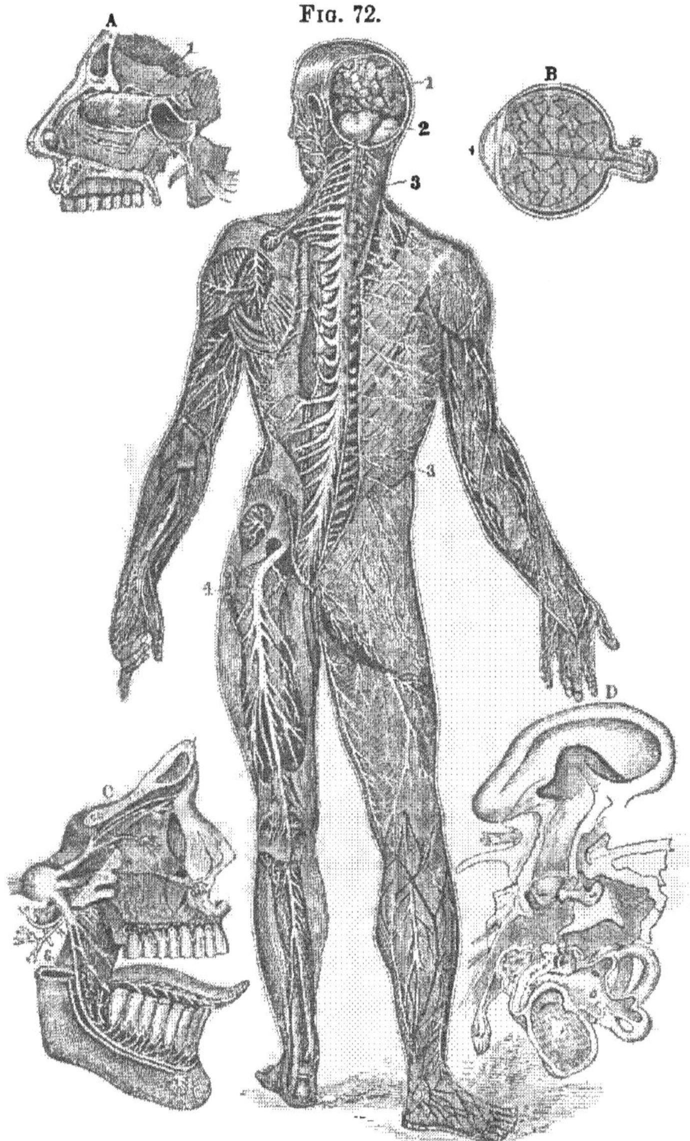

Fig. 72. A Representation of the Brain, Spinal Cord, and Spinal Nerves.—
1, The cerebrum. 2, The cerebellum. 3, 3, Spinal cord. 4, The sciatic nerve.

A. Apparatus of Smell.—1, 2, Olfactory nerve. B. Apparatus of Vision.—15, Optic
nerve. C. Distribution of the Trigeminal Nerve.—6, Nerve of taste. D. Apparatus
of Hearing.

matter; that at the base of the brain are a number of gray *ganglionic* masses (optic thalami, corpora striata, corpora quadrigemina, etc.); that the *pons* is in connection with the cerebrum, cerebellum, and, through the medulla, with the cord; that in the medulla there are gray masses; and that the cord has a gray central and a white outer layer. If a cross-section of the cord is made, a gray centre, with projecting horns and an upper and lower groove in the white matter, is presented. On the anterior under side of the cerebrum is seen projecting forward a small, elongated, globular mass, the *olfactory lobe* of that side. Just back of it are seen two round, white cords, commencing to cross each other, the *commissure of the optic tracts.*

The skull is seen to be arched above, the under side of the arch having a uniform surface; below, it presents depressions, projections, and numerous openings. The large opening on the posterior part of the skull affords passage for the cord and blood-vessels, and is called the *occipital foramen.* The other openings serve for the entrance of arteries and outlets for the cranial nerves and the veins. In animals, at birth, the bones of the cranial arch are frequently cartilaginous, but those at the base are always *ossified* at this stage of development.

Remove the skin from the neck and thorax and from the fore-limb of the opposite side from which half the skull was removed. Place the animal on its back. Cut the *pectoral muscles* (the muscles which hold the limb to the trunk) close to their insertion in the humerus, and allow the limb to fall from the trunk. Remove the loose cellular tissue between the limb and the neck-back region, and the many white cords of the *brachial nerve plexus* will be exposed. Carefully remove all loose areolar and muscular tissue. It is advisable to preserve the arteries in position. Trace the *nerves* to the inter-vertebral places of exit. Number the vertebræ from the head. By the removal of the cellular tissue, the dissecting out of some and the cutting of other muscles, the nerve and the neighboring arteries can be traced in their distribution down the limb. Observe that the nerve-trunks are placed on the inner side of the limb, that they lie between muscles and are deeply embedded in areolar tissue, and that they are distributed to all tissues of the limbs, including the membranes of the joints. In the neck dissect out the *pneumogastric trunk.* Trace its branches to the different parts of the respiratory tract, to the heart, and to the stomach.

Dissection of the remainder of the animal:

Open the *thorax,* as directed in Chapter V.

Dissect out and trace the branches of the arch of the *aorta.*

Examine the *heart.* (See paragraph 89.)

Dissect the respiratory tract, as directed in Chapter VI.

Dissect the *abdominal* and *pelvic* organs, as directed in Chapter VIII.

Dissect the motor apparatus, as directed in Chapter XIV.

Hardening of the Brain.—Pass 60 per cent. alcohol through the vessels of the brain, and irrigate the ventricles with the same. Place the mass in 55 per cent. alcohol, and gradually increase the strength up to 95 per cent. Thus hardened, it can be better handled and more successfully dissected. Small cubes of different parts of the brain and sections of the cord may be placed in alcohol No. 1, to prepare for microscopic work. Make a number of transverse sections of the hardened cervical spinal cord. Endeavor to secure sections passing through the nerve-roots; stain with hæmatoxylon and clear with carbolic acid. Note the anterior and posterior fissures; the pia mater of the cord; the anterior and posterior roots; the anterior, posterior, and lateral columns of white matter; the gray matter, with its horns; the central canal; the commissures, etc. Study the fibres in hardened specimens, and the cells and fibres in teased fresh specimens.

The Head.

339. The framework of the head is made up of twenty-two bones, of which eight enter into the formation of the *skull*, or brain-case, and fourteen into that of the *face*. (Table of bones, Chapter III.)

FIG. 73.

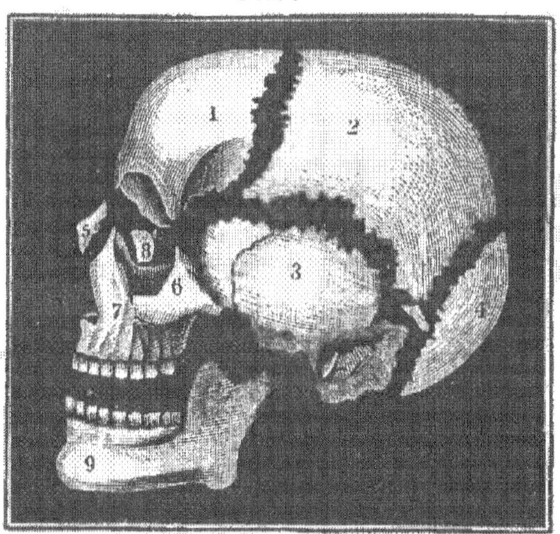

FIG. 73. BONES OF THE HEAD.—1, Frontal bone. 2, Parietal bone. 3, Temporal bone. 4, Occipital bone. 5, Nasal bone. 6, Malar bone. 7, Upper Jaw. 8, Os unguis. 9, Lower Jaw (maxilla).

The bones of the *face* are irregular in form, and, with the exception of the lower jaw, are closely and firmly joined to one another and to the adjacent bones of the skull. Beneath the frontal bone are the two deep quadrangular cavities, called the *orbits*, which contain the eyeballs, the tear-apparatus, and the protective organs of the eyes; in

339. What of the facial bones? Of the orbits and their contents? Of the nasal region? What are located in other depressions?

the middle of the face, projecting upward between the inner walls of the orbits, are the two deep *narrow channels* containing the organs of smell, and in the lower part of the same, the broad nasal *passages.* The nasal passages (429) are separated from the cavity of the *mouth* by the hard palate. In the depressions and small cavities of the face are located glands, nerves, and blood-vessels.

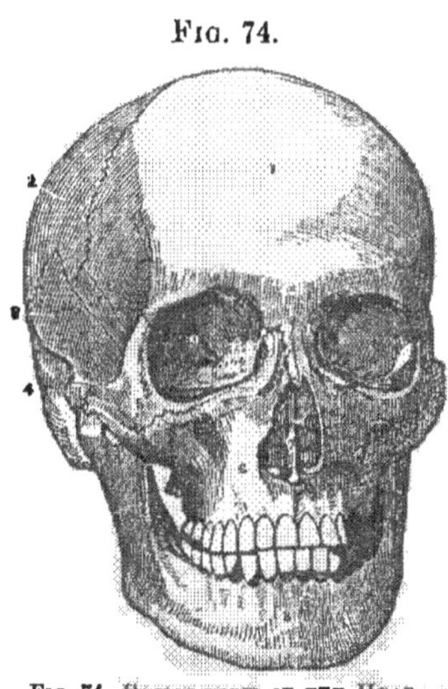

Fig. 74.

Fig. 74. FACIAL VIEW OF THE HEAD.— 1, 2, 3, The bones of the skull. 4, The zygomatic process of the temporal bone. 5, The malar (cheek) bone. 6, The superior maxillary bone (upper jaw). 7, The vomer, that separates the cavities of the nose. 8, The inferior maxillary bone (lower jaw). 9, The cavity for the eye. 10, The teeth.

340. The eight bones of the adult *skull* are firmly joined together. The bones forming the *vault* of the skull (the *frontal,* the two *parietals,* and the *occipital*) are united together by the serrated form of union called the *suture* (Fig. 119). The bones of the vault are made up of an outer layer of tough, resisting bone, an intermediate layer of cancellated bone, and an internal layer of brittle bone. The inner surface of the vault is smooth, and shows channelled places for the passage of blood-vessels. The bones of the *base* of the skull (*occipital, sphenoid, frontal, temporal,* and *ethmoid*) are crowded firmly in apposition. In the interior, the base has many elevations and depressions and numerous holes.

---

340. How many bones in the skull? What of the vault? Of sutures? Of bony plates? Of the base? Of the openings?

The former correspond to the form of the brain, and the latter serve for the passage of nerves and blood-vessels. The skull contains and protects the *brain*, its nerves and membranes.

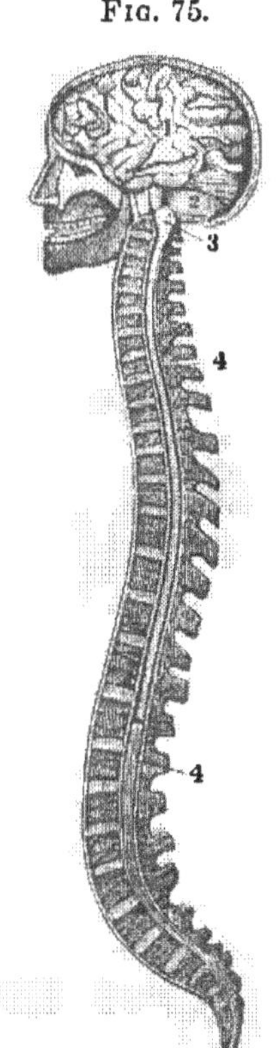

Fig. 75.

341. *In the arrangement of the skull* for the protection of the brain, the oval form (the form best adapted to resist pressure equally applied on all sides); the thickened base, where the most important part of the brain lies; the strong and narrow prominences, both in front and back, where most exposed to violence; the tough and hard plates, to resist the penetration of sharp substances; the intervening spongy layer, to diminish vibrations; the separate bones and the serrated unions of the external plates, also to lessen shocks; the simple contact of plane edges in the internal vitreous plate, where zigzag edges would be easily broken; the projections, depressions, and apertures for the safe passage of nerves and blood-vessels,—all combine to accomplish the one object, *protection*.

342. The Vertebral Column (149) is made up of a series of bones, called *vertebræ*. Each vertebra consists of a solid part (*body*), of an open ring (*foramen*), and of three major projections (*processes*), the one pointing backward being called the *spinous process*, and the two lateral ones, *transverse processes*. There are twenty-four movable vertebræ,—seven cervical, twelve dorsal, and five lumbar. The sacrum, in the embryonic stage, is made up of five vertebræ, and the coccyx of four (247). Between the movable vertebræ disks of fibro-cartilage are interposed. The vertebræ are all bound together by bands of tissue, called *ligaments* (509).

Fig. 75. A Section of the Brain and Spinal Column. —1, The cerebrum. 2, The cerebellum. 3, The medulla oblongata. 4, 4, The spinal cord in its canal.

343. The Spinal Canal is formed, in the natural state,

by the succession of these rings of bone. It extends from the back part of the base of the skull nearly to the lower end of the vertebral column. The cranial cavity and the spinal canal communicate through the *occipital foramen.* This canal contains the *spinal cord* (364), its membranes and vessels. Its intervertebral openings give exit to thirty-one pairs of nerves.

FIG. 76.   FIG. 77.

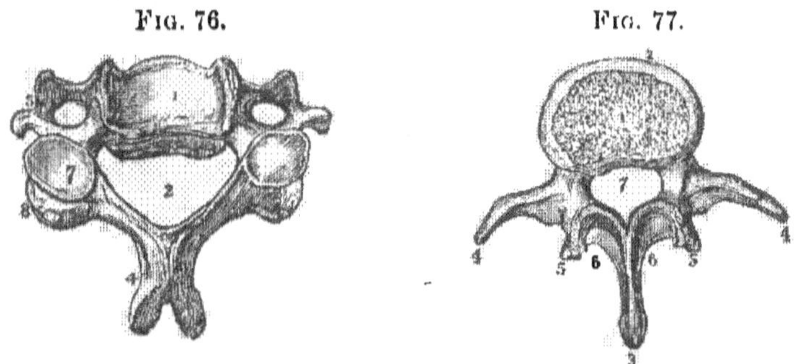

FIG. 76. A VERTEBRA OF THE NECK.—1, The body. 2, The foramen. 4, The spinous process, cleft at its extremity. 5, The transverse process. 7, The inferior articulating process. 8, The superior articulating process.

FIG. 77. A LUMBAR VERTEBRA.—1, The cartilaginous substance that connects the bodies of the vertebræ. 2, The body. 3, The spinous process. 4, 4, The transverse processes. 5, 5, The articulating processes. 7, The foramen.

THE NERVOUS SYSTEM.

344. This system in man includes the *cerebro-spinal system* and the *sympathetic system.* The former is composed of the brain and spinal cord and the nerves leading from them to the skin, muscles, and organs of the body. The sympathetic system is made up of ganglia, connecting fibres, and nerves. Its nerves are distributed to the vis-

---

348. What is the extent of the spinal canal? What is found in the canal?

344. What does the nervous system include? What is embraced in the former? In the latter? To what are the nerves of the latter distributed?

cera and to the vascular system, and also are in connection with the cerebro-spinal system.

345. NERVE-FIBRES AND NERVE-CENTRES. — The nerves are made up of white *nerve-fibres* (78), bound together by traces of delicate areolar tissue. The nerve-centres (ganglia) are composed of gray *nerve-* or ganglionic cells (80) and white nerve-fibres.

346. The FUNCTIONS OF THE NERVOUS SYSTEM are— (1) *sensation,* common, as of the skin, and special, as of the eye, the ear, etc. ; (2) the regulation of all the *motions* of the animal body ; (3) the manifestation through its centres of *thought, will, intelligence,* and the *faculty of language ;* (4) the exercise of a controlling influence over the *nutritive, vascular,* and other mechanisms, the proper working of which is essential to the continuance of life.

347. The function of the nervous system is innervation. It receives impressions and transmits impulses. Its centres receive, record, and act upon impulses, and originate new impulses. The reception, origination, and transmission of nervous impulses are necessary for the proper maintenance of life and continuance of the functions of the various organs. Through the action of the end-organs of the nerves, of the nerve-fibres, and of the great centres, the mind of man is made conscious of external phenomena and of his relation thereto. Through the action of centres in the brain, he is made conscious of himself and of his own mental actions.

348. The nerves only transmit impulses. All other nerve-tissue functions are performed by the cells of the centres (83). If a ray of colored light enters the eye, the

---

345. Of what are nerve-fibres composed? Nerve-centres?

346. What are the functions of the nervous system?

347. Give a function of the nervous system. Nervous impulses.

348. What do the fibres do? The cells? How does sensation occur? How motion? How brain-action?

end-organ of the nerve of sight (retina) receives a peculiar impression, an impulse is transmitted to the receiving centre in the brain, and the activity becomes manifest as a state of consciousness,—a *sensation*.   A brain-centre may originate an impulse, which, being sent to a certain muscle, manifests its activity as *motion*.   A brain-centre may originate an impulse, which, being transmitted to another centre, manifests its activity as an *idea*, an *emotion*, or a mental *sensation*.

349. IMPULSES.—The power of initiating vital impulses, independent of any immediate disturbing event or stimulus from without, is one of the fundamental properties of protoplasm (9).   The power of initiating nervous impulses is a distinctive function of the ganglionic nerve-cells (84).   The impulse is known by its action.   Its nature appears to be that of an explosive discharge.   The building up, the storage, and the setting free of the impulse appear to demand the use of much energy.   The continued setting free of the explosive is followed by a sensation of weariness, a desire for a period of rest and recuperation.   This is well seen in the deep sleep following the rapid and exhausting impulse-discharges of an epileptic attack.

THE CEREBRO-SPINAL SYSTEM.

350. The entire BRAIN, or *Encephalon*, is chiefly made up of two parts,—an anterior upper part, called the *cerebrum*, and a smaller part, called the *cerebellum*, or little brain.   Besides these, there are the connecting parts, called the *peduncles*, the *pons*, and the *medulla*.   They are all seated within the skull.

351. The entire human brain weighs, on an average, in the adult female, 1262 grammes (44½ ounces), and in the adult male, 1410.36 grammes (49¾ ounces).   In extreme cases, the brain has attained

---

350. Of what is the brain composed?   Where situated?   What connecting parts?

the weight of 2012 grammes (74.8 ounces). In an idiot boy it weighed as low as 241 grammes (8¼ ounces), and in a female idiot forty-two years of age, 283.5 grammes (10 ounces). The maximum average in the European is observed between the thirtieth and fortieth years. In a European white, a brain must weigh at least 975 grammes (34.39 ounces) in the female, and 1133 grammes (39.96 ounces) in the male, in order to be capable of performing its functions. Professor Owen found the weight of the brain of a gorilla to be 425 grammes (15 ounces). In a healthy body the average proportion to the entire weight is as 1 to 41.

WEIGHT OF THE BRAIN IN SOME EMINENT MEN.

Name.	Age.	Profession.	Weight of Brain. Grammes.	Ounces.
Turgeneff	65	Author.	2012.00	(74.83)
Cuvier	63	Naturalist.	1829.96	(64.54)
Byron	36	Poet.	1807.00	(63.73)
Lejeune Dirichlet	54	Mathematician.	1520.00	(53.61)
Agassiz	66	Naturalist.	1513.97	(53.40)
Fuchs	52	Pathologist.	1490.00	(52.87)
Gauss	78	Mathematician.	1492.00	(52.62)
Dupuytren	58	Surgeon.	1436.00	(50.65)
Hermann	51	Philologist,	1358.00	(47.90)
Haussmann	77	Mineralogist.	1226.00	(43.24)

The brain increases, other things remaining the same, in proportion to the vascular activity of which it is the seat. This is the reason that the brains of certain criminals and lunatics have been found so large. In most cases, the physiological activity, of which intelligence is the result, has the most influence on brain-development.

352. The CEREBRUM consists of two lateral hemispheres united by a thick, broad band of white nervous tissue (*corpus callosum*). They are sustained below by stalks of nervous substance, called *peduncles*. The whole of its free surface is composed of a layer of gray nervous matter. This layer, about one-fifth of an inch in thickness, is moulded into numerous tortuous and complicated elevations, called *convolutions*. This layer is made up of nerve-cells (80), with numerous fine white fibres. The bulk of

---

352. Describe the cerebrum. The convolutions.

the cerebrum is composed of white nerve-fibres, which fibres ultimately connect with the fibres in the gray layer.

353. Within the hemispheres and below the corpus callosum are certain cavities, called *ventricles.* By the old anatomists these were held to be the residence of the "animal spirits." Lying in front

Fig 78.

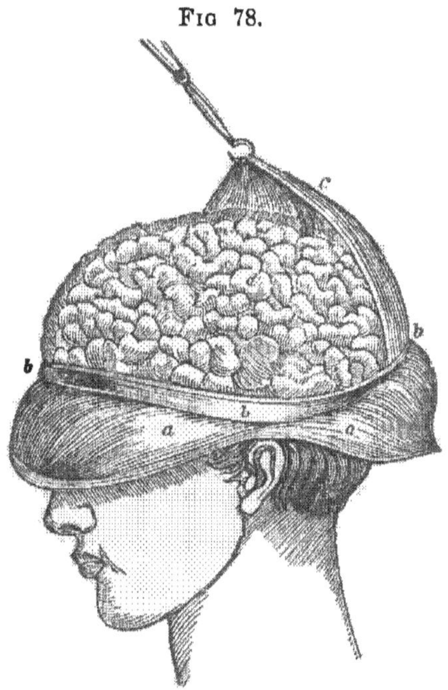

Fig. 78 REPRESENTS A CONVOLUTED CEREBRAL HEMISPHERE.—*a, a,* The scalp turned down. *b, b, b,* The cut edge of the bones of the skull. *c,* The external strong membrane of the brain (dura mater), suspended by a hook. *d,* The left hemisphere of the brain.

of the peduncles, but projecting into the lateral ventricles, are two masses of gray matter, the *corpora striata* in front and the *optic thalami* behind. Resting on the back part of the peduncles are four small eminences, called the *corpora quadrigemina* (Fig. 80, 1, Fig. 81, 28). On the under side of the front lobe of the cerebrum are seen two small, ovoid masses of gray matter, the *olfactory lobes.*

354. The initiative acts of thought pass through the gray substance; consequently the greater the amount of gray substance, and of surface upon which it can be developed in a continuous layer,

the more power the truly intellectual phenomena acquire. Hence the gray surface is folded and contorted so as to increase its extent. The arrangement of the swellings is definite. The fundamental convolutions are constant throughout the human species; the secondary parts, or folds, exhibit variations. The brain of the fœtus

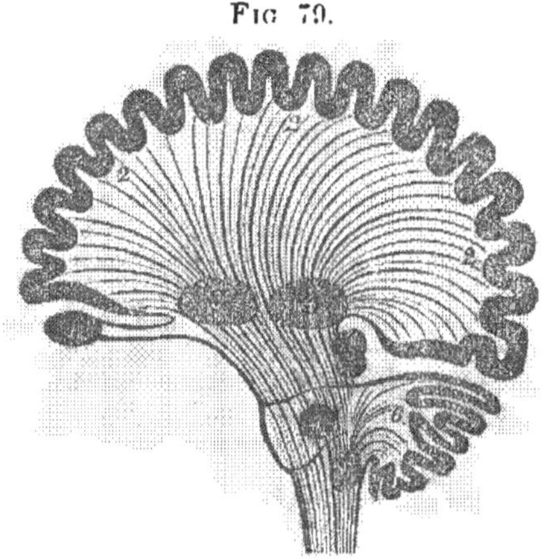

FIG. 79.

FIG. 79. DIAGRAM OF HUMAN BRAIN, IN VERTICAL SECTION, showing the situation of the different ganglia and the course of the fibres.—1, Olfactory ganglion. 2, Hemisphere. 3, Corpus striatum. 4, Optic thalamus. 5, Tubercula quadrigemina. 6, Cerebellum. 7, Ganglion of tuber annulare. 8, Ganglion of medulla oblongata.

at the beginning is smooth ; at the seventh month the convolutions are simple ; at birth the folds are simple ; later, the complicated folds are rounded out. The convolutions become enlarged and more complex as age advances, in proportion to the activity of the organ. Large and simple convolutions are a sign of idiocy ; small convolutions, with numerous foldings, are a sign of intellectual capacity.

FUNCTIONS OF THE SUPERIOR PARTS OF THE BRAIN.

355. If the cerebral lobes be removed from a frog, he seems to possess no *volition*. If his flanks be now gently stroked, he will croak, and the croaks will follow regularly

355. What effect has the removal of the cerebral lobes on a frog ? What occurs when the lobes are intact ? What is volition ?

after each stroke.   He can swim, can keep his balance on
a tilted board, will avoid places which are dimly lighted,
can pass from the water to a floating stick, can eat, drink,

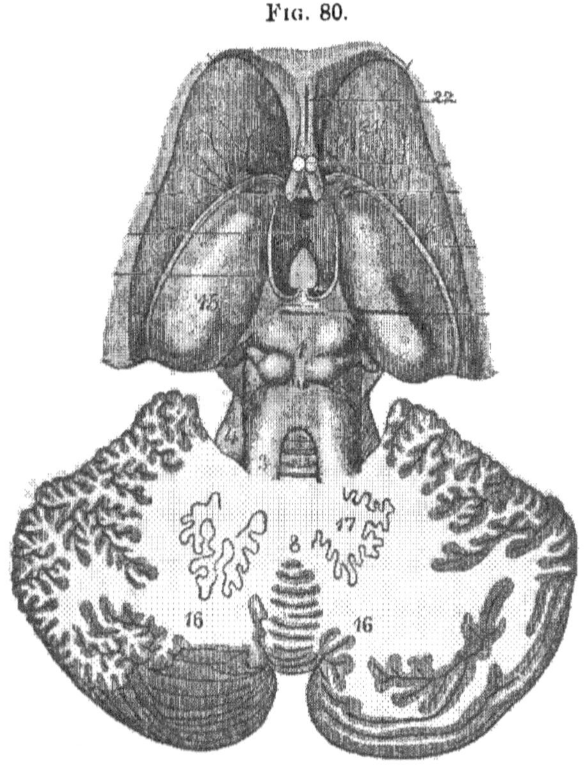

Fig. 80.

Fig. 80 (*Leidy*). CORPUS CALLOSUM REMOVED AND CEREBELLUM CUT OPEN IN MEDIAN
LINE.—1, Quadrigeminal body. 3, Superior peduncle of the cerebellum. 4, Superior
portion of the middle peduncle. 8, The cerebellum. 15, Thalamus. 16, Hemispheres
of the cerebellum. 17, Dentated body. 21, Corpus striatum. 22, Fifth ventricle between
the layers of the pellucid septum.

and sleep well; but he does not move unless stimulated
from without.   If the flanks of a normal frog be stroked,
he may or he may not croak.   His actions cannot be predi-
cated.   He has cerebral lobes.   He possesses *volition*.   The

mutilated frog is a machine, and nothing more; the other is a machine governed and checked by a ruling will.

356. When the cerebral lobes are removed from a bird, its movements appear like those of a clumsy, stupid, drowsy bird. Left alone, it will remain quiet for a long time; placed on its back, it will regain its feet; thrown into the air, it will fly with precision and in a definite direction; disturbed, it will shift its position; kept alive for some time, it cleans its feathers: in short, it appears to be in full possession of a bird's powers, except satisfactory indications of intelligence and definite will-power.

357. FUNCTIONS OF THE CEREBRUM.—In the *human brain* the impulses which cause the varied movements of the body, as walking, grasping, balancing, etc., arise in the pons, the medulla, and the parts of the hinder brain. In the nerve-cells of the *convolutions* arise the impulses which set in motion, retard, or stop the impulses arising in the inferior centres of the brain. The nerve-cells of the convolutions are the seat of *volition*, of *consciousness*, of *educated intelligence*, and of the *faculty of language*. These powers are injured or lost from experimental sections, disease, or destruction of these parts.

358. FUNCTIONS OF THE CONVOLUTIONS.—Men have lost by accident large masses of cerebral material upon *one side*, and, after recovery from their wounds, have suffered little or no impairment of the mental functions. The healthy brain-tissue is not sensitive to ordinary irritation, as pricking, cutting, or mild electric currents. A series of careful experiments by Hitzig, Fritsch, Ferrier, and others have shown that there is a connection between the faradic-

---

356. What of the action of a bird which has lost its cerebral lobes? What faculties are lost?

357. Where do "movement-impulses" arise? Where is the seat of "originating impulses"? Of what are the convolution-cells the seat? What proof?

electric stimulation of certain areas of the brain-surface and certain definite muscular movements. These experiments make it quite certain that there is a localization of function in the brain-surface. It has been noticed that *aphasia* (the loss of articulate speech) is almost always associated with disease of the hinder portion of the third convolution. In a vast majority of cases the disease is on the left side of the brain. In *microcephales*, who have never been able to learn to speak, the third frontal convolution has been found atrophied. Hence it is inferred that in these convolutions—not in the muscles, or in the motor nerves, or in the motor centres of the brain—the fundamental phenomenon of articulate speech is located (495).

In 1877, when house-surgeon at Boston City Hospital, I had under my charge a man suffering from compound comminuted fracture of the left vault. Eleven pieces of bone were removed, leaving a hole about one and a half inches in diameter. The man lived eighty-three days, retaining his mental faculties, speech, and motion up to the last week. After the primary inflammation had subsided, the cerebral tumor was insensible to gentle manipulation. During waking hours it was gorged with blood and projected; during deep sleep it became pale, and partially sank into the cranial cavity. A laborer in New Hampshire was tamping a charge of powder into a rock, when, by a premature discharge, the rod (three feet seven inches long, one and one-fourth inches in diameter, and weighing about thirteen pounds) was driven into the left side of the face, near the angle of the jaw, passed through the front part of the cranial cavity, and emerged through the frontal bone in the median line, driving bone and brain before it. The man became delirious and comatose, but subsequently recovered, although with loss of sight in the left eye. Later, this man drove coach in Chili for my acquaintance, Mr. J. Allen, the manager of the American Line. Twelve years after the accident the man lost his life in California. The skull is now in the Harvard University Medical Department Museum. Fischer reports (*Deutsche Zeit. für Chir.*, 1883) the case of a carbine iron ramrod entering the chest to the right of the fourth dorsal vertebra, passing through the neck, the base of the skull, and the brain, and projecting thirty centimetres out of the left side of the head. The ramrod was driven back into the neck by blows of a hammer, and removed. The patient recovered, losing sight in the right eye, however.

359. **Bilateral Action.**—In general, both cerebral hemispheres probably act together, each part being respectively associated by its nerve-connections. One hemisphere has been shown to be sufficient for the exhibition of all the mental functions, and to exert a due influence on the body. It is possible that the right and the left brain may be at the same time engaged in different trains of ideas. Why are most persons *right-handed?* Why is the faculty of language more often exercised from the left side? According to M. Broca, the left hemisphere, which presides over the movements of the right side of the body, owing to the decussation (365) of the nerves near their origin, has, from the first, a greater amount of

activity. This primary excess of activity extends to all the functions of which this hemisphere is the seat, and notably to that of articulation. There are persons who originally, or after a disease in the left hemisphere, speak with their right brain; in the same way, there are some who were originally left-handed, and others who have become left-handed in consequence of loss of, or inability to use, the right hand.

360. RAPIDITY OF CEREBRAL ACTION.—To determine this, the person experimented upon makes a signal as soon as he perceives a stimulus. The stimulus used may be a sound, a flash of light, or an induction (electric) shock. The moment of applying the stimulus and the moment of making the signal, as by pressing on an electric button, are recorded on a paper ribbon moved by clockwork at a known uniform speed. The interval between the two points is carefully measured, and the fraction of time accurately calculated. This interval of time is called the "reaction period." The length of this period varies in every person according to the nature and disposition of the stimulated end-organ.

361. The "reaction period" of astronomers has long been known. It is known that two men watching the same star under the same circumstances are not able to record its transit over a line at the same moment. Between the years 1814 and 1834 the "reaction period" of Struve was from .04 to 1.08 seconds longer than that of Bessel. It is known by astronomers that the individual "reaction period" varies, and that they are not always able to record the contact of stars equally sharply. This has given rise to the so-called "personal equation" of observers. Donders has determined the reduced "reaction period" to be—feeling one-seventh, hearing one-sixth, and sight one-fifth of a second. Exner has shown that it takes an intelligent person less than one-tenth of a second to perceive and to will.

362. FUNCTIONS OF THE SUPERIOR GANGLIA.—The *corpora striata* and the *optic thalami*, often called the "basal ganglia," are the great means of communication between the cerebral hemispheres on the one hand and the peduncles on the other. As the great mass of the peduncular fibres connect in an indirect manner with the external gray layer through the basal ganglia (a few fibres are found, however, to pass directly), these nerve-masses appear to act as "middle-men" between the cerebral convolutions and the

rest of the brain. It cannot at present be stated definitely what is the nature of the mediation which either body respectively effects. Injuries or lesions of these ganglia of one side cause loss of motion and of sensation on the opposite side of the face and body. When both are injured, the will is unable to cause action below the ganglia, or the consciousness to be influenced by impulses from below.

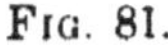

Fig. 81.

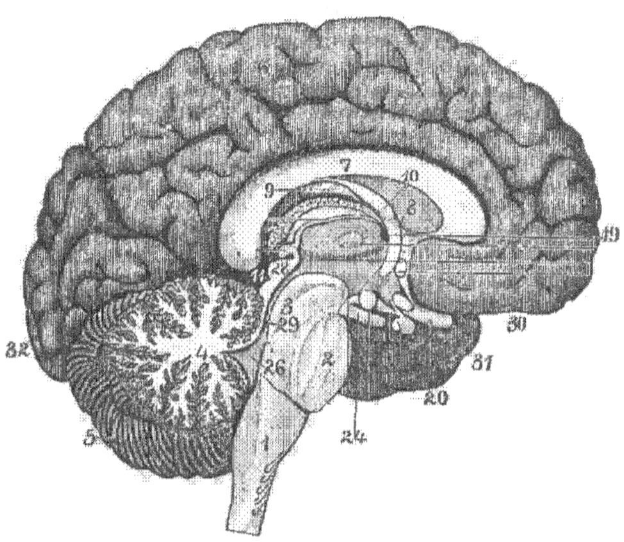

Fig. 81 (*Leidy*). SECTION OF THE BRAIN ALONG THE GREAT LONGITUDINAL FISSURE.—1, Medulla oblongata. 2, Pons. 3, Crus of the cerebrum. 4, Arborescent appearance in section of the cerebellum. 5, Left hemisphere of the cerebellum. 6, Inner surface of the left hemisphere of the cerebellum. 7, Corpus callosum. 8, Pellucid septum. 9, Fornix. 10, Anterior crus of the fornix. 19, Foramen of communication between the third and lateral ventricles. 20, Optic nerve. 24, Oculo-motor nerve. 26, Fourth ventricle. 28, Quadrigeminal body. 29, Entrance from the third to the fourth ventricle. 30, 31, 32, Anterior, middle, and posterior lobes of the cerebrum.

In the vicinity of the front eminences of the *corpora quadrigemina* are seated the centres for the co-ordination of the movements of the eyeballs (466), and for the contraction of the pupil (459). These two centres work together. If the eminences of one side are removed, the animal loses sight on the same side. All experiments indicate that these nervous eminences are the *centres* of *sight* (462).

The *olfactory lobes* are concerned in the sense of smell. Odorous particles present in the air in the upper nasal chambers, acting on the epithelium of these lobes, produce sensory impulses, which, ascending to the brain, give rise to the sensations of smell (430).

Fig. 82.   Fig. 83.

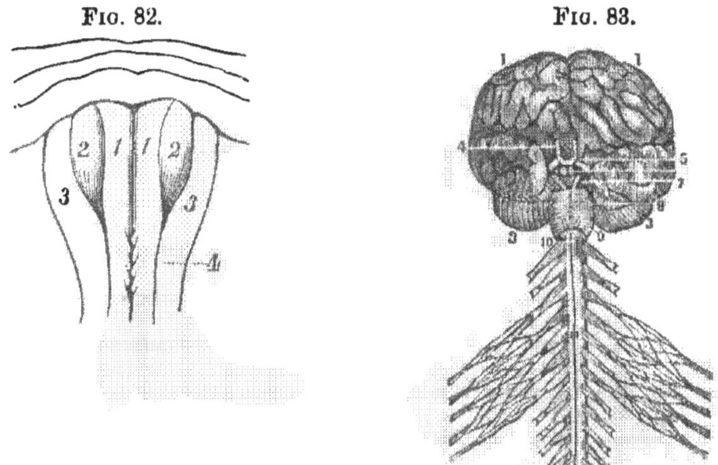

Fig. 82. (*Dalton*). MEDULLA OBLONGATA OF HUMAN BRAIN, anterior view.—1, 1, Anterior pyramids. 2, 2, Olivary bodies. 3, 3, Restiform bodies. 4, Decussation of the anterior columns. The medulla oblongata is seen terminated above by the transverse fibres of the pons Varolii.

Fig. 83. ANTERIOR VIEW OF THE BRAIN AND SPINAL CORD.—1, 1, Hemispheres of the cerebrum. 3, 3, Cerebellum. 4, Olfactory nerve. 5, Optic nerve. 7, Third pair of nerves. 8, Pons. 9, Fourth pair of nerves. 10, Lower portion of the medulla oblongata. 11, Spinal cord.

363. The CEREBELLUM, or little brain, is situated beneath the back lobes of the cerebrum. It is made up of gray nerve-matter without and white matter within. Its surface is crossed by numerous furrows, which vary in depth. A slight notch in front and behind marks it off into two hemispheres. A vertical section brings the tree-like arrangement of the white matter into view.

364. The SPINAL CORD is the cylindrical long mass of

---

363. The cerebellum? Location? Appearance? Divisions? Appearance of interior?

364. The spinal cord? Location? Extent? Enlargements? Speak of the color and the fissures.

nerve-matter contained in the spinal canal (343). It extends from the pons to the first lumbar vertebra, from whence it is continued as gray filaments into the sacrum.

Fig. 84.

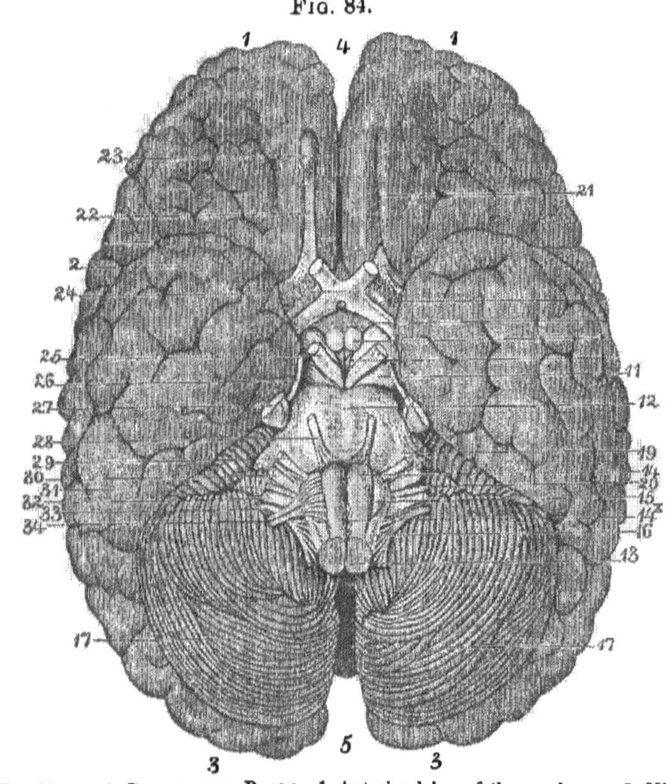

Fig. 84 (*Leidy*). BASE OF THE BRAIN.—1, Anterior lobes of the cerebrum. 2, Middle lobes. 3, Posterior lobes. 4, 5, Anterior and posterior extremities of the great longitudinal fissure. 11, Crura of the cerebrum. 12, Pons. 13, Medulla oblongata. 14, Pyramidal bodies. 14*, Decussation. 15, Olivary body. 16, Restiform body. 17, Hemispheres of the cerebellum. 19, Crus of the cerebellum. 20, Pneumogastric lobule of the cerebellum. 21, Fissure which accommodates the olfactory (1) nerve (22). 23, Bulb of the olfactory nerve. 24, Optic commissure. 25, Oculo-motor (3) nerve. 26, Pathetic (4) nerve. 27, Trifacial (5) nerve. 28, Abducent (6) nerve. 29, Facial (7) nerve. 30, Auditory (8) nerve. 31, Glosso-pharyngeal (9) nerve. 32, Pneumogastric (10) nerve. 33, Accessory (11) nerve. 34, Hypoglossal (12) nerve.

At the lower part of the neck and in the lumbar region it presents enlargements. From these enlargements the

nerves of the lower limbs branch off. Many nerves .from
the external parts of the body terminate in the cord. The
cord does not fill the canal, but is held in place by its membranes. It is white without and gray within, the reverse
of which is seen in the brain. It is divided by front and
rear fissures into a right and a left portion.

365. The MEDULLA OBLONGATA is the upper enlarged
part of the spinal cord. It extends from the upper border
of the first vertebra to the pons. It is divided by fissures
into a right and a left portion, and the latter by grooves into
four *columns.* Many of the fibres of the anterior column
(motor in function) cross over and make connection with
the cerebral hemisphere of the opposite side. This is the
decussation of the anterior columns of the cord. Special
deposits of gray matter are found in the interior (Fig. 79).

366. The PONS, or "bridge," is the bond of union of the
various parts of the brain connecting the cerebrum above,
the medulla, and, through it, the spinal cord below, and the
cerebellum behind (Fig. 84, 12).

367. MEMBRANES OF THE CEREBRO-SPINAL SYSTEM.
—The skull and spinal canal are lined by a continuous tough
membrane called the *dura mater.* This acts in the skull as
a kind of periosteum (16), and in both portions it smooths
off the bony roughnesses. The inner surface of the dura
mater is in contact with a thin membrane, the *arachnoid.*
The *pia mater* is a very vascular membrane, which dips into
all the depressions of the brain and cord, and in the nourishment of which it assists.

---

365. What of the medulla oblongata? Extent? Fissures? What
is the decussation? Gray matter?

366. Speak of the pons.

367. What is the dura mater? For what does it serve? What of
the arachnoid? Of the pia mater?

368. Between the arachnoid and the cord is a considerable space, which is called the *sub-arachnoidean space*. It is largest at the lower part of the canal. It communicates with the ventricles of the brain, and contains an abundant serous fluid. This secretion is sufficient in amount to expand the arachnoid and to fill completely the interior of the dura mater. This fluid forms a water-bed for the delicate structures of the cord and the internal ganglia of the brain. When the blood-pressure in the brain suddenly becomes too great or too small, the fluid is forced out of the ventricles into the spinal portion, or *vice versa*. Thus it regulates the degree of pressure on the brain and spinal-cord centres. When this fluid is suddenly withdrawn, great brain-disturbance ensues.

369. FUNCTIONS OF THE INFERIOR PARTS OF THE BRAIN.—Experiments and disease-action show that the nervous machinery required for the execution of bodily movements (both visceral and skeletal) is present after complete removal of the cerebral hemispheres. When the brain is reduced to the corpora quadrigemina and cerebellum, with the peduncles and the pons, the mammal is able to execute all ordinary movements. When the parts between the hemispheres and the medulla are removed (*i.e.*, the pons, peduncles, and ganglia), a large number of complex movements are no longer executed: the animal can no longer balance itself; it lies helpless on its side, and can only perform simple movements when disturbed. If the medulla of a mammal is removed or destroyed, death ensues.

370. In the inferior parts of the brain are situated the nerve-centres, which *originate* and *adjust* the impulses necessary to complex body-movements, as running, bal-

___

369. If the cerebral lobes are removed, what is the effect? If the pons, peduncles, and ganglia? If the medulla?

370. What impulses arise in the inferior parts of the brain? What external controlling influences? What internal? What of cerebral influences?

ancing, writing, breathing, digestive movements, etc. The outer movements are carried out by motor nervous impulses arising in these nerve-centres, yet these centres are influenced, arranged, and controlled by impulses received from the outside through the senses of touch, sight, hearing, etc. In digestion, respiration, etc., the action of these centres is influenced by the impulses coming from the digestive tube, the lungs, etc. In bodily movements *executed under the will*, the cerebral hemispheres simply put this machinery in action.

371. The *peduncles* of the cerebrum serve as the chief means of communication between the spinal cord and the superior parts of the brain. The *peduncles* and the *pons* are intimately connected with the co-ordination of movements. Complex bodily movements can be executed in the absence of the optic thalami, the corpora striata, and the cerebral hemispheres, but not in the absence of other parts of the brain. Injury to one side of the pons commonly causes paralysis of the muscles of the same side of the face and of the muscles of the limbs of the opposite side of the body. Hence the crossing over of impulses, beginning in the spinal cord (376), is gradually completed as the impulses pass through the pons.

372. The *cerebellum* is an important organ of co-ordination (393). It receives motor and sensory impulses, and combines, influences, and adjusts them to produce correct movements. When this organ is severely injured, disorderly movements result; when it is removed, an almost total loss of control over body-movements supervenes. It is quite probable that its functions are especially connected with the equilibrium impulses proceeding to the higher centres from the semicircular canals (475).

373. The *medulla oblongata* is the link between the middle and lower spinal cord and the brain. The motor impulses from the cerebrum cross to the opposite side in the medulla. The majority of the " centres" for various reflex, protective, and organic functions are seated in this portion of the cord. The principal centres are the " respiratory" (184), the " vaso-motor" (135), the " heart inhibitory" (128), the " artificial glycogenic" (308), the " deglutition" (261), the " gastric" and the " vomiting" (266), etc.

374. FUNCTIONS OF THE SPINAL CORD.—If the cord of a dog be severed in the region of the back, the hind limbs remain flaccid and motionless. Stimulation of the hind foot evokes no symptoms of pain and calls forth no motions. The dog, if frightened, is unable to cause motions in his hind quarters. Stimulation of the lower cord at the point of section calls forth irregular movements in the hind limbs; stimulation of the upper cord at the same point gives rise to symptoms of pain, movements of the muscles near the section, and regulated movements above. If the animal recovers from his wound, the cord-sections not becoming united, and if the hind feet be stimulated, a series of regulated, definite movements will be produced,—that is, *reflex action.* These reflex movements are often powerful, varied, and complex (82).

375. The HUMAN SPINAL CORD is the nerve-link connecting the spinal nerves with the parts within the skull. It is a mere instrument for executing cerebral commands. It transmits outgoing and incoming impulses. The conductor is not simple, but is carried out by a system of relays (377). The path of least resistance is that of the white fibres, and it is inferred that motor impulses ordinarily, and the sensory for most of the way, pass over the white tracts of their own side. The cord is the great seat of the centres for REFLEX ACTION. The reflex centres of the cord control the sphincters of the bladder and rectum, exert a protective influence over the body, and execute

---

374. What effect results from cutting the spinal cord? What is the influence of later stimulation? What are reflex action movements?

375. What is the spinal cord? What can it do? What is the path of least resistance? What use does the brain make of the cord? What do the reflex centres control?

involuntary movements of the limbs, as the sudden withdrawal of a burnt finger, even in opposition to the will, or the withdrawing of the tickled foot during sleep or during deep mental action. The cord does not appear to possess automatic centres (84).

376. *As to the course pursued* by different impulses,—of volition, of touch, of general sensation, of pain,—there is much indefiniteness. The statements of the results arrived at by different experimenters are conflicting and unsatisfactory. According to Schiff and his followers, the purely volitional impulses (motor) pass along the antero-lateral columns, and the purely tactile along the posterior columns of the same side; while the gray matter can transmit in all directions impulses of sensation and such outgoing impulses as are parts of reflex action. According to Brown-Séquard and others, the sensory impulses pass from the nerves along a certain length of the posterior columns, then cross over to the gray matter of the *opposite side*, in which they ascend to the brain; the volitional impulses, having crossed in the pons (371) and medulla (373), descend in the antero-lateral columns, keeping to the same side.

377. *Experiments show* that the gray matter of the cord is physiologically continuous; that it is marked out by physiological barriers of resistance into nervous mechanisms; that these mechanisms carry out co-ordinated muscular movements and associate incoming impulses with these movements,—that is, REFLEX ACTION. It is inferred that a volitional impulse for the production of a given body-movement, as of making a step, descending from the brain by the white tracts, passes into the gray matter of the cord at the place where the physiological mechanism for the execution of the given movement is located, and then emerges in the proper nerve; and that the incoming impulse, as from the foot, passes at first into the mechanism with which that part is associated in producing a frequently-recurring reflex action, and that the impulse then travels up to the brain by a more direct tract than the gray mass.

378. *The brain uses the mechanism* of the cord to do the coarse work of most body-movements, employing inferior brain-centres to supervise and control the action of the cord-mechanism. The more drilled and disciplined the cord-centres, the less the oversight demanded of conscious brain-action. An untrained cord, as in a

child, acts hesitatingly. An idiotic spinal cord only learns and executes under constant supervision, and quickly forgets its lessons. A healthy cord learns readily, remembers correctly, and executes the movements so well that in time little brain-supervision is demanded.

379. A SENSORY NERVE is a thread of communication between the sensitive cells of the external end-organ and the eminently automatic (84) or central cell. If a small object be applied to an appropriate end-organ, like the tip of the finger, the cerebral cen-

FIG. 85.

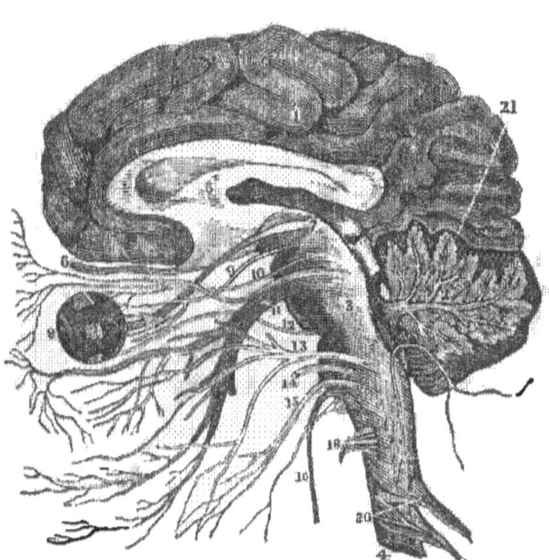

FIG. 85, A VERTICAL SECTION OF THE CEREBRUM, CEREBELLUM, AND MEDULLA OBLONGATA, showing the relation of the cranial nerves at their origin.—1, The cerebrum. 2, The cerebellum, with its arbor vitæ represented. 3, The medulla oblongata. 4, The spinal cord. 5, The corpus callosum. 6, The first pair of nerves. 7, The second pair. 8, The eye. 9, The third pair of nerves. 10, The fourth pair. 11, The fifth pair. 12, The sixth pair. 13, The seventh pair. 14, The eighth pair. 15, The ninth pair. 16, The tenth pair. 19, The eleventh pair. 18, The twelfth pair. 20, Spinal nerves. 21, The tentorium.

tres recognize the sensations to which an educated mind applies the terms "pressure," "form," "hardness," etc. If the connecting nerve now be cut, and the same body be applied to the cut nerve-trunks, a sensation of pain only is recognized at the cerebral centres.

380. By a MOTOR NERVE is to be understood the thread of communication between the automatic or nerve cell of the centre and its muscular end-process (85). When a stimulus is applied to the centre of the given nerve, the transmitted impulse gives rise to a muscular contraction (87). The velocity of a motor impulse in the arm of man is about thirty-three metres (one hundred and eight and one-fourth feet) per second. The velocity of sensory impulses in man has not yet been well determined. In most cases the velocity of the impulses is retarded by cold and accelerated by heat. As yet, experiments have not shown that a purely motor trunk may act as a sensory trunk, and *vice versa.*

381. The CRANIAL NERVES pass from the central nervous system (the pons and medulla, principally) outward by openings in the skull. They are arranged in twelve pairs, and distributed to the organs of special sense (Chapter XII.), to certain muscles of the face and neck, to the larynx, pharynx, heart, lungs, stomach, and intestines.

382. FUNCTIONS OF THE CRANIAL NERVES.—In these nerves the motor and sensory tracts are far less mixed than in the spinal nerves. The nerves of the senses of smell (first), sight (second), and hearing (eighth), are purely sensory. The third, fourth, sixth, and eleventh are purely motor. The others are mixed to a greater or less degree. Of the *mixed cranial nerves,* the fifth, seventh, and tenth are most important (Figs. 84, 85).

The *fifth,* or *trifacial,* contains the motor fibres to the muscles of mastication; the vaso-motor fibres of the head and face; the secretory fibres to the tear-glands; the dilated fibres of the pupils. It is the general nerve of sensation to the head and face and most of the mucous membrane of the mouth. Its first branch is distributed

---

380. What is a motor nerve? What is the velocity of a motor impulse? Of a sensory influence?

381. Speak of the cranial nerves. What is a cranial nerve? How many? To what distributed?

about the orbit, the second about the superior maxilla, and the third to the inferior maxilla. It is the nerve of the special sense of *taste* (426) to the front part of the tongue. It is the nerve concerned in toothache and facial neuralgia.

383. The *seventh*, or *facial* is the nerve of facial expression, being distributed to the muscles of the face. It emerges from the skull beneath the external ear. In paralysis of this nerve, the facial parts are drawn to the sound side, the eye is not fully closed, and the troubled side loses expression. The *tenth*, *pneumogastric* or *vagus*, is the motor nerve for the muscles of the pharynx, of the œsophagus, of the stomach, of the intestines, and of the larynx; it is the vaso-motor nerve of the lungs, and the inhibitory nerve of the heart. It is the sensory nerve of the air-passages, the pharynx, the œsophagus, and the stomach. It influences the respiratory and vaso-motor centres of the medulla, also the secretion of saliva and the pancreatic fluid. The cranial nerves play a very important *rôle* in the mechanism of human life. When healthy, they perform important duties with precision; when diseased, they make life far from pleasant.

Fig. 86.

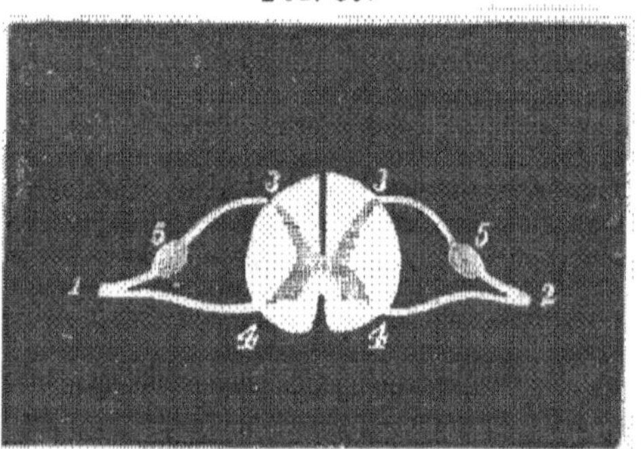

Fig. 86. Transverse Section of Spinal Cord.—1, 2, Spinal nerves of right and left sides, showing their two roots. 4, Origin of anterior root. 3, Origin of posterior root. 5, Ganglion of posterior root.

384. The Spinal Nerves are arranged in thirty-one pairs. Each nerve arises by two roots,—the *anterior*, or motor-impulse-transmitting root, and the *posterior*, or sensory-impulse-transmitting root. The latter has an embedded *ganglion*, behind which the two roots unite into one *nerve*. The nerve, thus formed, passes from the spinal

---

384. How many spinal nerves? How many roots? How do nerves leave the canal? To what distributed? Their function?

canal by an intervertebral opening. The spinal nerves are distributed to the viscera, muscles, and skin below their point of exit. They transmit both sensory and motor influences.

385. All *spinal nerves* are composed of motor and sensory fibres. When a spinal nerve is divided, the stimulation, as by heat, scratching, electricity, etc., of the trunk-end causes a sensation in the conscious centres, or a reflex action in another muscular area; stimulation of the distal end causes muscular contractions in its own area. When the *anterior root* only is cut, the muscles supplied by that nerve cease to be caused to contract either by the will or by reflex action, while the structures to which the nerve is distributed retain their sensibility. If the trunk-end is stimulated, no sensory effect is produced; if the distal end, the muscles are caused to contract. When the *posterior root* is cut, the muscles to which the nerve is distributed may be caused to contract by the exercise of the will or through reflex action; but the parts to which it is distributed lose their sensibility. If the trunk-end is stimulated, sensory effects are produced; if the distal end, no sensory effects or movements occur. The *ganglion* on the posterior root appears to be concerned only in the nutrition of the nerve.

Fig. 87.

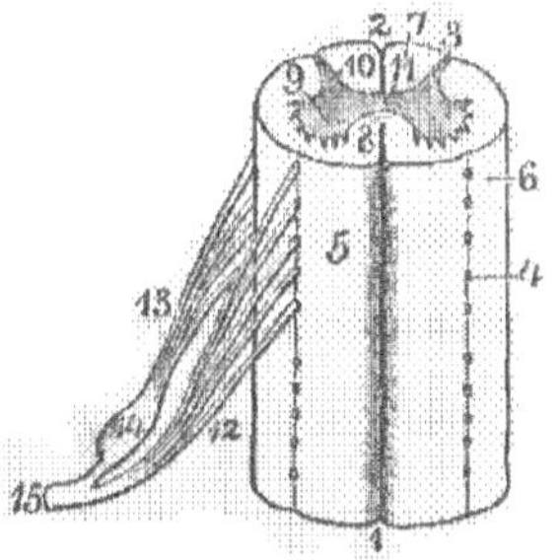

Fig. 87 (*Leidy*). Segment of the Spinal Cord.—1, Anterior median fissure. 2, Posterior median fissure. 3, Postero-lateral fissure. 4, Antero-lateral fissure. 5, Anterior column. 6, Lateral column. 7, Posterior column. 8, Anterior commissure. 9, Anterior horns of the gray substance. 10, Posterior horns. 11, Gray commissure. 12, Anterior root of a spinal nerve springing by a number of filaments from the antero-lateral fissure. 13, Posterior root from postero-lateral fissure. 14, Ganglion on the posterior root. 15, Spinal nerve formed by the union of the two roots.

If the nerve-ganglion be excised the whole posterior root degenerates, as well as the sensory fibres of the mixed nerve. When the posterior root is cut between the ganglion and the cord, the cord portion degenerates. If the anterior root be cut, the motor nerves in the distal portion degenerate. The knowledge of these facts led Waller to employ excision and cutting to determine accurately the distribution of sensory and motor fibres. In 1811, Charles Bell distinguished between the motor and sensory fibres. In 1822, Magendie showed the functions of the anterior and posterior roots. These discoveries laid the foundation of modern nerve physiology. In 1832, Marshall Hall's experiments established the theory of reflex action.

386. The SYMPATHETIC SYSTEM (344) consists of two chains of ganglia (gray nerve-masses), one on each side of the vertebral column. This double chain extends through the deep parts of the neck into the chest and abdomen. The ganglia communicate with one another, with the spinal cord, with the ganglia seated in or on the viscera of the thorax and abdomen, and with certain of the cranial nerves. The nerve-fibres of this system are distributed to the muscular fibres of the blood-vessels (vaso-motor).

387. FUNCTIONS.—The sympathetic system presides over the viscera of the body. It has been named the "nutritive nervous system." It exerts its influence over the viscera and the body at large by the control it exercises over the calibre of the blood-vessels. Its ultimate branches are called the *vaso-motor nerves* (134), and through them the vaso-motor centre (373) makes its influence felt. This system is assisted by, and is subordinate to, the cerebro-spinal system.

388. SUMMARY.—The functions of motion, of sensation,

FIG. 88. A BACK VIEW OF THE BRAIN AND SPINAL CORD.—1, The cerebrum. 2, The cerebellum. 3, The spinal cord. 4, Nerves of the face. 5, The brachial plexus of nerves. 6, 7, 8, 9, Nerves of the arm. 10, Nerves that pass under the ribs. 11, The lumbar plexus of nerves. 12, The sacral plexus of nerves. 13, 14, 15, 16, Nerves of the lower limbs.

FIG. 89 REPRESENTS THE SYMPATHETIC GANGLIA, AND THEIR CONNECTION WITH OTHER NERVES.—A, A, A, The semilunar ganglion and solar plexus, situated below the diaphragm and behind the stomach. This ganglion is situated in the region (pit of the stomach) where a blow gives severe suffering. D, D, D, The thoracic (chest) ganglia, ten or eleven in number. E, E, The external and internal branches of the thoracic ganglia. G, H, The right and left coronary plexus, situated upon the heart. I, N, Q, The inferior, middle, and superior cervical (neck) ganglia. 1, The renal plexus of nerves that surrounds the kidneys. 2, The lumbar (loin) ganglion. 3, Their internal branches. 4, Their external branches. 5, The aortic plexus of nerves that lies upon the aorta. The other letters and figures represent nerves that connect important organs and nerves with the sympathetic ganglia.

386. Of what does the sympathetic system consist? Where found? What connections? How distributed?

387. What are its functions? What control does it exercise? What portion influences its action?

Fig. 88.

Fig. 89.

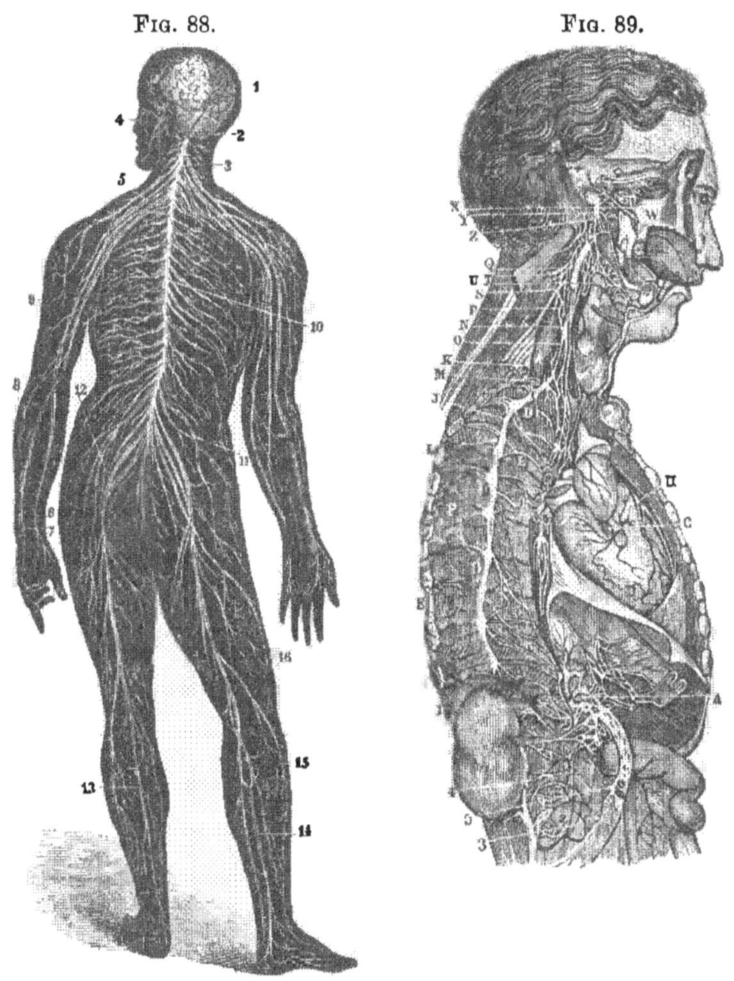

of the regulation of actions, of the special senses, as well as of digestion, absorption, nutrition, circulation, respiration, secretion, and excretion, are placed more or less under the control of the nervous system. This system of nerve-centres and of impulse-conducting fibres plays the part of an excitor and regulator in regard to the functions of the other tissues. The paths and the centres of all the functions of the body are structurally associated. The anatomical links, the nerves, are exceedingly numerous, and intricate in distribution. The physiological relations between all parts, even the most distant, are most intimate, and are also interdependent.

389. As a result of the close anatomical connection and physiological relation, all parts of the body are more or less in sympathy with one another. The odor from the engine-room of a steamer excites nausea; the thought of a savory dish causes a flow of saliva; the sight of an animal in pain induces a painful sensation in the mind; a sudden mental emotion accelerates or retards the beat of the heart; disease in one eye often leads to a similar malady in the other; a severe burn induces ulceration of the duodenum, etc. During life, under the excitation and regulation of the nerve-centres, an active co-ordination of all the parts of the body is sustained, and the organism is enabled to execute the duties for which it was designed,— growth, work, and the continuance of the species.

390. SUMMARY (*Continued*).—

Cerebrum.—Psychical faculties: perception, ideation, reasoning, emotion, volition, and the faculty of language.

---

388. What functions are under nervous control? What part does it play? What of the anatomical links? Physiological relations?

389. What are the duties of the organism?

390. Write on the slate a summary.

Olfactory lobes.—Sense of smell.

Optic thalami, } "Middle-men" between the peduncles
Corpora striata. } and the cerebral centres.

Corpora quadrigemina.—Centre for sight, centre for co-ordination of eyeballs and pupil.

Peduncles, } Parts of communication concerned in co-
Pons. } ordination.

Cerebellum.—Important organ of co-ordination.

Medulla.—Seat of centres for various organic functions.

Spinal cord.—Conductor of impulses, centre of certain reflex movements.

Ganglia.—Centres of automatic nerve-action.

Nerves.—Conductors of impulses.

End-organs.—Receivers of impressions.

391. SPASMS, or CONVULSIONS, are involuntary contractions of the skeletal muscles, varying widely as regards their intensity. When accompanied by severe pain, they are known as *cramp*. They are caused by irritations acting on some portion of the nervous system, causing the explosive discharges in the nerve-centres known as *impulses* (349). In children, gum-irritation (in teething) and digestive irritation are the most common causes; in adults, the presence of irritants in the blood, in the alimentary tube, or in the fleshy parts. *Tetanus*, or "lock-jaw," is commonly started by some irritant, as a splinter in the flesh, or a drug, like strychnia. *Paralysis*, or palsy, is the suppression of the transit of motor impulses to a certain extent. It may be general, involving most of the body, or local, as in wrist-drop. It results from degeneration or disease in the central cells, from pressure upon or injury to the central cells, or from section or pressure of the nerves in their course.

392. *Hemiplegia* is one-sided paralysis. In most cases, the muscles of the arm, the leg, the trunk, and the lower part of the face indicate the suspension of motor-impulse conduction. In the majority of cases the seat of mischief is within the skull. The most common factor is the escape of blood into the cerebral tissues. The escaping blood rends apart the tissues, or its accumulation presses upon the soft structures, thus stopping cell-action. The absorption

of the clot is frequently followed by a partial recovery of the motor functions. *Paraplegia* is a paralysis of both sides of the lower part of the body. It commonly results from injury or disease of the spinal cord. The lesion of the cord frequently follows injury to or malformation of the vertebral column. It may occur at any part of the cord. The nearer the medulla the seat of the trouble, the greater the inconvenience, as well as the danger to life. Paralysis may be *local*, as in facial paralysis, due to sudden chilling of the face, or to the cutting of the nerve. All forms of sensation may be more or less impaired, lost, exalted, or perverted, as in *anæsthesia, hyperæsthesia, neuralgia*, etc.

393. CO-ORDINATION is the adjustment of the outgoing impulses from a nerve-centre to the incoming impulses. The adjustment of the nervous impulses to the duties at hand obliges the muscles to contract in proper order, at the proper time, and to the proper extent, thus occasioning orderly, purposeful movements (515). The interval between the arrival at the central cells of the incoming impulses and the departure from them of the outgoing impulses is a busy time for the protoplasm of the nerve-cells of the centre. During this interval many processes, chemical and physiological, of which at present we know little or nothing, are being carried out.

394. HABIT.—This is the disposition which the organism acquires from the frequent execution of certain acts to repeat these acts until some more powerful forces intervene. The influence of habit over the ordinary operations of the central system is well known. Owing to having stated hours for eating and drinking, the sensations of hunger and thirst are rarely experienced at other periods of the day. The user of tobacco and alcoholics, the votary of opium, or chloral, or hashish, is subject to the same influence. The user invariably feels the urgent need of the customary stimulant or sedative when its ingestion is even slightly delayed. In some persons, the interruption of an accustomed habit so affects their mental actions that they will undergo inconveniences and will run physical and social risks rather than not indulge the habit (dipsomania). A habit once firmly fixed cannot be turned aside without causing deep inconvenience to the entire system.

395. In explanation of the phenomena of habit, physiology can offer nothing definite. In the physical world, a force once acquired

will continue indefinitely if no more powerful force, or combination of forces, interfere with it. In the nervous system it may be, as a series of impulses acting on the centres call forth certain actions, that the impression of the impulse at the centre is not effaced with the accomplishment of the resulting act; that the arrival of the given series of impulses at the given centres at regular intervals deepens the impression; that the influence of these impressions becomes so deeply worked into the activity of the centres that the centres, after a time, become able to produce the associated actions without the arrival of impulses from without, and that thus a habit becomes fixed and influential.

HYGIENE.

396. For the proper performance of their functions the different organs of the body are dependent upon the impulses originating in the nerve-centres. Upon the integrity and proper working of all parts of the nervous system depends the healthy action of each part and of the whole. Owing to the intimate relations of the great nerve-centres to all organs, improper action or imperfect performance of duties by the organs is quickly and markedly manifested by irregular, spasmodic, abnormal, and even painful action of the superior centres. The physical condition of the system affects reflex action, co-ordinate action, sense action, and mental action. The highest health and vigor of the nervous system require—(1.) *A sound nervous organization by inheritance.* (2.) *A sufficient supply of normal blood.* (3.) *The judicious and regular exercise of the body and the brain.* (4.) *The ability to secure normal sleep and rest.*

----

396. What influence do nerve-impulses exert? What results from intimate relations and close connections? What are affected by the physical condition of the system? What is required for the highest health of the nervous system?

397. I.—A Sound Nervous Organization by Inheritance.—Every-day observation shows that children inherit not only the features, but the physical, mental, and moral constitution of their parents. Even those utterly ignorant of the laws of transmission are wont to estimate the child according to its family: favorably, if of a "good family" or "good blood;" unfavorably, if of a "bad family" or "bad blood." Every formation of body, internal and external, all intellectual endowments and aptitudes, and all moral qualities, are or may be transmissible from parent to child. If one generation is missed, the qualities may appear in the next generation (*atavism*). A guilty secret may thus reveal itself long after the active participators in it have passed from this life.

398. It is important to notice that not only the natural constitution of the parents may be inherited, but their acquired habits of life, whether virtuous or vicious; and especially is this true of the vicious. Even when the identical vice does not appear, there is a morbid organization and a tendency to some vice akin to it. Not only is the evil tendency transmitted, but what was the simple practice, the voluntarily adopted and cherished vice, of the parent, becomes the passion, the overpowering impulse, of the child. A person thus is often handicapped for life by the mistakes and faults of his ancestors.

399. M. Morel sketches the history of four generations as follows: "*First Generation.*—The father was an habitual drunkard, and was killed in a public-house brawl. *Second Generation.*—The son inherited his father's habit, which gave rise to an attack of mania, terminating in paralysis and death. *Third Generation.*—The grandson was strictly sober, but was full of hypochondriacal and imaginary fears of persecutions, etc., and had homicidal tendencies. *Fourth Generation.*—The fourth in descent had very limited intelli-

397. What expression of a great truth? How do we estimate persons? What is transmitted? What is atavism?

398. What tendencies may be transmitted? What results?

gence, and had an attack of madness when sixteen years old, terminating in stupidity nearly amounting to idiocy; with him the race probably became extinct."

400. "Habits of growing *drunkenness* in parents have the effect of inclining the children to grow up instinctive drunkards, and the first children born, ere the habits are confirmed, are free from the vice which holds the younger children fast in a disgraceful thraldom."—*Fothergill.* "Of three hundred idiots in Massachusetts, Dr. Howe referred one hundred and forty-five directly to intemperance. A like proportion of insanity finds a similar reference. If we add to these all the degrees of weakness, imbecility, and deterioration which lie between these extremes of idiocy and insanity on the one hand and sound manhood and sound-mindedness on the other, what a dreadful and unending entail have we as the product of this one vice [of the parents] !"—*Bascom* (245, 408).

401. Says a famed physician, after long and close observation of the evil effects of *tobacco,* "If the evil ended with the individual who, by the indulgence of a pernicious custom, injures his own health and impairs his faculties of mind and body, he might be left to his enjoyment, his fool's paradise, unmolested. This, however, is not the case. In no instance is the sin of the father more strikingly visited upon the children than in the sin of tobacco-smoking. The enervation, the hysteria, the insanity, the dwarfish deformities, the consumption, the suffering lives and early deaths, of the children of *inveterate smokers* bear ample testimony to the feebleness and unsoundness of the constitution transmitted by this pernicious habit" (412).

402. Should we trace the effects of the whole list of vices, it would be with equally sad results. Even of the great love of *money-getting,* a celebrated physician writes, "I cannot but think, after what I have seen, that the extreme passion for getting rich, absorbing the whole energies of a life, does predispose to mental degeneration in the offspring, either to moral defect, or to moral and intellectual deficiency, or to outbreaks of insanity."—*Maudsley.*

403. Any kind of nervous disease in the parents, whether natural or acquired, seems to predispose to innate feebleness in the child. The offspring of "fast" parents are too often weakly and delicate. The disease received by inheritance may appear at birth, it may not appear until a definite period after birth, or it may lie dormant until

p

brought out by an extraneous exciting cause. The hereditary tendency to diseases is intensified by the intermarriage of those suffering from the same affection, as of phthisis, insanity, neuralgia, etc.; by the marriage of those closely related; by the marriage of the very young; or by the marriage of those of very unequal ages. It therefore behooves every one to see that his family shall not suffer from the sins and follies of his generation. By judicious education, and a strict obedience to physical and mental regimen, a naturally defective constitution may be improved.

404. II.—A SUFFICIENT SUPPLY OF NORMAL BLOOD. —The nerve-centres are not only delicate in structure and easily influenced, but are very vascular. The circulation of the blood in the centres is rapid and very essential. The tissue-changes in the protoplasm of the blood are rapid. The brain, though weighing less than one-fortieth of the body, is said to receive one-fifth of the blood expelled by the left ventricle. Hence it is that impurities in the blood so rapidly affect the superior nerve-centres. Therefore it is of the highest importance, for the proper working of the nervous system, that the blood be sufficient in amount, contain all the nutrient elements (214, 114), be properly oxygenated (181), be relieved of all products of tissue-waste at the earliest possible moment (316), and that impurities and foreign materials (alcohol, chloral, morphia, etc.) be rapidly eliminated. Whatever deteriorates the quality of the blood impairs the health of the nervous system.

405. *The effects of poor ventilation* are soon manifest in the nerve-centres,—drowsiness, dulness, headaches, nausea, etc. An *improper food*, or a good food improperly pre-

---

404. Why is a supply of normal blood needed? What of the brain blood-supply? What is therefore essential?

405. What results from imperfect ventilation? From a poor or bad diet? From bad bread?

pared, is not well assimilated, and the blood, in turn, is not put in condition to afford proper tissue-food. The effects of a bad diet are most marked in brain-workers, as distinguished from hand-workers. No teacher can teach well, no lawyer can plead well, no clergyman can preach well, who habitually takes improper food. Poor *bread* in the United States is said to cause more physical mischief than alcohol. An improper diet not only induces dyspepsia (281), but influences the brain-centres, causing confused, morbid emotions and weakened will-power.

406. *For the integrity of the working* of the nerve-centres, it is important that the *excretory* apparatus of the skin, of the lungs, of the bowels, and of the kidneys be in good working order. The retention in the blood of the products of normal tissue-waste induces headache, confusion of ideas, dimness of vision, nausea, and, in some cases, delirium, stupor, and death (305). The circulation in the blood and the slow elimination of the active principles of certain drugs and foods have a most injurious influence upon the action of the nerve-centres during the presence of the poisons in the blood, and even after their passage from the blood by way of the urine, the breath, and the perspiration.

407. STIMULANTS AND SEDATIVES.—At present a number of drugs useful in the alleviation of pain, in the meeting of certain surgical and medical emergencies, and in the prolonging of life, are extensively used by the people for their stimulating or their quieting effects on the central nervous system. At first a small quantity produces

---

406. What result from imperfect excretion? From the presence of poisons?

407. What do the people largely use? What is the effect of a small quantity? Of continued use? Of a larger quantity? What is said of the craving?

the characteristic and desired effect; later, the system having become accustomed to the presence of the foreign agent in the blood, a larger dose must be employed to get the desired stimulation or sedation (394). These drugs, in definite, small doses, are fatal poisons; but the system becomes so habituated to them as to endure with immunity doses which if taken at first would produce rapid death. Under their voluntary, continued use, the system is educated into a craving for them. This craving becomes so strong that the will-power of the consumer is unable to resist the demand for the degrading, baneful drug, though the injurious effects are felt and acknowledged.

408. ALCOHOL (241) taken into the system effects rapid changes in the working of the nerve-centres. When taken continuously, it impairs the nutrition of these centres. Each successive indulgence increases the abnormal nutrition and strengthens the demand for alcoholics (397). Impaired cell-nutrition induces imperfect, abnormal, or perverted action,—mental, organic, muscular. As a result of the deterioration of nutrition in the superior brain-centres, the power to resist the craving for intoxicants grows feebler and feebler, and at the same time the intellectual and physical powers are diminished. The effect on the nervous system of the abuse of the intoxicating principle of all spirituous liquors ranges from drunkenness and acute poisoning, through alcoholic mania, acute and chronic alcoholism, to dipsomania. The diseased condition caused by intoxicating drinks in the parents tends to induce nervous enfeeblements in the offspring, as epilepsy, insanity, imbecility, neuralgia, etc. (400, 401). Bruehl-

---

408. Effect of alcohol upon the nerve-centres? Of impaired cell-nutrition? What is the range?

Kramar maintains that the inebriety of the father has a more baneful effect on the offspring than the intemperance of the mother.

In *drunkenness*, the early mental and physical exhilaration, the irregular action of mind and body, the loss of control over the head and limbs, the deep, narcotic sleep, as well as the succeeding muscular and mental depression, the nausea and perverted sensations following the debauch, are, painfully, too well known. In *acute poisoning*, the influence may be so powerful as to cause dangerous sleep, loss of sensation, coldness of the surface of the body, feeble pulse, and speedy death. In *mania*, there is a fixed delusion at times, especially in those who have inherited a love for ardent spirits. *Acute alcoholism* ("the horrors") is characterized by tremor, restlessness, wakefulness, and a disturbed, anxious expression of the features. In this state, there is a want of appetite, frequent and feeble pulse, a marked depression of spirits, an inability to concentrate the mind on any subject; the affected person becomes vacillating, suspicious, quarrelsome, and cowardly. He has frightful dreams, hallucinations of hearing, seeing, smell, and taste. In *chronic alcoholism* as the result of the steady use of intoxicants for a considerable period, there is a striking deterioration of physical health, together with mental and bodily debasement. The memory and judgment are weakened, the different faculties of the mind are in abeyance. The person becomes untruthful, cunning, or cowardly, indifferent to the wants of those dependent on his exertions; often suffers from deep mental depression, with suicidal tendencies; the end is frequently general paralysis or dementia. In *dipsomania*, there is an uncontrollable impulse, "thirst" for alcoholics. It is a form of insanity. From a physiological point of view, it is hard to reform "chronic inebriates." Their nerve-centres have become so perverted in their action that they have lost self-control; the inherited coupled with the cultivated appetite demands a resistance beyond their powers.

409. CHLORAL is a hypnotic. It is a recent and a most seductive drug. The people have rapidly learned that it produces sleep and relieves restlessness and "nervousness." It is resorted to in order to produce sleep, as alcohol is to drown shame, and opium to deaden pain, and thus the "chloral habit" often becomes as pernicious as the "opium habit." Persons commencing with small doses become habituated to it, and are compelled to use larger and larger doses, until they are enslaved to the drug-craving.

In *chronic chloralism* there is marked muscular weakness, especially of the legs; there is feeble action of the heart, cold extremities, a tendency to profuse sweating, and peculiar cutaneous symptoms. Under its use the consumer becomes dull and dreamy, the will-power vanishes, the judgment is impaired, and the intellectual faculties are blunted. It is a dangerous drug. From it there are a large number of recorded cases of poisoning and death. It is often cumulative in its action. It should be used only under the direction of an educated medical man, and continued only while under his care.

410. HASHISH, or Indian Hemp, when given in full doses, produces a feeling of exhilaration, with a condition of revery. In the East it has long been employed as an exhilarating intoxicant,—a producer of deep sleep with an unconsciousness to pain. It induces a sense of prolongation of time,—that is, ideas are evolved with extraordinary rapidity. Its use may lead to catalepsy and to convulsions. It is not as pernicious in its effects as opium, yet its habitual use is not devoid of danger to the nervous system. It is an ingredient in several nostrums for the production of euthanasia in the advanced stages of phthisis.

411. OPIUM and its derivative *morphia* are most useful and most dangerous. The number of habitual consumers of morphia and opium appears to be on the increase in the United States, as well as in China and the East. In therapeutic doses, opium induces a quieting effect, accompanied by a peculiar dreamy condition. It is commonly stated that after taking opium there is a stage of increased mental activity. This is seen most frequently in those who take it habitually as a stimulant. The habitual opium-taker becomes spare of body, his appetite diminishes, his skin grows sallow and parchment-like, and the functions of portions of the glandular system are in abeyance. There is a marked deterioration of the will-power and of the memory, a manifest inclination to deceive and lie about the habit, a noticeable lack of attention to proper business, and a decided change in the moral tone. Actual mania or dementia may result from the long-continued use of the drug. To produce the desired effect, the amount of the drug used has to be steadily increased. The inability to get the drug in sufficient amounts and at the proper time causes mental and physical torments.

The hypodermic method of taking morphia is the most dangerous, both immediately and remotely. The opium-smoking method is less injurious than any other form of the opium habit. In the opinion of Dr. H. Kane, opium-smoking works less harm to the individual and to the community than alcoholism. A dangerous combination of tobacco and opium in the form of cigars and smoking-tobacco has recently come into use, by which the bad features of both drugs are made more seductive and more dangerous.

412. TOBACCO is a poison that modifies the energies, and not the structure, of the nervous system. It is an evasive

poison; no traces are stamped on the body, such as the "hob-nail liver" produced by alcohol. It, however, has a baneful effect on but a minority of *adults* who use it in moderation; and when the use of the weed is abandoned by adults, the worst effects generally disappear rapidly. In smoking, carbonic acid, carbonic oxide, several ammonias, and crude *nicotin* are drawn into the air-passages. Portions of the two latter enter the blood-current, circulate with the blood, work mischief in the nerve-centres, and are principally eliminated by the kidneys. The poisonous effect on the system is induced by the ammonias and the nicotin. The marked evil effect in adults is upon the mucous membrane of the air-passages: the tonsils are enlarged, the throat becomes red and dry: in short, the "smoker's sore throat" is established. The reports of the effects of tobacco on the digestive and nutritive functions are conflicting (286). Tobacco alone merely produces feebleness of vision, but tobacco and alcohol not unfrequently cause "tobacco amblyopia." In general, more intellectual work can be done without tobacco than with it.

On the youthful and the immature, the effects of tobacco, in what form soever taken, are pernicious. The processes of nutrition are diminished and the growth stunted; the innervation of the heart is disturbed; its action becomes weak, irregular, and intermittent, causing palpitation, faintness, and dizziness; muscular co-ordination is impaired, for it is said that youthful smokers cannot draw a "clean straight line." Certain glands, at first, are stimulated, especially by cigarette-smoking, but later become markedly

412. Why is tobacco called an evasive poison? What results from smoking? What are the active poisonous agents? Describe the "smoker's sore throat." What is the effect on the young? Why is tobacco a bane to youth? What conclusion?

debilitated; the power of concentration of mind is lessened, the intellectual activity is said to be impaired, and the whole individual is crippled. Tobacco is a bane to the youth of the world. No boy from ten to fifteen years old can practise smoking or chewing the weed without becoming mentally and physically less efficient when he reaches his majority than he otherwise would have been. Tobacco is not a food. Its consumption in the system does not evolve energy or heat, though it may enable a man accustomed to using it to continue work for a longer period when the accustomed food is protracted. For all young people, and for most adults, it would be healthier not to use tobacco in any form as an indulgence or a solace.

413. III.—THE JUDICIOUS AND REGULAR ACTION OF ALL PARTS OF THE ORGANISM.—*Exercise* (519) *of the skeletal muscles is an indispensable condition* for health of the brain and nervous system. Exercise compels the blood to flow more freely and fully, stimulates the excretory organs, sharpens the appetite, induces the taking in of more food and promotes its absorption and assimilation, and thus the blood offered to the cells of the nerve-centres is made richer, clearer, and more invigorating. The effect of insufficient exercise is felt in the brain, through the resulting indigestion and the deficient excretion by the bowels, lungs, and kidneys, as mental dulness and heaviness, impaired memory, impairment of the power of concentration, headache, neuralgic pains, etc. In persons who are merely sedentary, having little occasion for active thought, this want of exercise is sufficiently mischievous; but where there is great mental activity the mischief is

---

413. What results from muscular exercise? How does deficient exercise affect the brain? What of business-men? Of the English nobility? Of mental conditions affecting bodily health?

vastly increased. Hundreds of ministers, lawyers, and counting-room employés shorten their days because of this neglect. Especially is this the case in America. The English nobility, notwithstanding their many indulgences, are a long-lived race, and this is doubtless owing to their spending so much time in open-air exercise. That the bodily organs may be directly affected by impressions purely mental does not admit of doubt. Of this fact the skilful physician never loses sight; for a hopeful, healthful influence of the mind may be made a remedial agency quite as powerful as that of drugs, batteries, and baths.

414. *Mental Exercise.*—Regular and systematic mental exercise is essential to the health of the brain-cells. The nerve-cells need careful, methodical, graduated exercise, in order to increase their activity and efficiency. As the gymnast becomes expert not by spasmodic efforts, but by accurate, persistent drill, so must the mental athlete gain his power by the regular performance of such exercise as he is able to bear. The gymnast at first feels pain in his muscles, but he has only to persevere, with proper intervals of rest, and what was at first difficult becomes easy, while power is gained for severer feats. A person unaccustomed to mental gymnastics feels headache and confusion at first, but frequent repetition makes easy and natural the hitherto laborious efforts. By exercise the nerve-cells will gain that firmness which increases their capability for action.

415. The *amount of mental exercise* should be adapted to the health and age of the individual. If from any cause the nervous system be weakened, an amount of exercise which would be quite harmless to one in health may prove disastrous. The nerve-

---

414. What is the effect of systematic muscular work? Of systematic mental work? What influence on the brain-cells?

tissue of children and youths needs care; for overwork that in the adult is followed by fatigue, easily removed by rest, in the child may result in irreparable injury. Much evil undoubtedly arises from school-children remaining too long in cramped or otherwise restrained positions in ill-ventilated, poorly-lighted, improperly-desked school-rooms; but much more results from the excessive and premature strain to which the youthful brain is often subjected under the greater variety of instruction which is imparted under modern systems of education. Parents and teachers should not fail to remember that there are important differences in the quality of different brains. In some children the mental reaction to impressions is sluggish and incomplete; in others, again, the reaction is rapid and lively, but evanescent, so that, though quick at perception, they retain ideas with difficulty; while in others there is that just equilibrium between the internal and external in which the reaction is exactly adequate to impression. These differences should be taken into account.

416. EDUCATION.—The researches of Dr. Chaussier showed only one hundred and twenty-two out of twenty-three thousand two hundred newly-born infants to possess abnormal bodily peculiarities of any kind. Every child's mental future depends on that which it has inherited from its ancestors, upon the influences received from books at school and at home, and from the examples about it. If possible, the early book-knowledge should be inculcated at home. The minutes devoted to the study of one subject should be few, but the work should be earnest and the repetitions frequent. Dr. Chadwick is of the opinion that a child from the age of five to seven can attend to one

---

415. How should mental work be proportioned? What of the nerve-tissue of children? What evils in the modern school system? Speak of mental reactions. Effects of the forcing system.

416. Upon what does a child's mental future depend? What of early mental work? What is Dr. Chadwick's opinion? What injurious influences in school-life?

subject fifteen minutes; from seven to ten years, about twenty minutes; from ten to twelve, about twenty-five minutes; and from twelve to sixteen, about thirty minutes. The day-school is preferable for children to the boarding-school, with its atmosphere of discipline and routine. One of the great causes of overstraining in youth is the offering of prizes for the best exhibit in the faculty of memorizing. Of the causes of the physical deformities produced in school-life, bad air (sewer and once-breathed), poor lights, constrained positions, too long hours, and want of active, interesting exercise are most prominent.

417. *Let the drill of school-children and youth* be confined to a few subjects. Restrict those subjects in the public schools to the topics which are needed by the average citizen in ordinary life,—a knowledge of arithmetic, letter-writing, geography, history, human physiology and hygiene, plant-life, and animal life. Let the drill be vigorous, thorough, and progressive. Require the culture to be not of the memory alone, but of the powers of observation, of comparison, and of reasoning. Take the necessary time to accomplish a few things well. Let the study be intensive, not trivial and prolonged. Allow frequent intervals for rest, or for changes of position. Also instruct the young how to use properly the tools employed in daily adult life. By such a course the brain-centres will be in a state of sound health, and will be fitted for continuous enduring mental labor during youth, maturity, and age. But permit the brain-centres to be weakened in childhood and youth by diffusive studies, by prolonged lounging and dawdling over books, by cultivation of memory of words, by the production of a brain-dyspepsia, and the brain must ever work weighted and held back by ill-trained and perhaps permanently diseased centres.

418. HARMONIOUS DEVELOPMENT OF GIRLS.—The effect of the modern educational forcing system on boys is faulty enough, but more censurable on girls. The overwork that is forced on the miss entering her teens, from dress and the customs of society, in connection with the varied studies and exercises mapped out in the graded and higher schools, exhausts the nervous energies, stunts a proper physical development, and leaves the brain clogged with unassimilated material, which soon vanishes from want of a slower and more sterling culture. The vital energies and nerve-force which are thus dissipated should be devoted during youth to the consolidation of the physical system and invigoration of the mind. To have a healthy, well-balanced mind, the body must be strong and symmetrically developed. The culture of the feelings should be in harmony with the intellect. If either sex needs a high, harmonious development more than the other, physically, mentally, and morally, it is the woman. It is due to the home, due to the future of the country.

419. Says Dr. Ray, "I have no hesitation in saying that, of all the means for preserving health, there is nothing more sure, or better suited to a greater variety of persons, than *habits of regular and systematic mental occupation* of some dignity and worth. In this proposition I would embrace all those kinds of employment which pass under the general name of *business*, and which, little as we are disposed to recognize the fact, bear the same relation to the health of the mind that food, exercise, etc., do to the health of the body. Work is the condition of our being as active and progressive creatures.

420. "*The saddest effects of the absence of stated useful employment are seen among women of easy circumstances.* It is a poor view of woman's duties and capacities that confines her to a little busy idleness because the chances of fortune have placed her beyond the necessity of earning a living, and they must have but a narrow view of the exigencies of social life who believe that any woman of tolerable health and strength may not find abundant opportunities of that kind of work which affords no other recompense than the consciousness of doing good, and therefore to be done, if done at all, by those who can dispense with every other compensation. A life of idleness and luxurious ease can be no more honorable to one sex than to the other, and we know very well that in a man it creates no claims upon the respect and confidence of the community."

421. NORMAL SLEEP.—In sleep the prominent feature is the cessation of the automatic activity of the brain. All

---

421. What is the chief feature of sleep ? What has been observed ? What is Pflüger's idea ?

parts of the body share directly or indirectly in it: the pulse and respirations are slower; the intestines and the viscera are more or less at rest; the secreting organs are less active, and the temperature of the body is lowered. During sleep the cerebral vessels do not appear as gorged as during the waking hours. It cannot at present be stated what is the determining cause of this rise and fall of cerebral activity. Pflüger suggests that the marked intermission in brain-activity is due to an exhaustion of the oxygen stored up between the brain-cell molecules; that sleep is necessary for the maintenance of the functions of the brain; that during sleep the cerebral tissues lay up new stores of oxygen and other foods, in order to compensate for the disintegration and waste of the active hours. Sleep, after a day's labor, is deepest at its commencement.

422. The early hours of night afford the most refreshing sleep. The ventilation of the sleeping-room demands attention every night (207). The amount of sleep needed depends upon the age, health, natural temperament, and occupation of the individual. Pichegru is said to have slept only four hours out of twenty-four during one year's campaign. John Hunter, the anatomist, and Frederick the Great, required only five hours daily. The young and the aged need more sleep than the person of middle life; the sick, more than the well; those engaged in mental pursuits, more than those wearied by manual labor; persons of great sensibility, more than the sluggish natures whose normal condition is more nearly allied to sleep; women more than men. We may say, in general, that the time should not be less than from six to eight hours. Most persons, however, require a longer period.

423. BRAIN-WORK.—All good brain-work is accomplished by a brain having a reserve of strength sufficient to give buoyancy to the work. Thoroughly agreeable

mental work stimulates the recuperative faculty of the centres, and the supply of impulses seldom fails. In healthy centres the reserve of energy is kept up, and the brain increases in power for work and for endurance. The well-trained brain can do immense amounts of work and keep its condition; an ill-trained or non-trained brain, under less work, will give way. The condition which most commonly. exposes the reserve of mental energy to loss is worry. It is not mental work, but worry, that uses up the brain.

424. WORRY largely arises through the feeling of incapacity to perform the work at hand. By the wearing influence of worry the tone and strength of the mind are seriously impaired. As a result of worry, the nerve-mechanisms are thrown out of gear, and brain-action becomes discordant, and even painful. In school-life, the "cramming" of facts, the straining of the memory, the rivalry for prizes, the desire to do three years' work in two, with the lurking fear of failure before the mind; and in world-life, the struggles, the strifes, the combinations in business and in social circles, the envyings and emulations, constitute sources of worry. The induced abnormal cerebral action is manifested by headaches, confusion of thought, inability to fix the attention, failure of the memory, sleeplessness, and even pain. The impairment or failure of cerebral action indicates the need of *brain-rest.*

425. REST (529).—This is best secured by change of occupation. Idleness is the worst method of attaining rest. To a young person suffering from continuous headache, or

---

424. What is the cause of worry? What results from worry? Mention some sources of worry. What are indications for rest?

424. How can brain-rest be secured? What of idleness? In normal action? How with the laboring classes?

from wakefulness, moderate daily out-of-door work, not drugs, is indicated. All studies should cease. Amusement and muscle-work should occupy the waking hours. Only by a radical change can permanent cerebral mischief be averted. When the brain-action is normal, and no inconvenience is felt, mental rest may be secured daily by some kind of mental work which, without being fatiguing, requires just enough effort to impart interest, as a change from mathematics to languages or literature, or from these to music, painting, etc. Rest of the best kind is often afforded by diverting excursions and amusements. Among the laboring classes, amusements constitute almost the only practicable means for repairing the constant waste of nervous energy incident to monotonous toil and daily worries.

CHAPTER XII.

THE SPECIAL SENSES.

Taste.

426. The *tongue* (251), seated in the mouth, bears the chief *end-organs* of the sense of taste. The special nerves of taste are portions of the fifth and ninth cranial nerves

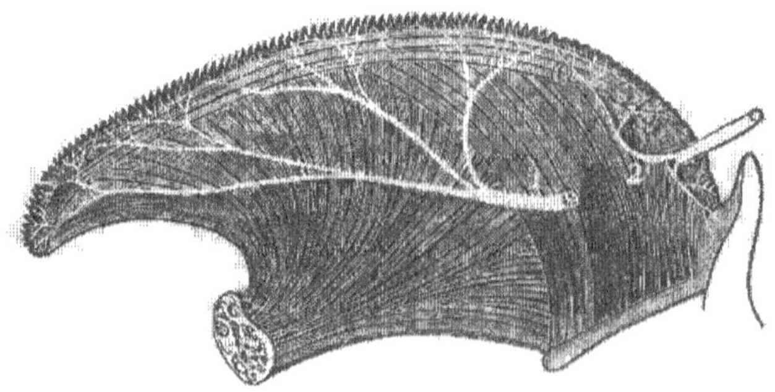

Fig. 90 (*Dalton*). Diagram of the Tongue, with its sensitive nerves and papillæ.—1, Lingual branch of fifth pair. 2, Glosso-pharyngeal nerve.

(382), which end in the papillæ of the mucous membrane of the tongue and palate. Minute blood-vessels, as well as nerves, pass into these papillæ. (See fine print under 251.)

427. Physiology of Taste.—It is essential for the development of taste that the substance experimented upon

---

426. What are the nerves of taste? What end in the papillæ?

427. What is essential for the development of taste? How is the sensation increased? When is it most acute?

should be dissolved. The effect is increased by rubbing the solution between the tongue and some hard body, as the roof of the mouth. The larger the surface, the more intense the sensation. A temperature of 22° C. (72° F.) is most favorable for the development of the sensation. Temperatures much above or below this lessen the sensation. Sweet substances have most effect when placed on the tip of the tongue; bitter, when placed on the back; and acid, it is said, on the edge.

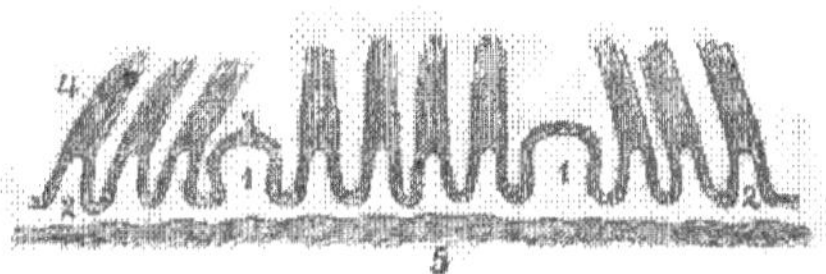

Fig. 91.

Fig. 91 (*Leidy*). DIAGRAM OF THE PAPILLÆ OF THE TONGUE, moderately magnified.—1, Capitate papillæ. 2, Conical papillæ. 3, Epithelium. 4, The same structure forming bunches of hair-like processes. 5, Areolar tissue.

428. Tastes may be classified as acid, saline, bitter, and sweet. Substances have the power of affecting the taste end-organs by virtue of their chemical nature. When the tongue is tapped, or a constant current is passed, a taste-sensation arises in the brain. The taste-sensation takes some time for its development after contact of the sapid body. Vintschgau determined the "reaction period" to be—for salines, .1598 second; for sugar, .1639 second; for acids, .1676 second; and for quinia, .2351 second. Von Wittich found it to be .1670 second for the constant current. The sensation endures for a considerable time, though this may be due to the substance remaining in contact.

Smell.

429. The *end-organs* concerned in the sense of smell are the nerve-filaments coming from the *olfactory lobes* (362). The nerve-filaments are distributed to the mucous

---

429. Speak of the end-organs concerned in smell. Describe the nasal passages. What of the membrane? Of the olfactory nerves? Of the fifth pair?

membrane lining the upper nasal passages. The nasal passages (see Fig. 38) extend from the opening of the nostrils in front to the pharynx behind. They are high, vaulted, narrow, and are separated from each other by a median partition, partly bony and partly cartilaginous. In the upper part of the vault are plates of bone hanging from the body of the *ethmoid* bone of the skull, and in the middle part a pair of scroll-like bones, the *turbinated*. Over these is stretched the very vascular nasal mucous membrane. The horizontal plate of the ethmoid, on which rest the olfactory lobes, has many holes, through which pass the nerves of smell. The nerve of sensation to the nasal mucous membrane is from the fifth pair.

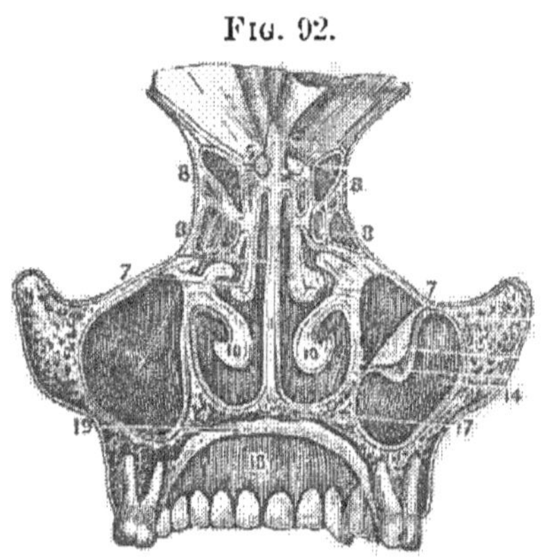

FIG. 92.

FIG. 92. A TRANSVERSE VERTICAL SECTION OF THE BONES OF THE FACE.—7, Middle turbinated bone. 8, 8, Ethmoidal cells. 10, 10, Inferior turbinated bones. 11, Vomer, covered by nasal mucous membrane. 14, Antrum. 17, Floor of nostrils and roof of mouth. 19, Mucous membrane of roof of mouth. 18, Anterior alveolar arch.

430. PHYSIOLOGY OF SMELL.—The olfactory end-organs are the only structures of the body upon which odors have a distinct effect. The sensory impulses produced in the olfactory end-organs, ascending to the brain, give rise to the sensation of smell. For the development of smell-impulses, the odorous particles must be conveyed to the membrane in a gaseous medium, as of the air. When the

***

nostrils are filled with rose-water, the odor of rose is not perceived. Each odorous substance causes a specific sensation. In ordinary breathing, through diffusion (176), portions of the incoming and outgoing air reach the olfactory end-organs. By sniffing, the odorous air is drawn higher up into the nasal passages, and thus influences a greater surface. The larger the affected surface, the more intense the sensation. We recognize the odor of cologne through

FIG. 93.

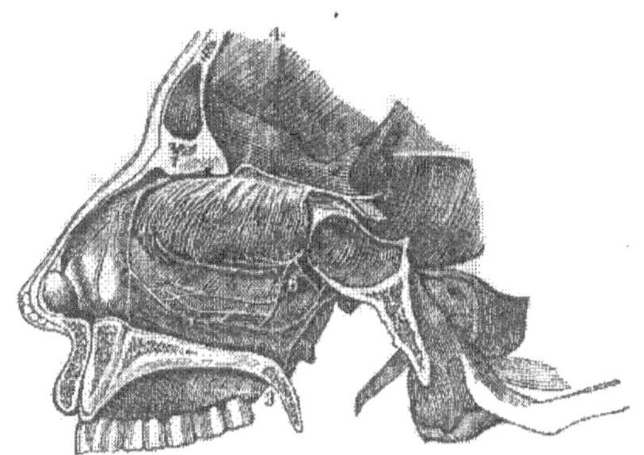

FIG. 93. A SIDE-VIEW OF THE PASSAGE OF THE NOSTRILS AND THE DISTRIBUTION OF THE OLFACTORY NERVE.—4, The olfactory nerve. 5, The fine divisions of this nerve on the membrane of the nose. 6, A branch of the fifth pair of nerves.

the olfactory nerve, and the pungency of ammonia through the fifth nerve. Time is required for the development and transmission of the impulses, and the sensation continues for some time. Under the constant influence of an odor or odors, the olfactory impulses are not perceived in the brain. This blunting of the sense of smell is noticed after remaining several hours in an atmosphere vitiated by tobacco-smoke and pulmonary and cutaneous exhalations, then going into the outer air and, after a few minutes, returning to the room. Hence it is that escaping gas and entering sewer-gas often fail to awaken the deep sleeper.

Audition.

431. The apparatus concerned in *hearing* consists of three parts,—the *external ear*, Fig. 94, 1 ; the *middle ear*, Fig. 94, 2 to 6 ; and the *internal ear*, Fig. 94, 6 to 13.

FIG. 94.

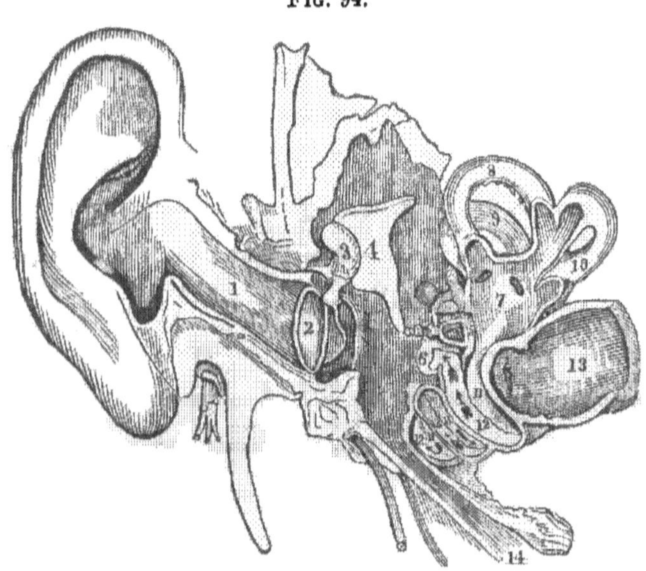

FIG. 94. A VIEW OF ALL THE PARTS OF THE EAR.—1, Meatus, or canal. 2, The membrana tympani. 3, 4, 5, The bones of the ear. 6, Membrane of the foramen ovale. 7, The central part of the labyrinth (vestibule). 8, 9, 10, The semicircular canals. 11, 12, The channels of the cochlea. 13, Auditory nerve. 14, The opening from the middle ear, or tympanum, to the throat (Eustachian tube).

432. The EXTERNAL EAR consists of the *pinna* and the *external auditory meatus*, or canal. The pinna is made up of a framework of firm, elastic cartilage, covered with skin, and attached to the sides of the head. It is provided

---

431. Of what is the hearing apparatus composed ?

432. Describe the pinna. What of its muscles ? Describe the meatus. What of its lining ?

with three feeble muscles, which in some persons are sufficiently developed to cause the movements of the pinna.
The meatus is a bony and cartilaginous canal, lined with
skin, leading to the interior of the *temporal* bone (Fig. 73).
It is about one and one-quarter inches deep, and terminates
at the *tympanum*. Its lining skin holds many stiff hairs,
numerous glands, which secrete a wax (cerumen) having a
bitter taste, and a few oil-glands.

433. The MIDDLE EAR, or TYMPANUM, is a small
chamber in the temporal bone. It contains air, certain
small bones, a few minute muscles, and nerves. It is separated from the meatus by a thin, oval-shaped membrane,
called the *membrana tympani.* It is lined with mucous
membrane. It communicates with many bony cells of the
temporal bone, with the internal ear by two openings,
which are closed in the natural state with membranes, and
through the *Eustachian tube* with the pharynx (158).
Hence, in catarrhs of the nasal passages and of the
pharynx, the disease-process often extends up the tube,
involves the middle-ear membrane, and gives rise to pain
and deafness. The bones are three in number,—the *malleus* (hammer), the *incus* (anvil), and the *stapes* (stirrup).
These bones weigh only a few grains, are covered with periosteum, have blood-vessels and nerves, give attachment to
minute muscles, and form movable joints.

434. The *malleus* is attached by its projecting process, called "the
handle," to the inner surface of the membrana tympani, and the
rounded part, or "head," is articulated with the thick part of the
incus. By its short leg the *incus* is attached to the back wall of
the tympanum, and by its long leg to the stapes. The *stapes* has a

---

remarkable resemblance to an iron stirrup. The foot-piece of the latter is attached to the membrane which closes the *fenestra ovalis*, or opening into the internal ear. These bones are so articulated to one another as to act as a single lever, the fulcrum being at the junction of the short leg of the incus with the wall of the tympanum, the long arm being in contact with the membrana tympani, and the short arm terminating in the base of the stapes. Hence the movement of the stapes is less than that of the membrana tympani.

Fig. 95.

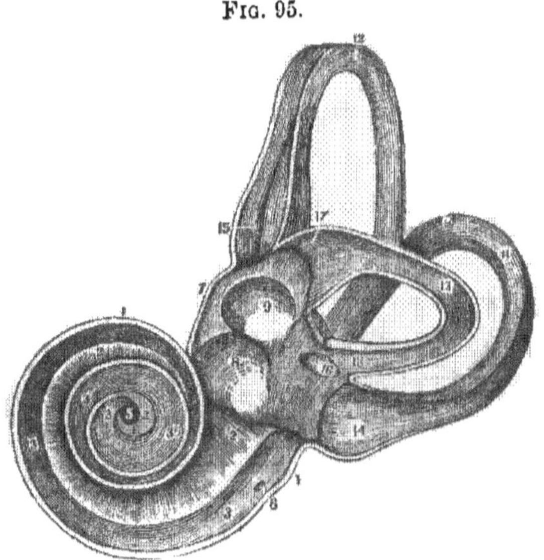

FIG. 95. A VIEW OF THE LABYRINTH LAID OPEN.—1, 1, Cochlea. 2, 3, Two canals, that wind two and a half turns around a hollow axis (5). 7, Vestibule. 8, Fenestra rotunda. 9, Fenestra ovalis. 11, 12, 13, 14, 15, 16, 17, 18, The semicircular canals. Highly magnified.

435. The INTERNAL EAR, or LABYRINTH, consists of several complex chambers and canals, each containing membranous and fluid contents and nerve-endings. The spaces occur in the hardest part of the temporal bone, in the base of the skull. These spaces communicate with one another,

---

435. What is the labyrinth? In what bone seated? What openings has it? Describe the chambers. Speak of the end-organs.

also with the middle ear, by two openings, the *fenestra ovalis* and the *fenestra rotundum*, and internally with the *internal auditory meatus*, which transmits the nerve of hearing from the brain to these spaces. These chambers consist of the oval-shaped *vestibule*, the three bony tubes of the *semicircular canals*, and a spiral, bony canal making two and a half turns, the *cochlea*, or "snail-shell." The *end-organs* of the auditory nerve are of two kinds, —the complicated *organ* of *Corti*, found in the cochlea, and the *epithelial* arrangements of *cells* and *hair-like organs* in the vestibule and the canals.

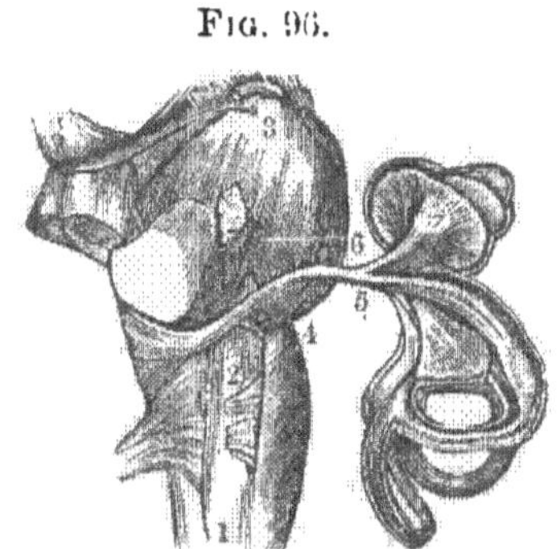

Fig. 96.

FIG. 96. A VIEW OF THE AUDITORY NERVE. —1, Spinal cord. 2, Medulla oblongata. 3, Lower part of the brain. 4, Auditory nerve. 5, A branch to the semicircular canals. 6, A branch to the cochlea.

436. SOUND, as sound, has no existence in nature. It cannot exist independent of a sense of hearing. When a tense string or wire, or a bar of steel, is struck, it is thrown into vibrations. These vibrations communicate movements to the adjacent air, water, or solids. The latter vibrations, conveyed to the end-organs of the ear, develop certain impulses. These impulses, reaching certain brain-centres, give rise to the *sensation of sound.* If the vibrations are less than thirty per second, or more than thirty-eight thousand per second, the sensation of sound is not perceived by man. The range of ordinary appreciation of tones lies between forty and four thousand vibrations per second.

---

436. What is necessary for the existence of sound? How is sound produced? How transmitted? How does the sensation arise? What of the appreciation of sound?

437. Sounds cannot be produced in, or propagated through, a vacuum. To produce or to transmit sound there must be some matter, as air, water, or solids, to be thrown into vibration. In *musical* sounds, the vibrations which cause them are periodical. When the vibrations are irregular, or the period is so complex as not to be appreciable, then the sensation produced is that of a *noise.* The human ear appreciates best the sound-vibrations which are transmitted through the air. It can and may receive sounds by the mouth and the nasal fossæ through the Eustachian tube, as when a vibrating tuning-fork is held between the teeth.

438. FUNCTIONS OF THE EXTERNAL AND MIDDLE EARS.—The *pinna* collects the waves of vibrations coming from various directions, and directs them into the meatus, and thence on to the *membrana tympani.* This membrane is very susceptible to air-vibrations, and is most readily thrown into corresponding movements when sound-waves reach it by the meatus. The loose articulation of the *ear-bones* prevents good bone-to-bone transmission of vibrations. But the series of bones acting together as one lever (434) transmits every vibration of the membrana tympani to the membrane covering the opening—fenestra ovalis—to the internal ear. The movements of the internal ear membrane are less than those of the membrana tympani, but the loss in amplitude is made up by a gain in force. Thus the sound-wave vibrations are intensified at the entrance to the labyrinth. The *Eustachian tube,* by permitting air to enter or to leave the middle ear by way of the pharynx, admits of equal pressure on the outer and inner surfaces of the membrana tympani. This arrangement, like the air-hole of a drum, enables the membrane to work equally well in the rare air of the mountain-top and the dense air of the deep mine.

---

438. What is the function of the pinna? Of the membrana tympani? Of the ear-bones? Of the Eustachian tube?

The tube also permits the secretions of the membrane of the middle ear to escape to the pharynx.

EXPERIMENT.—Close the nose and lips, fill the mouth-parts, and distend the cheeks with air, then go through the act of swallowing, but do not allow the air to escape by the mouth. After some practice, a peculiar pressure will be felt in both ears. Air has thus been forced from the pharynx through the Eustachian tube into the middle ear, and the membrane is forced outward. This sensation continues until, by the act of swallowing, the excess escapes. The aurist, by entering a peculiar tube into the Eustachian tube through the nostrils, is enabled to force air into the middle ear, and thus influence the membrane.

Close the mouth and nose, then, at the same time, swallow and inspire. Air will be drawn out of the middle ear, the membrane becomes drawn in, and a feeling of tension is produced. During the presence of an abnormal amount of air, or absence of a normal amount, the power of hearing is impaired, because the membrane cannot perform its normal function. If a person goes from the outer air at once into the condensed air of a caisson, there is great danger of the membrane being ruptured, owing to the unequal pressure. The same may be effected on coming out of the caisson, by reverse pressure.

439. PHYSIOLOGY OF HEARING.—The pinna, the meatus, the membrana tympani, the middle-ear cavity, the Eustachian tube, and the chain of bones, all work together to facilitate the reception of vibrations from without, and to transmit them correctly to the interior. This is their only function. The vibrations of the membrane at the base of the stapes are communicated to the fluids in the vestibule. The vibrations of this fluid are transmitted to the fluid in the cochlea and to the fluid and calcareous bodies within the membranes of the vestibule and semicircular canals. The physiological process of hearing only commences in the labyrinth. The end-organs of the auditory nerve in the labyrinth receive modified vibrations and generate *auditory impulses*. These impulses, passing over the auditory nerve and reaching certain parts of the brain, induce what we call *auditory sensation*. The appreciation of sound-waves is ultimately a mental act.

439. What parts serve only to transmit? By what are vibrations transmitted in the labyrinth? Where do the auditory impulses arise? Where the auditory sensations?

440. Whenever the fibres of the auditory nerve are stimulated, either by vibrations through the proper end-organs or by the direct application of stimuli,—electrical, chemical, or mechanical,—the result is always a sensation of sound. If sound-waves fall on the auditory nerve, they produce no sensory effect. Experiment shows that sound-waves must be brought to the auditory filaments through the proper end-organs to occasion in the brain the sensation of sound. The vibrations generated in the fluid, the *endolymph*, within the membranous canals and vestibule, are supposed to influence the auditory hairs and cells; the vibrations of the vestibular fluid, the *perilymph*, to influence the organs of Corti and the basilar membrane. Certain structures of the membranous semicircular canals are held to be the end-organs of the *sense of equilibrium* (475), and the organ of Corti is considered to be the end-organ of the labyrinth concerned in the *sense of hearing*.

441. AUDITORY SENSATIONS.—They are of shorter duration than visual sensations. When a visual sensation is repeated ten or more times a second the sensations become fused as one (463). The ticks of a pendulum beating one hundred a second are audible as distinct sounds. A well-trained ear can distinguish, through a long range of notes, the difference of a single vibration per second. The "reaction period" for sounds is about one-sixth of a second. In seeking for the cause of auditory sensations, we almost always refer them to the external world. We do not think of the sound as originating in the hearing apparatus. The judgment of the *distance* of sounds is quite limited. A sound of a known character we locate as near or far by its degree of loudness. The distance through which an unaccustomed sound has been propagated we can only vaguely surmise. The judgment of direction of sounds is also limited. In determining direction, the position of the head and the ear most affected are chiefly to be depended upon. The origin of the sound from the human voice is found to be more readily and accurately located than the vibrations from a musical instrument or from noise.

Sight.

Directions for Dissection.—Secure the eye of an ox or sheep. Observe: the transparent, bulging, glass-like *cornea* in front; surrounding and continuous with the cornea, the dirty-white *sclerotica*; and the thin *conjunctiva* adherent to the sclerotica as far forward as the corneo-sclerotic junction, and as far back as the junction of the eyelids with the ball, and on the inner side of the lids. Dissect away the fat from the posterior part of the ball, exposing the junction of the four recti (straight) muscles with the sclerotic and the round *optic nerve*. The latter does not enter the ball in the axis of the eye.

Puncture the cornea, and a small amount of limpid fluid, the *aqueous fluid*, escapes. With fine embroidery scissors cut the cornea from the sclerotic close to its union with the latter. The cornea is seen to be transparent, of nearly uniform thickness, and watch-glass-shaped. With the cut surface uppermost, examine the eye. Note: the *iris*, its free edge bounding the dark opening called the *pupil*, and resting on the anterior surface of the capsule of the lens. On the front surface of the lens make a shallow, cross-shaped incision. The tissue which retracts is the *capsule of the lens*. Under slight

FIG. 97.

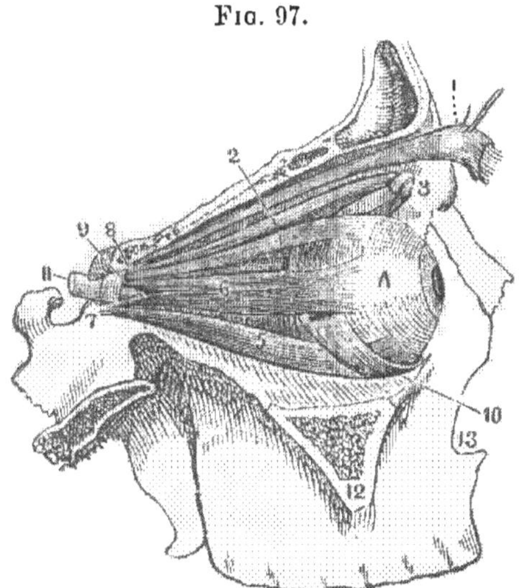

FIG. 97 (*Leidy*). MUSCLES OF THE EYE.—1, The palpebral elevator muscle. 2, The superior oblique. 3, The pulley through which the tendon of insertion plays. 4, Superior straight muscle. 5, Inferior straight muscle. 6, External straight muscle. 7, 8, Its two points of origin. 9, Interval through which pass the oculo-motor and abducent nerves. 10, Inferior oblique muscle. 11, Optic nerve. 12, Cut surface of the malar process of the superior maxillary bone. 13, The nasal orifice. A, The eyeball.

pressure with the handle of the scalpel the *lens* will escape from its capsule. Notice the difference in curvature between its front and rear surfaces, the firmness of its tissues, and its transparency. Cause a ray of light to pass through a fresh lens, and note its *refracting* power. Behind the bed in which the lens rested will be seen the glassy *vitreous humor*. Allow the vitreous to escape. Looking into the hollow of the ball, note: the entrance at the fundus of the *optic nerve*, and the blood-vessels radiating from that spot. Separate the inner thin membrane, the *retina*, from the next membrane, the *choroid*. Observe that the retina appears like an expansion of the optic nerve, and that most of the *black pigment* adheres to the choroid. At the anterior edge of the choroid, near its junction with the cornea, are seen the pale fibres of the *ciliary muscle*. Outside of the choroid is seen the *sclerotica* of the posterior part of the ball.

Microscopic Work.—The careful examination of the eyeball is one of the most remunerative labors of the microscopist. The study of the retina, however, is one of the most difficult problems. The fresh, still warm eyes of the ox or sheep are best. The injection run into the optic artery is preferably carmine or Prussian blue. In half an hour the work of dissection and examination may be commenced. Make transverse sections of the cornea and sclerotica. Tease out and examine in five per cent. saline solution or the aqueous humor bits of the various membranes. By such work much can be learned of the structure of the organ. The transparent structures require to be hardened and darkened, in order to make out the relations of one structure to another. (For details see Frey's "Microscopic Technology," Section 22.) Müller's eye-fluid—bichromate of potassa, 2 grammes; sulphate of soda, 1 gramme; distilled water, 100 grammes—is excellently adapted for hardening the unopened immersed eyeball. After a month's immersion, very handsome and useful sections can be made.

442. The ORGANS OF SIGHT in man consist of the *eyeballs*. The external protective apparatus consists of the *eyebrows*, the *eyelids*, the *lachrymal gland* and its *appendages*, and the *palpebral glands*. The eyeballs and the tear-glands are lodged in the bony cavities called the *orbits* (340).

443. The ORBITS are pyramidal in shape, having a quadrangular base. Their apexes are directed backward and inward. Near the apex of each orbit may be seen openings for the nerve of sight, the nerves of sensation and motion of the eye-parts and blood-vessels. In the orbit the eyeball rests on a cushion of fat, and is moved by the *ocular muscles*,—four straight muscles (*recti*) and two oblique (superior and inferior obliquus).

444. The EYEBROWS are the thick, fat ridges, studded with hairs, surmounting the orbits. The hairs are set obliquely outward. The EYELIDS are the two thin, movable covers of the eyeball. The upper one is the larger, and provided with a special elevator muscle. The free margins of the lids are bevelled and beset with *eyelashes*. The

442. What are the organs of sight? Name the protective organs.

443. Describe the orbits. Upon what do the eyeballs rest? How moved?

444. Describe the eyebrows. The eyelids. The eyelashes. The palpebral glands.

lashes of the upper lid curve upward, those of the lower, downward; hence there is no interlacing. Each eyelid consists of a thin, semilunar plate of cartilage, covered on the outside with thin skin and fibres of the muscle of the lids (*orbicularis palpebrarum*, Fig. 127), and on the in-

FIG. 98.

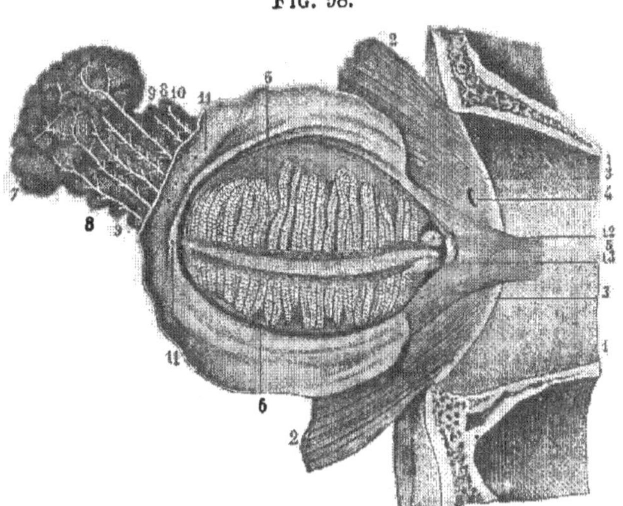

FIG. 98 (*Leidy*). THE LEFT EYELID AND LACHRYMAL GLAND, TURNED FORWARD AND INWARD, TO SHOW THEIR INNER SURFACE.—1, Upper and lower part of the orbit. 2, Portion of the palpebral orbicular muscle. 3, Attachment of this muscle to the inner margin of the orbit. 4, Perforation for the passage of the external nasal nerve. 5, Offset described as the tensor muscle of the eyelids. 6, Palpebral glands. 7, Posterior, and 8, anterior portions of the lachrymal glands. 9, 10, Ducts. 11, Orifices opening on the inner surface of the upper eyelid. 12, 13, Puncta lachrymalis.

side with the *conjunctiva* (448). On the inner surface of the cartilage are little grooves, which contain the minute *palpebral glands*. The oily secretion from these glands passes by minute ducts on to the free edge of the lids.

445. FUNCTIONS.—The *eyebrows* influence the amount of light reaching the eyes, slightly protect the eyeballs

445. What are the functions of the eyebrows? Of the lids and lashes? Of the palpebral glands?

from foreign bodies, and turn aside the perspiration flowing from the forehead. The *eyelids* and *lashes* prevent the entrance of an excess of light, and, by the rapid movements of the former, play an important part in the moistening and cleansing of the eyeballs. In *winking*, which may be voluntary, though usually reflex (82), foreign bodies are swept over the ball inward to the lachrymal lake. The *palpebral gland* secretion oils the edges of the eyelids, prevents their adhesion, and protects them from the action of the tears.

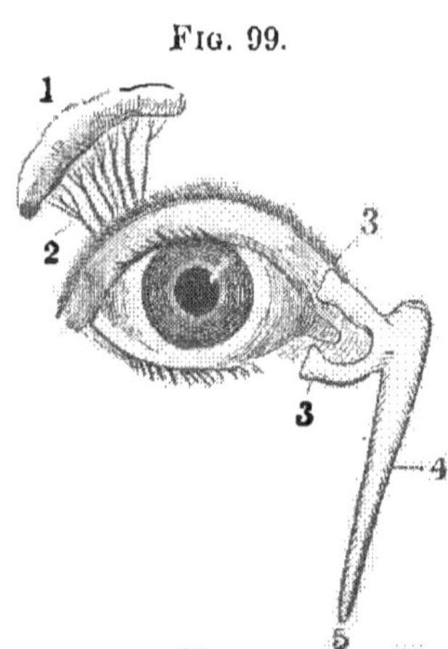

FIG. 99. VIEW OF LACHRYMAL GLAND AND NASAL DUCT.—1, The lachrymal gland. 2, Ducts leading from the lachrymal gland to the upper eyelid. 3, 3, Canaliculi. 4, The nasal sac. 5, The termination of the nasal duct.

446. The LACHRYMAL GLAND (Fig. 99) is a small almond-shaped body, found in a depression in the upper and outer part of the orbit, between the bone and the eyeball. Its ducts, from six to twelve in number, open on the inner surface of the upper eyelid, near the outer angle. Their secretion, the *tears*, is a clear, saltish, alkaline fluid, containing a little albuminoid matter.

447. LACHRYMAL CANALS.—On the margin of each eyelid, near the inner angle, is a little projection, having a small opening, the *puncta lachrymalis*. This is the commencement of the tear-canal. The short canals from the

---

446. Speak of the lachrymal gland. Shape. Location. Duct-secretion.

447. What is the puncta? What meet in the nasal sac?

puncta of the upper and lower lids meet in the nasal sac, from which the *nasal duct* conducts the tears to the lower part of the nose.

448. The CONJUNCTIVA is a mucous membrane (165). It lines the inner surface of the lids, covers the exposed surface of the eyeballs, dips into the orifices of the glands, and, through the nasal duct, is continuous with the nasal membrane. Hence, in colds of the nasal passages, the eyes are often red, irritable, and watery.

449. FUNCTIONS.—The secretions of the lachrymal glands and of the conjunctiva moisten the surface of the eyeballs and lids, facilitate the movements of the eyeball, and preserve the transparency of the cornea. The *tears* are the more abundant secretion. An increased flow of tears may · be oc-

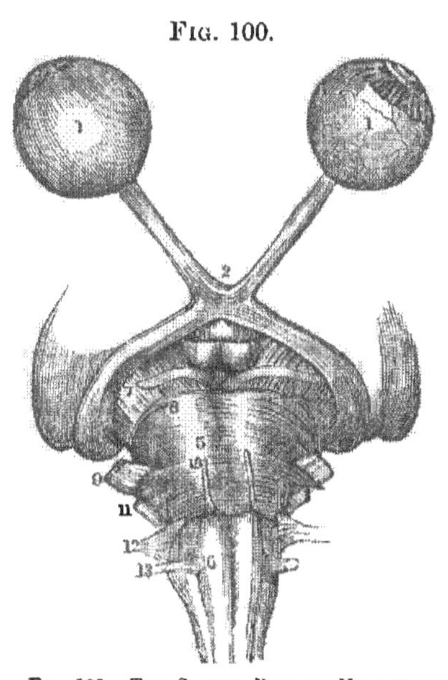

FIG. 100.

Fig. 100. THE SECOND PAIR OF NERVES.— 1, 1, Globe of the eye: the one on the left is perfect, but that on the right has the sclerotic and choroid coats removed, to show the retina. 2, Optic commissure. 5, The pons Varolii. 6, The medulla oblongata. 7, 8, 9, 10, 11, 12, 13, The origin of several pairs of cranial nerves.

casioned by a strong light, by irritants acting on the surfaces of the eye, nose, and tongue, as of dust, snuff, and pepper, and by vomiting, laughing, and crying. By constant efforts, the tear-glands can be educated to produce

---

448. Describe the conjunctiva. What occurs in colds?

449. What are the functions of the tears and mucus? How may the tear-flow be increased? What becomes of the tears?

large amounts of tears, as seen in lachrymose beggars, hypocrites, etc. In passing over the surface of the eyeball, a portion of the secretions is evaporated, but the larger part passes into the punctæ of the lids and is discharged into the nostrils. When mental emotions excite a flow of tears, the lady removes the surplus from the eyes and face with her handkerchief; but the gentleman, not wishing that his emotion should be marked, covers his face with his handkerchief—and blows his nose.

450. The EYEBALL is a strong, closed, membranous sac, rudely compared to a globe. It is about an inch in diameter. It is spherical in form, but has a segment of a smaller and more prominent sphere engrafted on its front part. Hence its front-to-rear diameter is longer than its side-to-side diameter. It is attached behind to the optic nerve, and is maintained in position by its muscles (443). It occupies a protected position in the orbit, and has an extensive range for vision. The *optic nerves* arise each on its side of the brain, but at the *commissure* (Fig. 84, 24) they communicate with each other.

451. MEMBRANES or TUNICS.—The eyeball is surrounded by a hard, firm membrane, the *sclerotica* (Fig. 101, *m*, *n*). In living persons, the front exposed segment of this membrane shining through the *conjunctiva*, *f*, *f*, is called the " white of the eye." In front it passes into the *cornea*, *h*, *h*, characterized by its glass-like transparency. It rises and bulges in the middle, like an old-fashioned watch-crystal, and through it light passes into the interior. Within the sclerotica is a thinner and more delicate mem-

450. Describe the eyeball. What of its position? What of its nerve?

451. Speak of the sclerotica. Of the cornea. Of the choroidea. Of the iris. Of the retina.

brane, the *choroidea, g, g.* It contains a large number of blood-vessels, and is black, owing to the presence of a large number of pigment-cells. This membrane joins in front the *iris, p, p,* which is seen to rest on the front surface of

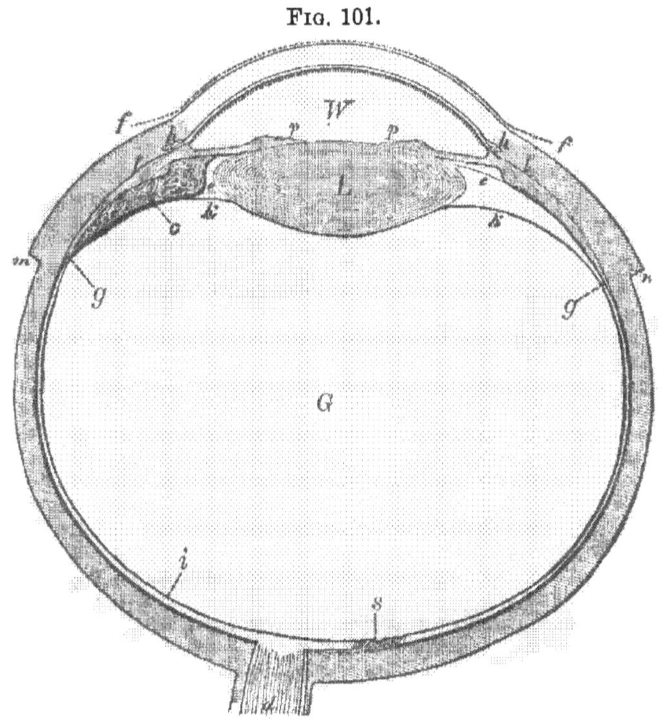

FIG. 101.

FIG. 101. HORIZONTAL SECTION OF RIGHT EYE (from *Helmholtz*).—W, Aqueous humor. L, Lens. G, Vitreous humor. f, f, Conjunctiva. h, h, Cornea. p, p, Iris. t, t, Ciliary muscle. k, k, Hyaloid membrane. c, Ciliary processes. e, e, Suspensory ligament. m, n, Sclerotica. g, g, Choroidea. i, Retina. s, Fovea centralis. d, Optic nerve.

the lens. This iris is seen in every normal human eye, and assumes a lighter or darker hue according to the number of its pigment-cells. The iris surrounds the dark opening, the *pupil.* Within the choroid is an exceedingly delicate membrane, the *retina, i.* It forms the continuation and extension of the *optic nerve, d,* the nerve of vision.　It contains the *end-organs* of the apparatus of vision.

452. IRIS.—The greater the number of the pigment-cells on the posterior surface of the iris, the darker is the "color of the eye." The variation in amount of the pigment is the cause of the different shades seen in the eye, ranging from the darkest brown to light blue and gray.　In the *albino,* the pigment is absent from the choroid, as well as from the hair and skin.　The iris of an albino appears whitish red, and the pupil of a bright red.　When exposed to a dazzling light, through reflex action, the eyelids are incessantly winking, owing to the retinal demand for a moderation of the light. The iris is provided with dilating and contracting muscular fibres. In the natural state, the pupil is constantly undergoing changes of diameter.　The instillation of a solution of atropia causes the pupil to become very large; of eserina, very small.

DEMONSTRATION AND EXPERIMENTS.—Select a boy having a large ocular fissure and a prominent eye.　Call the attention of the class to the *eyebrows,* the direction of the hair, the thickness of implantation as compared with some other boys, and the hairless tract, in most cases above the bridge of the nose, *eyelids,* and *eyelashes.*　Point out the method of the insertion of the lashes, the direction and curvature of the upper and lower rows, and the non-interlacement.　Gently pull down the lower lid.　Demonstrate the junction of the mucous membrane and the skin, the place of implantation of the lashes, the fifteen to twenty openings on the fine edge of the lid (outlets of the *palpebral gland ducts*), and the slight elevation on the margin near the inner angle, which has an opening (puncta). Gently seize the lashes of the upper lid, hold a small pencil on the upper lid from three-eighths to five-eighths of an inch from the margin, direct the student to look down, then quickly evert the lid.　Note the pink, moist mucous membrane, the *conjunctiva,* and the outline of the tarsal cartilage pressing on the conjunctiva.

When the eye is open, an elliptical space, the *fissure,* and at the outer and inner junctions of the skin of the upper and lower lids, the *canthi,* appear.　The fissure is almond-shaped in the pure Semites, large in negroes, and small in Mongolians.　In the Esquimaux, Chinese, and most of the Japanese, the internal canthus is lowered, while the external has an upward direction.　The internal canthus is covered by a fold of loose skin.　This fold is slightly stretched over the angle of the eyelids, and covers the caruncle, which is visible in the Americo-Europeans, and forms a kind of third eyelid, in the form of a crescent.　The small triangular space at the inner canthus, the *lacus,* contains a small, reddish, conical body, the *caruncle.*　This is the source of the whitish secretion which collects at the inner angle.

Point out the loose, clear, white, thin *conjunctiva* overlying the sclerotica; the white or yellowish-white *sclerotica,* the clear, transparent *cornea,* the black *pupil,* and the various-hued *iris.*　Place a lamp to the right and a little in front of the face of the student. With a convex lens between the lamp and the eye, direct a pencil of rays on to the cornea.　Then call attention to the *cornea,* its form and scleral junction, the *anterior chamber,* containing the *aqueous humor,* the *iris,* and the *lens.*　Note the ready contraction and dilatation of the pupil under varying amounts of light.

Request, if convenient, an oculist to demonstrate to the class the fundus of the eye from the normal model of the phantom, pointing out the *retinal vessels*, the *blind spot*, and the *yellow spot*. Then, if possible, permit the students to observe the interior of the living eye by the aid of the ophthalmoscope.

Look with one eye intently through a small hole in a card at the bright blue sky. Move the card very rapidly from side to side, or up and down. The eye sees on the cards the shadows of the fine capillary retinal vessels. Hence the end-organs of the retina are behind the blood-vessels (462). Remove the objective from a microscope. Look into the eye-piece, and move the head rapidly from side to side, when the shadows of the retinal vessels will be perceived by the eye.

Close the left eye. Hold a sheet of white paper having a central black dot before the right eye. Fix the eye on the black spot. Dip a quill-pen in black ink, and move its point gradually in one direction from the black spot. At a certain distance, the black spot of ink will no longer be seen. Make a dot. Continue the movement outward, and the ink-spot again comes into view. Make a dot. It will now continue in sight until it passes from the field of vision. Make similar trials along other meridians. Connect the black places by lines. An irregular figure will be drawn, circumscribing an area of the field of vision within which rays of light produce no visual sensation. This indicates the presence of a blind spot in the eye (462).

453. FUNCTIONS OF THE TUNICS.—The *sclerotica* and *cornea* determine the form of the eyeball, and support and protect the delicate parts in the interior. Through the posterior part of the former pass the optic nerve and the retinal vessels, and into it are inserted the muscles which move the eyeball. The former is not transparent, but a strong light directed through it illuminates the interior. The *cornea* permits the ray of light from the outer world to enter the eye. The *choroidea* absorbs the strong rays of light, and thus assists in making a clearer image on the retina. The *iris*, by changing the size of the pupil, regulates the amount of light entering the eye, acts as a diaphragm to cut off the rays which are not parallel to the principal stream of light, and aids in near vision. The *retina* contains the microscopic rods and cones, the *end-organs* of vision. The end-organs change the impressions of light into the impulses which occasion in the brain the *sensation of vision.*

453. What are the functions of the sclerotica? Of the cornea? Of the choroidea? Of the iris? Of the retina?

454. MEDIA AND LENS.—The space between the posterior surface of the cornea and the anterior surface of the lens and iris is filled by the *aqueous humor*, *W* (Fig. 101). This humor consists of about five drops of a limpid fluid resembling water. Directly behind the iris is the *lens, L*, which resembles a thick burning-glass. In the normal eye it is clear as crystal. In the disease called *cataract* it becomes more or less opaque. The lens is more bulging, or convex, on its rear surface than on its front surface. It is enclosed in the *capsule* of the lens, which is held in place by an elastic membrane, the *suspensory ligament, e, e*. The space, spheroidal in shape, between the back surface of the lens and the front surface of the retina is filled by the *vitreous humor, G*. This is a clear, gelatinous mass, surrounded by a fine thin membrane.

455. FUNCTIONS OF THE MEDIA AND LENS.—The eye is a camera. It consists of a series of lenses and media arranged in a dark chamber, in which the iris acts as a diaphragm. The object of this apparatus is to form on the retina a distinct image of objects placed before the eye. The rays of light on entering the eye traverse in succession the cornea, the aqueous humor, the lens, and the vitreous humor. The rays of light are strongly bent out of their course—*i.e.*, are *refracted*—at the front surface of the cornea and at the front and rear surfaces of the lens. The many rays of light coming from the field of view are thus concentrated on the limited field of the retina.

EXPERIMENT.—Remove the front convex lens from a pair of opera-glasses, or procure a convex lens with a gradual curve. Hold it opposite a window, and place a piece of white paper behind it to act as a screen. A small reversed picture of the window-frame

454. Where is the aqueous humor found? Speak of the lens. How is it held in place? Describe the vitreous humor.

455. What is the eye? What is its function? Through what do rays of light pass? How are they influenced? What results?

will appear on the paper. If the paper be moved to a certain distance, varying with each lens, the picture will become clear and distinct, yet with color-rings about the edges. At that distance from the lens the paper is said to be *in focus*. If the paper be moved nearer to, or farther from, the lens, the picture becomes blurred, and the paper is said to be *out of focus*.

Visit a photographer's studio. Request him to point out and name the uses of the essential parts of the camera,—the blackened box, the ground-glass screen, the lens, the diaphragm, and the apparatus for adjusting the lens and the screen to the object. Watch him place the camera and then work the ground-glass screen into the proper focus. When all is ready, put your head under the curtain of the camera and study the reversed image depicted on the glass.

Carefully remove the sclerotica and choroidea from a small portion of the back of a bullock's eye, near the entrance of the optic nerve. Place the prepared eye in the end of a tube, blackened in the interior, which closely fits the globe of the eye, having the cornea forward. You will be enabled to see a distinct reversed image on the retina of the illuminated object in front of the cornea.

456. LIGHT.—The sun is the chief source of light. The principal sources of earthly light are combustion, friction, and electricity. Bodies which are not luminous, like most natural objects, are rendered visible by the light which falls upon them. The rays of light move in straight lines. The luminous power diminishes as the square of the distance through which it passes,—*i.e.*, the illumination is nine times as powerful at one foot as it is at three feet from the source of light. The sunlight is white. It may be decomposed by a prism or a convex lens into several colored lights.

457. REFRACTION.—When parallel rays of light pass from one medium to another, as from air through water and glass to air again, in a direction perpendicular to the media, they continue to move on in the same lines; if, however, they enter the media obliquely, or enter a medium having a curved or prismatic surface, they are bent out of their course,—*i.e.*, are *refracted*. Rays of light coming

---

456. Mention sources of light. How do light-rays move? How does the power decrease? What of sunlight?

457. Explain the phenomenon of refraction of light. What is its connection with clearness of vision?

from a large object and passing through a double convex lens, like the lens of the eye, are bent towards the central axis of the lens, and form a small reversed image on a screen placed behind the lens, but nearer to the lens than is the object. If the screen be placed at the focus of the lens, the image will be clear and distinct; if not, the image will be blurred.

458. ACCOMMODATION.—When the photographer has placed his camera in a favorable position in order to secure a clear image on the ground glass, he moves the lens, or the screen, or both, backward or forward until the reversed image of the object appears clearly on the glass screen. In the camera the refractive power of the lens is fixed, and the diaphragm is changeable, but the distance between the lens and the screen is adjustable. In the human eye, the distance between the refractive surfaces and the screen (retina) is fixed, the diameter of the opening of the diaphragm (pupil) and the refractive power of the lens are adjustable. In adapting our eyes to form on the retina a clear, sharp image of a near object, we are conscious of an effort. In this adaptation,—1, the pupil contracts; 2, the front surface of the lens becomes more convex; and, 3, the refracting power of the lens is thus increased. In looking from a very near object to a distant object, no effort is needed in the normal eye; the forced pupil-contraction ceases, and the lens assumes its natural shape. *Accommodation* is the adjustment within the eye in order to permit a clear and distinct image to be formed on the retina.

EXPERIMENT.—In a dark room hold a candle on one side of the eye, about eighteen inches distant. Let the observer stand on the opposite side of the front of the eye. Let the examined eye rest at ease. Three images of candle-light will appear,—one from the surface of the cornea, an erect image from the anterior surface of the lens, and a reversed image from the posterior surface of the lens. If now the person being examined looks at an imaginary near object, the first and third images keep their position and relative brightness, but the second image advances and becomes dimmer, and the pupillar margin of the iris inclines slightly forward. When the eye is allowed to adjust for distant vision,—*i.e.*, assumes the position of ease,—the second image recedes and becomes brighter, and the others retain their position and relative brightness. Hence, in accommodation, the anterior surface of the lens becomes more convex; the cornea does not change its form, and the posterior portion of the lens neither advances nor recedes.

459. MECHANISM OF ACCOMMODATION.—The lens is elastic. The suspensory ligament (454) keeps the lens tense and its front

surface somewhat flattened. In accommodation for near objects, the contraction of the ciliary muscle (Fig. 101, *t, t*) pulls forward the choroid coat and the ciliary processes and slackens the suspensory ligament, and thus the lens is allowed to bulge forward, in virtue of its elasticity. When the lens is removed, as for cataract, the ability to accommodate is lost. Accommodation is a voluntary act. But few persons can effect it at will unless they are aided by visual sensations resulting from turning the attention to a near object.

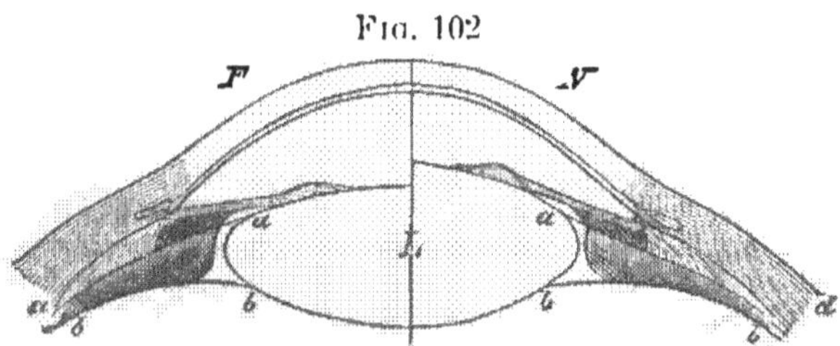

Fig. 102.

Fig. 102. Diagram showing Change in Front Shape of Lens in Accommodation (from *Helmholtz*).—*L*, Lens. *N*, The lens adjusted for near vision. *F*, The lens adjusted for normal vision.

The contraction of the pupil which takes place at the time of the accommodation results from an associated action of the central nervous system. The mechanism for the association of accommodation and contraction of the pupil appears to be located in the corpora quadrigemina (362). In looking from a distant object to one very near, we are conscious of an effort; when looking from a very near to a distant object, there is a sense of relaxation or relief.

EXPERIMENT.—Fix two needles upright in a yard-stick or a similar bit of wood. Place the needles about thirty inches apart. Hold the stick on a level with the eye, and in such a manner as to have the needles nearly in a line, and the nearest very close to the eye. Direct the attention to the far needle, then glance at the near needle: the former appears distinct, the latter blurred. Direct the attention to the near needle, then glance at the far needle: the converse is noticed. In the first instance, the image of the far needle is focussed on the retina, but the focus for the near needle is *behind* the retina; hence the blurred image on the retina (457). When the image of the near needle is focussed, the focus for the far needle is in *front* of the retina, and diffusion circles are formed on the retina.

If the near needle be gradually brought nearer and nearer to the eye, we find that greater and greater effort is required to see it; the eye is rolled in, the pupil contracted, and the accommodation mechanism forced to its limits, till at last no effort can make a clear image on the retina. The position of the needle now marks the limit of *accommodation for near objects*. If the person be "near-sighted," the object can be brought yet nearer to the eye and still produce a clear image. If the object be removed gradually from the "near-sighted" eye, a point is very soon reached at which the image becomes blurred. This marks the limit for accommodation for the given eye for *far objects*. If the object be gradually removed away from a normal eye, the image continues clear so long as the object is in sight. Hence the *far point* for the near-sighted is near at hand; for the normal eye, at an infinite distance.

Test the eyes of the pupils by a set of *Snellen's test-types*. These are a series of types arranged according to the size of the letters, ranging from No. I. to No. XX. No. I. is seen by a normal eye at a distance of one foot, at an angle of 5′; the letters of No. II. are seen at two feet distance, at the same angle; and so on, up to No. XX. The accompanying test-line is No. X., and should be easily read at ten feet by the normal eye. Some pupils may be able to read it at eleven or more feet distant (463).

V Z B D F H K O S

460. NEAR LIMIT AND FAR LIMIT.—In the normal (*emmetropic*) eye the near limit of accommodation is about 10 or 12 centimetres (3.9 to 4.7 inches) from the cornea, and the far limit, for practical purposes, at an infinite distance. In the "short-sighted" (*myopic*) eye the near limit is about 5 or 6 centimetres (1.9 to 2.4 inches), and the far limit only shortly removed from the eye. In the "flat eye" (*hypermetropic*) the near limit is at some distance away, and a far limit of accommodation does not exist. This ocular defect is quite common in school-children. In the "long-sighted" eye of old people (*presbyopic*) the near point is at some distance away, but the eye is unable to focus it, and the far point is at an infinite distance. In the *normal* eye, when no effort of accom-

FIG. 103.

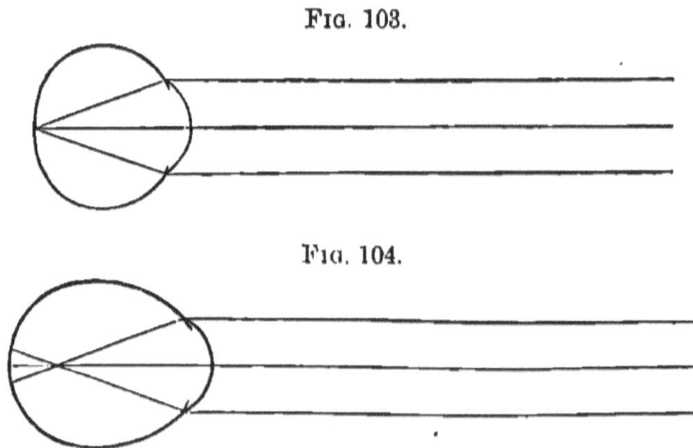

FIG. 104.

modation is made, the principal focus of the eye lies on the retina (Fig. 103); in the *near-sighted* eye, in front of it (Fig. 104); and in the *flat* eye, behind it (Fig. 105). The near-sighted eye and the flat eye are abnormal eyes. The former condition may rise from

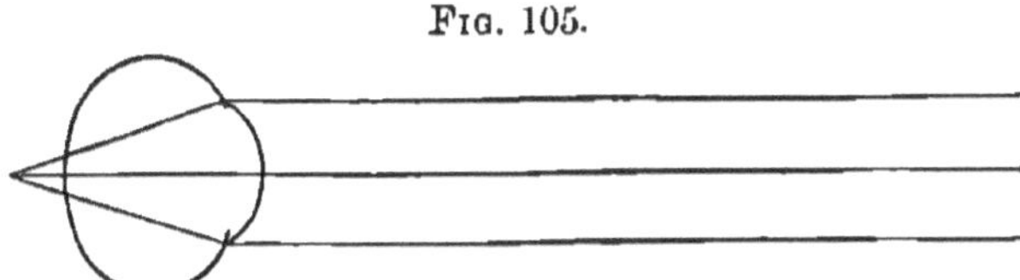

FIG. 105.

too convex a cornea, too convex anterior surface of the lens, spasm of the mechanism of accommodation, or from too great length of the long axis of the eyeball. The latter condition is the most common factor. This defect is corrected by using concave glasses. The flat eye possesses too short an antero-posterior axis. Its defect is corrected by using convex glasses.

461. IMPERFECTIONS OF THE EYE.—What is known as a normal eye is not a perfect optical instrument. *Spherical aberration* exists more or less, owing to the irregularity of the refractive power of the lens from the centre to the circumference. This is not entirely corrected by the narrowing of the pupil. Most eyes are more or less *astigmatic*, owing to unequal curvature of the cornea. When the cornea is most convex in the vertical meridians, horizontal lines are brought to a focus sooner than are vertical lines, and *vice versa.* An astigmatic person can often see letters made up of vertical and oblique lines distinctly, but not, at the same time, horizontal lines. A slight amount of *chromatic aberration* has been detected. The lens does not appear to be constructed to obviate this defect. In the vitreous humor are often seen *muscæ volitantes*, which appear as beads, streaks, patches, granules, etc. Occasionally radiate figures, corresponding to the arrangement of the fibres of the lens, appear in the field of vision.

462. VISUAL SENSATIONS AND PERCEPTIONS.—Light falling on the rods and cones of the retina excites *sensory*

---

462. What arise in the retina? What becomes of the impulses? How does a sensation arise? How a perception? What portion of the retina is involved? How is the field of vision interpreted? What of the blind spot? Of the yellow spot?

impulses. Concerning the manner of production of the impulses in the retinal structures, nothing at present is known. These impulses pass over the fibres of the optic nerve to the corpora quadrigemina (362). From thence impulses reach the cerebral centres, produce changes in the protoplasm, and give rise to what we call a *visual sensation.* In the mind the sensations are co-ordinated into *perceptions.* The sum of these sensations constitutes the *field of vision.* The structures in which the visual impulses arise lie behind the retinal blood-vessels. The image on the retina is inverted; the top is bottom, the right is left, etc. When the field of vision is interpreted by touch, there is a mental re-inversion of the image-perception. At the point where the optic nerve enters the eye is located the *blind spot.* The region of most distinct vision is the *fovea centralis* of the yellow spot. This spot lies at a spot corresponding to the axis of the eye (Fig. 101).

463. A VISUAL SENSATION has a duration longer than that of the stimulus. The sensation of a flash of light lasts much longer than the time occupied by the light-vibration acting on the retina. If two flashes occur near enough together, they occasion a single sensation. In order to prevent fusion, the interval with the faint light must be more than one-tenth of a second; with a strong light, more than one-thirtieth to one-fiftieth of a second. It is easier to distinguish differences of brightness between two faint lights, as of a dip and of a spermaceti candle, than between two bright electric lights. Most people see two stars as one when the distance between them subtends an angle less than 60″. Hisschmann could distinguish objects 50″ distant from each other. *Snellen's test-types* are constructed on the principle of having the limbs and subdivisions equal in breadth to one-fifth of the height. The letters are of such a height as to be seen by a normal eye under a visual angle of 5′. Hence each limb of the letters is seen under a visual angle of 60″. *Color-sensations* depend on the wave-length of the rays falling on the retina in a given time, and on the amount of white light falling on the same retinal area at the given time. White light

dilutes the colored light sensations. The three primary retinal sensations correspond to what we call red, green, and violet. The sensation of color is more distinct in the centre of the retina than near the circumference.

464. COLOR-BLINDNESS is an incapacity on the part of the visual organs to respond to the stimulus which one of the three kinds of light is calculated to produce. White is not white to the color-blind. To the "red-blind" it is a mixture of green and violet; to the "green-blind," of red and violet. It is well known that persons vary in the power of distinguishing color. Some persons regard as similar colors which to others are distinct. The most common form is the inability to distinguish green and red from each other. "Green-blindness" and "violet-blindness" are quite rare. "Red-blindness" is quite common. The "red-blind" in railroad and steamer service learn to distinguish red from green lights by one of them being bright and the other dim. Too often, on foggy nights, this test fails them, an accident happens, and they are discharged for drunkenness, carelessness, etc., when the fault was color-blindness. Hence it is of importance that all line-men and deck-officers should be tested as to their ability to distinguish quickly red from green, especially at night. Holmgren's variously-colored worsted test is the most satisfactory.

465. AFTER-IMAGES.—If the eye is directed to the sun, the image of the sun is present for a long time after the eye is turned away. If the eye is directed for some time to a white image on a black background, and then turned to a white wall, a similar image in gray is seen on the wall. The appearance of the gray image is explained as the result of retinal exhaustion. The steadfast gaze at the white object has exhausted the retinal area which appreciates white, and when the rays from the white wall strike on this exhausted area they are not appreciated,—that is, there is a dark sensation space,—but the white rays on the adjacent areas reach over the exhausted areas, and a gray image is perceived. When a red patch is looked at and exhaustion results, the negative image is green; orange, blue; yellow, an indigo-blue. A blending of the three primary colors, as seen in the sensation produced by a rapidly-revolving chromatic top, produces a sensation of white.

466. BINOCULAR VISION.—Having two eyes, we receive from every object two sets of sensations, but under ordinary conditions

we perceive only one object. By squinting we can so influence the field of the retina as to render the perception double. The single-ness of perception depends upon the image of the object falling upon similar areas of the retina at the same time, and the resulting sensations being blended into one perception. The two eyes move together, upward or downward, to the right or to the left, con-verge for near vision, and diverge to parallelism for far vision. We cannot diverge the eyes beyond parallelism of the axes: hence the two images of any object must fall on corresponding parts of the retinæ. The mechanism for the co-ordination of the movements of the eyeballs in order to secure one perception is located near the corpora quadrigemina (362).

Binocular vision affords man the means of forming visual judg-ments concerning the form, size, and distance of objects. Single-eye judgments are more liable to error than binocular. One eye supplies that part of the visual field which is lacking in the other. By a long series of associations of visual sensations, those derived from the movements of the eyeballs, and those derived from touch, we are enabled to form, by the eyes alone, judgments concerning objects of the external world.

Touch.

467. The SKIN (48) contains the principal *end-organs* of the sense of touch. The mucous membrane contains end-organs for the sense of touch for a short distance only from its junction with the skin at the mouth, nostrils, etc. A hot or cold liquid, or a hard or soft body, in the mouth occasions a definite sensation ; either of them in the stom-ach or intestines, only a general sensation of *pain*. As to the exact nature of the end-organs in the skin there is still doubt. At one time the " tactile corpuscles," and at another the " end-bulbs of Krause," have been regarded as the specific organs of touch.

---

467. What are found in the skin and mucous membrane ? What of mucous-membrane sensations ? What are the end-organs of touch ?

468. If the optic nerve is stimulated in its course, the brain recognizes a sensation of light; if the auditory nerve, of sound; if the gustatory nerve, of taste; if a general nerve, of pain (379). If the *end-organ* the retina be stimulated by its appropriate stimulus, light, the brain recognizes a definite perception in its field of vision; if the end-organs of the labyrinth, a definite perception of sound; if the end-organs of the nerve of taste, a definite perception of sweet, acid, etc.; if the end-organs of the skin or parts of the mucous membrane, a definite perception of *pressure* or of *temperature*. We judge of the weight or the hotness or coldness of a body, because the end-organs in the skin enable the brain to perceive how much it presses, or how hot or cold it is when compared with the part of skin in contact with the same. Further than this the skin organs do not afford us information as to the nature of the body. An induction shock and the prick of a needle in the skin give rise to similar sensations and perceptions.

469. SENSATIONS OF PRESSURE.—(1.) We can distinguish the difference of pressure between one and two ounces as well as between ten and twenty. (2.) When two touch-sensations follow each other sufficiently near, they become fused. Thus, if the tip of the finger be placed on a slowly-revolving notched wheel, each notch will be felt; if the speed be increased sufficiently, the sensations are fused into one prolonged sensation. (3.) If the hand be placed on the table, and weights be piled on the same, the increment of drachm-weights will scarcely be noticed, while that of

---

468. Speak of general stimulation. Of special stimulation. What do the skin-organs recognize?

469. Speak of differences of pressure. Of near touch sensations. Of the application of weights. Of variations of pressure. Of sensitive parts.

pound-weights will soon become painfully evident. (4.) Variations of pressure are more readily distinguished when they follow in succession than when they occur at the same time. The end-organs of the palmar surfaces of the fingers and of the forehead are more sensitive to pressure than those of the sole of the foot, of the thigh, or of the fore-arm.

470. SENSATIONS OF TEMPERATURE.—In judging of the temperatures of bodies, or of different parts of our own body, we start with some part, as of the hand, as a standard. The more gradual the change of the temperature, the less the sensation. Plunging into and withdrawing the hand from hot water excites acuter sensations than keeping the hand quiet in the water. The sensations of slight cold are more noticeable than those of slight heat. The range of most accurate determination seems to lie between 27° C. and 33° C. (80.6° F. and 91.4° F.). The cheeks, temples, tongue, and lips are more sensitive than the hand. The legs and trunk are least sensitive.

471. LOCALIZATION OF SENSATION.—When any part of the body is exposed to a notable variation of pressure or temperature, consciousness perceives that a particular part of the body has been touched or heated. We refer the sensation to the place of the origin of the impulse, not to the outer world, as in sight, hearing, smell, etc. The power of localizing sensations varies in different parts of the body and in different individuals. As a general rule, the more movable parts, as of the tip of the tongue, the lips, the tips of the fingers, etc., most readily discriminate

---

470. How do we judge of temperature? What sensations are more noticeable? What parts are most sensitive?

471. How are sensations localized? What parts are most acute? How is improvement explained? What may be learned?

sensations. The improvement of touch through tactile exercise is explained by a more exact limitation of the areas of sensation within the brain, not by the development of new end-organs or nerves in the skin. By the cultivation of this sense, guided and corrected by the other senses, especially that of sight, we are enabled to build up ideas concerning the form, the roughness or smoothness, the plane or round surfaces, the hardness or softness, and the hotness or coldness of objects. By culture the sense of touch can be wonderfully improved, as is shown in the delicate touch of the skilled mechanic and the knowledge acquired by the blind.

EXPERIMENTS.—With a pair of sharp-pointed dividers test the sensitiveness of the skin. Place the two limbs at such a distance apart as shall, when both are pressed simultaneously, excite the sensation of two pricks. Push the limbs nearer and nearer, until the two points will excite only one sensation. Repeat the tests for different parts of the body. It will be found that the tip of the tongue, the palms of the last phalanx and of the second phalanx of the finger, are the most sensitive, and that the back, the sternum, the forearm, and the back of the hand are the least sensitive parts of the human body.

On the forearm determine the closest distance of the divider-points which will excite two sensations. Press a heavy ring on the part, and within the ring apply the points; only one sensation will be noticed; that is, the neighboring sensation has obscured the previous double sensation. At another part determine by *light* pressure the nearest distance for two sensations. Now press heavily, and only one sensation will be recognized. Light pressure gives a clearer sensation than heavy pressure.

Blindfold a person. Place a marble, or other smooth, uniform body, between the forefinger and middle finger; the presence of one body will be recognized. Bend the middle finger over and beyond the forefinger, and then place the marble in the fork thus formed, so that it touches the radial side of the forefinger and ulnar side of the middle finger; the presence of two bodies will be recognized. This is an error of judgment, because, in ordinary affairs, these two portions of the skin cannot be touched by one object at the same time.

Muscular Sense.

472. If the hand and arm be placed on the table, and if different weights be placed on the palm, a person can crudely estimate differences in the weight by *pressure* sen-

472. How does pressure indicate weight? How do we estimate the weight of small bodies? What is the muscular sense?

sations. If the person holds the weight or given body in the hand, free from the table, he not only feels pressure, but is aware of muscular exertion to hold and to lift the body. Through the nerve-connections he is made conscious of this resistance. By a combination of pressure sensations and muscular exertion sensations, man is able to form quite accurate judgments of the weight of bodies. The *muscular sense* is the sense which informs us of the amount of the resistance to muscular action.

473. The muscular sense is quite necessary for the proper guidance of all bodily movements, as of walking, as of prehension, as of all kinds of handiwork, etc. In all bodily movements consciousness is aware of the amount of contraction to which the muscles are put. This is well illustrated, when we make up judgments as to the size of an object, by the movements of the eyeballs, aided by sight. Consciousness is aware of the muscle or group of muscles put into action and of the amount of that action. It is also aware of the condition of the muscles, whether light and buoyant, or heavy, tired, and painful. The seat of the *end-organs* of this sense has not yet been determined. Certain physiologists have located them in the terminals of the nerves in the muscles; others, in the central nervous system, and affirm that the changes in the centres affect consciousness by giving a conception of the effort expended in arranging the incoming and outgoing impulses.

Sense of Equilibrium.

474. The movements of our bodies are governed and guided by a conscious appreciation of our body and of its relation to surrounding objects and the atmosphere. This appreciation is largely made up of visual sensations, of muscular sense, and of touch sensations. When this appreciation is disturbed, as in swinging or rapidly turn-

ing, our equilibrium is not secure,—we become dizzy, stagger, and reel, are unable to co-ordinate our bodily movements or to adapt ourselves to the position of things about us; yet no perversion of sight alone, or touch alone, or muscular sense alone, occurs.

EXPERIMENTAL RESULTS.—When the horizontal, membranous, semicircular canals of a pigeon are cut, the bird continually moves its head from side to side; when one of the vertical ones, up and down. When one side only is operated upon, the trouble soon passes away. When both sides are operated upon, the condition persists. In the latter case, if the bird is calmed, the movements do not appear. If the bird is disturbed, or if it attempts to move, these peculiar movements are exaggerated. If the mutilated bird is thrown into the air, it flutters and falls in a confused manner. If balanced and quieted and placed at rest, it places its head in a constrained position. If it is now disturbed, its movements become irregular, and it is unable to execute combined co-ordinate movements. It has difficulty in getting at food which it may see, and then in picking up the food. If food is placed within its beak, it eats it with avidity. If the bird is placed in a heap of grain, guided by contact sensations, it feeds well. It can also clean its feathers and scratch its head, being assisted by tactile sensation from all parts of the body. It sees well. It appears to hear well. No paralysis has been detected in any group of muscles. It cannot co-ordinate its movements. It acts like a dizzy bird. In rabbits, section of membranous portions of the semicircular canals produces loss of co-ordination.

475. The *semicircular canals* are placed in planes, at nearly right angles to one another. Hence the pressure of the endolymph (440) on the membranous canals in any position of the head, or variation of movements of the head, would be different in each of the three canals. If the epithelial cells and hair-like organs of the membranous canals do recognize impressions from the movements of the contained fluids, if the impressions are converted into impulses, which, transmitted over the auditory nerve, are not of an auditory nature, then it is possible to conceive that the impulses thus generated in the canals by the movements of the head, becoming changed into sensations, may enable consciousness to judge of the movements which gave rise to them. Hence it is held that in the human semicircular canals are probably located the *end-organs* which build up the impulses concerned in the *sense of equilibrium* (372).

HYGIENE.

476. OF THE TONGUE.—The sense of taste (426) becomes perverted by the abuse of condiments and stimu-

---

476. How is the sense of taste injured? How is it improved? What of the influence of tobacco?

lants and the endless admixture of different articles of food. In children this sense is usually acute. By careful training the sense may become of great commercial value, as seen among the tea-tasters connected with the tea-houses of China and Japan. The use of wholesome and simple foods and drinks is advantageous to the sense. If not perverted, it often gives timely warning of the presence of injurious substances in foods and drink. The use of tobacco and hot-spiced foods is hurtful.

477. OF THE NOSTRILS.—The sense of smell (430) is an endowment not so much for pleasure as for protection. It is one of the most delicate and most available tests of the impurity of the air. We should not endeavor to blunt its powers by keeping its end-organs in an atmosphere of offensive smells, either by an act of the will or by using a powerful and more agreeable odor, like musk, to mask the offensive compounds, but rather, accepting its warnings, remove from such offensive surroundings. The sense of smell is blunted by the use of snuff, by the immoderate use of smelling-salts and powerful perfumes, and by the persistent inhaling of smoke, dust, and the odors arising from the decaying vegetables in the cellar, and the mephitic odors from the sewers and cesspools.

478. OF THE EAR.—Infants are deaf at birth; but the sense of hearing (439) is soon developed. No organ contributes so much to the intellectual development of the child as the ear. This is well shown in the mental backwardness of those of lasting congenital deafness compared

---

477. What of the sense of smell? How may it be blunted?

478. What of the sense of hearing? What of its influence on the mental growth? Effect of cultivation? How is hearing impaired? What of the internal ear? How should wax be removed? What of foreign bodies? Of cotton plugs? Of ear-boxing?

with those born blind. In youths and adults this sense is capable of great improvement. By its cultivation the blind are able to judge with considerable accuracy the distance of moving bodies, and the Indian to distinguish sounds inaudible to the untrained civilized ear.

Hearing is often impaired by colds and resulting inflammations. External and middle ear diseases may be excited by wetting the hair of the head and drying it too slowly, by clipping the hair too closely in the cold season, by frequent exposure of the head and neck to draughts of cool air, by perforation or rupture of the tympanic membrane, by immoderate tobacco-smoking, and by the extension of inflammation from the nasal pharynx through the Eustachian tube to the middle ear. The internal ear is well protected from external agencies and injuries by its position deep in the hardest portion of the temporal bone. We can do little or nothing to assist nature in its protection.

In health, the wax of the canal dries, scales, and falls out. The hardened wax should not be dug out of the ear, for fear of injury to the membrana by the steel or ivory pins; nor should the meatus be washed with water and strong soap. If the wax is hardened, run in a few drops of warm oil or glycerin, then carefully syringe with tepid soft water, taking time and using sufficient water. No foreign body, as a bean, corn, etc., should be permitted to remain long in the meatus (see Chapter XV.). The introduction of a pledget of cotton into the meatus to prevent "catching cold" is not judicious. The pledget not only impairs hearing, but its presence lowers the natural powers of resistance against cold. The ears of children ought not to be boxed. The sudden compression of the air in the canal may rupture an over-fragile tympanic membrane.

In case of ear-maladies, avoid "patent medicines," and consult the best aurist or surgeon in your vicinity.

479. OF THE EYE. *Management in Infancy.*—The number of blind persons in every community is large. In Massachusetts, in 1875, there was one to every five hundred and eighty-eight of the population; in Japan, in the same year, one to three hundred and twenty-six. In a very considerable number of cases the loss of sight dates from the first few days or weeks of life. The majority of those who so early become blind bring into the world good, useful eyes. The causes of infantile sore eyes and blindness are carelessness and ignorance, rather than diseases and injuries. The attendants of the child, from the time of its advent until it can care for itself, neglect proper precautions about light, cleanliness, and temperature. During the first few weeks of life the infant cannot shelter the eyes from dazzling *light:* hence too much care cannot be taken with regard to the position of the child to light. The *cleansing* of the eyes should receive early and careful attention. The washing should be done with simple warm soft water and soft bits of clean old linen. Exposure to cold currents of *air,* and to air fouled by the presence of soiled, damp clothes, by smoke, dust, and once-breathed air, often affects the eyes of infants injuriously.

480. *Management in Childhood.*—In adults it is well known that there are differences in respect to the distance, the acuteness, and the duration of vision. Careful studies

---

479. Speak of the number of blind. What is the chief cause of blindness? To what should attention be directed? Speak of washing. Mention certain injurious influences.

480. What has been noticed in adults? In weak children? What do the people notice? What do they not detect? What is noticed frequently in flat eye?

of the eyes of children, and especially of the eyes of weak children, have shown that the departure from the normal state of the eye is early, and, in a city or town community, of quite frequent occurrence. Among the people, the spots on the cornea, cloudiness of the humors, cross-eye, etc., attract attention, but the commencing short eye or the presence of flat eye is not noticed, and thus the inability to perceive objects is often attributed to obstinacy and stupidity in the child, rather than to his inability to see distinctly. In flat-eyed (hypermetropic) children, squinting of the in-turned variety is of quite frequent occurrence. The membranes of the eyes of weak children, especially those living in the city, are feeble. If such children are induced to stay in-doors, to look at small objects, to play with fine dissected puzzles, to cut out small pictures, etc., the weak tunics of the eyes tend to be stretched backward during forced accommodation, and near-sightedness results (460). For this reason, the practice of teaching children to read and to write at too early an age, as at five years or younger, is to be condemned. The probability of harm to the eyes during early school-life is diminished with every year added to life before the child enters school or commences the continued use of his eyes on fine work. Children should not be compelled to fix the gaze for long periods on their books. In reading, and more especially in writing, they should not be permitted to allow the head to fall too far forward, as this position impedes the return-flow of blood from the head. With print or script of the usual size, the paper should never be less than ten inches from the normal eye.

481. *Management in the Student Period.*—When a scholar can see well within a certain limit, but has less than normal vision beyond this point, *myopia* is to be suspected. A

myopic student should always wear glasses. Not only will his eyes then give him longer service, but he will be able to see more, to learn more of the world about him, and to know more. A short-sighted person who does not use proper glasses loses a large proportion of the pleasures of existence. Flat-eyed students should be early provided with glasses. Students should not use books with stinted margins and printed in small and closely-compressed type on very poor paper. The "blackboards" now used in the school-room should be painted green, to avoid too striking contrast. The desks ought to be assigned so that the pupil will be enabled to have his work about twelve inches from the eyes, and this with little stooping. Students should not be compelled to read, to write, or to draw by an insufficient light, and more especially during twilight. If the position of the seats and the means of illumination cannot be improved, then the order of exercises ought to be changed, in order to favor the eyes. Close visual attention should be demanded for short periods only. Change of the body-position, moving from one room to another, five minutes' calisthenics every hour, and occasional glances out of the window, are beneficial. For the health of the eyes, as well as for that of the body in general, out-of-door sports should be encouraged. Experience shows that the power for sustained visual effort is markedly dependent on the general vigor of the muscular system. In the choice of a life-work for the young, the capabilities of the eye should be considered; for eyes which would in a few years fail a compositor, copyist, or watchmaker would do good service for a gardener or a farmer.

481. What marks the state of near sight? What of the use of glasses? Speak of books; of desks; of light; of the change of exercises; of position; of sports; of choice of life-work.

482. In the *adult period* the eyes have become consolidated, but yet they suffer from a variety of causes,—as from general weakness of the body, from deterioration of the blood, from determination of the blood to the brain and eyes, from mechanical or chemical injuries, from impure, vitiated, and smoky air, from uncleanliness, from excessive use, from the want or misuse of spectacles, from defective or excessive illumination, etc., etc. In all visual troubles, endeavor to find the cause. If possible, remove the cause and use appropriate agents; if not, then mitigate the condition as much as possible by using the type-writer, writing-frames, suitably-tinted paper, optical devices, and appropriate medication.

483. *Illumination.*—Solar light is as congenial and necessary to the eye as food to the digestive organs. Prolonged exclusion from sunlight, as by confinement in dark cells, is weakening and highly injurious. On the other hand, vision has been weakened or destroyed by sudden exposure to the dazzling light. Temporary loss of sight has resulted from the reflection of bright sunlight, as from a mirror or other polished surface. The eyebrows, the lids, and the lashes chiefly protect the eyes from excessive light from above; hence, for solar lighting of rooms, low windows, bright, reflecting floors, and white blinds should be avoided. Dazzling light, insufficient light, unsteady light, as in a jolting railway-carriage, light with shadows, light falling directly into the eyes, one and all, are improper

---

482. Causes of eye-troubles in adults? What can be done?

483. Speak of solar light. Of deprivation of light. Of too bright light. What should be avoided in room-lighting? Mention improper kinds of illumination. Danger of twilight. Speak of artificial illumination. How may the bad effects of heat be mitigated? What of eye-work?

lights. Large windows and large panes of glass are desirable in all workrooms. Solar light is preferable to any artificial light for continued regular eye-work. Evening twilight is a dangerous light, for the eyes are already weary from the efforts of the day, the amount of illumination is on the decrease, and the strain on the eyes becomes more and more intense in the endeavor to make out the fading characters.

At present one of the best artificial methods of illumination is the argand-burner student-lamp or the argand-burner gas table-light. The best kind of a shade is of white porcelain having a green outer covering. The position of the lamp which is most favorable for the eyes is to the left front of the worker, having the flame slightly above the level of the eyes. If the heat from the large argand-burner is objectionable, a flat cell, eight inches square and half an inch thick, its sides being formed of plate-glass and its cavity filled with a filtered saturated solution of alum, may be placed in front of the lamp, to intercept the heat-rays. If the eyes become dry and hot, a wet sponge may be placed near the lamp. If possible, all work which is trying to the eyes should be done under solar light. Reading demands greater visual effort than copying, and copying than ordinary writing.

STATISTICS.—The report of Dr. Risley shows that in Philadelphia, in the primary schools, there are 4.27 per cent. of myopes; that the percentage steadily increases as the pupils pass to higher grades in the public school system, and that in the highest grade there are 19.33 per cent. of myopes. Drs. Loring and Agnew found that in New York City there were 3.5 per cent. in the youngest classes and 26.78 per cent. in the highest. Dr. Derby reports, as the result of the examination of four consecutive classes at Amherst (Massachusetts) College: Average age at entrance, 19; at graduation, 23.

	At entrance.	At graduation.
Manifest hypermetropia	30	47
Myopia	90	120
Emmetropia	125	87
	254	254

34 per cent. were myopic at entrance, and 47 per cent. at graduation. In 32 cases

the myopia remained stationary, and in 58 cases it increased. At St. Petersburg, the range of myopia was from 13.6 per cent. in the preparatory classes to 42.6 per cent. in the highest; at Lucerne, from 0. per cent. in the children of seven years to 61.5 per cent. in those of twenty-one years; and at Breslau, from 0.4 per cent. in the first half-year students to 63.3 per cent. in the highest classes. Observations and reports show that in myopic eyes the percentage of other eye-diseases is greater than in normal or hypermetropic eyes; that myopic eyes suffering from astigmatism had the greatest tendency towards other eye-maladies; that myopic eyes are chiefly recruited from eyes having defects of refraction, especially hypermetropic and astigmatic; and that the degree of myopia varies, not with each pair of eyes, but with each eye. Hence the importance of ascertaining, at the commencement of school-life, the condition of each eye, the presence or absence of errors of refraction, and, if present, the degree of the departure in each eye.

484. *Myopia, or Near Sight.*—The myopic person cannot see to the horizon or to the fixed stars; but he can see quite clearly within a certain fixed limit. The belief that short-sighted eyes are good and strong eyes, that myopes need not use spectacles for reading or other near work if they can see to work without them, and that myopia improves with age, is an erroneous one. The chief malformation in myopia is an elongation of the eyeball. The most efficient cause of this elongation is the muscular tension on the balls during forced continued inturning of the eyes when engaged on fine work or working under poor light. If this strain be continued, the bulging will steadily increase, and the myopia will be rendered "progressive" and more and more troublesome. When once started, and if not counteracted, it provides for its own increase. The prevention of the increase and the correction of the refractive defect are to be accomplished by the use of proper spectacles. The latter do not increase the sharpness of vision, but keep the work farther from the eyes, prevent the convergence strain, stop the posterior bulging, and correct the optical defects (460).

485. *Prevention of Eye-Diseases.*—Secure pure and clear air. Tobacco-smoke, smoke, and dust are very injurious to most eyes. The washing of the eyes with clear, soft spring-water or with clean river-water is often beneficial. Hot water should be used only under the directions of a

485. Influence of air? Of washing? Of borax-water? What of weak children? Of defects of vision? Of frames? Of weak sight?

skilled surgeon. If there is a smarting, irritating, gritty sensation at night, after work, drop into each eye, before retiring, five drops of a solution of borax, ten grains to the ounce, in camphor-water. All foreign bodies should be promptly and carefully removed from the eye-surfaces. (See Chapter XV.) Weak children should not be sent to school until they have been brought into a state of fair health and strength by out-of-door pursuits. All defects of vision should be promptly treated,—the short-sighted organ with concaves, and the easily-fatigued, painful, dim-seeing, flat organ with appropriate convexes. Persons having such eyes should use glasses at all times. Spectacle-frames are preferable to eye-glasses, or "nippers," for constant use. The use of the single, quizzing glass is not advisable. Some cases of "weak sight" (*asthenopia*) are benefited by prolonged rest. In other cases, especially where the failure rests with the muscles, reading at fixed intervals for definite lengths of time is beneficial.

486. OF THE FINGERS.—By common usage, the special organ of the higher tactile sense (469) is the hand. It is admirably fitted for this office by reason of the number, size, arrangement, and abundant nerve-supply of its papillæ. At the tips of the fingers the delicacy of touch may be highly developed. By education of the finger-tips the blind learn to read raised letters, to distinguish impressions on coins, and even to detect shades of color. By care the fingers can be given greater scope for sense-activity. The dry, hard skin may be made more pliable by using tar or oat-meal soap, applications containing glycerin, and wearing gloves at night. The fingers, if delicacy of touch is

---

486. What of the seat of the sense of touch? Speak of this sense in the blind. Of the nails.

desired, should be washed no oftener than absolutely necessary. They should never be put in hot water. By the
use of glycerin ointment, rubber gloves, cotton flannel, and
friction, frequent washing may be avoided. For cleansing
the fingers, use fine soap, ammonia-water, and a brush. It
is preferable to file rather than cut nails. The nails of
children should be carefully attended to. The under surfaces of the nails are best cleaned with a toothpick or an
ivory cleaner. A well-formed, well-kept nail aids the tactile sense of the finger-tips, and also enhances the beauty
of the wonderful mechanism, the hand.

CHAPTER XIII.

THE LARYNX AND VOICE.

(For dissection, see Chapter VI.)

487. The LARYNX (160) is the special organ of voice in man. It is a kind of hollow chamber, extending from near the root of the tongue to the first ring of the trachea. The framework of the larynx is made up of four cartilages. Within this framework, extending from front to rear, are two thin elastic bands, covered by mucous membrane, called the *vocal cords*.

488. Of the four cartilages composing the larynx, the *thyroid* is the largest, and consists of two lateral, quadrangular, wing-like plates, which meet in front and form the prominence called *pomum Adami* (Adam's apple). The cartilage is connected with the hyoid bone above, and with the cricoid cartilage below.

The *cricoid* cartilage somewhat resembles a signet-ring. Its front half is narrow and convex, and its rear half broad. This cartilage connects above with the thyroid cartilage by an articulation which permits the latter to move downward and forward and the reverse. Below, it is attached to the first ring of the trachea by membrane.

The *arytenoid* cartilages are two in number, small, triangular, and curved. They are placed on the summit and back part of the cricoid, with which they form movable articulations. These articulations permit these cartilages to be partly revolved, to be drawn near the middle line, and to be elevated to a limited extent.

489. Looking down into the larynx, two folds of its lining membrane are seen passing from the rear to the receding angle of the thyroid in front. These are the superior, or *false vocal cords*. They

---

487. Speak of the larynx. Of what is it made? What does it contain?

are not concerned in the production of voice. Below these folds are seen the *true vocal cords*. The latter are made up of elastic tissue (24), are covered by mucous membrane, and form two sharp ridges or projections, turned towards each other. These projections have very fine and smooth edges, which are placed accurately on the same level. Between the vocal cords is a somewhat triangular opening,

Fig. 106.   Fig. 107.

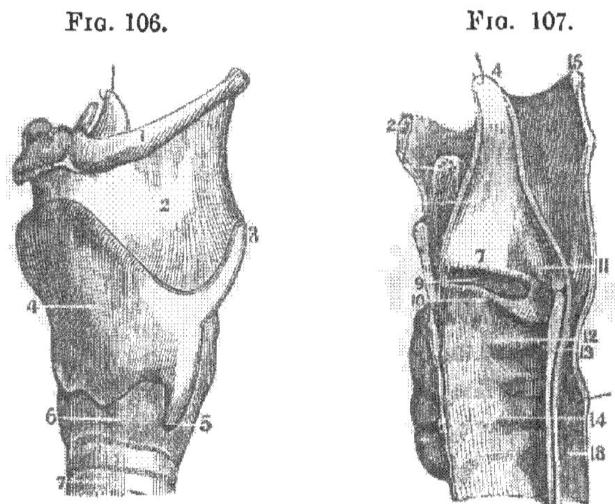

Fig. 106. A SIDE-VIEW OF THE CARTILAGES OF THE LARYNX.—1, The os hyoides (bone at the base of the tongue). 2, The membrane that connects the hyoid bone and thyroid cartilage. 3, 4, 5, The thyroid cartilage. 6, The cricoid cartilage. 7, The trachea.

Fig. 107. A VERTICAL SECTION OF THE LARYNX.—2, The os hyoides. 4, The apex of the epiglottis. 7, The superior vocal cord. 9, The ventricle of the larynx. 10, The lower vocal cord. 11, The arytenoid cartilage. 12, 13, The cricoid cartilage. 14, The trachea. 18, The œsophagus.

wider behind than in front, which is called the *glottis*. The cords are stretched between the recessed part of the thyroid and the anterior angle of the arytenoids. The latter are acted upon by five pairs of muscles and the single *arytenoideus*. The latter causes the cords to approach each other and to become more tense. The *crico-thyroid* is the chief tensor muscle of the cords. Above the true vocal cords, on each side, is a cavity called the *ventricle*. All parts of the interior of the larynx are lined with mucous membrane, and, with the exception of that on the cords, the latter is studded with mucous glands (166).

490. PRODUCTION OF SOUND.—Whenever a solid body is thrown into vibrations, provided the latter are of a certain strength and follow one another with a certain rapidity, the sensation of sound is produced in the ear. If the vibrations are less than eight per second, or more than thirty-eight thousand, they produce no definite distin-

Fig. 108.

Fig. 109.

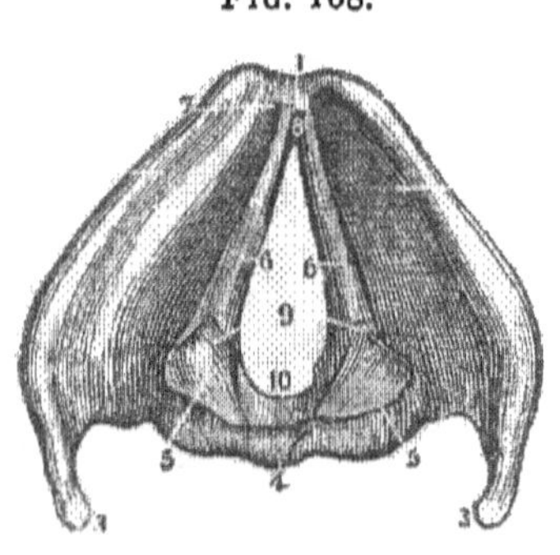

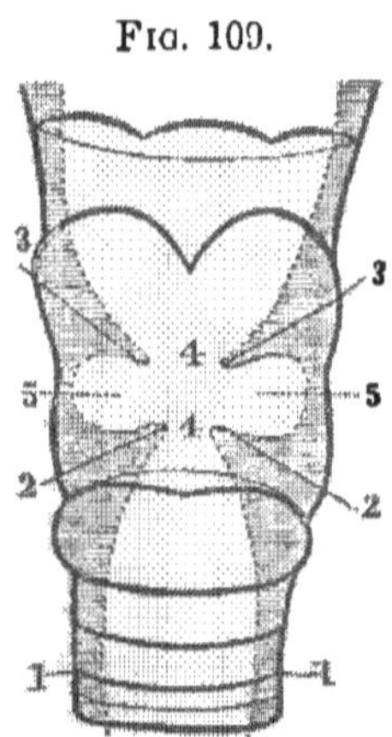

FIG. 108. A VIEW OF THE LARYNX, SHOWING THE VOCAL LIGAMENTS.—1, The anterior edge of the larynx. 4, The posterior face of the cricoid cartilage. 5, 5, The arytenoid cartilages. 6, 6, The vocal cords. 7, Their origin within the angle of the thyroid cartilage. 9, Their termination at the base of the arytenoid cartilages. 8, 10, The glottis.

FIG. 109. AN IDEAL SECTION OF THE LARYNX.—1, The trachea. 2, 2, The lower vocal cords. 3, 3, The upper vocal cords. 4, 4, Rima glottidis, or glottis. 5, 5, Cavities between upper and lower vocal cords,—the ventricles.

guishable effect on the nerve of hearing. When the vibrations exceed a definite number per second, the ordinary ear cannot distinguish between two near sounds. The *pitch* of a sound is determined by the number of vibrations in a given space of time; the *strength*, by the extent of the action of the vibrating body. In the violin, the vibrations of the stretched strings; in the wind instru-

490. How does sound arise? What of the appreciation of sound? What of pitch? Of strength? Of different instruments?

ment, the successive condensations and rarefactions of the air in the tube; and in the tongued instrument, the combined action of the vibrating tongue and the impulses communicated by it to the air, are the sources of sound.

491. THE SEAT OF VOICE.—Experiments on living animals, the result of observations after surgical operations on the air-passages, and the study of the larynx in action by means of the laryngoscope, show that the true vocal cords are the essential organs for the production of voice. In ordinary tranquil breathing, the cords are widely separated and the glottis has a triangular form. The glottis increases slightly in size during each inspiration, and contracts somewhat during expiration. During the production of pure vocal sounds the arytenoid cartilages are said to become erect, to approach and almost touch each other; the posterior portion of the glottis becomes completely closed, and the anterior portion appears as a fine fissure, about one-hundredth of an inch wide, and the cords thus approximated are seen to be thrown into vibrations.

492. THE VOICE.—A current of air, driven by a more or less prolonged expiratory movement (175), throws into vibrations the vocal cords, which have been already approximated and made of the proper tension by muscle-action within the larynx. The rapid movements of the cords impart vibrations to the column of air in the larynx, pharynx, mouth, etc., above the cord, and thus give rise to the sound called *voice*. The chambers and recesses above the cords modify the sounds produced by the vibrations of the cords. *Loudness* depends on the strength of the ex-

---

491. What are the essential organs in voice? What is the condition of the parts during breathing? During vocal sound-production?
492. How is a vocal sound produced? What modify the sounds? What of the muscular influences?

piratory current; *pitch*, on the length and tension of the vibrating cord; and *quality*, chiefly on the physical nature of the cords. Intrinsic (to the larynx) muscular action produces variations in the tension of the cords, determines the length of the cord which may vibrate, and the width of the glottis, all the changes working together to produce differences in the vocal sounds.

493. The length of the cords is constant, or varies only with age. The length determines the range only, and not the note given out at any time. The shrill voice of the child is determined by the shortness of the cords in infancy. In the male, at the age of puberty a rapid development of the larynx takes place, with an elongation and thickening of the cords, leading to a change in the range of the voice. The voices of the soprano, tenor, and barytone depend on the respective lengths of the vocal cords. The *tension* of the cords is variable. The chief tensor muscle is the crico-thyroid. It has a nerve-supply distinct and separate from the other muscles of the larynx, and is the most important muscle concerned in the production of voice. When its special nerve is cut on one side, it becomes impossible to produce high notes.

494. MUSCULAR CO-ORDINATION.—Almost every movement, within or without the larynx, concerned in the production of voice, is effected by two or more muscles working in concert. The controlling centre of these movements is seated in the gray substance at the base of the *fourth ventricle* of the brain (Fig. 81, 26). If this portion be compressed, as in certain forms of apoplexy, or injured, vocalization is impeded or suppressed, though the laryngeal apparatus remains in a perfect condition. Singers need not only flexible cords, strong respiratory and laryngeal muscles, and a ringing resonance of the air-passages,

494. Speak of co-ordination in voice. How effected? What do singers need? What of the influence of external sounds? What of mutes?

but a well-cultured nerve-centre. In the culture of this centre it is found that the impulses acting from the centres of hearing on to the vocal centre are of prime importance in the accurate management of the voice (394). Deficiency in this respect is commonly expressed in the phrase, such and such a person "has no ear." The muteness of the totally deaf is seldom due to defects in the laryngeal apparatus, but to their inability to recognize sound-waves and thus to receive impulses from the centres of hearing. By the patient imitation of the facial expression they are taught to speak.

495. SPEECH, or the utterance of articulate sounds, is a distinctive characteristic of man. Animals have voice; man alone has speech. The raven may be taught to speak by rote, but man alone attaches meaning to the word-sounds and phrase-sounds he employs. Speech is a modification of the vibrations generated in the larynx in their outward passage through the cavities of the mouth and nose. The nerve-centres which control the power of speech, acting through or upon the centres of voice, appear to be seated on the left side of the brain, in the hind part of the third frontal convolution (358). The faculty of speech is natural, but its exercise is an art. Pressure or injury to this part of the brain does not necessarily stop vocalization, does not prevent the expression of thought by writing or by signs, but does prevent articulate speech.

496. ARTICULATE SOUNDS are divided into vowels and consonants. The true *vowels*, or open sounds, are generated in the larynx. They are uninterrupted vocal tones, modified in the outward passage by alterations in the length and

---

shape of the pharynx, mouth, and lips. When the back entrance to the nostrils is not closed, the tones acquire a *nasal quality*. The *consonants* are entirely formed in the parts above the **vocal cords**. They are produced by the expiratory current of air being in various ways interrupted or modified in its course through the throat and mouth.

497. *Whispering* is speech without the employment of the vocal cords, and is effected principally by the tongue, teeth, and lips modifying the expiratory current. *Sighing* is produced by the parts seated above the cords. If the vocal cords are brought into action, the sigh is changed into a *groan*. *Lisping, stammering*, and *stuttering* are due to errors in the action of the organs of speech. Stammering is almost always caused by irregular action of the nerve-centres.

HYGIENE.

498. *Recitations* and *reading aloud* are useful and invigorating muscular exercises. They call into varied action most of the muscles of the trunk. The movements of the thorax in full inhalation and graduated expiration act beneficially in enlarging the capacity of the lungs; and the movements of the diaphragm and the abdominal muscles communicate to the digestive apparatus a healthy and invigorating stimulus. If the voice be raised, and the vocalization made as rapid as possible, the muscular effort becomes great, and even exhausting. Vocal exercise should not be carried to the point of exciting soreness or fatigue, either in the thoracic organs or in the larynx. Until the lung-capacity and the laryngeal capabilities are drilled into

497. Speak of whispering. Of sighing. Of groaning. Of stammering.

498. What is the influence of reading aloud? Of sustained rapid vocal work? Speak of vocal drill. Of posture.

accord, the periods devoted to the exercises should be brief, and the intervals for rest of such a length as fully to rest all the parts (529). The drill of the organs, in order to produce purer and higher tones, should be gradual and

Fig. 110.   Fig. 111.

Fig. 110. An improper position, but one not unfrequently seen in some of our common schools and in some of our public speakers.

Fig. 111. The proper position for reading, speaking, and singing.

progressive; otherwise the laryngeal apparatus may be seriously impaired. During vocal exercise the erect posture should be maintained.

499. About the fourteenth or fifteenth year the voice becomes irregular and harsh, the high notes are not well

sounded, and the grave tones make their appearance. At this time the voice of the boy changes to that of the man, and that of the girl becomes fixed in that of the woman. During this transition period, exercise of the voice in singing ought to be moderated, or entirely suspended, in order to prevent laryngeal affections.

Gymnastics and calisthenic exercises are invaluable aids in the culture and development of the voice, and should be sedulously practised when opportunity renders them accessible. But even a slight degree of physical exercise, in any form adapted to the expansion of the chest and to the freedom and force of the circulation, will serve to impart energy to the muscular apparatus of the voice, and clearness to its sounds.

CHAPTER XIV.

THE MOTOR APPARATUS AND LOCOMOTION.

Directions for Dissection.

SECURE the limb of a dog, pig, rat, or other mammal. Remove the skin. Observe the *areolar connective* tissue and the *fat* contained in the meshes. Remove all loose portions and fragments until the glistening, bluish-white *fascia*, which binds the muscles in place, is cleaned. Make an incision parallel to the axis of the limb through the fascia. Raise the fascia, and peel it off. Select a long, slender muscle. Carefully remove from it all connective tissue, taking care not to nick the muscular fibre. Separate it from the adjacent muscles by cutting out the intervening areolar tissue or fat. Trace and free it to its upper place of attachment, the *origin;* then downward, until it ends in the hard, firm cord, or band, the *tendon.* Trace the tendon by slitting up the fascia, which holds it in a smooth, lined groove, to its attachment in the part which is moved by its contraction. This point of attachment is called its *insertion.*

Note the thin membrane surrounding the muscle, the parallel component bundles of fibres, the little blood-vessels entering the bundles, and the disappearance of the red, elastic fibres in the white, non-elastic tendon. Observe the movements which the shortening of the muscle causes. Seek and dissect out the *antagonist muscle* or *muscles.*

The *joint.* Remove all muscle, fat, and connective tissue from about the joint. Observe the lateral, anterior, and posterior *ligaments,* if it is a "hinge-like joint." Saw the bone off about two inches below the joint. Then saw through the middle of this bone, the joint, and the upper bone, laying open the parts, as in Fig. 123. Note the investing membrane, the *periosteum;* the *compact* bone; the *cancellated* or open-work bone, near the joint; the soft, red, oily *marrow;* the *enlargement* and processes for muscular and ligamentous attachment, near the joint; the *cartilage* tipping the bone; the lateral firm, white, band-like *ligaments;* the white, viscid *synovial fluid;* and, perhaps, an internal round ligament, *movable cartilage,* and a mass of *fat.* Cut the lateral ligaments. Observe the smooth, moist surface, the internal layer of *synovial membrane.* Shave off a bit of bluish-white, translucent cartilage and compare it with a bit of bone.

Open another joint. Note that all joints, functions and position considered, are constructed equally well; that each joint is mechanically perfect; and that the animal machine is the only self-oiler which manufactures its own lubricants.

Take a long bone, as a sheep's rib, and put it in a vessel containing one part of muriatic acid and seven parts of water. Allow it to remain a few days. The earthy matter will be mostly dissolved out. The bone will now be flexible, and may be knotted. Place another bone in the fire. The animal matter is expelled, and the brittle "bone-earth" alone is left.

25*

THE MOTOR ORGANS.

500. The parts of the human body concerned in loco-motion consist of the *bones, joints, ligaments,* and *tendons* (passive in function), and the *muscles* and *nerve-centres* (active in function).

FIG. 112.   FIG. 113.

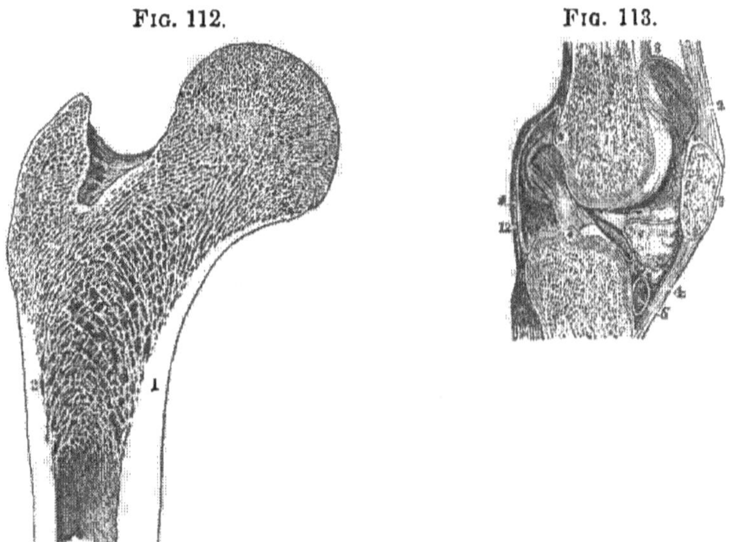

FIG. 112 (*Leidy*). LONGITUDINAL SECTION OF THE PROXIMAL EXTREMITY OF THE FEMUR, exhibiting the arrangement of the spongy substance.—1, 2, Positions in which the compact substance appears to resolve itself into a series of arches.

FIG. 113. A VERTICAL SECTION OF THE KNEE-JOINT.—1, The femur. 3, The patella. 5, The tibia. 2, 4, Ligaments of the patella. 6, Cartilage of the tibia. 12, The cartilage of the femur. * * *, The synovial membrane.

501. The BONES (16) are hard, somewhat elastic, and resistant. The *compact* bone is found in the shafts of the long bones (femur, tibia, humerus, etc.), and in other parts where strength is wanted. The *cancellated* structure

---

500. What parts are concerned in the production of motion?

501. Describe bone. Speak of compact bone. Of cancellated bone. Of the hollowness of bones. How are bones nourished? What is the periosteum?

is found at the ends of the long bones, in order to expand their surface at the points of junction and to serve better for the attachment of muscles.   The *hollowness* of the long

Fig. 114.

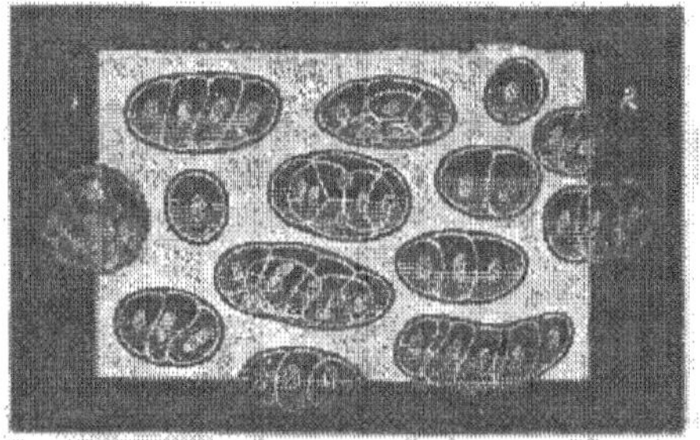

Fig. 114 (*Leidy*). CARTILAGE, section through the thickness of the oval cartilage of the nose.—1, Towards the exterior. 2, Towards the interior surface. Highly magnified. It exhibits groups of cartilage cells embedded in a homogeneous matrix.

bones endows them with greater comparative strength than if the same weight of bony tissue had been used in the solid form.   In certain. bones (frontal, sphenoid) the hollows contain *air;* in others, *marrow.*   The bony tissue is

Fig. 115.

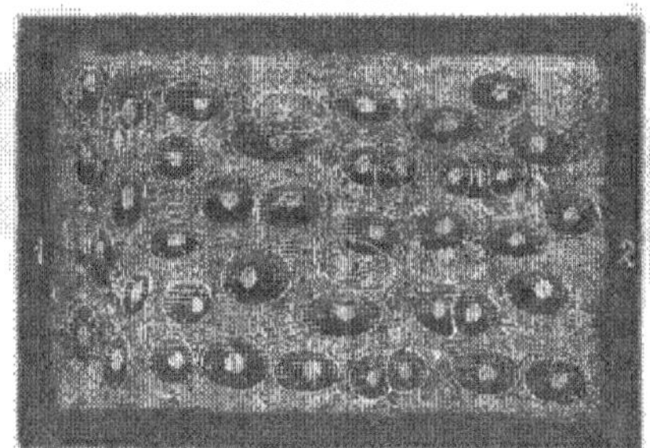

Fig. 115 (*Leidy*).   SECTION OF FIBRO-CARTILAGE FROM THE AURICLE OF THE EAR.—The cells are seen embedded in a fibrous matrix. 1. Exterior surface, where the cells are parallel to it. 2, Towards the middle. Highly magnified.

endowed with great innate strength and elasticity.   This tissue is very vascular.   Most of the blood enters by the vessels of the periosteum (16).   In the long bones there is usually an artery in the medulla.

502. Dry Bone consists of 33 per cent. of animal matter, 51 per cent. of calcium phosphate (bone-earth), 11 per cent. of calcium carbonate (chalk), and the rest of calcium fluoride, sodium chloride, and magnesium phosphate.

Fig. 116.

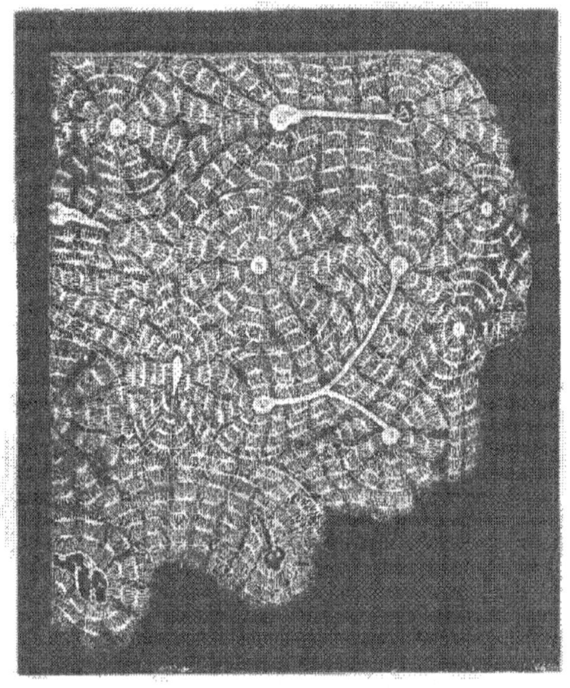

Fig. 116 (*Leidy*). Transverse Section of Bone from the Shaft of the Femur; highly magnified.—The large circular orifices are transverse sections of the *Haversian canals*, surrounded by concentric layers of osseous substance. Between the latter are seen the lenticular excavations, or *lacunæ*, intercommunicating by means of *canaliculi*.

503. Cartilage, under the microscope, presents a clear, slightly granular matrix, with nucleated corpuscles embedded in the same. The corpuscles are of a rounded form, or have flattened sides and rounded angles. Cartilage has no blood-vessels, but the matrix is permeated by nourishment coming from the vessels in the vicinity.

502. Of what is dry bone composed?

504. BONE-FORMATION.—Bone is formed from cartilage or from fibrous tissue. In the former case the change begins in the centre of the *cartilage*-mass. A certain part of the cartilage-matrix is absorbed, in order to form channels into which blood-vessels penetrate. Granules of lime salts are deposited from these blood-vessels on the walls of the channels and within the cartilage-corpuscles. The first deposit is usually dense and irregular in formation. If the channelled space increases, *cancellated* tissue is the result; if it becomes more filled with bone-salts, deposited in concentric layers gradually closing around the blood-vessels, *compact* bone is

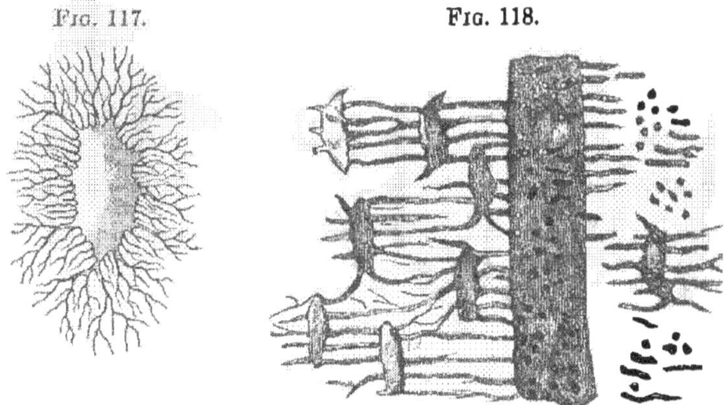

FIG. 117.　　　　FIG. 118.

FIG. 117 (*Leidy*). AN OSSEOUS LACUNA, exhibiting its numerous diverging canaliculi. Highly magnified.

FIG. 118 (*Lessing*). HAVERSIAN CANAL, lacunæ and connecting canaliculi.

produced. During life there is a continual deposition and re-absorption of bone. In the formation from *fibrous tissue* the bone-salts are directly deposited.

505. MICROSCOPIC CHARACTERS OF BONE.—The matrix of bone is impermeable to fluids, and hence bone contains nutrient canals. Compact bone is traversed by blood-vessels, which enter by the *Haversian canals*, which channels, for the most part, run lengthwise of the bone. The bone-tissue is arranged in concentric *laminæ*, or plates, around the Haversian canals. In transverse section of these canals, circles of *lacunæ* are seen surrounding the canals. The lacunæ are hollows in the laminæ, having exceedingly fine, ramifying tubes running in various directions, called *canaliculi*.

These little tubes inosculate with those of the adjacent lacunæ, allowing fluids to pass from one lacuna to another. Within the lacunæ are found nucleated masses, the *bone-corpuscles*, which are characterized by a multitude of fine processes occupying the canaliculi. An arrangement of bone-laminæ, containing lacunæ and canaliculi, around a central tube is called an *Haversian system*. The whole compact tissue of bone is an aggregation of such systems, the interstices being filled with fragments of similar laminæ.

FIG. 119.   FIG. 120.

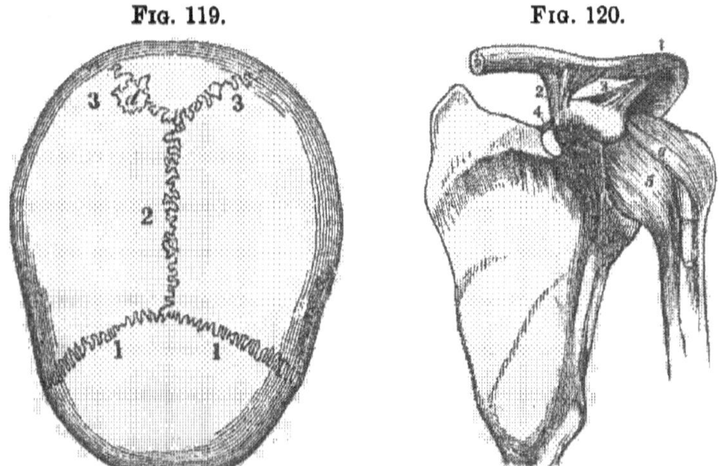

Fig. 119.—1, 1, Coronal suture. 2, Sagittal suture on the top of the skull. 3, 3, Lambdoidal suture.

Fig. 120.—2, 3, The ligaments that extend from the clavicle (1) to the scapula (4). The ligaments 5, 6, extend from the scapula to the first bone of the arm.

506. A JOINT, or ARTICULATION, is a junction of two or more bones. Joints permit the movements of the animal frame; they serve to deaden internal shock, produced by the contact of the body with external objects, and they contribute to the strength of the skeleton, especially of the back and the lower limbs, for a pillar of a given height and thickness has less power to resist vertical pressure than

506. What is a joint? What are the functions of joints? Kinds? Examples?

a number of shorter pillars built up one above the other
to an equal height. Joints are of two kinds,—*immovable*,
as of the frontal and parietal bones, or of the vomer with
the azygos process; and *movable*, as of the hip, shoulder,
and ankle.

507. In a MOVABLE JOINT the bones are merely in
contact with each other. The ends of the bones are usu-

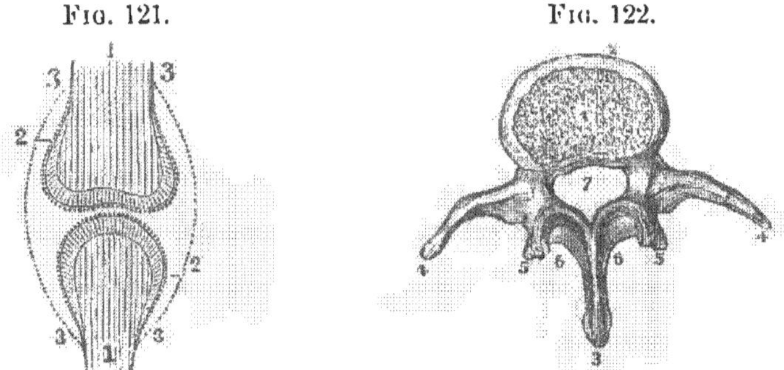

FIG. 121.   FIG. 122.

FIG. 121. DIAGRAM OF A JOINT.—1, 1, Extremities of bones. 2, 2, Terminal cartilages.
3, 3, 3, 3, The dotted line which indicates the outlines of the closed synovial sac.

FIG. 122. A LUMBAR VERTEBRA.—1, The cartilaginous substance that connects the
bodies of the vertebræ. 2, The body of the vertebra. 3, The spinous process. 4, 4, The
transverse processes. 5, 5, The articulating processes. 6, 6, A portion of the bony bridge
or arch that assists in forming the spinal canal (7).

ally expanded (Fig. 114). The end of one bone is commonly convex, and that of its companion bone concave.
The ends of the bone are covered by a thin layer of bluish-
white, elastic CARTILAGE (503). This cartilage is closely
adherent, and its free surface is highly polished. It serves
to deaden shock and to facilitate motion.

508. The SYNOVIAL MEMBRANE is a thin, delicate web,
arranged in the form of a short, wide tube. The ends of

507. Describe a movable joint. What is cartilage? What does
it do?

508. What is the synovia? Describe the secreting membrane.
What is the use of synovia?

the tube are attached to the margins of the articular surfaces of the bones; the outer surface is connected with the
inner surface of the ligaments, and the inner, cell-covered
surface secretes a fluid, called *synovia* (Fig. 113).   The
synovia is whitish, viscid, and glairy, and is much like the
white of an egg.   It serves to lubricate the surfaces of the

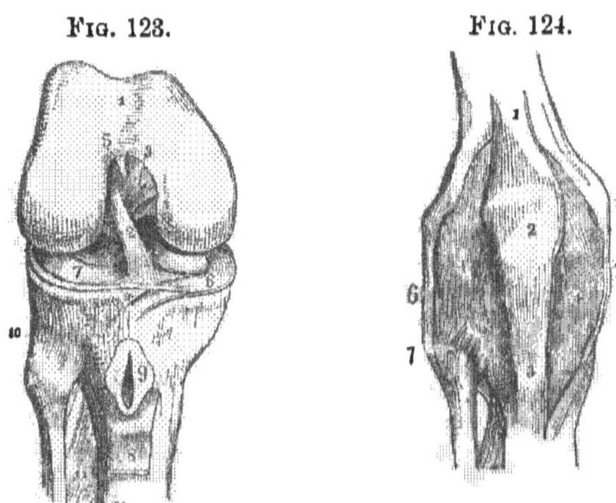

Fig. 123.   Fig. 124.

FIG. 123 (*Leidy*).   THE RIGHT KNEE-JOINT, laid open from the front.—1, Articular surface of the femur.   2, 3, Crucial ligaments.   4, Insertion of one of these ligaments into
the tibia.   6, 7, Internal and external semilunar fibro-cartilages.   8, Ligament of the
patella turned down, so as to exhibit the synovial bursa (9) beneath.   10, Superior tibio-
fibular articulation.   11, Interosseous membrane.

FIG. 124 (*Leidy*).   FRONT VIEW OF THE RIGHT KNEE-JOINT.—1, Tendon of the quadriceps extensor muscle.   2, Patella.   3, Ligament of the patella, or tendinous insertion of
the muscle just mentioned.   4, 4, Capsular ligament.   5, 6, Internal and external lateral
ligaments.   7, Superior tibio-fibular articulation.

cartilages (507), and thus prevents grating, lessens friction,
and minimizes the wear.   Its function is similar to that of
the oil used on the bearings of machinery.   BURSÆ consist of an areolar tissue sac containing a viscid fluid.   They
are found interposed between surfaces which move upon
each other, as of the gliding of a tendon (Fig. 113, 6) or
of the skin over projecting bone-surfaces.   A *bunion* is an

enlarged and inflamed bursa at the inside of the ball of the great toe.

509. LIGAMENTS.—Outside of the synovial membrane are to be seen the proper ties between the bones, called *ligaments*. They are composed of white fibrous connective tissue (Fig. 6). In certain parts they are broadly expanded, like membranes (Fig. 120, 5), as in the shoulder capsular

FIG. 125.

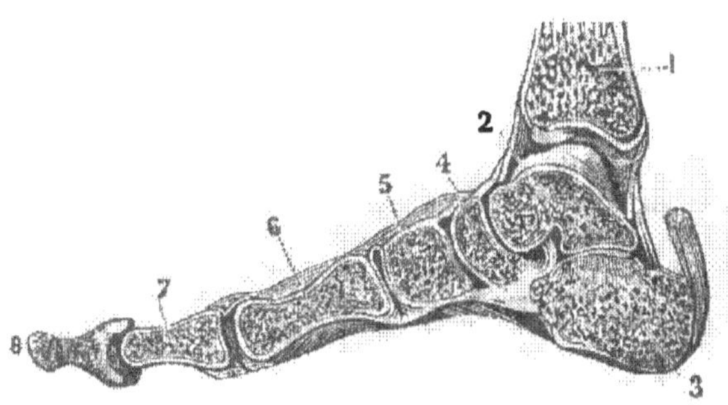

FIG. 125. A SIDE-VIEW OF THE BONES OF THE FOOT, SHOWING ITS ARCHED FORM. The arch rests upon the *heel* behind, and the *ball* of the toes in front.—1, The lower part of the tibia. 2, 3, 4, 5, Bones of the tarsus. 6, The metatarsal bone. 7, 8, The bones of the great toe.

ligament. In other parts they form bands of various shapes, as in and about the knee-joint. They tie the bones very firmly, yet permit much motion. In certain joints they are so arranged as to permit free motion in certain directions but limit it in others.

510. MOVABLE JOINTS are of three varieties,—planiform, hinge-like, and ball-and-socket. The *planiform* have more or less plane surfaces and gliding movements, as in the tarsal and metatarsal articulations of the foot. Such joints allow limited motion, deaden shock, impart elasticity and slight flexibility. The *hinge-like* permit motion in two directions in one plane, as in the elbow, ankle, and

509. What are ligaments? Speak of their forms. Of their function.

fingers. The ligaments on the sides of such joints are very strong, the other ligaments varying in size according to position. In the case of the fingers and of the ankle-joint, the tendons of certain muscles replace the ligaments. In the *ball-and-socket joint* there is a cup-like cavity lined with cartilage in the one bone, and a corresponding head-like extremity on the other, the bone being held in place by a membranous capsule. This kind of joint permits motion in all directions, as in the hip- and shoulder-joints.

511. INTERARTICULAR CARTILAGE.—In certain joints, plates of fibro-cartilage are found between the articulating surfaces, as between the lower jaw and the temporal bone, the clavicle and the sternum, and within the knee-joint (Fig. 123, 6, 7). They make the joint deeper, allow more freedom of motion, and tend to prevent dislocations. Cushions of fat are found in the knee- and hip-joints. Between the vertebræ are introduced thick cushions of elastic fibro-cartilage (Fig. 75).

512. TABLE OF THE PRINCIPAL SKELETAL MUSCLES.

(See Figs. 126, 127.)

THE HEAD.

Occipito-frontalis, moves the scalp.
Orbicularis palpebrarum, closes the eye.
Orbicularis oris, closes the lips.

Masseter, } elevate the lower jaw.
Temporal, }
Digastric, depresses the lower jaw.

THE NECK.

Sterno-cleido-mastoid, moves the head forward or to one side.
Trapezius (7), moves the head and neck backward.

THE TRUNK (anterior).

Diaphragm, muscle of respiration.
Pectoralis major, moves the humerus and scapula.
Serratus magnus, aids in violent respiration.
Intercostals, muscles of respiration.

Rectus abdominis, } bend the body forward.
Psoas magnus, }
Obliquus externus (26), } assists in violent expiration.
Obliquus internus, } bends the body forward.

---

511. What are interarticular cartilages? Their function? What of fat? Of vertebral cartilages?

Fig. 126.

OCCIPITO FRONTALIS
ORBICULARIS PALPEBRARUM
ORBICULARIS ORIS
MASSETER
FLEXOR CARPI RADIALIS
BICEPS
RECTUS FEMORIS
SARTORIUS
GRACILIS
RECTUS FEMORIS
ANNULAR LIGAMENT
ANNULAR LIGAMENT

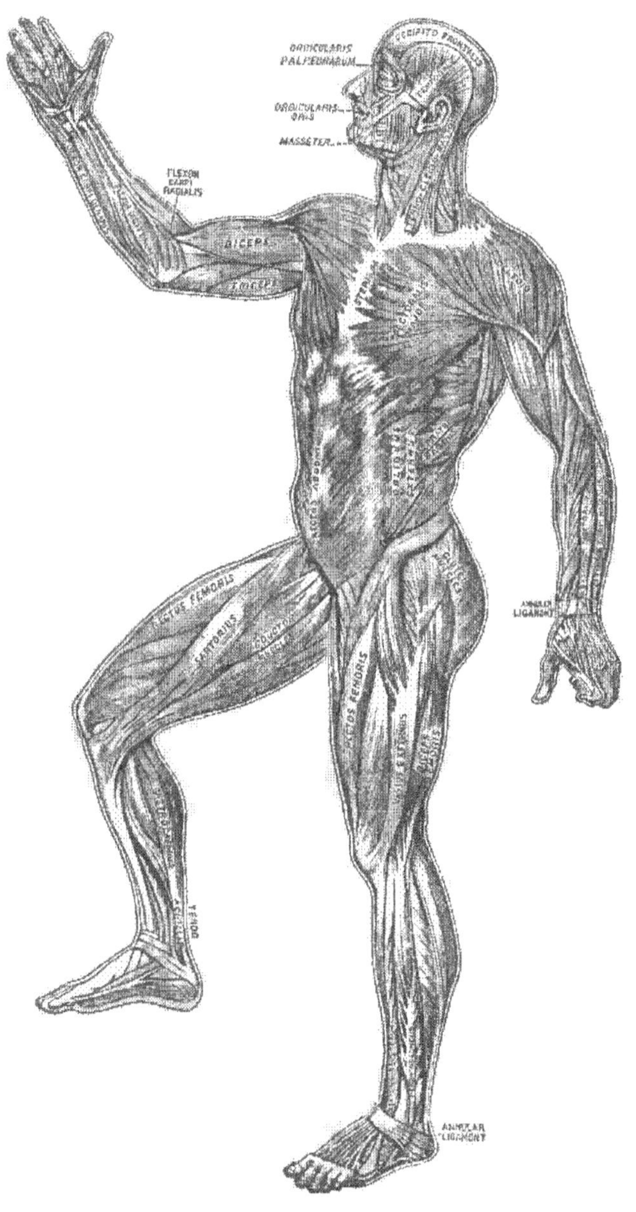

THE TRUNK (posterior).

Rhomboideus major,
Rhomboideus minor, } move the scapula backward.

Latissimus dorsi (24), moves the humerus downward and backward.

Serratus posticus inferior, muscle of expiration.

THE UPPER EXTREMITY.

Deltoid (8), elevates the arm.

Subscapularis,
Supra-spinatus, } rotate the humerus.
Infra-spinatus (12),

Brachialis anticus,
Biceps, } flex the forearm.

Triceps (10),
Anconeus, } extend the forearm.

Flexor carpi ulnaris and *radialis,* move the carpus.

Flexor digitorum, flex the fingers.

Extensor carpi radialis and *ulnaris* (21), antagonize the flexors.

Extensor digitorum (22), antagonize the flexors.

(Upward of thirty muscles act on the fingers.)

THE LOWER EXTREMITY.

Glutæus maximus (28),
Glutæus medius, } keep the body erect, rotate the thigh, move the thigh back-
Glutæus minimus, ward.

Psoas magnus,
Pectineus,
Iliacus, } raise the thigh. When the limbs are fixed, bend the body forward.
Adductor longus,

Rectus femoris,
Cruræus, } extend the leg. Their common tendons (*Quadriceps femoris*) contain the patella.
Vastus externus and *internus,*

Sartorius (tailor's muscle), flexes the leg on the thigh.

Biceps femoris,
Semi-tendinosus (30), } flex the leg.
Semi-membranosus,

Gracilis,
Abductors, } move the thigh inward.

Tibialis anticus,
Proprius pollicis, } flex the foot.

Gastrocnemius (32),
Soleus, } acting through the *tendo Achillis,* extend the foot.

Extensor digitorum,
Flexor digitorum, } move the toes.

(Upward of twenty muscles act on the toes.)

FIG. 127.

1
2
4
3
5
6
7
8
9
10
11
12
13
14
15
14
16
24
25
26
21
20
17
22
27
18
23
28
28
19
30
29
31
32
33

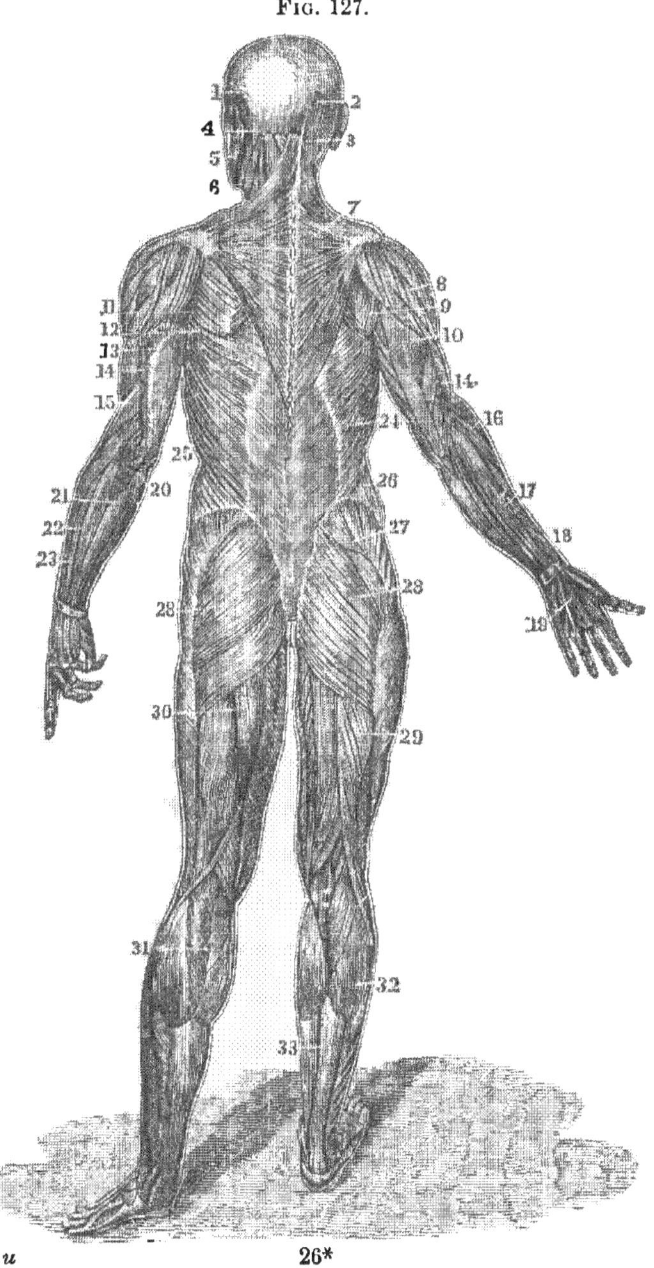

513. TENDONS OF MUSCLES.—The skeletal muscles are, for the most part, arranged to act on the bones as on levers.

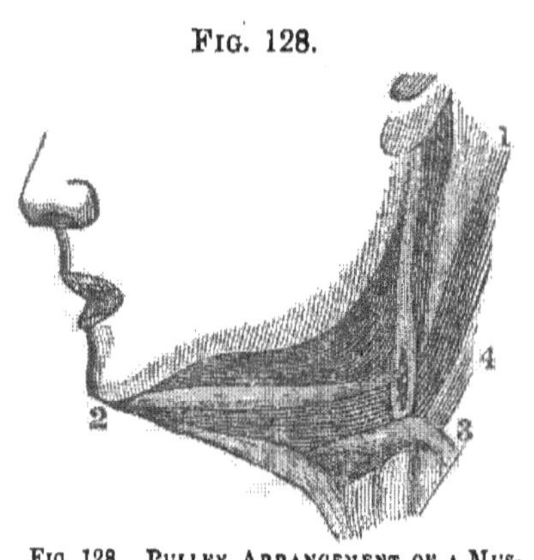

FIG. 128.

FIG. 128. PULLEY ARRANGEMENT OF A MUSCLE.—1, Digastric muscle attached to the mastoid process of the temporal bone behind the ear. 2, Its attachment to the lower jaw. 3, Hyoid bone. 4, The pulley arrangement of the digastric and stylo-hyoid muscles.

In most cases they are attached at both ends to the bones, in some places *directly*, as in the intercostals, at other places *indirectly*, as in the tendo Achillis (Fig. 126). Tendons are the white, flexible, strong, and nonelastic cords, or bands, in which the muscular fibres terminate (Fig. 17). The tendon by which a muscle arises (*origin*) enables a large number of bulky, muscular fibres to act from a definite point of the skeleton, whilst the tendon of attachment (*insertion*) transmits the muscular force to some other equally precise point of bone (Fig. 130, 4, 5). The tendons reflect the muscular force over the joints and other parts of the skeleton, as well as through loops (Fig. 128, 4); they economize muscular tissue, and they afford lightness and elegance, as is seen in the ankle and wrist.

514. ACTION OF MUSCLE (18, 19, 75, 76).—When the skeletal muscles swell and shorten their fibres, the part

---

513. What do the skeletal muscles do? How attached? What are tendons? What of the use of tendons of origin? Of tendons of insertion? What advantage results?

514. What results from muscular contraction? What differences in action? Give examples of the three orders. What of the third order? What of flexors? Of extensors?

into which they are inserted is moved. If both ends of the muscle are attached to soft parts, constriction usually results; if one end is attached to bone and the other to a soft part, the latter is moved; if both ends are attached to bone, the one offering the least resistance is moved, and the action is after the manner of levers: thus, the contraction of the muscle of the neck causes the head to move on the occipital condyles as *fulcrums*, and the heavy face is ele-

Fig. 129.

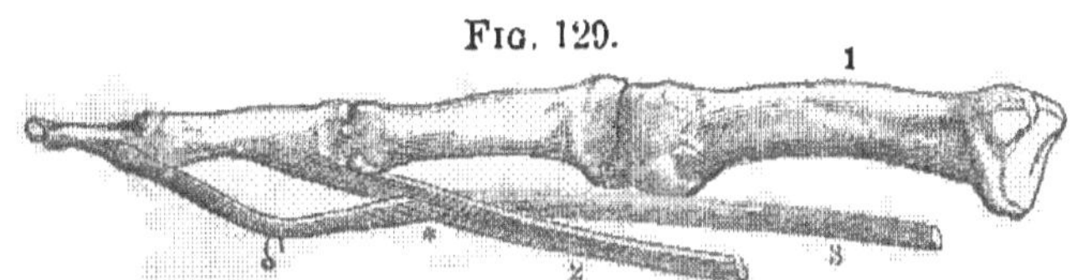

Fig. 129 (*Leidy*). METACARPAL AND PHALANGEAL BONES OF THE FINGERS, WITH THEIR TENDONS AND LIGAMENTS.—1, Metacarpal bone. 2, Tendon of the superficial flexor. 3, Tendon of the deep flexor, passing through a perforation (*) of the superficial flexor.

vated (lever of the first order); the toes resting on the ground, the *fulcrum*, the contraction of the muscles of the calf raises the body on the toes (lever of the second order); the contraction of the biceps and brachialis of the arm (Fig. 130) causes the forearm and hand quickly to approach the arm (lever of the third order). The latter order occurs most commonly in animal mechanics. Under this order, with a slight shortening of the muscle, great motion of the part, with rapidity and precision of movement, is secured, though with the expenditure of much force. In general, the *flexors* (like the biceps of the arm or of the leg) act at greater mechanical advantage than the *extensors*, like the quadriceps of the leg. In the extensors the power acts at all times obliquely, therefore they are larger and more bulky than the flexors.

515. CO-ORDINATE MOVEMENTS OF THE BODY.—In most movements several muscles act together in concert.

After contraction has ceased, gravity or elastic reaction in certain cases causes the parts to return to a state of equilibrium. In other cases, a set of *antagonistic* muscles are brought into action. Experience shows that the proper movements of the body depend more upon the proper co-operation of the muscles than upon the force of the contrac-

Fig. 130.

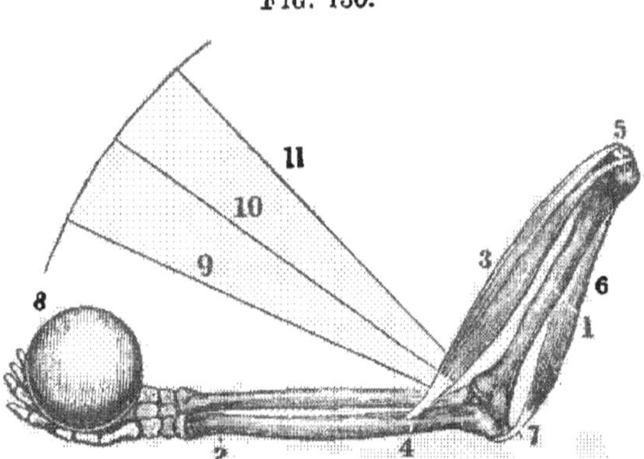

Fig. 130. Diagram of the Third Order of Lever.—1, The bone of the arm above the elbow. 2, One of the bones below the elbow. 3, The muscle that bends the elbow. This muscle is united, by a tendon, to the bone below the elbow (4); at the other extremity, to the bone above the elbow (5). 6, The muscle that extends the elbow. 7, Its attachment to the point of the elbow. 8, A weight in the hand to be raised. The central part of the muscle 3 contracts, and its two ends are brought nearer together. The bones below the elbow are brought to the lines shown by 9, 10, 11. The weight is raised in the direction of the curved line. When the muscle 6 contracts, the muscle 3 relaxes and the forearm is extended.

tions. The skilled blacksmith does a given job more quickly and with less fatigue than the unskilled, because he uses his powers to greater advantage. Experiments show that nearly all movements of the muscles are *co-ordinate* (593). In order to execute a composite motion, like a leap, the muscles must begin to work in the proper order, and the

---

515. How is equilibrium re-established? What does experience show? What of the composite movements in a leap? What of the mechanism?

energy of each muscle must increase, halt, and diminish, according to a proper order, so that the result shall be the correct position of the limbs, the just balance of the body, and the proper velocity of the centre of gravity in the right direction. The peculiar mechanism of the composite co-ordinate movements resides in the MOTOR GANGLION CELLS of the central nervous system (372). As yet, little is known of the process by which the human animal imparts a definite duration to the energy of the muscles.

516. SENSORY INFLUENCE.—The *motor ganglia* are constantly receiving information from the sensitive surfaces of the body. The impulses arising from external influences are constantly being sent inward to the *sensory ganglia* (394), from which they are reflected upon the motor ganglia, and may thus inhibit, accelerate, or modify the activity of the latter. The nerve-impulses from the mental centres, the optic centres, and the centres of sense of equilibrium (474) and of muscular pressure (370) appear to exert an influence on the motor ganglia, causing the latter to keep the muscles in a proper state of adjustment for the duty at hand, or to lose control of them. This is well seen in the positions, the perfect balance, the nicety of touch, the delicacy and celerity of motion, the susceptibility to mental disturbances, in the skilled billiard-player; in the trained horseman, when vaulting into the saddle of a moving steed; or in the composite movements of the wire-walker or the gymnast.

517. The ERECT POSTURE, in which the weight of the body is borne by the plantar arches (Fig. 126), is the result of co-ordinate contractions of the muscles of the trunk and legs. The object of these contractions is to hold the body in such a position as to keep

---

516. How do external conditions influence the motor ganglia? What is the influence of the other centres? Give examples.

the line of gravity within the area of the feet. A dead body will not remain standing when unsupported; the unconscious unsupported man falls; the growing child does not acquire the ability to stand erect until after months of constant practice, accompanied by numberless falls. Experience shows that the education of the co-

Fig. 131.   Fig. 132.

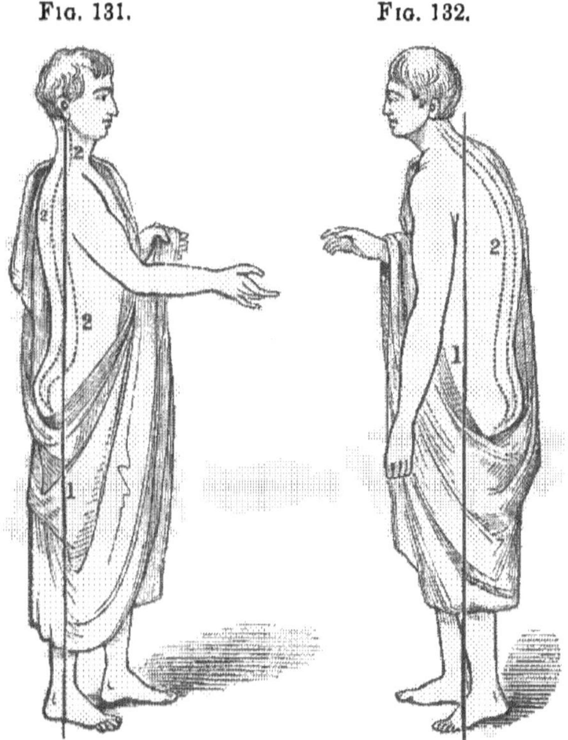

Fig. 131. Erect Position of the Body.—1, A perpendicular line from the centre of the feet to the upper point of the spinal column, where the head rests. 2, 2, 2, Spinal column with its three natural curves. The head and body are so balanced that the muscles are not kept in a state of tension.

Fig. 132. Stooping Position of the Body.—1, A perpendicular line. 2, Unnatural curved spinal column, and its relative position to the perpendicular line (1). The curved position of the body and lower limbs keeps the muscles in tension, which exhausts their energy.

ordinating motor ganglion cells in men is slow and tedious, and that in some cases (chorea) these centres are almost incapable of education.

In *walking*, there is a moment in which the body rests vertically on the foot of one leg, while the other is inclined back, with its heel raised and its toes resting on the ground. In motion, the weight of the body is transferred from one limb to the other alternately. Before the limb which is raised and advanced reaches the ground, the body is propelled forward by the straightening of the ankle of the foot which is behind.

In *running*, the heel is not brought to the ground; in walking, it is. In walking, the whole propulsive action is from the foot; in running, the knee and hip, being both greatly bent, give vast additional impulse. There is a space of time when neither foot of the runner is on the ground.

In *leaping*, all the joints of the lower limbs are flexed in preparation, and the impulse given by their sudden extension propels the body through the air. In leaping, the limbs are extended together; in running, they are extended alternately.

518. EFFECT OF MUSCULAR EXERCISE.—The *lung*-action is greatly hurried. The blood-flow is enhanced. The quantity of air inspired and of carbonic acid expired is wonderfully increased. The action of the *heart* rapidly increases in force and frequency, and the flow of blood through all parts of the body is augmented. The blood has been found to flow more freely and of richer quality through the vessels of the working muscle than through those of the quiescent muscle. The *skin* becomes red from the fulness of the vessels, and the perspiration is much increased. The increase of carbon excreted demands an increase of carbon to be given in the form of food, and hence the *appetite* is largely increased. The demand for meat and fats, rather than for carbo-hydrates, is noticed. The *digestion* improves, and the absorption becomes more perfect.

----

518. What is the effect of muscular exercise on the lungs? The heart? The skin? The appetite? The brain? The skeletal muscles? What microscopic changes?

A sufficiency of exercise makes the performance of *mental work* more perfect, renders the action of the nerve-ganglia quicker, readier, and more exact, and strengthens the ability to cope with mental obstacles. Under continued exercise the *smooth muscles* appear to be strengthened; the *skeletal muscles* become heavier, those of the right side keeping up the natural advantage over those of the left, as a rule; their strength increases with the work demanded of them up to a limit peculiar to each person; their capacity for endurance is enhanced, and their rapidity and precision in action are wonderfully augmented (87). Of the microscopic difference between worked and unworked human muscle but little is definitely known. The muscle-bundles and sarcolemma of worked cattle are thicker than the corresponding parts in fattening cattle.

519. DEFICIENCY OF EXERCISE.—Insufficient exercise causes the muscles to become smaller and softer, less energetic in their contraction, less precise in their action, less capable of endurance, and less powerful in their combined influence. The non-use may lead to excessive wasting, as seen in the bandaged limb some weeks after a fracture, or even to a change of sarcotic elements (71) into fat, as has been noticed after certain nerve-injuries. All the organs are influenced by the action of the skeletal muscles. Insufficient action of the voluntary muscles induces feebleness and a tendency to degeneracy in most of the tissues and organs.

This want of tone is shown in the pallor, coldness, dryness, and transparency of the skin; in the want of color of the mucous surfaces; in the dry and lustreless condition of

---

519. Effect of insufficient exercise? Of no exercise? How does deficiency of exercise make itself known? What parts do not suffer?

the hair; in the softness and flabbiness of the flesh; in the inability for sustained moderate exertion; in the ease with which irregular and difficult heart-action is induced; in the "shortness of breath" and the quickness of respiratory exhaustion; in the want of appetite and of ability to digest ordinary food; in the torpor of the bowels; in the deficient action of the kidneys; and in the state of the nervous system, characterized by indecision, want of buoyancy, and a feeling of inadequacy to cope with ordinary daily obstacles.

520. SYSTEMATIC EXERCISE.—The term "exercise" is usually restricted to the action of the skeletal muscles, but it should include the indirect culture of the nerve-centres and other organs by systematic movements. Of the importance to all persons of daily muscular exercise there can be no question. *The object of systematic exercise is the development and maintenance of a sound, symmetrical organism.*

521. The daily work of the blacksmith develops and strengthens the muscles of the arms and trunk, and especially the muscles of the right side; the work of the farm-laborer calls into action all the muscles, but some sets proportionally more than others; the drill of the dancer, those of the limbs; the work of the shoemaker, those of the arms; the practice of the boxer, those of the chest and arms, etc. In most cases, certain parts of the system become well or even excessively developed, while other equally important parts lag behind in growth and vigor. The heart- and lung-development of the blacksmith and laborer, the upper-extremity-culture of the dancer, the heart-,

---

520. What is systematic exercise?   Its object?

521. Give examples of one-sided development.   What may result from it?

o   27

lung-, and lower-extremity-development of the shoemaker and other persons following a sedentary line of work, are not proportional to those of their best physical parts. As the strength of the cable is only that of its weakest link, so the capabilities of the human body are only those of the weakest part called into action. If there is a one-sided physical development, then will the strong part, in the fulness of its power, tend to call upon the weak part for a sudden, sustained exertion beyond its power. The weak part endeavors, struggles, falters, wavers, breaks, and the whole structure topples, even in its apparent prime. It has been frequently noticed that the muscularly strong man often fails in life's work, where the weaker yet uniformly developed though perhaps not completely sound man succeeds. Too often the noted boxer, the heavy hitter, the successful oarsman, the celebrated gymnast, overtaxes the non-developed part, especially the heart and lungs, and in a few months becomes a physical wreck.

522. The Demands of Modern Life require a uniformly-developed, well-consolidated, well-balanced organism. It is a *sound body*, rather than a *strong body*, that is wanted. It should be the aim to establish such an accordance between heart, lung, muscle, stomach, kidney, and skin as will enable the possessor of the organism to perform the duties of life efficiently, regularly, and without marked physical inconvenience.

523. Physical Culture.—Homer observed that no man could acquire greater fame than by being strong in his hands, feet, and limbs. The Greeks aimed at the harmonious development of the individual. In their *gymnasia*, physical exercises were prescribed and

---

522. What is demanded by modern life? What constitutes **a sound** body?

regulated by law. Incessant methodical drill of the men for war was the normal condition of the Roman commonwealth. The army was named, from its dominant occupation, *exercitus.* In the age of chivalry, among the few, a high estimate was placed on the possession of a perfect body, and great care was observed in its attainment. With the advent of gunpowder, and the wide acceptance of the Church's doctrine of body-mortification in order to soul-perfection, there grew up a disregard of the conditions favorable to the body's well-being. This state of darkness prevailed on the continent of Europe until the present century, when Ling succeeded in introducing the "Swedish movement-cure." Primarily, this was designed to meet the needs of every imaginable disease, and had a certain measure of success. His followers developed out of it the modern system of *light gymnastics.* After the humiliation of Jena and Auerstadt (October, 1806), Stein devoted himself to the task of building up Prussia, of gaining more personal and property freedom for her masses, of elevating her serfs to citizens, of curbing the tyranny of caste, of developing an effective militia, and of acquiring territory. About the same time, a system of physical training, designed for the development of strong, serviceable men, was introduced in Prussia by Jahn. Strange as it may seem, this system of physical culture was opposed by the government, on the ground that it made the people less manageable and more intolerant of Church and State. But the people appreciated it. It grew in popular favor. The enthusiasm for body-training so advanced that in 1853 the Prussian government made "*turning*" a recognized branch of public instruction. Is it not fair to infer that the success of Prussia in Denmark, Austria, and France was quite as much due to the systematic general training of her people as to the carrying out of the civil systems of Stein? In England, more than in any other country in the world, *sports* have had a strong hold on the popular mind. All classes, the laboring class perhaps excepted, have always shown a great *practical* interest in walking, running, wrestling, swimming, riding, and other out-door exercises. The result of this is seen in the fine physical development of both sexes of the English upper and middle classes. The habits of exercise deeply impressed in cold, damp England follow them, and appear in their daily life in the enervating climates of Asia and Central America. The daily walk, ride, run, and other vigorous exercises, as well as the "tub," are characteristic of the energetic, pushing, enduring Anglo-Saxon the world round.

524. RELATIVE ADVANTAGES OF THE SYSTEMS.—The *Swedish system*, in which the exercises are limited to extremely simple although varied motions, undoubtedly gives rise to a moderate amount of muscular culture. Its routine, however, soon becomes monotonous. It does not call for that culture of the sense of muscular equilibrium, for that concordant action of the eye, of the central nervous system, and of the intellectual faculties, which are so highly desirable in the training of a sound body.

The *English system*, as its training takes place out of doors and in the country principally, and as it calls the eye, the brain, and the central nervous system into *interested* action, has much to commend it. It cultivates the muscular system; it calls for perseverance; it engenders courage, quickness to see and to decide, and celerity in action. It, however, tends too often to a one-sided culture, as the mountain climber, the runner, the wrestler, the rower, the rider, etc., is inclined to confine himself to the continued culture of his peculiar advantage, and becomes highly proficient in that respect, but neglects the culture of his weaker parts. Again, the English system requires conditions which are not easily attainable by the middle classes of the large towns.

The *German system* presents an ideal aim,—uniform, systematic culture. It is graded and adapted to every age and condition. It can be practised by all classes, even though living in densely-populated towns. It tends to a more equable perfecting of the muscular and sensory motor systems than either of the other systems.

525. INFLUENCE OF PHYSICAL CULTURE.—The census of 1880 showed that physical culture was a part of the school curriculum in three schools per one thousand in the United States. The bodily condition of many of the graduates of the high schools, public academies, private schools, and colleges is too well known to call for comment. That the want of physical training and a lack of knowledge as to personal care are largely responsible for the decreased efficiency of the educated young men and women of America, is beyond question. At Amherst College, early in the freshman year, a knowledge of the human body and of its requirements is inculcated, and throughout the collegiate course physical culture is a required part of the student's work. The result of this training is shown in the higher regard which the students have for their *personal* physical condition and hygienic surroundings; in a falling off in the ratio of sickness and invalidism, and a decrease in the proportion of three sick in the freshman year to one sick in the senior year, as the result of a four years' course. The statistics of certain schools for physical culture show that in classes made up of college students, school-boys, and city young ladies, under a six months' training, there was an increase of about two inches in the passive girth of the chest, of four inches in the expansive power, and of fifty cubic inches in the lung-capacity, besides a marked change in other parts of the system. Figures cannot begin to express the change in the physical and mental tone, resulting from the use of more air and a better digestion of the food taken, following a systematic drill.

526. SUPPRESSION OF BY-MOTIONS.—Watch a boy, strong in the arms, but unaccustomed to rope-climbing, attempt to ascend a rope hand over hand. He begins vigorously, but soon falters and struggles; his muscles tremble; his face becomes contorted; his legs perform choreic movements; his breath grows labored and irregular, and suddenly he descends. After a few weeks' drill he is seen to ascend the rope with comparative ease, the facial muscles calm, every joint locked, respiration labored, but regular. His training has enabled him to suppress by-motions, to concentrate his powers on the necessary motions, and, as a result, he accomplishes his task easily, promptly, and with the expenditure of much less energy. The suppression of by-motions, the accurate execution of the essential motions, the correct co-ordination of all the movements to the given end, and the apparent ease of execution, make the postures of the Japanese " geisha," the feats of the gymnast, the precision of the soldier, and the stroke of the billiard-player pleasurable sights.

---

526. What of by-motions? What does training accomplish?

527. JUDICIOUS SYSTEMATIC EXERCISE makes the muscles stronger, more agile, and more enduring; the extremities more flexible, efficient, and obedient; the skin more supple and a better protection; the central nervous system better fitted for complicated efforts; and the mind better able to increase its own powers for work and endurance. The usefulness of such a training is experienced in many situations in life. In emergencies of unexpected danger,—fire, shipwreck, accidents by carriage and rail, etc.,—the superiority resulting from that presence of mind and fertility of resources which are conferred by the consciousness of physical strength and trained nerves and rapid action makes this training of inestimable value.

528. CONDITIONS FOR EXERCISE.—By exercise is to be understood the frequent repetition of a more or less complicated action of the body, with the co-operation of the mind, for the purpose of being able to perform it better. During exercise the action of the lungs must be perfectly free. The clothing must be so arranged as to preclude the least impediment to the free play of the chest and abdomen. The amount of pure air supplied must be unlimited: hence it is better to exercise in an open shed, or entirely out of doors.

As soon as the respirations become labored, or if there be sighing respiration, rest must be taken. The heart should be gradually accustomed to its work. In order to bring the heart's action and the lungs' capacity to take the blood into accord, all exercise should be entered upon slowly and gradually. The breathlessness of the untrained

---

527. What results from systematic exercise? What advantage?

528. What is exercise? What primary conditions? What signs of danger? Management? What of the heart-action? What of the skin? Of shoes? Of food? Of drink?

runner who starts off at the height of his speed is due to blood congestion of the lungs. Hence, in endeavoring to reach a fire, with the intention of doing good, " make haste slowly." The heart's action must be closely watched. Excessive rapidity of the pulse (one hundred and twenty to one hundred and forty beats in the minute), or inequality or irregularity of the beats, points to the need of rest, and later to a more gradual order of exercise. Occasionally, a sudden excessive effort leads to rupture of the walls of the heart.

The skin should be kept very clean. During exercise the skin may be thinly clad. In the intervals of exertion, and immediately after, it should be so well covered as to prevent the least feeling of coolness of its surface. Flannel is best adapted for an exercise suit. The shoes should give plenty of room all around the foot; the sole should be thinnest and narrowest at the " waist," where elasticity is wanted, should be broad and thick at the " tread," where protection is most required, and the heels should be low and broad. A well-formed large foot is a far pleasanter sight than the smallest one distorted.

Food should not be taken immediately before or directly after exercise. Water is the best fluid to train on. Cold water may be taken moderately, and often, during exercise. When overheated, it is best to wash out the mouth frequently, and later to drink moderate amounts.

529. REST (425) is essential at frequent and regular intervals. The length of the period of rest should be such as to enable the muscles to regain their tone and to work with ease and vigor. The interval of rest enables the blood

529. What of the length of the periods of rest? What is the object? Management after exercise?

to remove the products of tissue-change from the centres of activity (muscle- and nerve-ganglia), and to permit the system, especially the muscles, to lay up a new store of oxygen, for during action the oxygen brought in the blood is not sufficient for the demand of the fleshy elements (87). After exercise, sponging with tepid water to remove the dust and the dried products of perspiration, vigorous rubbing, and putting on a dry under-suit are advisable.

530. KINDS OF EXERCISE.—The kinds of exercise should be selected according to the physical wants of the individual. The object in all cases is the production and the keeping up of a sound, well-balanced organism. The exercises suitable for a given individual can be determined only after a physical examination and a consideration of the evident needs of the system. The hap-hazard method of taking up a line of exercise is not judicious. For a beginner, the exercises should be carefully prescribed and the conditions for exercise clearly laid down. All exercise, to be beneficial, must be pleasurable and give buoyancy to the mind as well as strength to the muscles. Walking, to be beneficial, should be so active as to excite free perspiration in ordinary weather. Croquet and the "constitutional walk" of the boarding-school file are of little physical benefit. In quick walking, running, and rowing (especially with the slide-seat), the work is mostly performed by the muscles of the trunk and lower limbs, and hence they should be supplemented by a line of movements calling the upper extremities into action, like Indian clubs, rope and ladder exercises, etc. Base-ball, cricket,

---

530. What is the object of exercise? How best effected? What of hap-hazard exercise? Of mental interest? Of walking? Of sports? Of lawn tennis? Of gardening? Of household work?

swimming, skating, boxing, wrestling, and the riding of a restive horse are most excellent forms of exercise. Lawn tennis, from a hygienic point of view, is the best of modern games. It calls into action the eye, the intellectual and the motor centres, and makes demands on most of the muscles of the body, and is therefore to be commended, especially for ladies. Daily work in the garden is a good form of exercise, if the person performs all the kinds of work there afforded. No kind of exercise is so well calculated to develop all parts of the body in woman, and to promote good health, as housework. The development of a well-knit frame, of firm fat, and of muscular strength should be encouraged in girls. Their health and happiness are not only promoted, but they will be better fitted for one of woman's most exalted missions in life,—maternity.

531. The AMOUNT OF EXERCISE should be adjusted to the age and physical condition of the person. All movements must be kept within the strength and capacity of the given individual. All exercise should stop short of muscular exhaustion. In infancy, freedom of movement should be allowed. The child ought not to be urged to walk because it has passed a certain number of months. Compelling a child to walk at an early date often leads to deformed legs and feet. Boys and girls should take part in the same sports, be trained in similar duties, and be required to take part in the same occupations. In after-life it will be of as much advantage for the boy to have a definite idea of in-door duties as for the girl to be acquainted with out-door pursuits. Prolonged, severe efforts should not

---

531. What general rule? Speak of exercise for infants. For boys. For girls. For young men and women. What is Dr. Parkes's conclusion? Speak of exercise for business-men. For invalids.

v

be demanded until the system is consolidated (about the twenty-first year). Young, immature men, subjected to the strain of a military life, easily succumb to fatigue, as did the later conscripts in the French armies of Napoleon I. During the period of early manhood and womanhood, such an amount of out-of-door exercise, in addition to daily duties, should be taken as will daily induce healthy sleep from 9 P.M. until 5.30 A.M. Dr. Parkes estimates that every healthy adult man ought, if possible, to take a daily amount of exercise in some way which shall not be less than one hundred and fifty tons lifted one foot. This amount of work is equivalent to a walk of about nine miles on the level. As ordinary daily occupations call for certain amounts of effort, probably a daily walk of five miles, in addition, would be sufficient exercise for a business-man. The amount and kind of exercise for invalids should be determined by the medical attendant. After illness the convalescent should use caution, so as not to exceed his slowly-gaining powers of body and mind. A slight over-exertion is very frequently the cause of a relapse in fevers.

532. POSTURE.—An erect posture in sitting and in walking should be maintained. The erect, easy carriage of the West Point cadet results from the careful, persistent drill on the parade and in the class-room and study-room. It is commenced in youth and is continued through early manhood, and, as a result, the bones are consolidated in correct positions and the muscles of the right and left sides become equally developed. The uniform drill of the muscles, especially those of the back and abdomen, in childhood and youth would dispense with the demand for corsets

---

532. What is the West Point training? Why are corsets in great demand? What of distortions?

and braces by the young and middle-aged of both sexes. For the want of proper exercise, distortion of the chest and spine often appears. It has been affirmed that, among the fashionably educated, not one woman in ten escapes deformities of the thorax and spine, followed by lung and heart troubles. Assuming improper positions for several hours

Fig. 133.   Fig. 134.

Fig. 133 REPRESENTS AN IMPROPER, but not an unusual, position when writing.
Fig. 134 REPRESENTS A PROPER position when writing.

daily, through a series of years, as is too often done by students, certain artisans, seamstresses, etc., together with one-sided exercise, does not fail to produce distortion.

533. It has been noticed that slate-carriers and porters, who carry burdens on their heads, unsupported by the hand, are erect, well-balanced men. The drill of carry-

533. Effect of carrying weights on the head? What may a student do to his own advantage? Test?

ing a book balanced on the head at intervals during the day cannot fail to be beneficial to students. Students should, at frequent intervals during the day, rise, loosen the garments about the thorax and abdomen, take several deep respirations, then place the palms together in front of the chest, on a level with the fourth rib, and sweep them in that plane around to the rear, endeavoring to strike the knuckles together. Repeat this several times. Upon rising, and before retiring, stand erect, heels together, the feet forming an angle of ninety degrees; raise the hands vertically over the head, fists closed, thumbs in contact, then, bending the back, endeavor to touch the floor with the knuckles without bending the knees. Repeat this several times. *Test.*—Stand erect, with the back to the wall of the room and the back of the head in contact with the same. The ease with which this can be done will gauge the progress towards an erect attitude.

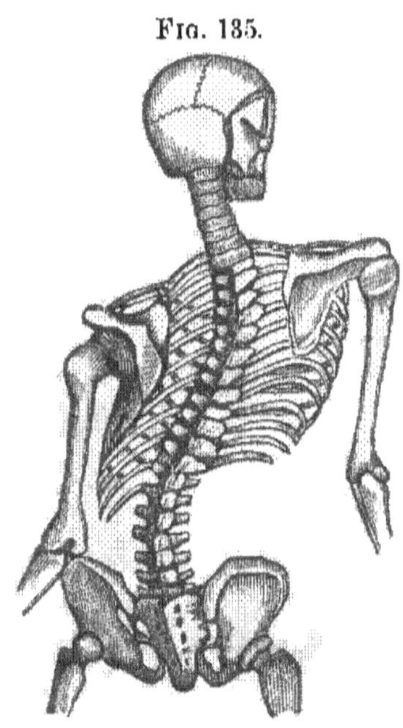

Fig. 135.

Fig. 135. A Deformed Thorax and Spinal Column.

534. TRAINING.—The object of training is to increase the breathing-power, to co-ordinate the heart-power to the blood-taking capacity of the lungs, to make the muscular

534. What is the object of training? How is it accomplished? What results? What may then be done?

action more vigorous and enduring, to increase the action of the eliminating organs, especially of the skin, and to lessen the fat. This is accomplished by a course of graduated exercises, such as induce free perspiration, with a diet rich in proteids but restricted as to carbo-hydrates, by care in the selection of beverages (water is best), and by abstinence from dissipation and from the use of stimulants and tobacco. The result of several weeks' work is a greater tissue-waste, a greater demand for proteids, fats, and pure air, a quicker renewal of the tissues, and a more vigorous living. A higher condition of health ensues. If, for the given individual, this is not carried to excess, the system can accomplish a severe, sustained physical exertion with greater safety than before the training. "The lives of most men are in their own hands, and, as a rule, the just verdict after death would be *felo de se*."

CHAPTER XV.

CARE OF THE SICK AND EMERGENT CASES.

535. In every home, however humble or dignified, woman is usually the Nurse. Nature seems to have endowed her in an especial manner to minister at the couch of disease and suffering. To be a good nurse requires a high type of womanhood; she should have both mental and physical power, blended with integrity and Christian trust.

If "good nursing is half the cure," how important that the daughter be early taught how to prepare drinks and nourishment, to administer medicine, and to perform the varied and important duties of the faithful nurse!

The physician well knows that his attentions upon the sick are unavailing unless the nurse *obeys* his directions. For a nurse, or immediate relatives or friends of the sick, to put their judgment in opposition to that of the physician, is not only arrogant, but endangers the patient.

The *room* for the sick should be selected where sunlight may enter, and as far from external noise as possible. It is poor economy, not to say unkind, to keep a sick man in a small, ill-arranged bedroom, when a more spacious and airy room is kept for only occasional "callers." All superfluous furniture should be removed from the sick-room.

536. In the first stages of disease, it is always proper treatment to *rest* both body and mind. It is wrong to tempt the appetite of a sick person: the disinclination for food is the warning of Nature that the system cannot well digest it.

The beneficial effects of *bathing* can hardly be overestimated, but the mode of the bath should be directed by the medical adviser. The best time, however, for bathing is when the patient feels most vigorous and is freest from exhaustion. Care is necessary to wipe dry the skin, particularly between the fingers and toes, and

326

also the flexures of the joints. Friction from a brush, a moreen mitten, or a dry flannel that has been saturated with salted water tends to relieve restlessness in patients. Air-baths have a tranquillizing influence.

537. *Quiet* should reign in the sick-room. No more persons should enter or remain in it than the welfare of the patient demands. It is the duty of the physician to direct when visitors should be admitted or excluded, and the nurse should enforce the directions. The movements of the attendants should be gentle: there should be no bustling to arrange the room at a fixed time; this should be done quietly and when it will give the least annoyance to the sick person. When a room requires sweeping, scatter over the carpet drained coffee-grounds; then keep the broom before you, giving a light, short brush; the dust will thus be prevented from rising above the couch. (It may be necessary to use a *damp* cloth in dusting the furniture, especially if the patient has disease of the lungs.) Creaking hinges should be oiled; shutting doors violently and heavy walking should be avoided. All unnecessary conversation should be deferred. If a colloquy must be carried on, let the tone be so high that the patient, if interested, can thoroughly comprehend it.

538. The *making of the bed* is often badly conducted. All bunches should be removed, the material of the bed laid even, and a thin quilt spread smoothly over a mattress. When convenient, have the head of the bed northerly, and so situated, at least, that the sick person may look on something more pleasurable than a table of glasses and phials. A nurse should never manifest impatience in arranging the pillows, but should try to adapt them to the comfort of the weary patient.

539. *All utensils* employed in the sick-room should be kept clean. Water designed for the patient to drink should not stand long in an open glass or pitcher, but, if convenient, should be given fresh from a *spring* or well. A very sick person is fatigued by being raised to receive drinks; hence, a bent tube or a cup with a spout should be used.

Both the *apparel and the bed-linen* should be changed more frequently in sickness than in health, and oftener in acute than in chronic diseases. All clothing should be well dried and warmed by a fire previous to being put on the bed or the patient.

No agent is of more importance to the sick-room than *pure air;*

hence the nurse, with all convenient speed, should remove everything that can emit an unpleasant odor. She should be chary of keeping ripe fruit or bouquets of flowers any length of time in the sick-chamber. When a disinfectant is needed, procure at the druggist's chloride of lime. To change quickly and effectively the air of the sick-room, cover the patient's bed with an extra blanket and closely envelop his head and neck, except the mouth and nose; the door and windows can then be safely opened for a short time. After the windows are closed, retain the extra coverings on the patient until the room is of proper warmth. Unless duly protected, the patient should never feel *currents of air*, although *fresh air* should be constantly admitted into the sick-room.

A well-adjusted thermometer is indispensable, as the feelings of the patient or nurse are not to be relied on as a true index of the *temperature* of the room. Regulating the warmth of the patient is one of the many duties of the nurse. There is a "sweating temperature;" when this is exceeded, perspiration will cease, if it has been present; also it will not take place during a high temperature. The patient should no more be allowed to complain of *too much heat*, without an attempt at its reduction, than he should be permitted to remain chilly when a change is possible.

540. The *nurse* should not confine herself to the sick-room longer than six hours at a time. She should exercise daily in the open air, also eat and sleep as regularly as possible. No doubts or fears of the patient's recovery, either by a look or by a word, should be expressed by the nurse in the chamber of the sick.

541. *Medicines assist* the natural powers of the system to remove disease. They should be given regularly, judiciously, and with cheerfulness. Life itself is often at the mercy of the nurse, and depends on the faithful discharge of her duty.

542. *Drinks* have a more decided influence upon the system than is generally admitted; hence the nurse should never depart from the quality of the drink, nor even exceed the due or prescribed quantity. Giving "herb-teas" without the sanction of the physician may cause serious evil.

543. The *food* of the sick should be prepared in the neatest and most careful manner, and the nurse ought to obey implicitly the physician's directions about diet. When a patient is convalescent, the desire for food is generally strong; great care, firmness, and

patience are required, that the food be prepared suitably and given at the proper time.

We append a few modes of preparing nourishment for the sick.

CRUST COFFEE.—Take light, sweet bread or crackers, and brown them *thoroughly*, as you would coffee-berry; when wanted for use, pour on them boiling water (the crusts will admit of several replenishings of boiling water); add sugar and cream to suit the condition of the patient.

GRUELS.—*Corn*-meal requires to be boiled several hours to be suitable nourishment for the sick. The mode of preparing gruel should be suited to the case and directed by the physician. Wheat-flour or oat-meal, farina, and sago can be prepared in less time, though they must be well cooked. Add salt while cooking.

Egg Gruel.—Take the yelks of two hard-boiled eggs; with a knife reduce them to a fine powder; beat this in a milk gruel made of rich new milk and wheat-flour; spices may be added when the condition of the patient permits.

BEEF TEA.—Meat contains principles that may be extracted, some by *cold*, others by *warm*, and still others by *boiling*, water; it should be cut very fine, and submitted for three hours each time, in succession, to half its weight of cold, of warm, and of boiling water; the fluids strained from the first and second macerations are to be mixed with that strained from the boiling process, and the mixture should be brought to a boiling heat to cook it; skim off the fat, and add a few drops of lemon-juice, with salt, for a flavor. Many of the "prepared foods" are to be commended.

FOOD FOR A BABE.—Cow's milk (Ayrshire is preferable) is a substitute for healthy human milk. In feeding—1st, let the babe draw from the bottle *warmed water* to its satisfaction; 2d, after a few minutes give it *fresh, undiluted*, properly-warmed milk to which a trace of salt has been added; 3d, have it suck *very slowly* all it will take. Some infants thrive on suitable diluted or condensed milk. Starchy or fibrous food should not be given until the child is seven months old.

544. POULTICE.—Mix the corn- or linseed-meal into a paste with hot water. On a piece of folded cloth place the paste to the thickness of half or three-fourths of an inch. Leave at least an inch of free margin between the paste and the edges of the cloth. On the upper surface place a piece of muslin or mosquito-netting of the

size of the surface of the paste. Now fold the free edges over the edges of the netting. Apply the netting side to the skin. On the outside place a layer of oiled paper, or oiled silk, or gum-cloth. If the wound is painful, sprinkle a few spoonfuls of laudanum over the poultice; if the wound is offensive, mix powdered charcoal in the paste.

545. OLIVE OIL.—In chest-diseases, Dr. Von Gieth, of Munich, uses olive oil in preference to poultices. Take a double fold of cotton cloth, sufficiently large to surround the trunk completely. Thoroughly saturate this with warm olive or cotton-seed oil. Apply this closely to the chest, shoulders, and abdomen. Over all draw a loose woollen shirt. Renew from time to time. The oil softens the skin and retains in the chest a uniform amount of heat.

546. The duty of the WATCHER is scarcely less responsible than that of the nurse, and, like the nurse, she should ever be cheerful, kind, firm, and attentive in the presence of the patient.

The watcher should be prompt, and reach the house of the sick at an early hour. Before entering the sick-room, she should eat a simple, nutritious supper, and also during the night take some plain food. She should be furnished with an extra garment, as a heavy shawl, to wear towards morning, when the system becomes exhausted.

The directions about the sick, especially the administration of medicine, should be *written* for the temporary watcher. Whatever may be wanted during the night should be brought into the sick-chamber or the adjoining room before the family retires to sleep, so that the slumbers of the patient shall not be disturbed by haste or searching for needed articles.

Sperm candles are preferable for the sick-room. Kerosene, in burning, emits a disagreeable odor, often annoying to the patient. All lights ought to be so arranged as not to be reflected in the part of the room where the sick person lies.

It is not necessary that watchers make themselves acceptable to the patient by exhausting conversation. If two watchers are needed, it is more imperative that they refrain from talking, and particularly from *whispering*.

Most sick persons have special need of nourishment about four or five o'clock in the morning.

547. When taking care of the sick, light-colored cotton or linen

clothing should be worn in preference to worsted apparel, especially if the disease is of a contagious character. It is always safe for the watcher to change her apparel worn in the sick-chamber before entering upon her family duties. Disease is often communicated by the clothing.

It can hardly be expected that the farmer who has been laboring hard in the field, or the mechanic who has toiled during the day, is qualified to render all those little attentions that a sick person requires. Hence, would it not be more benevolent and economical to employ and *pay* watchers who are qualified by knowledge and *training* to perform this duty in a faithful manner, while the kindness and sympathy of friends may be *practically* manifested by assisting to defray the expenses of these qualified and useful assistants?

POISONS AND THEIR ANTIDOTES.

548. POISONING, either from accident or from design, is of such frequency that every household should keep some available remedy, and every person should know *what to do* in such alarming contingencies. Nearly every poison has its antidote, which, *if used at once*, may prevent much suffering, and even avert death.

When known that poison has been taken into the stomach, the first thing is to evacuate it by the use of the stomach-pump or an emetic, unless vomiting takes place spontaneously.

As an emetic, ground *mustard* mixed in warm water is always safe. Take one tablespoonful to one pint of warm water. Give the patient one-half in the first instance, and the remainder in fifteen minutes if vomiting has not commenced. In the interval, let him drink copious draughts of warm water. Tickle the throat with a feather or the finger, to induce vomiting. After vomiting has begun, give mucilaginous drinks, such as flaxseed tea, gum-arabic water, or slippery-elm water.

If the patient is drowsy, give a strong infusion of cold coffee, keep him walking, slap smartly on the back, use electricity; it may be well to dash cold water on the head, to keep the patient awake. After the poison is evacuated from the stomach, to sustain vital action, give warm water and wine or brandy. If the limbs are cold, apply warmth and friction.

In ALL cases of poisoning, call a physician immediately, as the after-treatment is of great importance.

549.

POISONS.	ANTIDOTES OR REMEDIES FOR POISONS.
Aconite (Monkshood). Belladonna (Deadly Nightshade.) Bryony. Camphor. Conium ⎫ Cicuta. ⎭ (Water Hemlock). Croton Oil. Digitalis (Foxglove). Dulcamara (Bitter-Sweet). Gamboge. Hyoscyamus (Henbane). Laudanum. Lobelia. Morphine. Opium. Paregoric. Sanguinaria (Blood-Root). Savin Oil. Spigelia (Carolina Pink). Stramonium (Thorn-Apple). Strychnine (Nux Vomica). Tobacco.	For *vegetable* poisons give an emetic of *mustard;* make the patient drink freely of warm water; tickle the throat with a feather, to induce vomiting. Keep the patient awake until a physician arrives. Administer strong coffee freely.
Arnica.	*Vinegar* and water.
Prussic Acid. Bitter Almonds (Oil of). Laurel-Water.	Drink, at once, one teaspoonful of *water of hartshorn* (ammonia) in one pint of water.
Ammonia (Hartshorn). Potash. Soda.	*Vinegar* or *lemon-juice*, followed by sweet, castor, or linseed oil. Thick cream will answer as a substitute for oil. No emetic.
Iodine.	Starch or wheat-flour beaten in water. Give a mustard emetic.

POISONS.	ANTIDOTES OR REMEDIES FOR POISONS.
Saltpetre (Nitrate of Potassa). Chili Saltpetre (Nitrate of Soda).	Give, at once, a *mustard* emetic; drink copious draughts of warm water, followed by oil or cream.
Lunar Caustic (Nitrate of Silver).	Two teaspoonfuls of table-salt (chloride of sodium) mixed in one pint of water.
Corrosive Sublimate (bug-poison). White Precipitate. Red Precipitate. Vermilion.	Beat the *whites of six eggs* in one quart of cold water; give a cupful every two minutes. A substitute for white of eggs is *soap-suds* slightly thickened with wheat-flour. Emetics should not be given.
Arsenic. Cobalt (fly-powder). King's Yellow. Ratsbane. Scheele's Green.	Use a *stomach-pump* as quickly as possible, or give a mustard emetic until one is obtained. After free vomiting, give large quantities of *calcined magnesia*. The antidote for arsenic is *hydrated peroxide of iron*.
Acetate of Lead (Sugar of Lead). White Lead. Litharge.	Use a *mustard* emetic, followed by Epsom or Glauber's salt. The antidote is diluted *sulphuric acid*.
Antimony (Wine of). Tartar Emetic.	The antidote is ground *nut-gall*, or, as a substitute, oak or Peruvian bark, followed by a teaspoonful of paregoric.
Pearl-ash. Ley (from wood-ashes). Salts of Tartar	Drink freely of *vinegar* and water, followed by a mucilage, as flaxseed tea.

POISONS.	ANTIDOTES OR REMEDIES FOR POISONS.
Sulphuric Acid (Oil of Vitriol). Nitric Acid (Aquafortis). Muriatic Acid (Hydrochloric). Oxalic Acid.	Drink largely of water or a mucilage. It is important that something *be given quickly*, to neutralize the acid. The antidote is *calcined magnesia*. Chalk, lime, strong soap-suds, are substitutes for magnesia.
Matches (Phosphorus). Rat Exterminator.	Give two tablespoonfuls of *calcined magnesia*, followed by mucilaginous drinks.
Verdigris. Blue Vitriol.	The antidote is *cooking-soda*, or *white of eggs*. Drink milk freely.
Stings of Insects.	*Ammonia*, or cooking-soda moistened with water, applied in the form of a paste. The wound may be sucked, followed by applications of water.
Charcoal Fumes. Illuminating Gas. Sewer-Gas.	*Fresh* air and artificial respiration (557).

550. BLEEDING, or HEMORRHAGE.—The bleeding from an *artery* is characterized by the escape of a bright-scarlet frothy stream in *jets;* that from a vein, by the *trickling* of a steady current of dark blood; and that from the *capillaries*, by *oozing* from many divided points. The former may be controlled by judicious pressure in the course of the artery, or by direct pressure at the point from which the jets escape; the venous and capillary bleeding, by elevating the part and by pressure applied to the cut surface. Small vessels cut directly across readily contract, and the blood-current is naturally retarded and stopped. Crushed wounds rarely bleed freely. Bleeding from large arteries or large veins must be quickly controlled, or the great loss of blood will occasion death.

551. MANAGEMENT OF BLEEDING.—If from a *large artery*, place your finger on the jetting spot, elevate the limb, and keep the patient quiet; if from a *small artery* or vein, elevate the part, and wash off the dirt and clots with a stream of water. Apply (1) ice, or (2) direct a stream of hot water of a temperature of 46° C. to 49° C. (115° F. to 120° F.),—*i.e.*, the water must not be hotter than that in

FIG. 136.   FIG. 137.

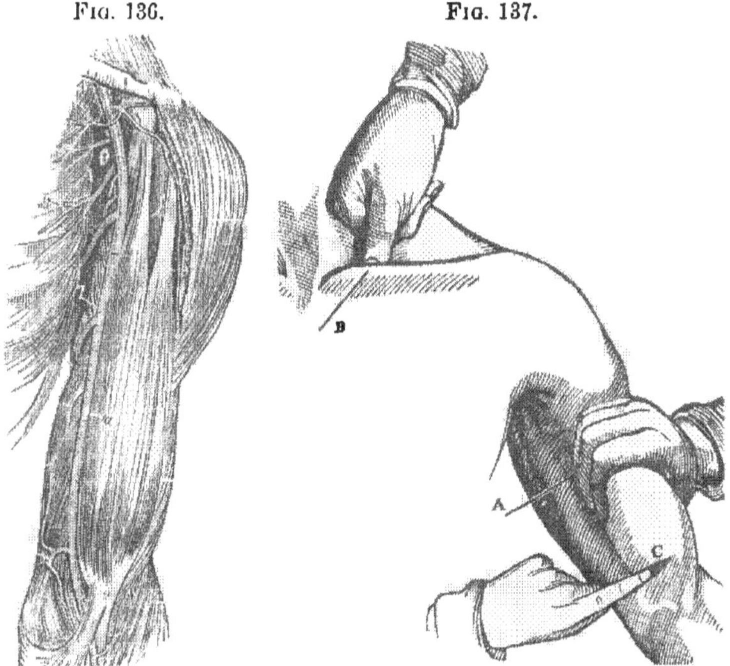

FIG. 136. TRACK OF THE LARGE ARTERY OF THE ARM.—1, The collar-bone.   9, The axillary artery.   10, The brachial artery.

FIG. 137. B, The manner of compressing the artery near the collar-bone. A, The manner of compressing the large artery of the arm with the fingers. C, The manner of compressing the divided extremity of an artery in the wound with a finger.

which you can hold the hand, and then gradually increase the temperature by the addition of water slightly hotter. In the case of internal bleeding, the temperature of the water may be raised from 46° C. gradually to 71° C. (115° F. to 160° F.). Use hot water freely. (3) Expose the part to the air. In the latter case, the natural contraction of the artery in connection with coagulation will control all moderate flow. Use no alum, or iron, or tannin, or other styptics. They retard future healing.

When the bleeding is controlled only by direct pressure in the wound, then apply the *field tourniquet* in the course of the artery above the wound, after which the finger on the jetting point may be removed. To make a field tourniquet, take a square piece of cloth, or a handkerchief, twist it corner-wise, and tie a hard knot in the middle. Place the knot over the artery, between the wound

Fig. 138.   Fig. 139.

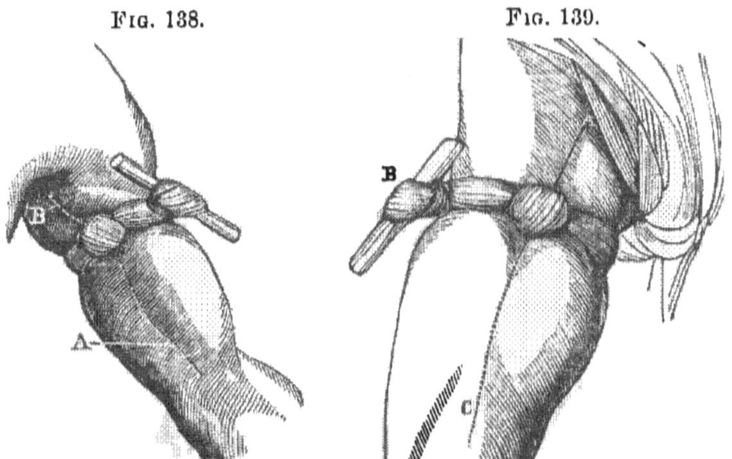

Fig. 138. METHOD OF APPLYING THE KNOTTED HANDKERCHIEF to compress a divided artery. A, B, Track of the brachial artery.

Fig. 139. A, C, Track of the femoral artery; the compress applied near the groin.

and the heart, carry the ends around the limb, and tie loosely. Place a stick under the handkerchief, near the last tie, and twist till the fingers can be removed from the compression without a return of the bleeding. (See Figs. 138 and 139.)

552. Having the bleeding under control, let the patient lie in a cool open room, with heaters to his feet. Keep him quiet. Keep anxious friends away from his side. If he desires, give him some nourishing drink, or water, especially the latter. If a surgeon cannot be secured, then, with a fish-hook attached to a penholder, or with a pair of small toothed pincers, pull out the large artery or large vein, and tie a silk or linen thread around the vessel between the hook and the flesh, making a "reef-knot," and allowing the

long ends to hang out of the wound. Remove the tourniquet, wash the wound, apply ice or hot water to the small bleeding-points, draw the parts together, and with a few turns of a bandage secure the parts in place. Allow the injured part to rest at ease on a pillow, covered with oiled silk, or oiled paper, or india-rubber, for the sake of cleanliness. Unless bleeding again occurs, do not change the dressing for forty-eight hours. On the third morning, carefully remove the stiffened cloths, previously softening them with tepid water, and cleanse the wound with warm water. In some cases, add to the warm water a little alcohol, or a few drops of carbolic acid.

Fig. 140.

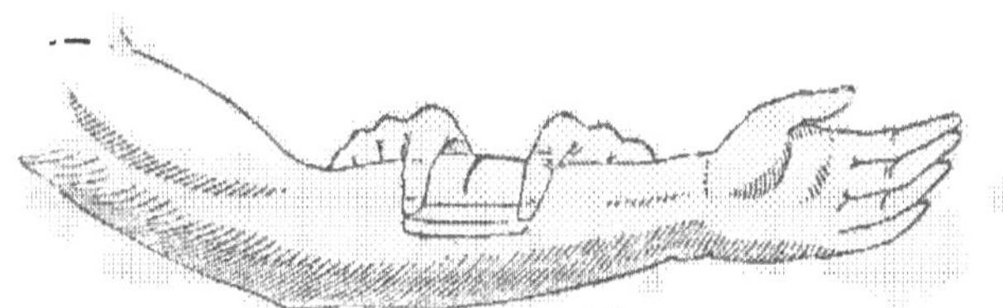

Fig. 140. Manner of applying adhesive strips to wounds.

553. In FLESH-WOUNDS, when no large vessel is divided, wash the parts with cold water, and, when bleeding has ceased, draw the incision together, and retain it with strips of adhesive plaster, not more than a quarter of an inch in width. Then apply a loose bandage. Avoid all ointments, "healing salves," and washes. In removing the dressing from the wound, both ends of the plaster should be raised and drawn *towards* the incision. To lessen the liability of a reopening, a proper position for the union should be regarded. If the wound is between the knee and the ankle, and on the anterior part, extend the knee and bend up the ankle; if on the posterior part, reverse the movement; and, in general, suit the position to the case. In severe wounds of the extremities,—arm or leg, —splints of wood or tin, well padded with cotton batting and covered with oiled silk, should be applied, in order to keep the adjacent joints locked and the irritated muscles from continually twitching. By keeping the parts quiet, the tendency to healing is assisted.

The union of the divided parts is effected by the action of the blood, and not by salves or ointments. The only object of the dressing is to keep the parts together and protect the wound from air and impurities. Nature performs her own cure. Small wounds seldom need a second dressing, and should not be opened until the incisions are healed.

554. BLEEDING AT THE NOSE (*Epistaxis*).—When due to an injury, it soon ceases; when due to plethora, it is often of benefit, and should be checked only when it becomes too copious. When occurring in a feeble person, it is often quite serious.

FIG. 141.

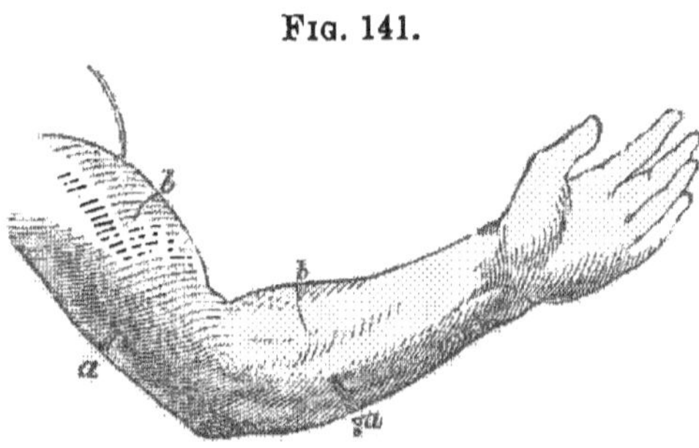

FIG. 141. *a, a,* Representation of wounds on the back part of the arm and forearm. *b, b,* Wounds of the anterior part of the arm and forearm. By bending the elbow and wrist, the incisions at *a, a,* are opened, while those at *b, b,* are closed. Were the arm extended at the elbow and wrist, the wounds at *a, a,* would be closed, and those at *b, b,* would be opened.

Management. — Sit up. Keep the head elevated. Raise the arms vertically at full length above the head. *Breathe through the mouth.* Have a cloth or sponge held under the nostrils, but do not bend forward. Apply ice to the nose, the middle of the forehead, and the nape of the neck. If it does not soon cease, then allow a stream of cold water, containing a teaspoonful of cooking-soda and a teaspoonful of table-salt to the pint of water, to flow in at one nostril and out at the other, the mouth being kept open all the time. Employ a nasal douche apparatus for this purpose. If this fails, and if a surgeon cannot be secured, the nostrils must be plugged. Cut a piece of sponge, as large as the nostril will admit, in a rounded form. Attach it to a cord. Push it into the nostrils as far back as the pharynx (Fig. 38). Make a number of similar pieces of sponge. With a darning-needle on the cord, thread one piece after another, and force them one by one into the nostril, until it becomes filled. This will control the bleeding. Remove after forty-eight hours by pulling out one at a time. Bleeding from the cavity from which a tooth has been recently extracted can be controlled by packing it with a paste of plaster of Paris.

555. BROKEN BONES, OR FRACTURES.—While the patient is lying on the ground, *cut* off the garments and the boots. Do not increase the pain by pulling them off. Gently but firmly pull on

the parts below the fracture until the arm or limb reaches its full length. Hold it quietly in this new position. This movement will pull the bone-fragments from the torn flesh, will prevent sharp, painful muscular contractions, and will give the patient some ease. Let another procure some thin strips of board, or lath, or straight sticks, or hollowed pieces of tin or sheet-iron, or even common straw cut to the length of the limb. Place some cloth or grass, in the form of even pads, above and below the broken part, then adjust around the parts a layer of the sticks, or laths, or bits of shingle, or straw, and then secure them above and below the break by cords or straps. Permit the splints to extend beyond the joints above and below. Now the man may cease pulling on the limb, and the patient can be transported home with comparatively little suffering, even in a springless wagon. A person suffers less when borne by two or four men on a shutter than in an ordinary hack or express-wagon. At home, the patient should be placed on a mattress which rests on slats. The spring, the wire, or the rope bedstead is not well adapted for the treatment of fractures of the lower extremities. Place a thick quilt on the mattress, then a rubber sheet, and a cotton sheet over all. When the bones have been adjusted as nearly as possible in position, the surgeon's work is not done. The keeping of the parts in the proper position demands daily educated care for several weeks. Hence the surgeon should be retained until the parts are again consolidated in the position found most practical. A broken bone can rarely be made as good, in form, shape, position, and usefulness, as the uninjured bone. The bad results in the treatment of many fractures are more dependent on the wilfulness, irritability, and meddling of the patient than on want of skill on the part of the surgeon.

556. BURNS AND SCALDS.—A *burn* is caused by the application of concentrated heat to the body; a *scald*, by the application of hot or boiling liquids. The effect varies according to the intensity and duration of the application. It ranges from simple redness to destruction of the part. The extent of the surface involved is also an important factor. When more than half the body is involved, death usually results.

When only a small patch of the skin is involved, in order to prevent blistering, apply *cold* water continuously until the smarting ceases, or plunge the part in a basin containing water and cooking-soda. Cut off garments which are in contact with the injured parts. Use care, so as not to remove the epidermis. Prick the lower outer edge of the blisters, and allow the water to run out. In moderate burns and scalds, apply cloths soaked in water containing all the cooking-soda it will dissolve. Do not remove the cloths, but keep them constantly wet. If cooking-soda is not at hand, apply strong soap-suds. The alkali of the soap soon deadens the pain. If the burn is extensive, put the patient into a warm bath, and raise the temperature of the water until he is comfortably warm. Give him some hot alcoholics and some opium preparation. After extensive burns, as from coal oil, the hot bath is the best place to live and to sleep in.

Do not remove the dressings for some days,—not until they are loosened by the discharges, or until they become very offensive. When the first dressing is removed, the character of the injury will determine the subsequent dressing. It may be carbolic acid in sweet or cotton-seed oil, one part to ten; or zinc ointment; or equal parts of lime-water and linseed oil; or flour dredged on the surfaces. In all cases keep the patient warm, give nutritious foods, administer alcoholics and opium as needed, and keep the parts quiet and clean. To prevent deformities, follow the instructions of the surgeon as to position and dressings.

557. ASPHYXIA, as from *drowning* or from breathing *illuminating gas*, etc.—Treat the patient at once, and on the spot. Place him in an open space. Do not permit the people to crowd around. Remove all obstructions to the passage of air to and from the lungs by cleansing the froth and mucus from the mouth and nostrils. If the person has been pulled out of the water, raise him up by the limbs, to allow all fluids to escape. If he has been pulled out of an atmosphere of choke-damp, of gas, of charcoal fumes, of chloroform or ether vapors, elevate the extremities, in order to assist the flow of blood towards the head and heart. Remove all close-fitting articles of clothing from the neck and chest. If natural respiration has ceased, employ the SILVESTER METHOD, as follows:

558. (1.) The body being laid on its back (either on a flat surface, or, better, on a plane inclined a little from the feet upward), a firm cushion or some similar support should be placed under the shoulders, the head being kept in a line with the trunk. The tongue should be drawn forward, so as to project a little from the side of the mouth; then the arms should be drawn upward until they nearly meet above the head, the operator grasping them just above the elbows, and then at once lowered and replaced at the side. This

should be immediately followed by moderate pressure with both hands upon the lower part of the sternum. This process is to be repeated about twelve or fourteen times in the minute.

(2.) As soon as natural respiratory movements recommence, cease the employment of artificial means, unless the efforts are feeble and imperfect. Should no natural respiration supervene, a dash of hot water (120° F.) or cold water may be used.

(3.) Maintain the temperature of the body by friction, warm blankets, and, when possible, by warm water (106° F.) or air-bath, keeping the head where a circulation of pure air may be maintained.

(4.) As soon as the patient can swallow, give warm milk, beef tea, tea, or coffee, with a tablespoonful of some spirit, or these may be injected by the stomach-pump.

(5.) When respiration is restored, put the patient into a warm bed, with hot bottles to his feet, and encourage sleep; but let him be watched, in case of secondary or relapsing apnœa, at the slightest symptom of which let friction and even artificial respiration be employed. Give volatile stimulants, such as spiritus ammoniæ aromaticus (*Bryant*).

559. Dr. Voisin, of Paris, reports the absolute certainty of restoring to life persons who have remained under water from a few seconds to five minutes. These results have been attained at Paris in cases of water-drowning accompanied by asphyxia, as well as by syncope. He ascribes them to the vigorous carrying out of the Silvester method; to the application of warmth by heaters to the entire surface of the body; to the use of warm baths and cold douches; to keeping the patient quiet in bed for some hours after restoration; and to the efforts of a trained and disciplined staff.

560. PREVENTION FROM DROWNING.—In the water the human body weighs about a pound. When it is a question of life or death, do not attempt to raise your body out of the water. One or both hands placed on a block of wood, a stool, or a chair will enable a person to keep the mouth and nose out of the water. This is all that is of vital importance until aid arrives. All persons should be trained, when in the water, to know and to have faith in its buoyant powers. In case of a wreck, know that an overturned or water-filled wooden boat will sustain more persons in the water than it will carry. Do not permit any one to climb on it, for that will jeopardize the safety of all hanging on to the wrecked boat.

561. BODIES IN THE EXTERNAL EAR.—The sooner a foreign body is out of the external auditory meatus the better. To remove *wax*, introduce a few drops of glycerin and water into the meatus for two or three nights; then, with an ear-syringe, direct a stream of tepid water into the meatus obliquely against the walls, and thus the water will get behind the wax and wash it out. To direct the stream against the wax does but little good, and to direct it against the membrana tympani does positive injury. To remove peas, beans, beads, etc., is often a work of difficulty, for the outer third of the meatus is wide, the middle third contracted, and the inner third enlarged. (See Fig. 94.) The passage, having bony walls, cannot be expanded.

If vegetable or animal materials remain, by the absorption of water they expand, and thus render their removal more difficult. Sometimes the body can be washed out by getting water back of the object. In other cases it may be floated out by filling the meatus with warm oil. If these fail, make a loop of twisted iron wire, introduce it into the ear, against one of the sides of the passage, turn it half around, noose the body, and jerk it out. If an insect or worm enters the meatus, fill the passage with warm oil, and the intruder will leave.

562. BODIES ON THE SURFACE OF THE EYEBALL.—When foreign bodies, as dust, cinders, etc., lodge upon the surface of the ball, or beneath the lids, do not rub the part. Hold the lids open, while the eye is rolled either up and down or from side to side. In this way the fragment may be removed. If not, hold up the upper lid and blow the nose; if this fails, seize the lashes of the upper lid and draw it away from the eye, then look down, and push the lower lid beneath the upper, and thus the lashes may brush out the body. If this is ineffectual, place a small pencil under the eyebrow, and quickly, by aid of the eyelashes, turn the upper lid over the pencil. Remove the offending body, if possible, with the corner of a moistened handkerchief. If this fails, summon a surgeon to remove the body. After the removal of the body, drop into the eye a drop of castor oil. This will ease the gritty sensation which persists after the removal of the foreign material.

563. FROST-BITE.—Frost-bite is usually manifested first upon parts unprotected by covering, as the face or ears, and especially the nose. In such case the skin first becomes red, from congestion of the dilated capillary vessels; next it becomes bluish, from arrest of the circulation, and afterwards of a dead-white hue. To restore circulation and sensibility, rub the frozen part with snow, or apply iced water. Keep the sufferer at first in a cold room, and let the return to a higher temperature be *gradual* and cautious, else *gangrene* may supervene.

564. HERNIA, OR RUPTURE.—A person who has hernia should never be allowed to become constipated (164). If the hernia comes down and cannot be replaced, place the sufferer on a bed. Apply ice in a rubber bag, or ice rolled in a single layer of flannel, over and about the parts. Wait an hour. Give the patient a Dover's powder. Place one or two pillows under the shoulders, flex the

thighs on the abdomen, raise the swelling, and endeavor by gentle manipulations to cause the parts last out to return first. If this does not succeed, place the patient with his abdomen resting on the back and his limbs over the shoulders of a strong man. Then let the man slowly rise. By this manœuvre, gravity tends to pull the escaped contents back into the abdomen. If this fails, send at once for the ablest surgeon in the vicinity. The danger following in the course of strangulated hernial contents cannot be overestimated.

565. RETENTION OF URINE.—Place the sufferer in a hot bath, or employ the Simpson bath (47). Administer two Dover's powders, or two grains of opium. Usually micturition will soon be induced. If not, after half an hour in the bath, remove the patient to a warm bed. Apply over the pubis cloths wrung out of hot water upon which camphor has been sprinkled. Send for a surgeon.

566. SIMPSON'S BATH. See ¶ 47, Chapter III.

567. WOUNDS.— *Wounds punctured* by the human teeth, by dogs and cats; from rusty nails, thorns, etc. As the deep parts so injured cannot be reached in order to be cleansed, apply over and about the entrance a poultice of bread, or of linseed or corn meal (544). Change once in four to six hours. This treatment favors the formation of pus, hinders healing at the surface, and tends to draw the foreign materials from the base of the wound.

Wounds from Suspected Mad Dogs or Mad Cats (Rabies).—Cauterize at once freely with lunar caustic (nitrate of silver), or pour into the wound a strong acid or alkali. Do not kill the dog or cat. Keep it in confinement, and thus ascertain if it is really mad. By this means much mental anxiety may be avoided. Mental stimulants must be freely administered, and the person's mind diverted.

Wounds from Poisonous Serpents.—Give whiskey, brandy, or rum freely. Apply at once ligatures, or tight cords, around the parts, between the wound and the heart. Tie them very tight. Cut open the wound, to favor bleeding. Suck the wound: if you have no sore in the mouth, you run no risks. Then apply caustics or a live coal. The patient may drink from one to three pints of whiskey or brandy. The man dying from snake-bite perishes from rapid exhaustion of nerve-force: hence stimulate. If water of ammonia is at hand, add four or six teaspoonfuls to each pint of liquor. Sustain the powers by nourishing food, like milk and eggs.

Wounds from Insects.—Apply cooking-soda made into a paste. Strong water of ammonia is, however, more efficacious. Olive oil often makes an excellent application. If these are not at hand, cover the bitten part with flour paste.

568. *Irritation from Ivy-Poison* (Rhus).—Apply constantly to loose cloths placed over the parts a lotion composed of carbolic acid, one part; sulphite of soda, six parts; and spring-water, seventy parts.

569. *Sunstroke.*—"More properly Heat-stroke, because it takes place on cloudy days and under any circumstances of exposure to great heat in a debilitated condition of the body, arising from over-exertion or frequently from intemperate habits. A large green leaf worn in the hat, or a moist light handkerchief, very certainly prevents sunstroke. *Symptoms:* The person falls suddenly, as in a common fainting-fit, but the head is very hot; so, at once take the patient to the shade, and pour a continuous stream of cold water on the head, crosswise, in every direction, so as not to fall on one spot. Mustard plasters may be applied to the spine and stomach alternately. The Egyptians pour salt water over the head and ears."

GLOSSARY.

THE NUMERALS DIRECT ATTENTION TO THE NUMBERED PARAGRAPHS,
TO WHICH THE STUDENT IS ADVISED TO REFER.

Ab-do'men. (246.) [L. *abdo*, to hide.] That part of the body which lies between the thorax and the bottom of the pelvis.

Ab-dom'i-nal. Pertaining to the abdomen.

Ab-du'cens. [L. *ab*, from, and *duco*, to lead.] Drawing to a different point. The nerve of the rectus externus of the eyeball.

Ab-duc'tor. [L. *abduco*, to lead away.] A muscle which moves certain parts by separating them from the axis of the body.

Ab-lu'tion. The act of washing.

Ab-nor'mal. [L. *ab*, from, and *norma*, a rule.] Contrary to the general order.

Ab-sorp'tion. (276.) [L. *ab*, and *sorbere*, to suck up.] The process of taking into a vessel or into the system.

Ac-com-mo-da'tion. (158.) The act of fitting or adapting, as in vision.

Ac-e-tab'u-lum. [L. *acetum*, vinegar.] The socket for the head of the thigh-bone,—so called from its resemblance to an ancient vessel for holding vinegar.

A-chil'lis. A term applied to the tendon of the two large muscles of the leg.

A-cro'mi-on. [Gr. *akros*, highest, and *omos*, the shoulder.] A process of the scapula that joins to the clavicle.

Ad-duc'tor. [L. *adduco*, to lead to.] A muscle which draws one part of the body towards another:—opposed to *abductor*.

Ad'e-noid. (294.) [Gr. *aden*, a gland.] Tissue resembling gland tissue.

Ad'i-pose. (25.) [L. *adeps*, fat.] Relating to fat.

A-e-ra'tion. [Gr. *aer*, air.] The act of supplying with air.

Af'fe-rent. (81.) [L. *ad*, and *fero*, I carry.] Conveying inward, as from the skin to the spinal cord.

Air'-Space. (203.) Cubic space allowed men or animals in habitations.

Al-bi'no. (452.) [L. *albus*, white.] An individual of any race of men having white hair and skin and a peculiar redness of the pupil of the eye.

Al-bu'men. (217.) [L. *albus*, white.] The chief constituent of the white of egg.

Al-bu'mi-noids. (217.) A class of principles resembling albumen.

Al'co-hol-ism. (408.) A series of diseased activities produced by the use of alcoholics.

Al'i-ment. (216.) [L. *alere*, to nourish.] Food; nutriment.

Al-i-ment'a-ry Ca-nal'. (249.) The musculo-membranous tube into which nutriment is taken to be digested, and by which it is conveyed through the body, the useless parts to be evacuated.

Al-ve'o-lar. [L. *alveolus*, a socket.] Pertaining to the sockets of the teeth.

Am-bly-o'pi-a. [Gr. *amblus*, obscure, and *ops*, the eye.] Impairment of vision; weakness of vision.

A-mœ'ba. See ¶ 6.

A-mœ'boid. [Gr. *ameibo*, I change, and *eidos*, resemblance.] A term applied to spontaneous changes of shape and position in cells.

Am-mo'ni-as. (412.) Compounds containing ammonia (NH_3) or derivatives of ammonia.

Am'pli-tude. Largeness; the degree of motion.

Am-pul'la. A dilatation; an enlargement at one end of the semicircular canals of the ear.

An-æs-the'si-a. (370.) [Gr. *an*, against, and *aisthanomai*, I feel.] The absence of sensation, especially of touch.

A-nas'to-mose. (105.) [Gr. *ana*, through, and *stoma*, a mouth.] To unite as vessels or branches; to inosculate with one another.

An-a-tom'i-cal. Relating to the parts of the body when dissected or separated.

A-nat'o-my. [Gr. *ana*, through, and *tome*, a cutting.] The description of the structure of animals. (The word *anatomy* properly signifies dissection.)

An'gu-li. [L. *angulus*, a corner.] A term applied to certain muscles on account of their form.

An'nu-lar. [L. *annulus*, a ring.] Having the form of a ring.

An-tag-o-nis'tic. An agent producing an effect contrary to that of another agent.

An-te'ri-or. [L. *ante*, before.] Situated before the median line:—opposed to posterior.

An'te-ro-Lat'e-ral. Pertaining to front and side.

An'te-ro-Pos-te'ri-or. From front to rear.

An'thro-poids. [Gr. *anthropos*, man, and *eidos*, form.] The name given to the manlike apes,—gorilla, chimpanzee, ourang, and gibbon.

An-ti-scor-bu'tic. (225-233.) [Gr. *anti*, against, and *scorbutus*, scurvy.] A substance or influence which prevents or mitigates scurvy.

An'trum. [L., a cave.] A cavity in the superior maxillary bone, the entrance to which is smaller than the bottom.

A-or'ta. (99.) [Gr. *aorte*; from *aer*, the air, and *tereo*, to keep.] The great artery that arises from the left ventricle of the heart.

Ap'er-tures. Mouths or openings.

A'pex. The point or extremity of a part, as of the heart.

A-pha'si-a. (358.) [Gr. *a*, without, and *phemi*, to say.] Speechlessness.

Ap-nœ'a. (188.) [Gr. *a*, without, and *pneo*, I respire.] Absence of respiratory movements.

A-po-neu-ro'sis. [Gr. *apo*, from, and *neuron*, a nerve.] The membranous expansion over muscles and tendons. The ancients called every white tendon *neuron*, a nerve.

Ap-pa-ra'tus. [L. *apparo*, to prepare.] An assemblage of organs designed to produce certain results.

Ap-pend'a-ges. [L. *ad*, and *pendeo*, to hang from.] Something connected to a part.

Ap-pen'dix. [L. *ad*, and *pendeo*, to hang from.] Something appended or added.

Ap-po-si'tion. (340.) Accurate contact; a setting to.

A'que-ous. [L. *aqua*, water.] Pertaining to or like water.

A-rach'noid. (367.) [Gr. *arachne*, a spider, and *eidos*, form.] Resembling a spider's web:—applied to a part of the brain.

Ar'bor. [L.] A tree. *Arbor Vitæ*, the tree of life,—a term applied to a part of the cerebellum.

A're-as. The spaces or portions of an organ or system.

A-re'o-lar. (22.) [L. *area*, a void place, an open surface.] Pertaining to the interstices between the fibres composing organs.

Ar'gand. The burner invented by Argand, of Geneva, in 1782.

Ar'rack. An intoxicant made from the palm and rice by the East Indians.

Ar'te-ry. (105.) [Gr. *aer*, air, and *tereo*, to keep; because the ancients thought that the arteries contained only air.] A tube through which blood flows.

Ar-tic-u-la'tion. (506.) [L. *artus*, a joint.] The union of bones with each other. Also, the forming of syllables by the organs of speech. See *Voice* (402).

A-ryt'e-noid. (488.) [Gr. *arutaina*, a ewer, and *eidos*, form.] The name of a cartilage of the larynx.

As-cen'dens. [L.] Ascending; rising.

As-phyx'i-a. [Gr. *a*, without, and *sphyxis*, pulse.] Originally, want of pulse; now used for suspended respiration, or apparent death.

As-sim-i-la'tion. (307.) The process of making food-stuffs like the components of the organs and tissues.

As-so-ci-a'tion. Union of activities for a given purpose.

As-the-no'pi-a. (485.) [Gr. *asthenia*, weak, and *ops*, the eye.] Weakness of sight.

A-stig'ma-tism. (461.) [Gr. *a*, without, and *stigma*, a point.] Irregular refraction of the eye, producing a blurred image.

At'ro-phied. [Gr. *a*, without, and *trophe*, nourishment.] Diminution in bulk of a part.

A-tro'pi-a. (452.) The active principle of *Atropa Belladonna*, or deadly night-shade.

Au-di'tion. [L. *audio*, to hear.] Hearing.

Au'di-to-ry. (439.) Pertaining to the sense or organ of hearing.

Au'ri-cle. [L. *auricula*, the external ear; from *auris*, the ear.] A cavity of the heart.

Au-to-mat'ic. Acting of itself:—applied to an action of a body, the causes of which appear to lie in the body itself.

Au-tom'a-tism. See ¶ 84.

Ax-il'la. [L.] The armpit.

Ax'il-la-ry. Belonging or relating to the armpit.

Az'ote. [Gr. *a*, without, and *zoe*, life.] Nitrogen,—one of the constituent elements of the atmosphere: so named because it will not sustain life.

Band'-Ax-is. (78.) The central portion of the nerve-fibre.

Bane'ful. Having poisonous qualities.

Bar'y-tone. [Gr. *barus*, heavy, and *tonos*, tone.] A male voice whose compass is between that of the tenor and the base.

Base of Skull. The foundation or support of the brain.

Bath. (47.) The immersion of the whole or a part of the body in some medium, as water, mud, or sand.

Bi'ceps. [L. *bis*, twice, and *caput*, a head.] A name applied to muscles with two heads at one extremity.

Bi-cus'pids. (254.) [L. *bis*, two, and *cuspis*, a point.] Teeth that have two points upon their crown. Premolars.

Bi-lat'er-al. [L. *bi*, and *lateralis*, pertaining to the side.] Referring to two sides.

Bi-noc'u-lar. (466.) [L. *bis*, two, and *oculis*, eye.] Relating to both eyes.

Bi'o-plasm. (9.) [Gr. *bios*, life, and *plasso*, to form.] The physical basis of life.

Bi-pen'ni-form. [L. *bis*, two, and *penna*, a feather.] Having fibres on each side of a common tendon.

Blis'ter. (28.) A collection of serous fluid under the epidermis.

Bolt'ed. (285.) Insufficiently masticated and insalivated food hastily swallowed.

Brach'i-al. [L. *brachium*.] Belonging to the arm.

Bre'vis, Bre'vi-or. [L.] Short. Shorter.

Bron'chi-a, *pl.* Bron'chi-æ. (163.) [L.] A division of the trachea that passes to the lungs.

Bron-chi'tis. [L.] An inflammation of the bronchial mucous membrane.

Buc-ci-na'tor. [L. *buccinum*, a trumpet.] The name of a muscle of the cheek:—so called because used in blowing wind instruments.

Buoy'an-cy. The quality of floating, as on water.

Bur'sæ Mu-co'sæ. [L. *bursa*, a purse, and *mucosa*, viscous.] Small sacs, containing a viscid fluid, situated about the joints, under tendons.

Bu-tyr'ic Ac'id. (219.) The name of an acid obtained from butter.

C. The chemical symbol of carbon.

Ca. The chemical symbol of calcium, the base of calx or lime.

Cæ'cum. [L. blind.] The name given to the commencement of the colon.

Cal'cis. [L.] The heel-bone.

Cal'ci-um. [L.] The metallic basis of lime.

Cal'i-bre. The diameter of a tube.

Cal-is-then'ics. [Gr. *kalos*, beautiful, and *sthenos*, strength.] Exercises pursued for the development of ease and beauty of motion.

Cal'lus. (311.) Unnatural thickness and hardness of the outer skin.

Ca-lor'ic. (189.) [L. *calor*, heat.] The agent inducing the sensation of heat.

Cam'e-ra. [L., a chamber.] The dark box used in photography.

Can-a-lic'u-lus, *pl.* **Can-a-lic'u-li.** (505.) [L. *canalis.*] A small channel.

Can'cel-la-ted. (501.) [L. *cancelli.*] Having a latticed appearance.

Ca'nine. (454.) [L. *canis*, a dog.] Pertaining to a dog, as dog-teeth, eye-teeth.

Can'thus. [Gr. *kanthos.*] The angle formed by the junction of the eyelids.

Cap'il-la-ry. [L. *capillus*, a hair.] Resembling a hair; a small tube.

Cap'sule. (456.) [L. *capsula*, a little chest.] A membranous bag enclosing a part.

Ca'put. [L.] The head. *Caput coli*, the head of the colon.

Car'bo–Hy'drates. (220.) Compounds made up of C, H, O, like starch, sugar, etc.

Car'bon. [L. *carbo*, a coal.] Pure charcoal. An elementary combustible substance.

Car'bon Com'pounds. Chemical compounds whose base is carbon.

Car-bon'ic Aç'id. A gas produced by perfect combustion of carbon in oxygen.

Car-bon'ic Ox'ide. (195.) A colorless gas formed under imperfect combustion.

Car'di-ac. (68.) [Gr. *kardia*, the heart.] Relating to the heart, or to the upper entrance of the stomach.

Car'ne-a, *pl.* **Car'ne-æ.** [L. *caro, carnis,* flesh.] Fleshy.

Ca-rot'id. [Gr. *karos*, lethargy.] The great arteries of the neck that convey blood to the head. The ancients supposed drowsiness to be seated in these arteries.

Car'pus, *pl.* **Car'pi.** [L.] The wrist.

Car'ti-lage. (503.) A pearly-white, glistening, elastic substance found adherent to bones.

Car'un-cle. [L. *caro*, flesh.] The small red body at the inner angle of the eye.

Ca'se-in. (217.) [L. *caseus*, cheese.] The principal nitrogenous portion of milk. The constituent of cheese.

Cat'a-lep-sy. [Gr. *katalambano*, to seize.] A total suspension of sensibility and voluntary motion; a trance.

Cat'a-ract. [Gr. *katarrasso*, to fall down.] Obstructed vision, due to disease of the crystalline lens or its capsules.

Ca-tarrh'. [Gr. *katarreo*, to flow down.] A profuse secretion from a mucous surface, as in a cold.

Cau-ca'si-an. One of the races of men.

Ca'va. [L.] Hollow. *Vena cava*, a name given to the two great veins of the body.

Cell. (8.) The anatomical unit.'

Cell-Body. (8.) The central mass of protoplasm.

Cel'lu-lar. [L. *cellula*, a little cell.] Composed of cells. See *Areolar.*

Cel'lu-lose. (221.) The chief component of plants.

Ce-men'tum. (201.) A portion of the outer layer of the teeth.

Cen-tim'e-tre. The hundredth part of a metre, or 0.394 of an English inch.

Cer-e-bel'lum, *pl.* **Cer-e-bel'la.** (363.) [L.] The hinder and lower part of the brain, or the little brain.

Cer'e-bral. [L. *cerebrum*, the brain.] Belonging to the brain.

Cer-e-bra'tion. The action of the brain during mental or moral manifestation.

Cer'e-bro-Spi'nal. Relating to the brain and spine.

Cer'e-brum. (352.) [L.] The front and large part of the brain. The term is sometimes applied to the whole contents of the cranium.

Cer'vi-cal. Relating to the neck.

Cer'vix. [L.] The neck.

Chem'is-try. (1.) The science of the statics and dynamics of atoms.

Chest. [Sax.] The thorax; the portion of the body from the neck to the diaphragm.

Chlo'ral. (400.) [*Chlor*, from chlorine, and *al*, from alcohol] Prepared by the action of chlorine on alcohol. A hypnotic.

Chlo'ral-ism. (400.) The condition resulting from using chloral.

Chlo'rine. [Gr. *chloros*, green.] A gas, so named from its color.

Chon'drin. (216.) [Gr. *chondros*, cartilage.] Gelatin obtained from cartilage:—a proteid.

Chor'da, *pl.* **Chor'dæ.** [L.] A cord. An assemblage of fibres.

Chor'dæ Ten-din'e-æ. (97.) The tendon-like cords found in the interior of the heart.

Cho-roi'de-a. (451.) [Gr. *chorion*, skin.] The second tunic of the eyeball.

Chro-mat'ic Ab-er-ra'tion. (461.) [Gr. *chroma*, color, and L. *ab*, from, and *erro*, to wander.] Irregular refraction of color-rays.

Chyle. (278.) [Gr. *chulos*, juice.] A nutritive fluid, of a whitish appearance, which is made from food by the action of the digestive organs.

Chyl-i-fi-ca'tion. [L. *chylus*, chyle, and *facio*, to make.] The process by which chyle is formed.

Chy-lo-poi-et'ic. [Gr. *chulos*, juice, and *poieo*, to make.] Connected with the formation of chyle.

Chyme. (276.) [Gr. *chumos*, juice.] A kind of grayish pulp formed from the food in the stomach.

Ci-ca'trix. (32.) [L.] The scar of a healed wound.

Cil'i-a. [L., plural of *cilium*.] Eyelashes.

Cil'i-a-ted. (68.) [L. *cilia*, eyelashes.] Having hair-like projections.

Cin-e-ri'tious. [L. *cinis*, ashes.] Having the color of ashes.

Cir-cu-la'tion. (124.) [L. *circulatio*, a going round.] The name given to the motion of the blood through the different vessels of the body.

Cl. The chemical symbol of the element chlorine.

Clav'i-cle. [L. *clavicula*, from *clavis*, a key.] The collar-bone:—so called from its resemblance in shape to an ancient key.

Clei'do. A term applied to some muscles that are attached to the clavicle.

Clot. (122.) [Dut. *kluit*, a mass or lump.] Soft or fluid matter becoming thicker or more solid, as a concretion of stagnant blood.

Co-ag-u-la'tion. (120.) [L. *coagulo*, to curdle.] The process of producing a thickened state in albuminoid fluids.

Co-ag'u-lum. [L.] A coagulated or curdled substance.

Coc'cyx. [Gr.] An assemblage of small bones attached to the sacrum.

Coch'le-a. [Gr. *kochlo*, to twist; or L. *cochlea*, a screw.] A cavity of the ear resembling in form a snail-shell.

Cœ'li-ac. [Gr. *koilia*, the belly.] Belonging to the belly.

Col'ic. Acute pain in the abdomen, aggravated at intervals.

Col'loid. [Gr. *kolla*, glue, and *eidos*, form.] Resembling glue.

Co'lon. [Gr. *kolon*, curtailed.] A portion of the large intestine.

Col'or-Blind'ness. (464.) Daltonism.

Com-bus'tion. (191.) [L. *combustio*, a burning.] Burning. The chemical union of oxygen with other elements or compounds.

Com-mis'sure. (450.) [L. *con*, together, and *mitto*, *missum*, to put.] A point of union.

Com-mu'nis. [L.] A term applied to certain muscles working together.

Com-plex'us. [L. *complector*, to embrace.] The name of a muscle that embraces many attachments.

Com-press'or. [L. *con*, together, and *premere*, *pressum*, to press.] A term applied to some muscles that compress the parts to which they are attached.

Con'di-ments. (224.) [L. *condire*, *conditum*, to season.] Substances taken with food to improve flavor or to promote digestion.

Con-duc'tion. The passage of heat or electricity from one particle to another.

Con'dyle. [Gr. *kondulos*, a knuckle, a protuberance.] A prominence on the end of a bone.

Con-junc-ti'va. (448.) [L. *con*, together, and *jungo*, to join.] The membrane that covers the front of the eyeball.

Con'so-nants. (496.) Letters which cannot be perfectly sounded without the aid of a vowel.

Con'stant Cur'rent. The electric current developed from direct chemical action. Voltaic electricity.

Con-sti-tu'tion. (399.) [L. *con*, together, and *statuo*, to set.] The particular frame or temperament of the human body.

Con-sump'tion. (208.) [L. *consumo*, to waste away.] A wasting away of the tissues. Usually applied to phthisis of the lungs.

Con-ta'gion. (200.) [L. *con*, with, and *tango* or *tago*, to touch.] The communication of disease by contact or the inhalation of the effluvia of a sick person.

Con-trac'tile. (77.) [L. *con*, together, and *traho*, *tractum*, to draw.] Possessing contractility.

Con-trac'tion. The shortening of living fibre on the application of stimulus.

Con-va-les'cent. [L. *convalesco*, to grow strong.] Recovering health after disease.

Con'vex. Swelling on the exterior surface into a round or spherical form.

Con-vo-lu'tion. (352.) [L. *con*, together, and *volvo*, *volutum*, to roll.] The tortuous eminences of the cerebrum. The irregular twistings of the intestines.

Con-vul'sion. (379.) [L. *convello*, to pull together.] Violent agitation of the limbs or body.

Co-or-di-na'tion. See ¶ 393.

Cor'a-coid. [Gr. *korax*, a crow, and *eidos*, form.] A process of the scapula shaped like the beak of a crow.

Co'ri-um. (28.) [Gr. *chorion*, the skin.] The true skin.

Corn. (31.) [L. *cornu*, a horn.] A horny hardness of the epidermis.

Cor'ne-a. (451.) [L. *cornu*, a horn.] The transparent membrane in the fore part of the eye.

Cor'o-na-ry. [L. *corona*, a crown.] Applied to vessels, nerves, etc., which encircle parts.

Cor'po-ra. [L., plural of *corpus*, a body.] The name given to eminences or projections found in the brain and some other parts of the body.

Cor'po-ra Quad-ri-gem'i-na. (353.) [L.] The four oval-shaped bodies of the base of the brain.

Cor'pus Cal-lo'sum. (352.) [L., the hard body.] The white bond of union of the cerebral hemispheres.

Cor'pus-cle. [Dim. of L. *corpus*, a body.] A small body, as a blood-disk.

Cos-met'ics. (40.) [Gr. *cosmeo*, to adorn.] Medicines supposed to beautify and improve the complexion.

Cos'tal. [L. *costa*, a rib.] Relating to the ribs.

Cramp. (379.) Spasmodic contraction of the muscles independent of the will.

Crep-i-ta'tion. [L. *crepito*, to crackle.] The sound caused by pressing cellular tissue containing air. A small crackling noise.

Crib'ri-form. [L. *cribrum*, a sieve, and *forma*, form.] A plate of the ethmoid bone, through which the olfactory nerves pass to the nostril.

Cri'coid. (488.) [Gr. *krikos*, a ring, and *eidos*, form.] A name given to a cartilage of the larynx, from its form.

Crys'tal-line. (454.) [L. *crystallinus*.] The crystalline lens, one of the media of the eye. It is convex, white, firm, and transparent.

Cu'bi-tus, *pl.* **Cu'bi-ti.** [L. *cubitus*, the elbow.] One of the bones of the forearm:—also called the *ulna*.

Cu'boid. [Gr. *kubos*, a cube, and *eidos*, form.] Having nearly the form of a cube.

Cu'mu-la-tive. A term applied to the violent action from drugs which supervenes after the taking of several doses with little or no effect.

Cu-ne'i-form. [L. *cuneus*, a wedge.] The name of bones in the wrist and foot.

Cus'pid. (254.) [L. *cuspis*, a point.] Having one point:—applied to a tooth.

Cu-ta'ne-ous. [L. *cutis*, the skin.] Belonging to the skin.

Cu'ti-cle. (99.) [L. *cutis*.] The external layer of the skin; the epidermis.

Cu'tis Ve'ra. (28.) [L. *cutis*, the skin, and *vera*, true.] The internal layer of the skin; the true skin.

Cys-ti-cer'cus. (232.) [Gr. *kustis*, a bladder, and *kerkos*, a tail.] The tailed bladder-worm:—one stage in the life of the tapeworm, or *Taenia*.

Dal'ton-ism. (464.) Color-blindness.

Dan'druff. (43.) Pityriasis. An oil-gland disease:—particularly applied to the scurf at the roots of the hair of the head.

De-coc'tion. [L. *de*, down, and *coquo*, *coctum*, to boil.] A preparation made by boiling substances in water to extract their virtues.

Dec-us-sa'tion. (365.) [L. *decusso*, to cross.] Union in the shape of an X or cross.

De-gen-er-a'tion. [L. *degenero*, to be worse than one's ancestors.] A diseased change in the structure.

Deg-lu-ti'tion. (261.) [L. *deglutitio*, to swallow down.] The act of swallowing.

De-lir'i-um. [L. *deliro*, to rave.] Wandering of the mind, as seen in fevers.

De-lir'i-um Tre'mens. (408.) Trembling delirium; "the horrors."

Del'toid. [Gr. *delta*,—the Greek letter Δ, —and *eidos*, form.] The name of a muscle that resembles in form the Greek letter Δ.

Den'tal. [L. *dens*, a tooth.] Pertaining to the teeth.

Dep-o-si'tion. The act of throwing down, as of lime salts in cartilage.

Der'mis. (28.) [L., from *derma*, the skin.] The skin.

Der'moid. [Gr. *derma*, the skin, and *eidos*, form.] Resembling the skin.

De-scen'dens. [L. *de*, down, and *scando*, to climb.] Descending, falling.

Dex'trin. A gum-like substance derived from starch.

Di-a-be'tes. (308.) [Gr. *dia*, through, and *baino*, to go.] An abnormal and diseased flow of urine.

Di'a-phragm. [Gr. *diaphragma*, a partition.] The midriff,—a muscle separating the chest from the abdomen.

Di-ar-rhœ'a. [Gr. *diarrheo*, to flow through.] A morbidly frequent evacuation of the intestines.

Di-ar-thro'sis. [Gr. *dia*, through, and *arthron*, a joint.] An articulation which permits the bones to move freely on each other in every direction.

Di-as'to-le. [Gr. *diastello*, to put asunder.] The dilatation of the heart when the blood enters it.

Di-e-tet'ics. (333.) That part of medicine which relates to diet or food.

Dif-fer-en-ti-a'tion. The production of diverse parts from a germ by a process of development.

Dif-fu'sion. (176.) [L. *diffundo*, *diffusum*, to spread.] The gradual mixing of gases or of fluids when in contact or separated by porous walls or divisions.

Di-ges'tion. [L. *dis*, apart, and *gero*, to bear.] The process of preparing foods in the alimentary canal for absorption into the blood-current.

Dig-i-to'rum. [L. *digitus*, a finger.] A term applied to certain muscles of the extremities.

Di-la'tor. A muscle which dilates certain parts.

Dip-so-ma'ni-a. [Gr. *dipsa*, thirst, and *mania*, madness.] An insatiable desire for intoxicants.

Dis-charge'. An increase of material from a part that secretes a fluid.

Dis-in-te-gra'tion. The breaking up into parts.

Dis'tal. (385.) [L. *disto*, to stand apart.] Applied to the farthest extremity of a part.

Dis-tri-bu'tion. (385.) The parts to which a nerve or an artery is apportioned.

Di-ur'nal. (321.) [L. *dies*, day.] During the day.

Dor'sal. [L. *dorsum*, the back.] Pertaining to the back.

Drop'sy. (22.) An abnormal collection of fluid in the areolar tissue.

Duct. (250.) [L. *duco*, *ductum*, to lead.] A canal or tube.

Du-o-de'num. (261.) [L. *duodenus*, of twelve fingers' breadth.] The first portion of the small intestine.

Du'ra Ma'ter. (367.) [L. *durus*, hard, and *mater*, mother.] The outer membrane of the brain.

Dys'en-ter-y. [Gr. *dus*, bad, and *enteria*, intestines.] A discharge of blood and mucus from the intestines, attended with tenesmus.

Dys-pep'si-a. (281.) [Gr. *dus*, bad, and *pepto*, to digest.] Indigestion, or disordered state of the digestive organs.

Dysp-nœ'a. (188.) [Gr. *dus*, difficult, and *pnea*, to breathe.] Labored or difficult respiration.

E-con'o-my. [Gr. *oikos*, a house, and *nemo*, to arrange.] The total of the arrangements necessary to the animal system.

Ef'fer-ent. (81.) [L. *effero*, to carry out.] Conveying from the central portions outward.

Ef-flu'vi-a. [L., from *effluo*, to flow out.] Exhalations or vapors coming from the body, and from decaying animal or vegetable substances.

E-ges'ta. (319.) [L., from *egero*, to cast out.] The natural excretions, like urine, excrement, etc.

E-las-tiç'i-ty. (69.) [Gr. *elauno*, to impel.] A property impelling a body of itself to return to its normal form.

E-lim-i-na'tion. [L. *e*, out of, and *limen*, a threshold.] Expulsion or discharge from an organ, a tissue, or the system.

Em-a-na'tion. [L. *emano*, to issue from.] The miasm from putrid materials.

Em'i-nen-ces. (302.) [L. *e*, out of, and *mineo*, I project.] Projections on the surface of an organ.

Em-me-trop'ic. (460.) [Gr. *em*, in, *metron*, a measure, and *optomai*, I see.] Pertaining to emmetropia, or the condition of the normal eye.

E-mo'tion. [L. *e*, out of, and *moveo*, to move.] Passion or delirium independent of the will.

Em-phy-se'ma. [Gr. *emphusao*, to inflate.] Collection of air in the areolar tissue under the skin, or in the interlobular lung-tissue.

Em-py-reu-mat'ic. (230.) [Gr. *empureno*, to kindle.] Having the taste or smell of slightly-burnt animal and vegetable substances.

E-mul'sion. (274.) Oil divided and held in a state of fine drops in a water containing an alkali or a mucilage.

En-am'el. The smooth, hard substance which covers the crown or visible part of a tooth.

En-ceph'a-lon. (350.) [Gr. *egkephalon*, the brain.] The contents of the skull; the brain.

En-do-car'di-um. (95.) [Gr. *endon*, within, and *kardia*, the heart.] The lining membrane of the heart.

En'do-lymph. (440.) [Gr. *endon*, within, and *lympha*, water.] The fluid in the internal ear.

End'-Or'gan. The outer terminal mechanism of a sensory nerve.

En-dos-mo'sis. [Gr. *endon*, within, and *osmos*, impulse.] The transmission of fluids through membranes inward.

En-er-va'tion. (402.) [L. *enervo*, to weaken.] A weakened condition of the nervous system.

En-tail'. (402.) [Fr. *entailler*, to cut deep.] A legacy transmitted from generation to generation.

E-pen'dy-ma. [Gr.] The membrane which lines the ventricles of the brain.

Ep-i-dem'ic. [Gr. *epi*, upon, and *demos*, the people.] An extensively prevalent disease.

Ep-i-der'mis. (28.) [Gr. *epi*, upon, and *derma*, the skin.] The superficial layer of the skin; the cuticle.

Ep-i-glot'tis. (160.) [Gr. *epi*, upon, and *glotta*, the tongue.] A cartilage of the larynx, which covers the glottis during deglutition.

Ep'i-lep-sy. [Gr. *epilambano*, to seize upon.] Sudden attacks of convulsions, with deep sleep and mouth-frothing.

Ep-i-the'li-um. (156.) [Gr. *epi*, upon, and *thele*, a nipple.] The upper cell layers of a mucous or serous membrane.

E-qui-lib'ri-um, Sense of. See ¶¶ 372, 474, and 475.

Es-e-ri'na. (452.) The active principle of the Calabar bean, *Physostigma*.

Eth'moid. (341.) [Gr. *ethmos*, a sieve, and *eidos*, form.] A bone of the skull.

Eu-sta'chi-an Tube. A channel from the fauces to the middle ear; named from Eustachius, who first described it.

Eu-tha-na'si-a. An easy death.

Ex-ci'sion. [L. *ex*, out, and *scindo*, *scissum*, to cut.] The cutting out of a part.

Ex'cre-ment. [L. *excerno*, to separate.] Matter excreted and ejected; alvine discharges.

Ex-cre'tion. (303.) [L. *excerno*, *excretum*, to sift out.] The process of separation of effete materials.

Ex'cre-tive. (330.) A principle found in the excrement.

Ex-ha'lant. [L. *exhalo*, to send forth vapor.] Having the quality of exhaling or forcing out air.

Ex-pec-to-ra'tion. (195.) [L. *ex*, out, and *pectus*, the breast.] The act of ejecting from the air-passages mucus and other matters from the lungs by coughing, etc.

Ex-pi-ra'tion. (174.) [L. *expiro*, *expiratum*, to breathe forth.] The act of expelling air from the air-passages.

Ex-ten'sion. [L. *ex*, out, and *tendo*, to stretch.] The act of restoring a limb to its natural position after it has been flexed or bent.

Ex-ten'sor. (514.) [L.] A term applied to a muscle that serves to extend any part of the body:—opposed to *Flexor*.

Eye'-Piece. The portion of the compound microscope placed in the upper part of the tube.

Fa'cial. [L. *facies*, the face.] Pertaining to the front and lower part of the head.

Falx. [L. *falx*, a scythe.] A process of the dura mater shaped like a scythe.

Fa-rad'ic Cur'rent. The interrupted electric current; the electricity of induction.

Fas'ci-a. (20.) [L. *fascis*, a bundle.] The white fibrous expansion around muscles.

Fas-cic'u-lus, *pl.* **Fas-cic'u-li.** [L., diminutive of *fascis*, a bundle.] A little bundle of muscular fibres.

Fats. (219.) Vegetable and animal oils. They are mostly hydro-carbons.

Fau'ces. [L.] The cavity at the back of the mouth.

Fe. [L. *ferrum*, iron.] The chemical symbol of iron.

Fem'o-ral. Pertaining to the femur.

Fe'mur. [L.] The thigh-bone.

Fe-nes'tra, *pl.* **Fe-nes'træ.** (434.) [L.] A window:—a term applied to some openings in the internal ear.

Fer-men-ta'tion. [L. *fermento*, to leaven.] The spontaneous changes which watery solutions of organic matter undergo under atmospheric influences.

Fe'ver. (321.) A condition of the system characterized by continued elevation of the body-temperature, with disordered functions.

Fi'bre. [L. *fibra*.] An organic filament or thread which enters into the composition of animal and vegetable textures.

Fi-bril'læ. [L., diminutive of *fibra*.] The microscopic filaments of muscular tissue.

Fi'brin. (121, 217.) A proteid principle found in beef, blood, and vegetables. It usually exists in the form of tough, elastic threads.

Fi'bro-Car'ti-lage. An organic tissue partaking of the nature of fibrous tissue and that of cartilage.

Fi-brot'ic. (408.) Resembling fibrous tissue.

Fib'u-la. [L., a clasp.] The outer and lesser bone of the leg.

Fil'a-ment. [L. *filamenta*, threads.] A fine thread.

Fil'trate. That which has run through a strainer or filter.

Fil-tra'tion. (227.) Straining.

Fis'sure. (168.) [L. *findo, fissum*, to cleave.] A deep groove or depression.

Fl. The chemical symbol of fluorine.

Flat'u-lence. (334.) [L. *flatus*, wind.] A collection of gas in the stomach and intestines.

Flex'ion. [L. *flectio*.] The act of bending.

Flex'or. (514.) [L.] A term applied to a muscle that flexes or bends a part.

Flue. (201.) A tube or passage for air, cold or heated.

Fol'li-cle. [L. *follis*, a bag.] A small secreting cavity.

Fo-ra'men, *pl.* **Fo-ram'i-na.** [L., from *foro*, to bore a hole.] A small hole or opening.

Fo-ra'men Mag'num. [L.] The great opening in the occipital bone at the base of the skull.

Fore'arm. The part of the upper extremity between the elbow and the hand.

Fos'sa. [L., a ditch.] A cavity in a bone, with a large aperture.

Fo've-a Cen-tra'lis. (462.) [L.] The central depression of the retina, in the yellow spot.

Frac'ture. [L. *frango, fractum*, to break.] The solution of continuity of a bone; a break in a bone.

Fræ'num. [L., a bridle.] *Frænum linguæ*, the bridle of the tongue.

Fron'tal. [L. *frons*, the forehead.] Belonging to the forehead. The bone of the forehead.

Ful'crum. (514.) [L.] The fixed point about which a lever moves.

Func'tion. [L. *fungor*, to perform.] The appropriate action of an organ or system of organs.

Fun'dus. [L.] The bottom of anything, as of the eye or the bladder.

Fun'gi-form. [L. *fungus* and *forma*.] Having terminations like the head of a fungus or a mushroom.

Gan'gli-on, *pl.* **Gan'gli-a.** (84.) [Gr., a knot.] A collection of gray cells in the course of a nerve.

Gan-gli-on'ic Sys'tem. (386.) A name given to the nervous system of organic life.

Gas'tric. [Gr. *gaster*, the stomach.] Belonging to the stomach.

Gas'tro-Pul'mo-na-ry. (165.) Pertaining to lung and stomach regions.

Gas-troc-ne'mi-us. [Gr. *gaster*, the stomach, and *kneme*, the leg.] The name of a large muscle of the leg.

Gei'sha. A Japanese public dancer.

Gel'a-tin. (216.) [L. *gelo*, to congeal.] A proteid substance derived from bone, cartilage, etc., by long boiling.

Gen-er-a'tion. (399.) An age; people living at the same time.

Ging'ly-form. [Gr. *ginglymos*, a knife-like joint, and *eidos*, form.] An articulation that admits of motion in only two directions; hinge-like.

Gland. (250.) [L. *glans*, an acorn.] An organ whose function it is to secrete or separate some particular fluid from the blood.

Gle'noid. [Gr. *glene*, a cavity.] A term applied to some cavities of bones.

Glob'u-lin. (217.) A proteid constituent of the blood-corpuscles.

Glos-sa. [Gr.] The tongue. Names compounded with this word are applied to muscles of the tongue.

Glos-so-Pha-ryn'ge-al. (382.) Relating to the tongue and pharynx.

Glot'tis. (489.) [Gr.] The narrow opening at the upper part of the larynx.

Glu'cose. (221.) [Gr. *glukos*, sweet.] Grape-sugar. It may be obtained from starch by the action of acids, or of saliva.

Glu-tæ'us. [Gr.] A name given to muscles about the hip.

Glu'ten. (217.) [L.] Glue. The residue after wheat flour has been deprived of starch.

Glyç'e-rin. (210.) [Gr. *glukos*, sweet.] A yellow, transparent, syrup-like fluid, the chemical base of animal fats.

Gly'co-gen. (308.) [From *glucose*, and *gennao*, to produce.] A peculiar constituent of liver-tissue.

Gom-pho'sis. [Gr. *gomphos*, a nail.] The immovable articulation of the teeth with the jaw-bone, like a nail in a board.

Gout. (334.) Inflammation characterized by pain in the joints of the feet and hands.

Gran'ule. [L. *granum*, a grain.] A microscopic particle of matter.

Grape Sugar. (221.) Glucose.

Groin. The lower and lateral part of the abdomen.

Gums. The red, firm, solid tissues which adhere to the necks of the teeth.

Gus'ta-to-ry. (427.) [L. *gusto*, *gustation*, to taste.] Belonging to the sense of taste.

Gym-na'si-a. [Gr. *gymnasion*.] An establishment for bodily exercise.

H. The chemical symbol of hydrogen.

Hæ-mo-glo'bin. (180.) [Gr. *haima*, blood, and *globus*, a globe.] The iron compound of the red corpuscles.

Hal-lu-ci-na'tion. (408.) [L. *hallucinor*, *hallucinatus*, to mistake.] Mental error; delusion.

Ha'shish. (410.) A preparation of *cannabis Indica*, or Indian hemp.

Ha-ver'si-an. (505.) Pertaining to the canals of Havers found in bone-tissue.

Hem-i-ple'gi-a. (370.) [Gr. *hemisos*, half, and *plesso*, to strike.] Paralysis affecting one side of the body.

Hem'i-spheres. (352.) [Gr. *hemi*, half, and *sphaira*, a sphere.] The upper spheroidal portions of the brain, separated from each other by the falx cerebri.

Hem'or-rhage. (122.) [Gr. *haima*, blood, and *regnumi*, to burst.] A discharge of blood from an artery.

He-pat'ic. (270.) [Gr. *hepar*, *hepatos*, the liver.] Belonging to the liver.

Herb'age. (202.) Grasses.

He-red'i-ta-ry. (399.) [L. *hæres*, an heir.] Transmitted from parent to offspring.

He-red'i-ty. (399.) The predisposition or tendency to definite physiological actions derived from one's ancestors.

Her'ni-a. [Gr. *hernos*, a branch.] A rupture or breach. A tumor arising from the protrusion of a portion of the intestines through an opening in the abdominal walls.

His-tol'o-gy. [Gr. *histos*, tissue, and *logos*, discourse.] A description of the minute structures of the body.

Hom-i-ci'dal. Murderous.

Ho-mo-ge'ne-ous. [Gr. *homos*, equal, and *genos*, a kind.] Of the same kind or quality.

Ho-mol'o-gous. [Gr. *homos*, same, and *logos*, relation.] Of the same essential nature.

Hu'me-rus. [L.] The bone of the arm.

Hy'a-loid. A transparent membrane of the eye.

Hy'dro-Car'bons. (218.) Compounds of hydrogen and carbon. They include many of the group of fats and oils.

Hy'dro-gen. [Gr. *hudor*, water, and *gennao*, to generate.] A gas which constitutes one of the elements of water.

Hy-dro-pho'bi-a. [Gr. *hudor*, water, and *phobeo*, to fear.] A disease caused by the bite of a rabid animal; rabies.

Hy'gi-ene. (1.) [Gr. *hugieinon*, health.] The part of medicine which treats of the preservation of health.

Hy'oid. (160.) [*v*, a Greek letter, and *eidos*, form.] A bone resembling the Greek letter *v* in shape.

Hy-per-æs-the'si-a. (379.) [Gr. *hyper*, excessive, and *æsthesis*, sensibility.] Diseased increase of sensibility.

Hy-per-me-tro'pi-a. (460.) [Gr. *hyper*, above, *metron*, a measure, and *ops*, vision.] "Flat eye;"—opposite to *myopia*, or near-sight.

Hyp-not'ics. [Gr. *hupnos*, sleep.] Drugs having the power to induce sleep.

Hy-po-chon-dri'a-cal. [Gr. *hypo*, under, and *chondros*, a cartilage.] Having low spirits, a condition frequently connected with dyspepsia.

Hy-po-der'mic. [Gr. *hypo*, under, and *derma*, the skin.] A term used to denote the application of medicines under the skin.

Hy-po-glos'sal. (382.) Under the tongue. The name of a nerve of the tongue.

Hy-poth'e-sis. [Gr.] A supposition. A theory is an accepted hypothesis.

Hys-te'ri-a. A very complex morbid condition. It is probably a disorder of the nervous system.

I-de-a'tion. The action of the cerebrum in producing or evolving ideas.

Il'e-o-Cæ'cal Valve. (268.) The mucous fold at the junction of ileum and cæcum.

Il'e-um. (264.) [Gr. *eilo*, to wind.] A portion of the small intestine.

Il'i-ac. Pertaining to the haunch.

Il'i-um. The outer expanded portion of the innominate bone; the haunch-bone.

Im'pulse. (349.) That which passes over the nerve fibres from nerve-cell group to nerve-cell group.

In'cus. (433.) [L., an anvil.] The largest of the three bones of the internal ear.

In'dex. [L. *indico*, to show.] The forefinger; the pointing finger.

In-di-vid'u-al. In zoology, the sum of the product of a single ovum or egg.

In-duc'tion Shock. The sharp sensation induced by a sudden electric discharge from an induction coil.

In-ert'ness. (107.) Tendency to inaction.

In-flam-ma'tion. [L. *inflammo*, inflammatum*, to set on fire.] A disordered function, characterized by pain, heat, redness, and swelling.

In-fu'sion. [L. *in*, upon, and *fundo*, *fusum*, to pour.] A solution of the soluble principles of a substance obtained by the action of warm or cold water.

In-hi-bi'tion. (85, 128.) [L. *inhibeo*, I hold in.] The stopping or checking of an already present action.

In-ner-va'tion. (317.) The nervous influence necessary for the maintenance of life and the functions of the various organs.

In-nom-i-na'ta. (247.) [L. *in*, not, and *nomen*, name.] Parts which have no proper name.

In-os'cu-late. [L. *in*, and *osculatus*, from *osculor*, to kiss.] To unite, as two vessels at their extremities.

In-sal-i-va'tion. (258.) The process of mixing saliva with food during mastication.

In-ser'tion. (513.) [L. *insero*, *insertum*, to implant.] The attachment of a muscle to a bone or other part.

In-spi-ra'tion. (173.) [L. *in*, in, and *spiro*, *spiratum*, to breathe.] The act of drawing in the breath.

In-sta-bil′i-ty. [Chemical.] The tendency of complex animal and vegetable compounds to split up readily into simpler chemical compounds.

In-teg′u-ment. (20.) [L. *intego*, to cover.] The epidermis, rete, dermis, and subcutaneous areolar and fatty tissues taken together as forming a covering.

In′ter. [L.] Between.

In-ter-ar-tic′u-lar. (511.) [L. *inter*, and *articulus*, a joint.] Situated between the bones.

In-ter-cel′lu-lar. (163.) [L. *inter*, and *cellula*, a little cell.] Between the cellular spaces of tissues.

In-ter-cos′tal. [L. *inter*, and *costa*, a rib.] Between the ribs.

In-ter-mit′tent. (132.) [L. *intermitto*, to leave off from time to time.] Intermission. Irregularity of the interval of the beat of the heart.

In-ter-no′di-i. [L. *inter*, between, and *nodus*, a knot.] A term applied to some muscles of the forearm.

In′ter-stice. [L. *inter*, between, and *sto*, to stand.] The slight separation between organs or parts of organs.

In-ter-ver′te-bral. Between the vertebræ.

In-tes′tines. [L. *intus*, within.] The canal that extends from the stomach through the body, situated in the abdominal cavity.

In-tox′i-cant. (242.) [L. *in*, in, and *toxicum*, poison.] A substance which will induce drunkenness or inebriety.

In-trin′sic. [L. *intrinsecus*, on the inside.] Within the organ or part.

In-tus-sus-cep′tion. (10.) [L. *intus*, within, and *suscipio*, *susceptum*, to receive.] The taking of nourishment into the interior.

In-vol′un-ta-ry. Independent of the will or power of choice.

I′ris. (451.) [L., the rainbow.] The colored circle that surrounds the pupil of the eye.

Ir′ri-ta-ble. (77.) Capable of responding to a stimulus.

Ir-ri-ta′tion. (195.) [L. *irrito*, *irritatum*, to provoke.] Excessive action of an organ or tissue, causing a morbid increase of the circulation or disturbance of sensibility.

Is′chi-um. [Gr. *ischion*, the hip.] The portion of the innominata which serves as a support for the trunk when we are seated.

I′vo-ry. A hard, solid, fine-grained substance of a fine white color; the tusk of an elephant.

Je-ju′num. (264.) [L., empty.] A portion of the small intestine.

Ju′gu-lar. [L. *jugulum*, the neck.] Relating to the throat or neck:—applied to the great veins of the neck.

K. [L. *kalium*.] The chemical symbol of the element potassium.

Kil′o-litre. One cubic metre,—about 35.326 cubic feet.

Kou′mis. An intoxicant made from the milk of the mare. The Tartars suck it from a tuft of hair dipped into the fluid.

Kre′a-tin. (310.) A constant constituent of the juices of muscles.

La′bi-um, *pl.* **La′bi-i.** [L.] The lips.

Lab′y-rinth. (435.) [Gr.] The internal ear:—so named from its many windings.

Lach′ry-mal. (440.) [L. *lachryma*, a tear.] Pertaining to or secreting tears.

Lac′te-al. (277.) [L. *lac*, milk.] A small vessel or tube of animal bodies for conveying chyle from the intestines to the thoracic duct.

Lac′tin. (215.) [L. *lac*, milk.] Lactose, or milk-sugar.

Lac′to-Pro′te-in. (229.) An albuminoid substance found in milk.

La-cu′na, *pl.* **La-cu′næ.** (505.) [L. *lacus*, a ditch or hole.] Small pits in the mucous membrane; also in the bones.

La′cus. [L.] A small space in the inner angle of the eye between the lids.

Lam′i-na, *pl.* **Lam′i-næ.** [L.] A plate or thin coat lying over another.

Lar-yn-gi′tis. Inflammation of the larynx.

La-ryn′go-scope. [Gr. *larynx*, larynx, and *skopeo*, to look at.] An instrument by which the larynx can be viewed in the living subject.

Lar′ynx. (487.) [Gr. *larynx*.] The upper part of the windpipe. The organ of the voice.

La'tent. [L. *lateo*, to lie hid.] Concealed; waiting for a favorable opportunity.

Lat'e-ral. [L. *latus*, the side.] Belonging to the side.

La-tis'si-mus, *pl.* **La-tis'si-mi.** [L., superlative of *latus*, broad.] A term applied to some muscles.

La-trine'. A water-closet.

Le-gu'min. (217.) Cheese or vegetable casein found in peas, beans, etc.

Le'sion. [L. *lædo*, *læsum*, to hurt.] A wound, hurt, or vitiated condition of a part.

Leu'cin. (310.) One of the principal products of the decomposition of nitrogenous matter. It forms thin, white, flat crystals.

Le-va'tor. [L. *levo*, to raise.] A name applied to a muscle that raises the part to which it is attached.

Lig'a-ment. (509.) [L. *ligo*, to bind.] A strong, compact substance serving to bind one bone to another.

Lig'a-ture. (105.) A thread of silk, flax, silver, etc., suitable for tying arteries and veins.

Lig'nin. (230.) The woody fibre of vegetable substances.

Lin'e-a, *pl.* **Lin'e-æ.** [L.] A line.

Lin'gua, *pl.* **Lin'guæ.** [L.] A tongue.

Lobe. A round or projecting part of an organ.

Lob'u-lar, Lob'u-lat-ed. (163.) [L. *lobulus*.] Shaped like a lobe or lobules.

Lo-cal-i-za'tion. The act or power of locating a sensation.

Lon'gus, Lon'gi-or. [L., long, longer.] A term applied to several muscles.

Lo'tion. [L. *lotio*, a wash.] A medicated fluid used as an external application.

Lu'bri-cant. [L. *lubricans*.] That which makes smooth or slippery.

Lum'bar. [L. *lumbus*, the loins.] Pertaining to the loins.

Lu'men. [L., light, pupil.] The calibre of an anatomical tube or vessel.

Lu'na-cy. [L. *luna*, the moon.] Insanity in which there are lucid or normal intervals.

Lymph. (295.) [L. *lympha*, water.] A colorless fluid in animal bodies, contained in vessels called lymphatics.

Lym-phat'ic. A vessel of animal bodies that contains or conveys lymph.

Mag'nus, -na, -num. [L., great.] A term applied to certain muscles.

Maize. Indian corn (*Zea mays*).

Ma'jor. [L., greater.] Greater in extent or quantity.

Mal-aise'. [Fr. *mal*, ill, and *aise*, ease.] Discomfort; uneasiness.

Ma-la'ri-a. [Ital. *mala*, bad, and *aria*, air.] A term for the disease-inducing agents arising from decaying organic materials.

Mal-for-ma'tion. A deviation from the normal form of a part.

Mal'le-us. (433.) [L., a hammer.] A bone of the middle ear.

Mam'mal. [L. *mamma*, a breast.] An animal that suckles its young.

Ma'ni-a. (400.) [Gr. *mainomai*, to rage.] Madness; delirium not occasioned by fever-action.

Man'like Apes. The chimpanzee, gorilla, ourang, and gibbon.

Mar-gar'ic. (219.) An acid intermediate between palmitic and stearic acid of fats.

Mar'row. [Sax.] A soft, oleaginous substance contained in the cavities of bones.

Mas-se'ter. [Gr. *massaomai*, to chew.] The name of a muscle of the face.

Mas-ti-ca'tion. (238.) [L. *mastico*, to chew.] The act of chewing.

Mas'toid. [Gr. *mastos*, the breast, and *eidos*, form.] The name of a process of the temporal bone behind the ear.

Mas-toid'e-us. A name applied to muscles that are attached to the mastoid process.

Ma'trix. (34.) [Gr. *mater*, a mother.] The place or substance in which anything is formed.

Max-il'la. [L.] The jaw-bone.

Max'i-mus, -um. [L., superlative of *magnus*, great.] A term applied to several muscles.

Me-a'tus. [L. *meo*, to go.] A passage or channel.

Mech'an-ism. An assemblage of cells or parts to perform a special function or action.

Me-di-as-ti'num. A membrane that separates the chest into two parts.

Me'di-um, *pl.* **Me'di-a.** (467.) [L.] A transparent or translucent solid, fluid, or gas.

Me-dul'la Ob-lon-ga'ta. (365.) The commencement of the spinal cord.

Me-dul'la Spi-na'lis. The spinal cord.

Med'ul-la-ry. (16.) [L. *medulla*, marrow.] Pertaining to marrow.

Med'ul-la-ry Sub'stance. (39.) A line of colored, irregularly-shaped cells, which run through the centre of a hair.

Mem-bra'na. (26.) A membrane; a thin, white, flexible, skin-like expansion, formed by fibres interwoven like network.

Mes-en-ter'ic. Pertaining or belonging to the mesentery.

Mes'en-ter-y. (204.) [Gr. *mesos*, the middle, and *enteron*, the intestine.] The membrane in the middle of the intestines by which they are attached to the spine.

Met-a-car'pus. [Gr. *meta*, after, and *karpos*, the wrist.] The part of the hand between the wrist and the fingers.

Met-a-tar'sus. [Gr. *meta*, after, and *tarsos*, the tarsus.] The instep:—a term applied to seven bones of the foot.

Mg. The chemical symbol of magnesium, the base of magnesia.

Mi-cro-ce-phal'ic. [Gr. *mikros*, small, and *kephale*, the head.] Relating to persons having abnormally small heads.

Mi'cro-scope. [Gr. *mikros*, small, and *skopeo*, to look at.] An optical instrument employed in the study of minute objects.

Mid'dle-men. (382.) Agents between two parties; arrangers of impulses.

Mid'riff. [Sax. *mid*, and *hrife*, the belly.] See *Diaphragm*.

Min'i-mus. [L.] The smallest:—a term applied to several muscles.

Mi'nor. [L.] Less, smaller:—a term applied to several muscles.

Mi'tral. (93.) [L. *mitra*, a mitre.] The name of valves in the left side of the heart.

Mixed Nerve. (383.) A compound of motor and sensory fibres.

Mo-di'ous. [L. *modus*, a measure.] A cone in the cochlea around which the membranes wind.

Mo'lar. (254.) [L. *mola*, a mill.] The name of some of the large teeth.

Mo-lec'u-lar. Pertaining to molecules, a collection of elementary atoms joined together.

Mol'lis. [L.] Soft.

Mor'phi-a. [From *Morpheus*, the god of sleep.] The most important narcotic principle of opium.

Mo'tor, *pl.* **Mo-to'res.** [L.] A mover:—a term applied to certain nerves.

Mu'cous. Pertaining to mucus.

Mu'cus. A viscid fluid secreted by the mucous membrane, which it serves to moisten and defend; animal mucilage.

Mus'cæ Vol-i-tan'tes. (461.) [L., hovering flies.] Mote-like objects hovering in the field of sight.

Mus'cu-lar Sense. See ¶ 472. It is sometimes called the sixth sense.

My-o-lem'ma. [Gr. *mus*, a muscle, and *lemma*, a sheath.] The investing membrane of muscular fibre.

My-ol'o-gy. [Gr. *mus*, a muscle, and *logos*, a discourse.] A description of the muscles.

My-op'ic. (460.) [Gr. *muo*, to contract, and *ops*, the eye.] (Near-sighted persons partially close the eyes when looking at distant objects.) Relating to near-sight.

N. The chemical symbol of nitrogen.

Na. [L. *natrium*.] The chemical symbol of sodium, the base of soda.

Nar-cot'ic. (188.) [Gr. *narke*, stupor.] A medicine which induces stupor or sleep.

Na'sal. Relating to the nose.

Nau'se-a. [Gr. *naus*, a ship.] Any sickness at the stomach, similar to commencing sea-sickness.

Nerve. (380.) The fibres of the animal body which transmit impulses.

Nerve'-Cen-tre. (84.) A group of nerve-cells. It can originate, receive, and modify impulses.

Ner'vous-ness. Unusual impressibility of the brain-centres; "brain-fag."

Neu-ral'gi-a. (379.) [Gr. *neuron*, a nerve, and *algos*, pain.] Pain in the course of a nerve.

Neu-ri-lem'ma. [Gr. *neuron*, a nerve, and *lemma*, a sheath.] The sheath or covering of a nerve.

Neu-rol'o-gy. [Gr. *neuron*, a nerve, and *logos*, a discourse.] A description of the nerves of the body.

Nic'o-tin. (412.) The colorless, poisonous, and stupefying odorous oil extracted from tobacco.

Nor'mal. [L. *norma*, a rule.] Of the regular type or form.

Nu'cle-a-ted. Having a nucleus or central particle.

Nu-cle'o-lus. (8.) The small body seen within the nucleus.

Nu'cle-us. (8.) [L., a kernel.] The small mass seen within the cell-body.

Nu-tri'tion. (308.) [L. *nutrio, nutritum*, to nourish.] Assimilation; the act of nourishing.

O. The chemical symbol of the element oxygen.

Ob-jec'tive. The combination of small lenses at the lower end of the tube of the microscope.

Oc-cip'i-tal. Pertaining to the occiput.

Oc'ci-put. (341.) [L. *ob*, and *caput*, the head.] The back part of the head, formed by the occipital bone.

Oc'u-lar. (443.) Belonging to the eye.

Oc'u-lo-Mo'tor. (382.) The nerve or muscle concerned in moving the eyeball.

Oc'u-lus, *pl.* **Oc'u-li.** [L.] The eye.

Œ-soph'a-gus. (260.) [Gr. *oio*, to carry, and *phago*, to eat.] The name of the passage through which the food passes from the mouth to the stomach.

O-lec'ra-non. [Gr. *olene*, the ulna, and *kranon*, the head.] The elbow; the head of the ulna.

O'le-ic Ac'id. (219.) One of the acids of fat. It is a fluid.

Ol-fac'to-ry. [L. *oleo*, to smell, and *facio*, to make.] Pertaining to smelling.

Ol'i-va-ry. Like an olive:—a term applied to the eminences of the medulla.

O-men'tum. [L.] The caul.

O'mo. [Gr. *omos*, the shoulder.] The name of muscles attached to the shoulder.

Oph-thal'mic. [Gr. *ophthalmos*, the eye.] Belonging to the eye.

Oph-thal'mo-scope. [Gr. *ophthalmos*, the eye, and *skopeo*, to look at.] An instrument used in examining the interior of the globe of the eye.

O'pi-um. (411.) [Gr. *opos*, juice.] The concrete juice of the *Papaver somniferum*. It is a stimulant narcotic.

Op'tic Thal'a-mi. See ¶ 353.

Or-bic'u-lar. [L. *orbis*, a circle.] A circular or sphincter muscle.

Or'bit. (340.) The bony cavity in which the eye is placed.

Or-gan'ic. Having an organized structure; relating to organs.

Or'gan-ized. (122.) Having a defined structure.

Or'i-gin. (513.) The source of a muscle's attachment.

Os. [L.] A bone; the mouth of anything.

Os'mose, Os-mo'sis. (275.) [Gr. *osmos*, impulse.] The mixing of fluids through a moist membrane or porous substance.

Os'se-ous. Pertaining to bones.

Os-si-fi-ca'tion. (504.) The process of bone-formation.

Os'si-fy. [L. *os*, a bone, and *facio*, to make.] To convert into bone.

Os-te-ol'o-gy. [Gr. *osteon*, a bone, and *logos*, a discourse.] The part of anatomy which treats of bones.

O'vum. [L., an egg.] The germ before impregnation. It is the product of the ovary.

Ox-i-da'tion. (313.) The chemical union of oxygen with other substances; burning.

Ox'y-Hæ-mo-glo'bin. (181.) Oxygen loosely combined with hæmoglobin in the blood.

P. The chemical symbol of the element phosphorus.

Pab'u-lum. [L., from *pasco*, to feed.] Food; aliment; sustenance.

Pa-la'tum. [L.] The palate; the roof of the mouth.

Pal'lor. [From *palleo*, to be pale.] Paleness; loss of color.

Palm. The hollow or inside of the hand.

Pal'mar. [L. *palma*, the palm.] Belonging to the hand.

Pal-ma'ris. A term applied to some muscles attached to the palm of the hand.

Pal-mit′ic. (219.) A colorless, solid, tasteless body found in certain oils. It is an acid in action.

Pal′pe-bral. (444.) Belonging to the eyelids.

Pal-pe-bra′rum. [L. *palpebra*, the eyelid.] Of the eyelids.

Pan′cre-as. [Gr. *pan*, all, and *kreas*, flesh.] The name of one of the digestive organs.

Pan′cre-a-tin. The albuminous ingredient of the pancreatic juice.

Pa-pil′la, *pl.* **Pa-pil′læ.** (30.) [L.] Small conical prominences.

Pap′il-la-ry. (97.) Pertaining to the papillæ.

Pa-ral′y-sis. (379.) Abolition of function, whether of intellect, sensation, or motion.

Par-a-ple′gi-a. (379.) [Gr., benumbing of parts.] Palsy affecting one-half the body, usually the lower portion.

Pa-ren′chy-ma. [Gr. *pareycluio*, to pour through.] The substance contained between the blood-vessels of an organ.

Pa-ri′e-tal. (341.) [L. *paries*, a wall.] A bone of the skull.

Pa-rot′id. (257.) [Gr. *para*, near, and *otos*, genitive of *ous*, the ear.] The name of the largest salivary gland.

Pas′sive. Acted upon; not acting of itself.

Pa-tel′la, *pl.* **Pa-tel′læ.** [L.] The knee-pan.

Pa-thet′i-cus, *pl.* **Pa-thet′i-ci.** (382.) [Gr. *pathos*, passion.] The name of the fourth pair of nerves.

Path-o-log′i-cal. [Gr. *pathos*, disease, and *logos*, a discourse.] Belonging to disease, or to disease-action.

Pec′to-ral. [L.] Pertaining to the chest.

Pe′dis. [L., genitive of *pes*, the foot.] Of the foot.

Pe-dun′cles. (352.) [L. *pes*, *pedunculus*, diminutive of a foot.] The foot-stalks of the brain.

Pel′vis. (247.) [L.] The basin formed by the larger bones at the lower part of the abdomen.

Pep′sin. (262.) [Gr. *pepto*, to cook.] An ingredient of the gastric juice which acts as a ferment in the digestion of the food.

Pep′tone. (274.) A proteid soluble in water and not coagulable by heat.

Per-cep′tion. The act of receiving knowledge of external objects by impressions on the senses; intellectual discernment.

Per-i-car′di-um. (95.) [Gr. *peri*, around, and *kardia*, the heart.] A membrane that invests the heart.

Per′i-lymph. (440.) [Gr. *peri*, around, and *lympha*, watery fluid.] The fluid of the internal ear.

Per-i-mys′i-um. [Gr. *peri*, around, and *mus*, a muscle.] The investing membrane of a muscle.

Per-i-os′te-um. (16.) [Gr. *peri*, around, and *osteon*, a bone.] The white membrane investing the bone.

Per-i-stal′tic. (265.) [Gr. *peri*, around, and *stello*, I contract.] A movement like the crawling of a worm.

Per-i-to-ne′um. (246.) [Gr. *peri*, around, and *teinein*, to stretch.] A thin, serous membrane investing the internal surface of the abdomen.

Per-me-a′tion. [L. *per*, through, and *meo*, to pass.] The passing of a substance through the pores of a body.

Per-o-ne′al. [Gr. *perone*, the fibula.] Pertaining to the external bone of the leg.

Per′so-nal E-qua′tion. See ¶ 361.

Per-spi-ra′tion. (46.) [L. *per*, through, and *spiro*, to breathe.] Excretion by the skin.

Per-ver′sion. A departure or change from the normal action.

Pha-lan′ge-al. Belonging to the fingers or toes.

Pha′lanx, *pl.* **Pha-lan′ges.** [Gr. *phalanx*, an army.] Three rows of small bones forming the fingers or toes.

Pha-ryn′ge-al. Relating to the pharynx.

Phar′ynx. (158.) [Gr. *pharunx*.] The upper part of the œsophagus.

Phos′pho-rus. [Gr. *phos*, the light, and *phero*, to bear.] A combustible substance, of a yellowish color, semi-transparent, resembling wax.

Phren′ic. [Gr. *phren*, the diaphragm, or parts adjacent to the heart.] Belonging to the diaphragm.

Phthi′sis (pronounced thi′sis.) [Gr. *phthio*, to consume.] Pulmonary consumption.

Phys-i-ol'o-gy. (4.) [Gr. *physis*, nature, and *logos*, a discourse.] The science of the functions of the organs of animals and plants.

Pi-a Ma'ter. (367.) [L., tender mother.] The most internal of the three brain-membranes.

Pig-men'tum Ni'grum. [L.] Black paint. See § 451.

Pin'na. (482.) [L., a wing.] A part of the external ear.

Plas'ma. (122.) [Gr. *plasso*, to form.] The fluid in which the blood-corpuscles float; the serum.

Pla-tys'ma. (88.) [Gr. *platus*, broad.] A muscle of the neck.

Pled'get. A piece of cotton or lint rolled in an oval form.

Pleth'o-ra. (334.) [Gr. *pletho*, to be full.] Excessive fulness of the vessels or of the body.

Pleu'ra, *pl.* **Pleu'ræ.** (155.) [Gr. *pleura*, the side.] A thin membrane that covers the inside of the thorax and also forms the exterior coat of the lungs.

Plex'us. [L. *plecto*, to weave together.] Any union of nerves, vessels, or fibres, in the form of net-work.

Pneu-mo-gas'tric. (383.) [Gr. *pneumon*, the lungs, and *gaster*, the stomach.] Belonging to both the stomach and the lungs.

Pneu-mo-ni'tis. [Gr. *pneumon*, the lungs.] Pneumonia; inflammation of the lungs.

Pol'li-cis. [L.] A term applied to muscles attached to the fingers and toes.

Pons. (366.) [L.] A bridge. *Pons Varolii*, a part of the brain formed by the union of the crura cerebri and cerebelli.

Pop-lit'e-al. [L. *poples*, the ham.] Pertaining to the ham or knee-joint.

Por'tal. (163.) [L. *porta*, a gate.] Relating to the vessels entering the fissure of the liver.

Por'ti-o Du'ra. (382.) [L., hard portion.] The facial nerve; seventh pair.

Por'ti-o Mol'lis. [L., soft portion.] The auditory nerve; eighth pair.

Pre-hen'sion. [L. *prehendo*, *prehensum*, to lay hold on.] The act of grasping.

Pre-mo'lar. (254.) [L. *præ*, before, and *molaris*, molar.] The first two pairs of molar teeth; the bicuspids.

Pres-by-op'ic. [Gr. *presbus*, an old man, and *ops*, the eye.] Relating to the defective vision (long sight) of old persons.

Press'ure Sen-sa'tions. (469.) Tactile sensations.

Pro-bos'cis. [Gr. *pro*, before, and *bosko*, to feed.] The snout or trunk of an elephant or other animal.

Proc'ess. (343.) A prominence or projection.

Pro-fun'da. [L., deep.] Applied to vessels and nerves from their relatively deeper position.

Pro'te-ids. (215.) [From *Proteus*, who could assume different shapes.] A name given to a class of chemical compounds made exclusively by plants, and composed of C, H, O, N, S, with Ca and P.

Pro'to-plasm. (9.) [Gr. *protos*, first, and *plasma*, formed.] Bioplasm.

Pseu-do-po'di-a. (6.) [Gr. *pseudes*, false, and *pous*, a foot.] Blunt, finger-like processes.

Pso'as. [Gr. *psoai*, the loins.] The name of two muscles of the thigh.

Psy'chi-cal. [Gr. *psuche*, soul or mind.] Belonging to the mind or intellect.

Pty'a-lin. The active principle of saliva.

Pu'bic. Pertaining to the pubis.

Pul-mon'ic,
Pul'mo-na-ry, } [L. *pulmo*, the lungs.]
Pul-mo-na'lis. }
Belonging or relating to the lungs.

Pul'que (pronounced pool'kay). An alcoholic intoxicant made from the *Agave Mexicana* in Mexico.

Pulse. (144.) [L. *pello*, *pulsum*, to beat, to strike.] The beating of the arteries following the contraction of the heart-muscle.

Punc'ta. (447.) [L.] A point.

Pu'pil. A little aperture in the centre of the iris, through which the rays of light pass to the retina.

Py-lor'ic. (262.) Pertaining to the pylorus.

Py-lo'rus. [Gr. *puloros*, a gate-keeper.] The lower orifice of the stomach.

Quad-ra'tus. [L. *quadra*, a square.] Of a square figure; quadrate; quadrangular:—applied to certain muscles.

Ra′bi-es. [L. *rabio*, to be mad.] A disease caused by the absorption through a scratch or wound of the saliva of a mad animal, inducing *hydrophobia*, or dread of water.

Ra′di-ate. Having lines or fibres that diverge from a point.

Ra-di-a′tion. (319.) The direct passing away of heat into the air from a warm body.

Ra′di-us. [L., a ray, a spoke of a wheel.] The name of one of the bones of the forearm.

Ra′mus. [L.] A branch.

Re-ac′tion. (62.) The vigorous acting again of the vital powers after they have been depressed.

Re-ac′tion Pe′ri-od. See ¶¶ 360, 361.

Re′cent. (70.) New; fresh.

Rec′tum. (268.) The third and last portion of the intestines.

Rec′tus, *pl.* **Rec′ti.** [L.] Straight; erect:—a term applied to several muscles.

Re-cu-per-a′tion. Recovery; restoration.

Re-duc′ing A′gents. (180.) A term applied to chemical bodies whose action is the reverse of that of oxygen, like nascent hydrogen.

Re′flex Ac′tion. (82.) A term applied to certain movements executed independent of the will.

Re-frac′tion. [L. *re*, again, and *frango, fractum*, to break.] See ¶ 457.

Reg′i-men. [L. *rego*, to govern.] The systematic regulation of the food and drink.

Re′lays. (375.) Local nerve-mechanisms which, under the spur of slight impulses, carry into effect complicated activities.

Re-mak′s′ Nerve-Fibres. (79.) Named after a German physiologist.

Re′nal. (300.) [L. *ren*, the kidney.] Belonging to the kidney.

Re-pro-duc′tion. [L. *re*, again, and *produco, productum*, to bring forth.] The production by organized bodies of others similar to themselves.

Re-sid′u-um. [L.] Waste matter.

Res-pi-ra′tion. (177.) [L. *re*, again, and *spiro*, to breathe.] The act of breathing.

Re-spi′ra-to-ry Cen′tre. (185.) A nervous mechanism of the medulla.

Retch′ing. Continued efforts to vomit independent of the will.

Re′te Mu-co′sum. (29.) [L., mucous network.] The substance in the skin containing the pigment.

Re-tic′u-lar. [L. *rete*, a net.] Resembling a net.

Ret′i-na. (451.) [L. *rete*, a net.] The essential organ of sight. One of the coats of the eye, formed by the expansion of the optic nerve.

Ret′i-nal Ex-haus′tion. See ¶ 465.

Rhyth′mic. (133.) [Gr. *rhuthmos*, measured movement.] Succeeding one another at regular intervals.

Rick′ets. (335.) A disease of children characterized by a large head, crooked spine and limbs, tumid abdomen, and general debility.

Ri-so′ri-us. [L. *rideo, risum*, to laugh.] The laughing muscle of Santorini,—a thin muscle acting at the angle of the mouth.

Ro-tun′dum. [L.] Round; circular.

Ru′ga, *pl.* **Ru′gæ.** A wrinkle; a fold.

S. The chemical symbol of the element sulphur.

Sac′cu-lus. [L., diminutive of *saccus*, a bag.] A little sac.

Sa′cral. Pertaining to the sacrum.

Sa′crum. (247.) [L., sacred.] The bone which forms the posterior part of the pelvis.

Sa′ké. A light wine made from rice by the Japanese.

Sa-li′va. (257.) [L.] The fluid secreted by the salivary glands, which moistens the food and the mouth.

Sam-shoo′. An intoxicant used by the Chinese. It is made from rice by distillation.

San-guin′e-ous. [L. *sanguis*, the blood.] Bloody; abounding with blood; plethoric.

Sar-co-lem′ma. (71.) [Gr. *sarx*, flesh, and *lemma*, a covering.] The thin sheath enclosing muscular fibrils.

Sar′cous. (71.) [Gr. *sarx*, flesh.] Pertaining to flesh or to muscular fibre.

Sar-to′ri-us. [L. *sartor*, a tailor.] A term applied to a muscle of the thigh.

Sca'la, *pl.* **Sca'læ.** (435.) [L., a ladder.] Cavities of the cochlea.

Sca-le'nus. [Gr. *skalenos*, unequal.] A term applied to some muscles of the neck.

Scalp. The integument of the skull.

Scal'pel. [L. *scalpo*, to carve or scrape.] A small knife with a straight blade fixed in a flat handle.

Sca'phoid. [Gr. *skaphe*, a little boat.] The name applied to one of the wrist-bones.

Scap'u-la. [L.] The shoulder-blade.

Scap'u-lar. Relating to the scapula.

Sci-at'ic. [Gr. *ischion*, the haunch.] Pertaining to the loins:—applied to the large nerve of the loins and legs.

Scle-rot'i-ca. (451.) [Gr. *skleros*, hard.] One of the tunics of the eyeball.

Scur'vy. (225.) Scorbutus;—a disease of the general system, having prominent skin-symptoms.

Se-ba'ceous. (41.) [L. *sebum*, tallow.] Pertaining to fat.

Se-cre'tion. The act of producing from the blood substances different from the blood itself; the matter secreted, as mucus, bile, saliva, etc.

Se-cun'dus. [L.] Second:—a term applied to certain muscles.

Sed'en-ta-ry. [L. *sedere*, to sit.] Accustomed to sit much and long.

Selt'zer. Water impregnated with carbonic acid gas; also, water containing carbonates of the alkalies and alkaline earths; soda-water.

Sem-i-cir'cu-lar. (435.) Having the form of a half-circle:—applied to a part of the ear.

Sem-i-lu'nar Valves. (92.) [L. *semi*, half, and *luna*, the moon.] The name of the three festooned valves of the heart at the entrance of the great arteries.

Sem-i-ten-di-no'sus. [L. *semi*, half, and *tendo*, a tendon.] The name of a muscle.

Sen-sa'tion. (380.) The consciousness of the reception of an impulse.

Sep'tum, *pl.* **Sep'ta.** [L.] A membrane that divides two cavities from each other.

Se'rous. (156.) Thin; watery; pertaining to serum.

Ser-ra'tus. (172.) [L. *serro*, to saw.] A term applied to some muscles of the trunk.

Se'rum. (115.) [L.] The thin, transparent part of the blood.

Sew'er-Gas. (199.) The complex gases developed by decomposition of organic materials in sewers and cesspools.

Si. The chemical symbol of the element silicon, the chief ingredient of silex and sand.

Sig'moid. [Gr.] Resembling the Greek letter ς (sigma).

Si'nus. [L., a bay.] A cavity the interior of which is more expanded than the entrance.

Skel'e-tal Mus'cles. Muscles attached directly or indirectly to the bony framework.

Skel'e-ton. (17.) [Gr. *skello*, to dry.] The aggregate of the hard parts of the body; the bones.

Smell'ing Salts. Carbonate of ammonia.

Snel'len's Types. (463.) Types used to test the range of vision.

Soaps. (274.) Compounds made by the action of soda or potassa with fatty acids.

Soft Wa'ter. (479.) A water which readily yields a lather with soap; a water free from lime-salts.

So'lar. [L. *sol*, the sun.] Pertaining to, or derived from, the sun.

So-lu'tion. [L. *solvo*, *solutum*, to dissolve, to loosen.] Any substance dissolved in a liquid.

So-pra'no. The treble; the highest female voice.

Spasm. (379.) A sudden contraction of muscular fibres independent of the will.

Spe'cies. An assemblage or series of similar organic beings.

Sphe'noid. (341.) [Gr. *sphen*, a wedge, and *eidos*, likeness.] A bone at the base of the skull.

Spher'i-cal A-ber-ra'tion. (461.) Defects in the refracting power of the lens from the centre to the circumference.

Sphinc'ter. [Gr. *sphingo*, to restrict.] A muscle that contracts or shuts an orifice.

Spi'nal Ac'ces-so-ry. (382.) The eleventh cranial pair. It is accessory to the vagus nerve.

Spi'nal Cord. (384.) A prolongation of the brain.

Spine. A thorn. The vertebral column; the backbone.

Spi'nous. (343.) Pertaining to the vertebral column.

Spir'its. A name given to liquid products of distillation. The term is confined to the stronger beverages, like rum, gin, whiskey, brandy, etc.

Splanch'nic. [Gr. *splanchnon*, a viscus.] Pertaining to the viscera.

Splanch-nol'o-gy. [Gr. *splanchnon*, the bowels, and *logos*, a discourse.] A description of the internal parts of the body.

Splen'ic. Pertaining to the spleen or milt.

Sple'ni-us. The name of a muscle of the neck.

Split'ting-up. (213.) The breaking up of a complex organic molecule, under the influence of warmth and moisture, into compounds of a simpler chemical nature, like water, carbonic acid, etc.

Spon-ta'ne-ous. [L. *sponte*, of one's own free will.] Taking place without external stimuli.

Spu-tum, *pl.* **Spu-ta.** [L. *spuo, sputum*, to spit.] The matter which is coughed up from the air-passages.

Sta'pes. (433.) [L. a stirrup.] One of the bones of the internal ear.

Starch. (220.) [L. *amylum* and *fecula*.] One of the main proximate principles of seeds.

Ste'a-rin. [Gr. *stear*, suet.] One of the proximate principles of animal fat. It is solid at ordinary temperature.

Ster'num. The breast-bone.

Stim'u-lant. (237.) A drug or agent which excites the organic action of the animal system.

Stim'u-lus. Something which excites the tissues or parts to action.

Stra'tum. [L. *sterno*, to spread.] A bed; a layer of anything.

Stri'æ. (71.) [L. a groove, a crease.] Marks seen on certain fibres.

Sty'loid. [L. *stylus*, a pen.] Pen-like:—an epithet applied to processes that resemble a style, or pen.

Sub. [L.] Under; beneath.

Sub-ar-ach-noi'de-an. (368.) [L. *sub*, under, Gr. *arachne*, a spider's web, and *eidos*, form.] Situated under the arachnoid membranes.

Sub-cla'vi-an. [L. *sub*, under, and *clavis*, a key.] Situated under the clavicle.

Sub-cu-ta'ne-ous. [L. *sub*, under, and *cutis*, the skin.] Situated under the skin.

Sub-ja'cent. (156.) [L. *sub*, under, and *jacere*, to lie.] Lying under or beneath.

Sub-lin'gual. (257.) [L. *sub*, under, and *lingua*, the tongue.] Situated under the tongue.

Sub-max'il-la-ry. (257.) [L. *sub*, under, and *maxilla*, the jawbone.] Located under the jaw.

Sub-mu'cous. [L. *sub*, and *mucus.*] Placed under the mucous membrane.

Sub-or'di-nate. [L. *sub*, under, and *ordinare*, to set in order.] Placed in a lower order or position.

Sub'soil. (202.) The soil lying under the black or cultivated earth.

Su-i-ci'dal. [L. *sui*, of himself, and *cidium*, slaying.] Partaking of self-murder.

Sul'cus, *pl.* **Sul'ci.** A groove or trench, as of the surface of the brain.

Su-pi-na'tor. [L.] A muscle that turns the palm of the hand upward.

Sup-pos'i-to-ry. (292.) A medicated, butter-like mass placed in the rectum to be dissolved.

Su'ture. [L. *suo*, to sew.] The seam or joint that unites the bones of the skull.

Sym-met'ri-cal. The resemblance existing in many organs or parts situated on each side of the median line.

Sym-pa-thet'ic Sys'tem. (386.) The system of organic life; the ganglionic system.

Syn-ar-thro'sis. [Gr. *sun*, with, and *arthron*, a joint.] An immovable articulation.

Sy-no'vi-a. (508.) [Gr. *sun*, with, and *oova*, an egg.] The fluid secreted into the cavities of joints for the purpose of lubricating them.

Sys'tem. An assemblage of organs composed of similar tissues and intended for the same functions.

Sys-tem'ic. Belonging to the general system.

Sys'to-le. (125.) [Gr. *systello*, to contract.] The contraction of the heart and arteries for expelling the blood and carrying on the circulation.

Tac'tile. (467.) [L. *tactus*, touch.] Pertaining to the sense of touch.

Tal'lah. An alcoholic intoxicant made from millet by the Abyssinians.

Tar'sus. [L.] The posterior part of the foot.

Tem'per-a-ture. (470.) A definite or certain degree of sensible heat, as measured by a thermometer.

Tem'po-ral. (341.) [L. *tempus*, time.] Pertaining to the temple region.

Ten'don. [Gr. *teino*, to stretch.] A hard, insensible cord, or bundle of fibres, by which a muscle is attached to a base.

Ten'or. The higher of the two kinds of voices usually belonging to adult males.

Ten'sion. The state of being stretched; the state of being bent or strained into action.

Ten'sor. A muscle that extends a part.

Ten-to'ri-um. [L. *tendo*, to stretch.] A process of the dura mater which lies between the cerebrum and the cerebellum.

Te'res. [L.] Round:—a term applied to many organs, the fibres of which are collected in small bundles.

Test. In chemistry, anything by which the nature of a substance is distinguished.

Tet'a-nus. (75.) [Gr. *teino*, to stretch.] Spasms with rigidity, continuing for some time. The muscles of the jaw being involved, *lock-jaw* occurs.

The'in. (238.) [L. *thea*, the tea-plant.] The active principle of tea. It has a large percentage of hydrogen.

Tho-ra'cic Duct. (277.) The principal tube of the lymphatic system.

Tho'rax. (89.) [Gr.] That part of the skeleton that composes the bones of the chest; the cavity of the chest.

Thy'roid. (488.) [Gr. *thureos*, a shield.] Resembling a shield:—applied to a cartilage of the larynx.

Tib'i-a. [L., a flute.] The large bone of the leg.

Tis'sue. The texture or organization of parts.

Ton'ic Ac'tion. (378.) The state of a part when under moderate, continued, muscular-action pressure.

Ton'ics. Medicines which produce a gradual but permanent excitement of the vital functions.

Ton'sil. (251.) [L.] A glandular body in the throat or fauces.

Tra'che-a. [Gr. *trachus*, rough.] The windpipe.

Tract. (383.) The space, region, or course of fibres, as of the optic tract.

Train'ing. (634.) The preparing of an animal for sustained athletic exercises.

Tran'sit. The passage of a celestial body across the meridian wire of the telescope.

Trans-mis'sion. (399.) The passing of mental, moral, and physical peculiarities from father to son, son to grandson, etc.

Trans-mu-ta'tion. (360.) The act of changing one impulse into another impulse.

Trans-par'ent. Admitting the passage of rays of light, so that objects may be seen on the other side.

Tran-sude'. [L. *trans*, through, and *sudo*, *sudatum*, to sweat.] To pass through the pores of a substance, as sweat or other fluids.

Trans-verse'. (343.) Lying in a cross-direction.

Tra-pe'zi-us. The name of a muscle:—so called from its form.

Tri'ceps. [L. *tres*, three, and *caput*, a head.] A term applied to muscles that have three attachments at one extremity.

Tri-chi'næ Spi-ra'les. (232.) A species of minute worms which work their way through human muscles, causing pain, irritation, and exhaustion. They most commonly occur in hog's flesh.

Tri-cus'pid. (92.) [L. *tres*, three, and *cuspis*, a point.] The triangular valves in the right side of the heart.

Tri-gem'i-nus. (383.) The triple nerves. The trifacial nerve. The branches are *ophthalmic*, *supra-maxillary*, and *infra-maxillary*.

Troch'le-a. [Gr. *trochelia*, a pulley.] A pulley-like cartilage, over which the tendon of a muscle of the eye passes.

Trunk. The principal part of the body, to which the limbs are articulated.

Tu'ber-cle. [L. *tuber*, a bunch.] A pimple, swelling, or tumor on animal bodies. A morbid product occurring in certain lung diseases.

Tur'bi-na-ted Bones. [L. *turbo*, a top.] The convoluted bones of the nostrils.

Turn'ing. (523.) The German athletic exercise drill.

Tym'pa-num. (433.) [Gr. *tumpanon*, a drum.] The middle ear.

Ty'phoid Fe'ver. [Gr. *tuphos*, stupor, and *eidos*, form.] A fever resembling typhus, but having intestinal lesions.

Ty'ro-sin. (310.) [Gr. *turos*, cheese.] A product of pancreatic digestion, associated with leucin, having white and tasteless crystals. It may be made of casein.

Ul-cer-a'tion. The formation of an ulcer; an ulcer or sore; a solution of continuity.

Ul'na. [L.] A bone of the forearm.

Ul'nar. Relating to the ulna.

Um-bi-li'cus. [L.] The navel.

U-ræ'mi-a. (305.) [*Urea*, a constituent of urine, and Gr. *haima*, blood.] The presence of an excess of waste nitrogen compounds in the blood.

U-re'ter. [Gr. *ourein*, to conduct water.] The excretory duct of the kidneys.

U-re'thra. [Gr. *ourein*, to pass urine.] The membranous tube leading from the urinary bladder.

U'ric. [Gr. *ouron*, urine.] An acid contained in urine and in gouty concretions.

U'vu-la. A soft body suspended from the palate, near the aperture of the nostrils, over the glottis.

Vac'cine Vi'rus. [L. *vacca*, a cow, and *virus*, poison.] The material derived from heifers for the purpose of vaccination,— the great preventive of smallpox.

Vac'u-um. [L. *vacuus*, void, empty.] A space void of matter.

Va'gus, *pl.* **Va'gi.** (383.) [From *vago*, to wander.] Wandering. The pneumogastric nerve is called the vagus.

Valve. Any membrane, or doubling of any membrane, which prevents fluids from flowing back into the vessels and canals of the animal body.

Val'vu-læ Con-ni-ven'tes. (264.) [L., the converging folds.] The semilunar folds of the mucous membrane of the small intestine.

Va'sa Va-so'rum. (106.) [L., the vessels of the vessels.] The fine blood-vessels permeating the coats of the arteries and veins.

Vas'cu-lar. [L. *vasculum*, a vessel.] Pertaining to vessels; abounding in vessels.

Va'so-Mo'tor. (134.) [L. *vas*, a vessel, and *motor*, a mover.] That which causes movements or changes in the calibre of vessels.

Vas'tus. [L.] Great; vast:—a term applied to some large muscles.

Vault. The superior arch of the skull.

Veins. (107.) Vessels that convey blood *to* the heart.

Ve-na Ca'va. [L., hollow vein.] See ¶ 102.

Ve'nous. Pertaining to veins.

Ven-ti-la'tion. (204.) [From L. *ventilo*, *ventilatum*, to blow, or to fan.] The operation of causing the air to pass through any place for the purpose of expelling impure air.

Ven'tri-cle. [L. *venter*, the stomach.] A small cavity of the animal body.

Ver-mic'u-lar. [L. *vermiculus*, a little worm.] Resembling the motions of a worm.

Ver-mi-for'mis. (268.) [L. *vermis*, a worm, and *forma*, form.] Having the form and shape of a worm.

Ver'te-bra, *pl.* **Ver'te-bræ.** (343.) [L. *verto*, to turn.] A joint of the spinal column.

Ver'te-bral. Pertaining to the joints of the spinal column.

Ves'i-cal. [L. *vas*, a vessel or tube.] Pertaining to the urinary bladder.

Ves'ti-bule. (435.) [L., a porch of a house.] A cavity belonging to the ear.

Vi-bra'tion. [L. *vibro*, *vibratum*, to shake.] The very rapid movements which stretched cords or elastic bodies make when oscillating.

Vil'li, plural of **Vil'lus.** (264.) The small conical projections of the mucous membrane of the small intestine.

Vi'rus. [L., poison.] Foul matter of an ulcer; poison.

Vis'ce-ral. [L. *viscus*, *visceris*, a bowel.] Belonging to the viscera, or bowels.

Vis'u-al. [L. *video*, *visum*, to see.] Pertaining to, or used in, sight.

Vi'tal. [L. *vita*, life.] Pertaining to life.

Vit're-ous. (454.) [L. *vitrum*, glass.] Belonging to glass:—applied to a humor of the eye.

Viv-i-sec'tion. [L. *vivus*, alive, and *seco*, to cut.] Experiments requiring dissection of living animals to advance physiological knowledge.

Vo'cal. [L. *vox*, the voice.] Uttered by the voice; belonging to the vocal apparatus.

Vod'ki. An alcoholic intoxicant made from the potato by the Russians.

Vo'lar. [L. *vola*, the hollow of the hand or foot.] Belonging to the palm of the hand.

Vo-li'tion. [L. *volo, volitum*, to desire.] The act of willing or of choosing.

Vol-ta'ic. A term applied to the electricity evolved by the battery of Volta; the constant current.

Vol'un-ta-ry. [L. *voluntas*, the will.] Acting or moving in obedience to the will.

Vo'mer. [L., a ploughshare.] One of the bones of the nose.

Wa'ter-Bed. A case, or tick, made of water-proof cloth filled with water. Such a bed affords equable pressure.

Will. (394.) The faculty or power of choosing to do or not to do, to act or not to act.

Wis'dom Teeth. (254.) A name given to the last grinder teeth.

Wrist'-Drop. (379.) Loss of power in the muscles of the forearm in lead poisoning.

Zy-go-mat'i-ous. [Gr. *zygos*, a yoke.] A term applied to some muscles of the face, from their attachment to the zygoma.

INDEX.

Abdomen, 137.
    compression of, 117.
Aberrations, 265.
Absorption, 38, 40, 42, 100, 153, 159, 173.
Accommodation, power of, in the eye, 262.
    mechanism of, 262.
Acid, butyric, 121.
    hydrochloric, 147.
    lactic, 177.
    margaric, 121.
    oleic, 121.
    palmitic, 121.
Adenoid tissue, 165.
Adipose tissue, 29.
After-images of vision, 267.
Air, composition of, 106.
    contamination of, 110.
    effect of impure, 108.
    impurities, 107, 109.
Air-cells, 93.
Air-space, 112.
Albumen, 121.
Alcohol, action of, 133.
    composition of, 132.
    effects on the nerve-centres, 228.
    effects on the vascular system, 84.
    injurious effects, 134.
    not a preventive of disease, 134.
Alimentary canal, 139.
Aliments, proteid, 120.
Amœbæ, movements of, 18.
    properties of, 18, 19.
Anatomy, definition of, 15.
Aorta, 63.
Appendages of the eye, 252.
Aqueous humor, 260.
Arachnoid, 209.
Arachnoidean space, 210.
Arbor vitæ, 207.
Arteries, distribution of, 60.
    pulmonary, 64.
    renal, 169.

Arteries, structure of, 65.
    systemic, 64.
    table of, 66.
Arytenoid cartilage, 284.
Ascending aorta, 224.
Asphyxia, 340.
    Silvester method of recovery from, 340.
Assimilation, 173.
Astigmatism, 265.
Audition, 344.
Auditory canal, 244.
Auricles of the heart, 59.
Automatism, 53.

Bath, Simpson's, 37.
    sponge, 84.
    Turkish, 163.
Bathing, 44.
    beneficial effects of, 326.
    in disease, 46.
    modes of, 45.
    rules for, 47.
    time for, 46.
Bed and bed-linen of the sick, 327.
Bicuspid teeth, 142.
Bilateral action, 204.
Bile, its color and effect on fats, 151.
Bile-duct, 151.
Binocular vision, 268.
Bladder, gall, 151.
    urinary, 171.
Bleeding, or hemorrhage, 334.
    management of, 335.
Blind spot, 266.
Blood, amœboid movements of, 70.
    change of, in respiration, 100.
    chemical composition of, 70.
    circulation of, 73.
    condition of blood in respiration, 104.
    function of, 72.
    microscopic appearance of, 70.
    physical appearance of, 69.

Blood, supply for the brain, 226.
Blushing, 79.
Body, co-ordinate movements of, 308.
    suppression of by-motions of, 317.
Bones, chemical properties of, 296.
    formation, 297.
    microscopic character of, 299.
    number of, 23.
    structure of, 23, 294.
    table of, 25.
Brain, 198.
    culture, 234.
    functions of the inferior parts of, 210.
    functions of the superior parts of, 201.
    membranes of, 203.
    weight of, 198.
    work, 237.
Bread, influence of, 227.
Breathing, affected through the skin by
    cold, 104.
    frequency of, 103.
    through the nostrils, 105.
Bronchi, 93.
Bronchia, 93.
Bunion, 300.
Burns, treatment of, 339.

Calcium, 16.
Callus, 32.
Canal, alimentary, capacity of, 139.
    lachrymal, 254.
    spinal, 195.
Capillaries, 64.
    flow of blood in, 81.
    interchanges in, 82.
    retardation of flow, 81.
    structure of, 69.
    walls of, 69.
Carbo-hydrates, or starchy foods, 122.
Carbolic acid, 337.
Carbon, 16.
Carbonic acid gas, 100.
Cartilage, structure of, 296.
    use of, 299.
Cartilages of the larynx, 284.
Casein, 121.
Cells, ciliated, 50.
    epithelial, 90.
    growth and division, 20.
    nerve, 51.
    physiology of, 51.
    structure of, 19.

Cellulose, 122.
Cement, 143.
Cerebellum, structure of, 207, 209, 211.
Cerebro-spinal system, 196.
    membranes of, 209.
Cerebrum, functions of, 203.
    structure of, 199.
Chemistry, definition of, 15.
Chest, capacity of, 95.
Children, alcoholic effects on, 228.
Chloral, effects of, 229.
Chlorine, 16.
Chordæ tendineæ, 63.
Choroidea, 257.
Chyle, 155.
    movements of, 156.
Chyme, 153.
Cilia, 50.
Ciliary motion, 50.
Circulation of the blood, 55.
    effects of alcohol on, 84.
    proofs of, 82.
    pulmonic, 74.
    systemic, 74.
Clothing, adaptation of, 43.
    cleanliness of, 42.
    damp, 42.
    in disease, 43.
    kind of, preferable in the sick-room,
      331.
    night, 41.
    object of, 39.
    water-proof, 41.
    woollen, 83, 163.
Coagulation of blood, 71.
    how favored, 72.
Coccyx, 138.
Cochlea, 247.
Cocoa, 131.
Coffee, 131.
Cold feet, 41.
Colds, causes of, 80.
Colloids, 154.
Colon, 150.
Color of the arterial blood, 78.
    of the iris, 258.
    of the venous blood, 81.
    sensations of, 266.
Color-blindness, 267.
Commissure of the optic nerves, 236.
Compression of the thorax, 117.
Cones of the retina, 259.

Conjunctiva, 255.
Constipation, 164.
Consumption, 115.
Contractile tissues, 48.
Contraction, theory of muscular, 54.
Convolutions, cerebral, 199.
    functions of, 203.
Convulsions, 221.
Cooking, 126, 162.
Corium, 31.
Cornea, 256.
Corns, 32.
Corpora quadrigemina, 200, 206.
    striata, 200, 205.
Corpus callosum, 199.
Corpuscles of the blood, 70.
    action of, 101.
    chemical composition of, 71.
    origin and function of, 71.
Cosmetics, 35.
Cranial nerves, functions of, 215.
Cuspid teeth, 142.
Cuticle, 31.

Dandruff, 36.
Deglutition, 145.
Demands of modern life, 314.
Dentine, 143.
Dermis, 30.
Diaphragm, 89.
Diet and its energy, 178.
    for health, 123.
    tables of, 178.
Dietetics, 186.
Diffusion of gases, 99.
Digestibility of foods, 129, 130.
Digestion, 152–156.
    summary of, 157.
Drinks, 328.
Drowning, prevention from, 341.
Duct, bile, 151.
    Steno's, 140.
    thoracic, 155.
    Wharton's, 141.
Duodenum, 148.
Dura mater, 209.
Dyspepsia, 157.
    aids to, 162.
    prevention of, 163.
Dyspnœa, 101.

Ear, bones of, 243.
    external, 244.

Ear, foreign bodies in, 341.
    functions of external and middle, 248.
    hygiene of, 274.
    internal, 246.
    middle, 245.
    wax of, 245.
Education, at home and at school, 235.
Eggs as a food, 127.
Elasticity, 148.
Emetics, 331.
Enamel, 143.
End-bulbs of Krause, 268.
Endocardium, 62.
Endolymph, 250.
End-organs of the apparatus of vision, 198, 258.
    of the auditory nerve, 247.
    of the sense of touch, 268.
    seat of, 272.
Endurance, physical, 188.
Energy of the body, 176.
    loss of, 179.
    normal expenditure, 179.
    normal income, 179.
Epidermis, 30.
Epiglottis, 92.
Epithelium, 36.
Erect posture, 309.
Ethmoid bone, 194.
Eustachian tube, 245, 248.
Excretion, 183.
    integrity of working of the nerve-centres dependent upon, 227.
    of salts, 184.
    of urea, 183.
    of water, 184.
Exercise, adaptation of, 321.
    conditions for, 318.
    deficiency of, 312.
    in gymnastics, 302.
    kinds of, 320.
    mental, 233.
        amount of, 234.
    object of systematic, 313, 318.
    of the muscles, 232.
Exner on the rapidity of mental operations, 205.
Expiration, 99.
Eye, 250.
    hygiene of, 276.
    imperfections of, 265.
    management of, in adult period, 279.

Eye, management of, in childhood, 276.
    in student period, 277.
Eyeball, 256.
    foreign bodies on, 342.
Eyebrows, 252.
Eyelids, 252.
    function of, 254.
    punctæ of, 256.

Face, bones of the, 193.
Fascia, 27.
Fat, 27, 121, 174.
Feet, protection of, 41.
Fenestra ovalis, 246.
    rotunda, 247.
Ferments,—saliva, gastric, pancreatic, and
  intestinal juice, 152.
Fibre, cardiac, 49.
    gray nerve, 51.
    muscular, 26.
    striped, 48.
    tubular nerve, 51.
    unstriped, 49.
Fibrin, 70.
    animal and vegetable, 121.
Fingers, mechanism of the, 282.
Fish, 127.
Flesh, 23.
Fluorine, 16.
Follicles, hair, 31.
Food, accessory, 123
    amount of, 158, 188.
    changes in the digestion of, 152.
    deficiency of, 187.
    excess of, 186.
    for a babe, 328.
    for the sick, 328.
    frequency of taking, 160.
    source of the proteids, 120.
    table of values, 128.
    use of, 119.
    want of, 187.
Force of heart-beat, 76.
Fossæ, nasal, 243.
Fourth ventricle of the brain, 288.
Fovea centralis, 266.
Fractured bone, 338.
Freckle, 31.
Frequency of heart-beat, 76.
Frontal bone, 194.
Frost-bite, treatment of, 342.
Fruits, value for food, 129.

Function of inferior parts of brain, 369.
    of superior parts of brain, 201.

Gall-bladder, 151.
Ganglion, 53.
Ganglionic cells, 51.
Gases, diffusion of, 99.
Gastric juice, 147.
Germ-force, 21.
Glands, adenoid, 168.
    lachrymal, 254.
    lymphatic, 165
    mesenteric, 155.
    mucous, 94.
    oil, 36.
    palpebral, 254.
    salivary, 144.
    structure of, 139.
    thymus, 169.
Globulin, 121.
Glottis, 285.
Gluten, 121.
Glycerin, 121.
Glycogen, 151, 174.
Grains. food-value of, 128.
Granules, 16.
Grape-sugar, 151.
Gray matter of the spinal cord, 213.

Hæmoglobin, 71, 101.
Hairs, 33.
    color of, 35.
    structure of, 35.
Harmonious development, 235.
Hashish, 230
Health-diet, 123.
Hearing, apparatus for, 244.
    how impaired, 275
Heart, 59.
    acceleration of, 77.
    action of, 76.
    capacity of, 63.
    inhibition of, 77.
    motive power of, 61.
    structure of, 62.
    work of, 76.
Heat, loss of, 180.
    of the body in different climates, 181.
      in fever, 182.
      in health, 180.
    production of, 175.
    regulation of, 181.

Heat, source of, 180.
Hemiplegia, 221.
Hemorrhage, or bleeding, 334.
Hepatic artery and vein, 151.
Hernia, 343.
Histology, definition of, 15.
Home, site of the, 111.
Hunger, 185.
Hydro-carbons, 121.
Hydrogen, 16.
Hygiene, definition of, 15.
Hyoid bone, 92.

Ileum, 148.
Impulses, nervous, 52, 197.
        mechanism of, 222.
        vital, 198.
Incisor teeth, 143.
Income and outcome of the body, 177.
Incus, 245.
Indigestion, causes of, 158.
Infants' food, 328.
Inheritance, influence of, 224, 229.
Inhibition, 53.
Innominata, 138.
Insalivation, 145.
Insensible perspiration, 37.
Inspiration, 98.
Interarticular cartilage, 302.
Intercostal muscles, 88.
Intestine, large, 149.
        small, 148.
Iris, 256, 258.
Iron, 16.
Irritable tissues, 48.
Ivy-poison, remedy for, 344.

Jaw, lower, 141.
        upper, 141.
Jejunum, 148.
Joints, 299, 301.
Juice, gastric, 147.
        pancreatic, its effect on foods, 151.
Juices, digestive, 153.

Kreatin, 177.
Kidneys, effects of alcohol on, 172.
        functions of, 170.
        structure of, 169.

Labyrinth, 246.
Lachrymal glands, 254.
Lacteals, 154.

Lactic acid, 177.
Lacunæ, 297.
Laminæ, 297.
Large intestine, 149.
Larynx, 91, 284.
Leaping, 311.
Legumen, 121.
Lens, crystalline, 260.
        function of, 260.
Ligaments, 23, 195, 301.
Light, 44, 261.
Liver, functions of, 151.
        structure of, 150.
Lungs, 89.
        structure of, 94.
Lymph, 167.
        function of, 168.
Lymphatic vessels, office of, 172.
        structure of, 165.

Magnesium, 16.
Maize, 128.
Malar bones, 25.
Malleus bone, 245.
Marrow, 23.
Mastication, 145.
Meats, 127.
Meatus auditorius, 247.
Media, 260.
Medicine, how to be given, 328.
Medulla oblongata, 209, 211.
Membrana tympani, 245.
Membrane, fibrous, 30.
        mucous, 94.
        of the eye, 256.
        serous, 90.
Mesentery, 148.
Milk as a food-element, 125.
        chemical constituents of, 120.
Molar teeth, 142.
Motor nerve, 215.
Mouth, boundaries of, 140.
        its action in digestion, 145.
Mucous glands, 94.
Mucus, 94.
Muscles, 23.
        action of, 306.
        contraction of, 54.
        effect of exercise on, 311.
        intercostals, 88.
        object of training the, 324.
        of the eye, 251.

Muscles, physiology of, 50.
  table of, 302.
Muscular sense, 271.
Myopia, 281.

Nails, 32, 283.
  in-grown, 33.
Narcotics, 230.
Nasal passages, 91, 194.
Nerve-cells and fibres, 51, 197.
  afferent and efferent impulses of, 52.
  function of cells, 197.
  ganglionic cells, 51.
Nerve-centres, 53, 210.
  co-ordination of, 222.
  spinal, 216.
Nervous system, 196.
  functions of, 197, 218.
  hygiene of, 223.
  summary of, 218, 220.
  sympathetic or ganglionic, 196.
Nitrogen, 16.
Nose, bleeding at the, 338.
Nucleolus, 20.
Nucleus, 20.
Nurse, directions for the, 326, 328.
Nutrition, 173.

Occipital bone, 194.
Œsophagus, movements of, 145.
Oleic acid, 121.
Oil glands, 36.
Oils, from what derived, 121.
Olfactory lobes, 200, 206, 241.
Open fire, 113.
Opium, 230.
Optic nerve, 256.
Optic thalami, 200, 205.
Orbits, 193, 252.
Organ of Corti, 247.
Organs of sight, 252.
Osmosis of liquids, 153.
Oxidation of foods, effect of, 177.
  of wood, 176.
Oxygen, 16.
  action of, 102, 104.
  its entrance into the blood, 105.

Palate, 91.
Pancreas, structure of, 151.
Papillæ, 31.
Papillary layer, 31.
Paralysis, 221.

Paraplegia, 222.
Parietal bones, 194.
Parotid gland, 140.
Patella, 294.
Peduncles of the brain, 199, 211.
Pelvis, bony, 138.
  renal, 169.
Pepsin, 147.
Peptones, 147, 154.
Pericardium, 62.
Perilymph, 250.
Periosteum, 23, 295.
Peristaltic action, 149.
Peritoneum, 138.
Perspiration, 37.
  Simpson's method of producing, 37.
Pharynx, 91.
  structure of, 145.
Phosphorus, 16.
Physical culture, different systems of, 314.
  influence of, 316.
Physiology, definition of, 15.
Pia mater, 209.
Pigments of the skin, 30.
Pinna, 244.
Plasma of the blood, 70, 73.
Pleura, structure of, 80.
Poisons and their antidotes, 331.
Pons Varolii, 209, 211.
Portal vein, 64, 151.
Posture, 322.
Potassium, 16.
Poultices, 329.
Production of heat and energy, 175.
Proteid compounds, 17.
Proteids, food-stuffs, 121, 147.
Protoplasm, properties of, 20, 198.
Pseudopodia, 18.
Pulse, 82.
Pupil of the eye, 257.
Pylorus, 148.
Pyramids, renal, 169.

Quiet in the sick-room, 327.
Quizzing glass, 282.

Reaction period, 205.
Rectum, 150.
Red corpuscle, 71.
Reflex action, 52, 212.
Refraction of light, 261.

Reproduction of the amœba, 18.
Respiration, abdominal, 96.
 changes in blood, 69, 100.
 changes of air in, 100.
 labored, 98.
 mechanism of, 97.
 of the amœba, 19.
Respiratory centre, 103.
Rest, 238, 319, 326.
Rete mucosum, 31.
Retina, 257.
Rhythm of heart-beat, 73.
Ribs, 86, 98.
Rickets, 123, 187.
Root of the lungs, 94.
Running, 310.

Sacrum, 138.
Saliva, use of, 144.
Salivary glands, 144.
Salts as food, 123.
Sarcolemma, 48.
Sclerotica, 256.
Scurvy, 124.
Sebaceous glands, 36.
Secretion by the kidneys, 169.
 digestive, 147.
 of the skin, 38.
Sedatives, 227.
Semicircular canals, 247.
Semilunar valves, 60.
Sensation, localization of, 270.
Sensations of pressure, 269.
 of temperature, 270.
Sense of equilibrium, 272.
 of touch, 38.
Sensible perspiration, 37.
Sensory impulses, 213.
 influences, 309.
 nerve, 214.
Serum, its chemical composition, 70, 91.
Sewer-gas, 109.
Sick-room, selection of, 326.
Sighing, 101.
Sight, 252.
Silicon, 16.
Simpson's method for sweating, 47.
Sinuses of Valsalva, 63.
Skeleton, 23.
Skin, 30.
 a heat-regulator, 182.
 functions of, 38.

Skin, hygiene of, 39.
 papillary layer of, 31.
Skull, bones of, 194.
 arrangement of, 195.
Sleep, 236.
 when most refreshing, 237.
Sleeping-room, 84, 115.
Smell, 241.
 hygiene of, 274.
 physiology of, 242.
Sneezing, 86.
Soups, 47.
Sodium, 16.
Sound, 247, 286.
 articulate, 289.
Spasm, 221.
Speech, 289.
Sphenoid bone, 194.
Spinal canal, 195.
 cord, 196, 208.
 functions of, 212.
 nerves, 216.
Spleen, structure of, 168.
Stapes, 245.
Starch, food-stuffs, 122.
Starvation, 188.
Sternum, 68.
Stimulants, 130, 227.
Stomach, function of, 147.
 structure of, 146.
Striæ, 48.
Stuttering, 290.
Subarachnoid space, 210.
Sublingual gland, 144.
Submaxillary gland, 144.
Sugars, 122.
Sulphur, 16, 119.
Sunstroke, 344.
Suprarenal bodies, 169.
Sutures, 194.
Sweat glands, 36.
Sympathetic system, functions of, 218.
Synovia, 300.
Synovial membrane, 299.

Taste, 240.
 physiology of, 240.
 reaction period, 241.
Tea, 131.
Tears, 254.
Teeth, 142.
 care of, 160.

Tooth, effects of bad, 159.
 milk, 143.
Temperature of the sick-room, 328.
Temporal bone, 194.
Tendons, 306.
Ternary compounds, 17.
Tetanus, 221.
Thalami optici, 205.
Thirst, 185.
Thoracic duct, 155.
 respiration, 97.
Thorax, 58.
 enlargement of, 96.
 structure of, 86, 88.
Thyroid body, 169.
Tissues, adenoid, 165.
 adipose, 29.
 areolar, 28.
 connective, 28.
 elastic, 28.
 muscular, 48.
 nerve, 48.
 white fibrous, 28.
Tobacco, 83, 225, 230.
Tongue, hygiene of, 273.
 structure of, 140.
Tooth, structure of, 143.
Touch, 268.
Trachea, 92.
Tricuspid valves, 60.
Tubuli uriniferi, 169.
Tunics of the eye, 256.
 functions of, 259.
Tympanum, 245.

Unit, anatomical, 20.
 of heat, 178.
Unstriated muscle, 53.
Unstriped fibre, 49.
Urea, 151, 171, 173.
Uric acid, 175.
Urine, 170, 343.
Uvula, 91.

Vagi nerves, action of, 103.
Valves in the veins, 68.
 mitral, 61.
 semilunar, 60.
 tricuspid, 60.
Valvulæ conniventes, 149.
Vasa vasorum, 68.
Vaso-motor action, 79.

Veins, 64.
 blood-flow in, 81.
 inferior vena cava, 64.
 portal, 64.
 structure of, 68.
 superior vena cava, 64.
Velocity of blood-flow in the arteries, 78.
 of blood-flow in the veins, 81.
Ventilation, 112, 327.
 effects on the brain, 227.
Ventricles of the brain, 200.
 of the heart, 59.
 of the larynx, 285.
Vermiform appendix, 150.
Vertebra, 86.
 structure of, 86, 194.
Vertebral column, structure of, 86, 195.
Vestibule, 247.
Villi of the intestines, 154.
Visual sensation, 266.
Vital capacity of the lungs, 95.
 force, 21.
 impulses, power of, 198.
 knot, 103.
Vitreous humor, 260.
Vocal cords, 284.
Voice, 287.
 hygiene of, 290.
Volitional impulses, 213.
Vomiting, nervous mechanism of, 149.

Walking, 179, 310.
Want of food, 187.
 of useful employment, effects of, 236.
Waste products, 183.
Watcher, duty of, 330.
Water as food, 124.
 characteristics of good, 124.
 comparative value of, 125.
Wharton's duct, 141.
Whispering, 290, 330.
White corpuscles, 71.
Winking, 254.
Worry, 238.
Wounds, 334.
 by poisonous serpents, 343.
 flesh, 337.
 from insects, 344.
Wrist-drop, 35, 221.

Yawning, 104.
Yellow spot, 266.

Contanseau's Practical Dictionary of the French and English Languages. Composed from the French dictionaries of the Academy, Boiste, Bescherelle, etc., from the English dictionaries of Johnson, Webster, Richardson, etc , and from technological and scientific dictionaries of both languages; followed by abridged vocabularies of geographical and mythological names. By LÉON CONTANSEAU. Crown 8vo. Half roan. $1.20.†

Prof. Contanseau was induced to prepare this work in consequence of the great inadequacy of all previous French-English dictionaries to meet the wants of the student, which inadequacy was frequently brought to his notice during his professional career.

Contanseau's Pocket Dictionary of the French and English Languages. Being a careful abridgment of the Practical French and English Dictionary, preserving all the most useful features of the original work; followed by abridged vocabularies of geographical and mythological names. By LÉON CONTANSEAU. 18mo. Extra cloth. 60 cents.†

All the leading characteristics of the larger work have been retained in this abridgment, which was prepared for the purpose of affording those pupils, readers, and travellers who object to the size or expense of the former the benefit of a thoroughly good French and English dictionary of more portable size and at a lower price.

Neuman & Baretti's Pocket Dictionary of the Spanish and English Languages. Compiled from the last im proved edition. 18mo. Extra cloth. $1.08.†

Uniform in general style and appearance with the Pocket Dictionaries of Contanseau and Longman, containing every word likely to be met with by the traveller or the student.

Ancient Classics for English Readers. Edited by Rev. W. LUCAS COLLINS. 28 vols. Small 12mo. Fine cloth. 50. cts each. Also in sets of 14 vols. Cloth. $12.50. Half calf. $25.00.

1. Homer's Iliad. 2. Homer's Odyssey. 3. Herodotus. 4. Cæsar. 5. Virgil. 6. Horace. 7. Æschylus. 8. Xenophon. 9. Cicero. 10. Sophocles. 11. Pliny. 12. Euripides. 13. Juvenal. 14. Aristophanes. 15. Hesiod and Theognis. 16. Plautus and Terence. 17. Tacitus. 18. Lucien. 19. Plato. 20. Greek Anthology. 21. Livy. 22. Ovid. 23. Catullus, Tibullus, and Propertius. 24. Demosthenes. 25. Aristotle. 26. Thucydides. 27. Lucretius. 28. Pindar.

Foreign Classics for English Readers. Edited by MRS. OLIPHANT. 16mo. Extra cloth. $1.00 per volume.

The purpose of this series is to present in a convenient and attractive form a synopsis of the lives and works of the great writers of Europe—who they were and what they wrote. *Uniform with the Ancient Classics.*

Seventeen Volumes now Ready.

Groves's Greek and English Dictionary. Comprising all the words in the writings of the most popular Greek authors, with the difficult inflections in them, and in the Septuagint and New Testament. Designed for the use of schools and the undergraduate course of a college education. By Rev. JOHN GROVES. Revised edition. 8vo. Sheep. $1.80.†

The object of the compiler has been to produce a work which young Greek scholars could use with ease and advantage to themselves, but sufficiently full to be equally serviceable as they advanced.

Pickering's Greek and English Lexicon. Being a Comprehensive Lexicon of the Greek Language. Designed for the use of colleges and schools in the United States. By JOHN PICKERING, LL.D. 8vo. Sheep. $2.80.†

This work contains all the words in the Greek language, with their correct interpretation into English, and their different shades of meaning carefully distinguished and illustrated by citations from standard authors.

*Leverett's Latin Lexicon. Enlarged and im-*proved edition. Embracing the Classical Distinctions of Words, and the Etymological Index of Freund's Lexicon. By E. P. LEVERETT. 8vo. Sheep. $2.80.†

The Latin dictionaries now in common use, whatever may be said of the manner in which they do what they propose to do, are essentially deficient in the plan on which they are executed. This work by no means pretends to make up the defect, but aims chiefly to present the classical student with the results of the investigations of the most eminent lexicographers.

Longman's Pocket Dictionary of the German and English Languages. By F. W. LONGMAN. (Founded on Blakely and Friedländer's Practical Dictionary of the German and English Languages.) 18mo. Extra cloth. $1.08.†

"We have not seen any pocket dictionaries (German or English) that can bear comparison with this. It is remarkably compendious, and the arrangement is clear."—*London Athenæum.*

Lempriere's Classical Dictionary. Containing a full account of all the Proper Names mentioned in ancient authors, with Tables of Coins, Weights, and Measures in use among the Greeks and Romans; to which is prefixed a Chronological Table. A new and complete edition. 16mo. Fine cloth. $1.08.† 8vo. Sheep. $2.60.†

The original text of Lempriere has in this edition been carefully revised and amended, and much valuable original matter added. The work is now a complete Bibliotheca Classica, containing in a condensed and readily accessible form all the information required by the student upon the geography, topography, history, literature, and mythology of antiquity and of the ancients, with bibliographical references for such as wish to get fuller information on the subjects treated of.

Gardner's Latin Lexicon. A Dictionary of the Latin Language, particularly adapted to the Classics usually studied preparatory to a Collegiate Course. By FRANCIS GARDNER, A.M. 8vo. Sheep. $1.80.†

Sharpless and Philips's Astronomy, for Schools
and General Readers. By Prof. ISAAC SHARPLESS and Prof.
G. M. PHILIPS. Profusely Illustrated. 12mo. Half bound.
$1.00.†

"This book distances all its predecessors in the simplicity and lucid directness of its explanations as well as the natural arrangement of its thought. The book is thoroughly scientific in the best sense, thoroughly practical in the best sense, and replete with such diagrams and illustrations as are meant to and do aid in the explanation of the text. It is a book that ought to be in every American home."—*Philadelphia Times.*

Sharpless and Philips's Natural Philosophy.
By Prof. ISAAC SHARPLESS and Prof. G. M. PHILIPS, authors
of "Astronomy," etc. With numerous Illustrations. 12mo.
Half bound. $1.00.†

Among the many valuable features of the book will be found the following: Easy Experiments, Omission of Difficult Terms, Presentation of the Most Recent Results of Scientific and Practical Study, Suggestive Original Exercises, Practical Applications of the Principles Explained. The book will be found to contain clear *explanations,* abundantly illustrated, and prepared especially with reference to the convenience of teacher and scholar.

Greene's Lessons in Chemistry. By Prof. Wm.
H. GREENE, M.D., Editor and Translator of "Wurtz's Chemistry." 12mo. Half bound. $1.00.†

Perrin's Drill-Book in Algebra. Exercises for
Class-Drill and Review. Arranged according to subjects. By
MARSHALL LIVINGSTON PERRIN, A.M. 12mo. Cloth, limp.
Teachers' Edition, with Answers. 75 cents.† Scholars' Edition, Questions only. 60 cents.†

Walker's Object Lessons. The Handy Book of
Object Lessons. From a Teacher's Note-Book. By J. WALKER.
First and Second Series complete. 12mo. Extra cloth. $1.25.

Embracing Lessons on the following subjects, viz : THE ANIMAL, VEGETABLE, and MINERAL KINGDOMS; PHYSIOLOGY; PHYSICAL GEOGRAPHY; MANUFACTURES.
"The work is admirable in arrangement, simple and natural in method, and clear and comprehensive generally. Taken altogether, it is one of the best and most practical books in its kind that has as yet appeared."—*Boston Saturday Evening Post.*

Gow's Primer of Politeness: A Help to School
AND HOME GOVERNMENT. By ALEXANDER M. GOW, A.M.
12mo. Extra cloth, limp. 75 cents.

"His advice is enforced and made attractive by a judicious selection of appropriate anecdotes, so that his book is an edifying combination of instruction and entertainment. There is plenty of room for such a work, and we hope it will find an extensive sale."—*North American.*

Haldeman's Affixes. Affixes, in their Origin
and Application, Exhibiting the Etymologic Structure of English
Words. By S. S. HALDEMAN, author of "Outlines of Etymology," "Word-Building," etc. *New Edition.* 12mo. Extra
cloth. $1.50.*

THE READERS FOR YOUR SCHOOLS.

LIPPINCOTT'S
POPULAR SERIES OF READERS.
By MARCIUS WILLSON.

THIS SERIES OF READERS EMBRACES SIX BOOKS, AS FOLLOWS:

FIRST READER. With Illustrations. 96 pages. 12mo. Half bound. 20 cents.†

SECOND READER. With Illustrations. 160 pages. 12mo. Half bound. 33 cents.†

THIRD READER. With Illustrations. 228 pages. 12mo. Half bound. 44 cents.†

FOURTH READER. With Illustrations. 334 pages. 12mo. Half bound. 60 cents.†

FIFTH READER. With Illustrations. 480 pages. 12mo. Cloth sides. 90 cents.†

SIXTH READER. With Frontispiece. 544 pages. 12mo. Cloth sides. $1.00.†

They combine the greatest possible interest with appropriate instruction.

They contain a greater variety of reading matter than is usually found in School Readers.

They are adapted to modern methods of teaching.

They are natural in method, and the exercises progressive.

They stimulate the pupils to think and inquire, and therefore interest and instruct.

They teach the principles of natural and effective reading.

The introduction of SCRIPT EXERCISES is a new feature, and highly commended by teachers.

The LANGUAGE LESSONS accompanying the exercises in reading mark a new epoch in the history of a Reader.

The ILLUSTRATIONS are by some of the best artists, and represent both home and foreign scenes.

"No other series is so discreetly graded, so beautifully printed, or so philosophically arranged."—*Albany Journal.*

"We see in this series the beginning of a better and brighter day for the reading classes."—*New York School Journal.*

"The work may be justly esteemed as the beginning of a new era in school literature."—*Baltimore News.*

"In point of interest and attractiveness the selections certainly surpass any of the kind that have come to our knowledge."—*The Boston Sunday Globe.*

The unanimity with which the Educational Press has commended the Popular Series of Readers is, we believe, without a parallel in the history of similar publications, and one of the best evidences that the books meet the wants of the progressive teacher.

SANFORD'S
SERIES OF ARITHMETICS.

SANFORD'S ANALYTICAL SERIES.
COMPRISED IN FOUR BOOKS.

The Science of Numbers reduced to its last analysis. Mental and Written Arithmetic successfully combined in each Book of the Series.

By SHELTON P. SANFORD, A.M.,
Professor of Mathematics in Mercer University, Georgia.

FIRST BOOK.

Sanford's First Lessons in Analytical Arithmetic. Comprising Mental and Written Exercises. Handsomely and appropriately Illustrated. 16mo. Half roan. 20 cents.†

SECOND BOOK.

Sanford's Intermediate Analytical Arithmetic. Comprising Mental and Written Exercises. 16mo. 232 pp. Half roan 36 cents.†

THIRD BOOK.

Sanford's Common School Analytical Arithmetic. 12mo. 355 pp. Half roan. 64 cents.†

FOURTH BOOK.

Sanford's Higher Analytical Arithmetic; or, THE METHOD OF MAKING ARITHMETICAL CALCULATIONS ON PRINCIPLES OF UNIVERSAL APPLICATION, WITHOUT THE AID OF FORMAL RULES. 12mo. 419 pp. Half roan, cloth sides. $1.00.†

SANFORD'S
NEW ELEMENTARY ALGEBRA.

Designed for Common and High Schools and Academies. By Shelton P. Sanford, A.M. 12mo. Half roan. $1.00.†

From Prof. HUGH S. THOMPSON, *Principal Columbia Male Academy, Columbia, S. C.*

"Sanford's Arithmetics are superior to any that I have seen in the fulness of the examples, the clearness and simplicity of the analyses, and the accuracy of the rules and definitions. This opinion is based upon a *full* and *thorough test* in the school-room. To those teachers who may examine these Arithmetics with reference to introduction, I would especially commend the treatment of Percentage and Profit and Loss. No text-books that I have ever used are so satisfactory to teachers and pupils."

From Prof. B. MALLON, *Superintendent of Atlanta (Ga.) Public Schools.*

"I think they [Sanford's Arithmetics] are the best books on the subject ever published; and I trust it will not be long before they will be introduced into every school in our State. In my judgment they are the very perfection of school-books on Arithmetic."

CUTTER'S SERIES

ON

Analytical Anatomy, Physiology, and Hygiene,

HUMAN AND COMPARATIVE.

FOR SCHOOLS AND FAMILIES.

By CALVIN CUTTER, A.M., M.D.

During the past ten years more than two hundred thousand (200,000) have been sold for schools. This is the only series of works upon the subject that is graded for all classes of pupils, from the primary school to the college, the only one that embraces Anatomy, Physiology, and Hygiene for schools, and the only one arranged so as to be used advantageously with illustrating Anatomical Charts.

NEW SERIES.

First Book on Analytic Anatomy, Physiology, and Hygiene, Human and Comparative. 196 pp. With 164 Illustrations. 12mo. Half roan, cloth sides. 64 cents.†

Second Book on Analytic Anatomy, Physiology, and Hygiene, Human and Comparative. With QUESTIONS, DIAGRAMS, AND ILLUSTRATIONS for Analytic Study and Unific Topical Review. 309 pp. With 186 Illustrations. 12mo. Half roan, cloth sides. $1.08.†

New Analytic Anatomy, Physiology, and Hygiene, Human and Comparative. With QUESTIONS, DIAGRAMS, AND ILLUSTRATIONS for Analytic Study and Synthetic Review. 388 pp. With 230 Illustrations. 12mo. Half roan, cloth sides. $1.20.†

OLD SERIES.

First Book on Anatomy, Physiology, and Hygiene. Illustrated. 12mo. 56 cents.†

Anatomy, Physiology, and Hygiene. Illustrated. 12mo. $1.20.†

Human and Comparative Anatomy, Physiology, and Hygiene. By Mrs. E. P. CUTTER. Illustrated. 12mo. 36 cents.†

NEW OUTLINE ZOOLOGICAL CHARTS,

Or Human and Comparative Anatomical Plates. Mounted. (Including Rollers, etc.) Nine in number. Three feet long by two feet wide. $12.00.† Half set. Five in number. $7.20.†

TWO INVALUABLE
WORKS OF REFERENCE
FOR THE LIBRARY, SCHOOL, AND FAMILY.

LIPPINCOTT'S
GAZETTEER OF THE WORLD.

A Complete Pronouncing Gazetteer, or Geographical Dictionary of the World.

CONTAINING NOTICES OF OVER ONE HUNDRED AND TWENTY-FIVE THOUSAND PLACES

With Recent and Authentic Information respecting the Countries, Islands, Rivers, Mountains, Cities, Towns, etc., of every portion of the Globe; also the Census for 1880.

NEW EDITION, WITH SUPPLEMENTARY TABLES,

Showing the Population, etc., of the Principal Cities and Towns of the World, based upon the most recent Census Returns. One Volume. Imperial Octavo. Embracing 2680 Pages. Library Sheep. $12.00.

"It is the best work of its kind extant, and is a necessary supplement to any encyclopædia. The amount of information it contains is astonishing, and while, of course, condensed, it is all that is necessary for reference purposes."—*Chicago Tribune.*

"It has long stood far superior to all similar works through its uniform accuracy, exhaustive field, and evident purpose of the publishers to make it as complete and perfect as possible. It is the standard of standards."—*Boston Evening Traveller.*

LIPPINCOTT'S BIOGRAPHICAL DICTIONARY.

Lippincott's Pronouncing Dictionary of Biography and Mythology

Contains Memoirs of the Eminent Persons of all Ages and Countries, and Accounts of the Various Subjects of the Norse, Hindoo, and Classic Mythologies, with the Pronunciation of their Names in the Different Languages in which they occur.

BY J. THOMAS, A.M., M.D.

Complete in One Volume, Imperial 8vo, of 2345 Pages. Bound in Sheep. $10.00

"The most comprehensive and valuable work of the kind that has ever been attempted. An invaluable convenience."—*Boston Evening Traveller.*

"The most valuable contribution to lexicography in the English tongue."—*Cincinnati Gazette.*

"No other work of the kind will compare with it."—*Chicago Advance.*

THE STANDARD DICTIONARY

OF THE ENGLISH LANGUAGE.

Worcester's Unabridged

QUARTO DICTIONARY.

NEW EDITION, WITH SUPPLEMENT.

Fully Illustrated. With Four Full-page Illuminated Plates. Library Sheep, Marbled Edges. $10.00.

RECOMMENDED BY THE MOST EMINENT WRITERS.

ENDORSED BY THE BEST AUTHORITIES.

THE NEW EDITION OF

WORCESTER'S DICTIONARY

Contains Thousands of Words not to be found in any other Dictionary.

THE COMPLETE SERIES OF

WORCESTER'S DICTIONARIES.

QUARTO DICTIONARY. Profusely Illustrated. Library sheep. $10.00.
ACADEMIC DICTIONARY. Illustrated. Crown 8vo. Half roan. $1.50.†
COMPREHENSIVE DICTIONARY. Illustrated. 12mo. Half roan. $1.40.†
NEW COMMON SCHOOL DICTIONARY. Illustrated. 12mo. Half roan. 90 cents.†
PRIMARY DICTIONARY. Illustrated. 16mo. Half roan. 48 cents.†
POCKET DICTIONARY. Illustrated. 24mo. Cloth. 50 cents.† Roan, flexible. 69 cents.† Roan, tucks, gilt edges. 78 cents.†